SPACE MAGNATES

SPACE MAGNATES SERIES
BOOK 1

SAUL RAYBURN

First Edition: May 2024

Cover design by Cherie Chapman
ISBN: 978-1-963432-02-2 (ebook)
ISBN: 978-1-963432-01-5 (paperback)
Published by Luna Tick Entertainment LLC

Created with Vellum

SPACE MAGNATES

1

THE MAJOR

"Colonel, I must emphasize." Major Sinclair floated weightlessly inside the cramped operations deck. "The *Imperator* is one rail-gun discharge away from a catastrophic failure and burning up in the atmosphere."

"We have our orders, Major." Colonel Turunen held his hands in the pockets of his space suit, hovering on the other side of the deck. "The bombing runs over China have started. We must maintain our present course, ready to carry out orbital strikes."

Sinclair tightened her thin lips, considering her next words. The bright monitors behind the colonel made it difficult for her to read his face. If she could convince him not to fire until the end of their rotation three weeks from now, they would be transferred down to the surface, back under the cover of the North America Continental Missile Shield.

"Sir, we cannot fire the rail gun again. The heat radiators are cracked. Just one rupture can trigger—"

"Then cannibalize the radiators from a shuttle." He wiped sweat from his wrinkled forehead. The ventilation system struggled to operate, making the circular chamber feel like a sauna, irritating Sinclair to the point that she was ready to punch one of the monitors.

"Sir..." Sinclair glanced to her side, trying to hide her annoyance. "We are down to one operational shuttle. The other two have been salvaged for parts, per your orders. If the rail gun compromises the *Imperator*, not every spaceman will be able to abandon the spacecraft."

"Damn it, Major!" Turunen shouted. "What would you have me do?"

"Withdraw to a higher orbit," she replied. "Explain to SPACECOM that our rail gun is malfunctioning."

"Major Sinclair..." Turunen grabbed a handlebar bolted on the tactical console and pulled himself closer. "I will not be the commander who failed his mission because he didn't maintain his orbital precision bomber properly."

"The government has neglected the *Imperator*, not us." Sinclair counted with her fingers, raising her voice. "We are still eating expired rations. The barrel's heat radiators are months past their end of life. A third of our spacemen are performing poorly, many suffering from muscle atrophy. And there is much more I can point out. The government *doesn't* care about us."

"Watch your words, Major." He pointed at the large display, a global map littered with red and blue dots. "We must finish the war. It's time we kick China out of the Indian Ocean."

Sinclair cracked a few knuckles. "Then say our food supply is poisoned, incapacitating our spacemen."

Turunen studied her closely. Nervousness beat inside Sinclair's chest as she worried she'd finally crossed a line. But then she didn't care. She'd only joined the military to pay for engineering school, not to fight a war. At this point in the five-year-long war, if the United States Space Force went after every officer for a violation, the officer corps would be hollowed out.

"We don't falsify our records, Major. I could have you reprimanded."

The colonel pointed up with his eyes at the camera drilled into the cushion ceiling above them. He leaned over the tactical console and moved his lips without speaking: "Can you make the records show that?"

"I'm sorry, sir." Sinclair nodded. "I'll watch my words."

"Good." Turunen tapped the handlebar with his palm. "Keep the rail gun warm, Major."

Sinclair saluted, pushed off the floor, and glided toward the open hatch. The combat alarm shrieked urgently and flashed yellow lights before she made it out of the operations deck.

"Shit..." Sinclair spun around and heaved herself over to her station. She grabbed her helmet and gloves strapped to the wall and put them on, praying it was not a fire mission order. She tightened her blonde hair into a ponytail before putting the spheroidal helmet on.

Three officers flew onto the operations deck and dispersed to their stations.

"What we got?" Colonel Turunen floated up to his command seat.

"A fire mission order." Sinclair read her console, struggling to snap her helmet into the space suit's neck seal. "Straight from General Shugart. A heavy orbital strike on the coordinates provided."

"Prepare the *Imperator* for a fire mission," Turunen ordered.

Sinclair grunted, failing to get her helmet to click into place. "Damn piece of shit..." She smacked the glass with her hand. "Weapons, load explosive slugs!"

"Loading explosive slugs, Major!" The weapons officer punched buttons on the screen.

The neck seal popped as the helmet snapped into place. Twisting her gloves on with little struggle, she hoped she didn't break the neck seal. She tapped a button on her console, silencing the alarm.

"Engineering, sitrep!"

"Thrusters are clear and ready for activation." The engineer gave a thumbs-up.

"Navigations, target coordinates are 3-0 Delta, 4-9 Mike, 2-3 Sierra, November. 1-1-1 Delta, 0-0 Mike, 1-2 Sierra, Echo."

The navigator plotted on her orbital chart. "Coordinates confirmed, Major."

"Explosive slugs loaded and primed." The weapons officer

straightened his arms, clutching the rail-gun controls. “Ten minutes to target.”

Sinclair lifted her head up to Turunen, who was in his command seat.

“The *Imperator* is on standby and ready for your order, Colonel.”

“Put us in the correct orbital position.” Turunen nodded.

“Navigations, initiate course correction,” Sinclair relayed.

“Commencing course correction.” The navigator tapped a few buttons. “Thrusters firing.”

The *Imperator* rumbled, shaking the deck, generating vibration through Sinclair’s boots maglocked to the floor. The coordinates were in the eastern part of China. Sinclair zoomed in on the coordinates, and her lips separated, seeing the two-kilometer-long dam.

“Colonel, the target is the Three Gorges Dam.”

“The president did give General Shugart a blank check to finish this war.”

“Damn…we’re going to flood Central China.”

For minutes, the *Imperator*’s flight path on the orbital map slowly drifted from the Indian Ocean up to China’s interior. Sinclair concentrated on her breathing, bringing it back to a steady rhythm. She wanted to crack a knuckle, but the bulky gloves didn’t allow it.

Looking up at a camera feed, she saw the southern tip of India roll slowly beneath the spacecraft. They were minutes away from the target. If she was to convince him not to fire, now was the time.

She switched her comm channel to a direct line with Turunen. “Colonel, the *Revenant* is minutes behind us. Pass the fire order to them.”

“We will carry out the orders given to us,” Turunen said. “It’s too late for your idea.”

Sinclair tightened her lips again and looked away, wishing she had told him last week during their lunch break instead of this morning. She wanted to slap herself for waiting too long. Looking around the operations deck and imagining the dozen other spacemen on the *Imperator*, she realized the burden of responsibility for their lives weighed heavily on her shoulders.

They had bombed over fifty military targets in the past three years, without much hesitation or thought. The thousands of soldiers they had killed barely registered in her mind. But now, the spacecraft was on the brink of killing its crew, and she felt exposed.

The thrusters cut out once the dotted line crossed the coordinates, bringing the deck to a standstill.

"Course correction completed," the navigator said.

"Acknowledged, Navigations," Sinclair replied.

"The spacemen are suited up," the engineer said. "Major, ready to purge the air."

"Purge it."

Sinclair didn't feel the pressurized air being sucked into the vents, only seeing alerts on her helmet's HUD indicating the lack of breathable air in the operations deck.

"Five minutes to target, Major." The weapons officer tightly gripped the controls.

"Weapons, start the targeting package," Sinclair said.

"Developing the targeting package, Major." He unclutched his hand from the controls and typed in commands.

The software spit out dozens of flight paths for the explosive slugs, all curving at slightly altered angles to account for the *Imperator*'s orbital speed and Earth's rotation. The targeting system selected a curved line and beeped with confirmation.

"Target package is set." The weapons officer hovered his fingers over the red-colored safety switch. "Ready to take safety off."

"Stand by." Sinclair looked up at the countdown timer—just under two minutes.

Turunen stared at the displays. He appeared calm, likely seeing this as just another fire mission. Sinclair wondered if he was feeling the same weight on his shoulders as she did.

"One minute to target!" the weapons officer reported.

"Safety off," Turunen said.

"Safety off!" The weapons officer flicked the safety cover off but kept his finger away from the trigger.

Colonel Turunen sucked in a deep breath. "Transfer control to the *Imperator*."

"Transfer control to the *Imperator*." Sinclair passed the order on, surprised at how quickly she was able to say the words.

"The *Imperator* is now in control." The weapons officer pressed the red trigger.

Watching the timer count down, the muscles around her chest tightening, Sinclair thought she wasn't going to be able to breathe. She forced in and out a few breaths, mentally asking the *Imperator* to hold together.

The timer beeped.

"Firing!" the weapons officer shouted.

Sinclair grabbed a handlebar and clenched her teeth, ready for the violent tremors from the rail gun's kickbacks.

One second passed with stillness. Another second was silent. Feeling the lack of vibration in her legs was unsettling. Sinclair turned to the weapons officer. "Give me a—"

The *Imperator* twitched beneath the deck, followed by a muffled pop.

Alarms beeped from the engineering station, and the engineer said, "Major, we got breaches—"

A gray object cracked the floor open and shot through the weapons officer, smashing him against the ceiling, splitting his body into gory pieces.

"We've got explosions on the lower decks!"

"Where is it coming from?" Sinclair took her eyes off the mangled body pinned to the ceiling.

"It's—it's the rail gun," the engineer stuttered. "It's firing!"

Another discharge rattled the deck, and the weapon officer's body dropped from the ceiling, smashing into the floor and sending droplets of blood everywhere.

"Shut it down!" Sinclair climbed over her console, reaching for the weapons station. The rail gun fired a third time, blasting another set of debris through the deck.

The violent quake sent Sinclair flying across the deck, and the cushioned walls smashed against her back. She whelped at the pain in her neck and lower back. The rail gun fired, knocking her down to the floor.

"Shut it down!" Sinclair grunted.

The navigator was already at the weapons station, spreading her hands urgently over the buttons. "The controls aren't responding!"

"Cut its power!" Sinclair pointed at the engineer.

"I'm working it, Major!"

"Abandon ship!" Turunen jumped from his command seat.

"Sir, we need to shut down the rail gun," Sinclair replied, bracing herself against the rail-gun recoil. Another shake vibrated her hands.

"Abandon ship!" Turunen soared down to the engineering station and moved the engineer aside. "I'll take care of it."

After a couple discharges from the rail gun, the colonel turned his head, seeing the other three were still on the operations deck. "Move it!"

"You heard the commander!" Sinclair shouted. "Abandon ship!"

The two officers left the deck. Sinclair pressed the button to announce the order to abandon ship, triggering flashes of red lights. She pulled the handlebar and flew out of the room.

"Major Sinclair?" Turunen spoke in an unsettlingly calm voice.

"Sir?" Sinclair caught the edge of the hatch, bracing herself for the next recoil.

"Make it out of this alive." He fiddled with the engineering switches, not looking at her.

"Yes, sir."

"And, Sinclair?" Turunen turned, his old face red with anger. "Make the government pay for this." Salvia came out of his mouth, landing on his visor. "Never again."

The rail gun fired, and a second piece of debris burst through the deck. Sinclair flinched from the explosion and then brought her attention back to the colonel.

"I won't let this happen," she promised.

With fury, Sinclair flew down the corridor toward the emergency shuttle, careful not to let the walls hit her with each recoil of the rail gun. With the way the walls shook and moved, she recognized the *Imperator* was spinning uncontrollably, firing its rail gun in random directions down to Earth. She turned a corner and saw spacemen funneling into the shuttle.

The rail gun fired, and a piece of debris flew from the floor into Sinclair's helmet, cracking her visor. A hot piece slashed her neck, followed by a gush of dark, cold liquid inside her helmet.

She reached for her neck, but the helmet blocked her hands. Panic swarmed her mind, and she began hyperventilating, struggling to breathe. Her body spun around the corridor erratically. She slapped her helmet repeatedly, desperately trying to grab her neck. She screamed.

A strong grip wrapped her around the waist, pulling her through the corridor.

"It's okay, Major," Turunen said. "Some of us will get out of this alive."

"Sir..." she began, but blood clogged her throat.

Eyes fighting the urge to roll back, and feeling lightheaded, she struggled to follow what was happening or see where she was going. The copper-like taste of blood filled her mouth.

"Clear the path!" Turunen hollered.

Another set of hands grabbed her.

"Medic!" the colonel shouted. "The major is wounded!"

More hands grabbed her space suit and pulled her hard in one direction. The unexpected change from flashing red lights to a steady blue kept her awake. Seeing a row of black seats on both sides, Sinclair knew she was inside a shuttle.

"Step back, spacemen!" the colonel commanded. "The shuttle is full!"

"No," Sinclair mumbled, feeling the vibrations of the hatch closing. She raised her arm. "Sir..."

"Pressurize the cabin!" someone yelled. "I need her helmet off!"

Something hard banged against her helmet, rattling her head.

The shuttle jerked, went into a standstill, and fired its thrusters.

The acceleration only intensified her lightheadedness. Her eyelids grew heavy, and she struggled to keep them open.

Her helmet twisted off the neck seal, and cold air blasted into her face. Red droplets floated everywhere.

"Colonel..." she said as a painful pressure tightened around her neck.

"Hang on, Major!" a spaceman shouted in her face, hovering above her.

She barely heard the words and looked up. Before the darkness swarmed her vision, she saw on a monitor the plummeting *Imperator* firing explosive slugs at the planet below. How was Turunen going to evacuate all the spacemen they'd shared laughs with over the years? After a discharge, the orbital precision bomber swelled up and erupted into pieces. It exploded into a large debris field that drifted over the gentle blue atmosphere of Earth.

TWENTY YEARS LATER

2

THE MAGNATE

NYSE: VC 100.24 (-2.84%)

Michael Vanderheiden crossed his arms and admired the mural stretching from one end of the hallway to the other. All eight planets and their moons covered the wall, the colors intensified by the sun shining in through the glass ceiling above. The CEO, lean built with brushed-back brown hair and a trimmed beard, looked at Earth; its moon, Luna; and Mars. Only those planets had photonic platforms painted next to them. *Disappointing*, Vanderheiden thought. *We only built platforms at these planets before my retirement.*

The development of nuclear-thermal rockets had plateaued decades ago. This left the prosperity of the zero-g manufacturing complexes in low earth orbit and the mining colonies of Luna only possible for those who could afford the expensive rockets. Vanderheiden building the PhotonicWay changed everything.

Positioned in orbit around Earth, Luna, and Mars, photonic platforms fired powerful laser beams at spacecraft equipped with photonic engines, using the beam's heat to ignite the propellant mass inside the engine and generate thrust. This removed the need for spacecraft to carry an exorbitant amount of fuel, allowing them to carry more propellant mass, cargo, and personnel at a lower cost. The many dreams of tapping the natural resources of Luna and building colonies on Mars were realized.

Vanderheiden walked along the mural and came up to Neptune. Looking at the blue planet, he imagined photonic platforms orbiting over the dark but beautiful ice giant. *Someday, Vanderheiden Corporation will extend PhotonicWay's reach across the entire solar system.* He took a deep breath in through his nose. *And that will be my legacy.*

Laughter echoed from the opened doors down the hallway. Vanderheiden uncrossed his arms, readjusted his leather jacket, and walked to the PhotonicWay Command Center.

"Watch this! Watch this!" Gonzalez pointed at a video playing on his hand terminal, a glass tablet enclosed by a graphene cover. He had a metal-foam cast wrapped around his arm. Three of his operators huddled around him and leaned closer to the hand terminal's glass screen.

"And boom!" Gonzalez hooted. The others pulled their heads back, either groaning or chuckling.

"Damn..." one operator whispered.

Another operator saw Vanderheiden approach and pulled himself away from the huddle. "Hello, Vanderheiden! I'm Bakker...the new operator on the team." He extended his hand with a smile.

"Welcome to the team, Bakker." Vanderheiden shook it firmly and then looked at everyone else. "How is the PhotonicWay running today?"

The operators talked over each other. Vanderheiden glanced at the large screen in the back of the command center displaying a status card of each spacecraft running on the highway. The majority of the cards were green, with two yellows.

Vanderheiden turned to Gonzalez. "Why do we have yellows?"

"We have it in order," he replied. "Minor course corrections necessary."

"I want it all green by the end of the day."

Nicole, the most experienced operator, nodded and then smiled.

"Happy retirement, by the way! How does it feel leaving the company you built?"

"It'll be difficult leaving, but I'll make sure I leave the company in good hands." *I am burnt out. Running this company for ten years is too long.* Vanderheiden smiled at the operators. "Please excuse us."

After the operators returned to the workstations inside the large command center, Vanderheiden asked Gonzalez, "What had everyone laughing?"

"Oh..." He smiled. "You want to see the space dive I did in my wingsuit?"

Vanderheiden glanced at the metal cast on Gonzalez's arm. "And that's when this happened?"

"Ah..." He waved at him. "It's nothing."

Gonzalez played the video. The camera was attached to Gonzalez's helmet, and he wore a red wingsuit. He jumped out of a small space capsule hovering over eighty kilometers above Earth and dropped fast. Vanderheiden heard the bone crack when Gonzalez botched the landing after tripping over power lines.

"Gonzalez..." Vanderheiden lowered his chin. "As long as you are my chief operating officer, running the PhotonicWay, you will not end up in the hospital...especially if you want me to select you as my successor."

Gonzalez's ecstatic smile dropped. He nodded and put his hand terminal away.

"Let's go." Vanderheiden walked away. "Meeting in the Executive Chamber."

"Are the results in?"

Vanderheiden nodded. "And it's not good."

"Damn..." Gonzalez rubbed his nose.

Vanderheiden shoved the doors open and marched across the black tiles spread across the Executive Chamber. The blue skies of Houston, Texas, showed through the diamond-shaped glass panels on the walls and ceiling of the expansive room. A miniature statue of a photonic platform hung over the large wooden table that held a hologram projector.

The two other company chiefs were at the table. Arellano sat tall with her fingers interlocked calmly. The brunette executive was the corporation's first and only chief financial officer. Brunelli, the chief technology officer, leaned back in his chair with a hint of disgust on his face. He wore a golden necklace and a bright Hawaiian shirt with the top three buttons unfastened, revealing his hairy chest.

Vanderheiden came up to the table and tossed his hand terminal onto it. The black graphene cover clattered against the wood. Gonzalez grabbed a seat.

"So, it's official?" Vanderheiden looked at Arellano. "Our revenue and profit declined...again?"

Everyone turned to the chief financial officer. "Yes, it is official," she said.

"What is happening?" Vanderheiden sat down and pulled a red rubber ball out of his leather jacket's pocket.

"Our revenue is tied to the space economy's overall health, and all signs show a recession is coming. The higher tax rates from the Fairness Tax Act are going into effect soon, so our customers are cutting back on their budgets." Arellano shrugged her shoulders. "Our numbers were bound to take a beating."

"Our stock price is going to take a deep dive when we announce these results." Vanderheiden flicked his thumb. "The board is restless, and we don't need my successor to be on the hot seat at the start of their tenure."

Arellano nodded. "Our investors are getting nervous, too."

"We can blame it on the recession during the earnings call." Vanderheiden scooted his chair closer and put his elbows on the table. "Let's not make it three consecutive quarters of revenue decline."

He looked around the table, spinning the rubber ball in his hand. *Which one of you should succeed me? I must decide soon.* "Arellano, what's the latest on the military cargo contracts? Where are we on our legal protests?"

Brunelli locked his eyes on her.

"The story remains unchanged," she said. "Legal is facing political roadblocks. Shugart Technologies has an iron grip on the market. Their lobbyists have the militaries convinced they should keep their spacecraft on nuclear-thermal engines, not convert over to photonic propulsion."

"You need to push harder." Brunelli leaned forward. "Get more ruthless in your negotiations with the Pentagon."

"It's impossible to win the contracts." She turned her head. "The relationships between Shugart Technologies and the Pentagon goes back decades. As long as elected officials continue to get campaign donations from them, and retired military officers occupy Shugart's board, we'll never break into the defense industry."

"Well, then, hire better lobbyists." Brunelli pointed at her. "We'll play the damn political game if we need to."

"Hold it there, Brunelli." Vanderheiden raised the hand holding the rubber ball and spoke to Arellano. "You are saying it's impossible to get the cargo contracts? It is not like we are asking for flagship contracts."

Brunelli shook his head as Arellano replied, "Hiring the best lobbyists isn't enough. Our board has no retired officers or politicians with connections inside the government."

"General Sinclair," Gonzalez said.

"She wrote that white paper last year?" Vanderheiden asked. "Advocating for the space force to adopt photonic propulsion?"

Gonzalez smiled. "She could be our way into the defense industry."

Vanderheiden agreed. *This is good... Real good.* "Alright, I'll make some calls and try to get in touch with Sinclair. Any other ideas, Gonzalez?" *Maybe you are to be the new CEO...if you remain sober.*

Gonzalez shot his arm across the table and powered up the hologram projector, displaying the solar system and all the photonic platforms positioned around Earth, Luna, and Mars. The hologram zoomed in on the two gas giants.

"We should make the leap and deploy platforms at the outer planets. Start with Jupiter or Saturn. Give"—Gonzalez glanced quickly at Brunelli and Arellano—"the next CEO something great to start with."

Vanderheiden pondered the idea, squeezing the red ball. "Aside from research stations and military outposts, there is little economic activity in the outer system." He pointed at the hologram. "I'm not ready to extend a photonic line to the outer planets. Building and running the Martian line nearly bankrupted our company. We can't take that risk again."

"We have the financial caliber this time." Brunelli scoffed. "What happened to our dream of establishing photonic lines for all eight planets?"

"Financial reality," Vanderheiden shot back. "We almost lost this company when we deployed to Luna. And again when we extended to Mars."

"It's too risky," Arellano said. "Our stock is about to dip below one hundred. It takes years to travel to those planets. The time and cost to set up would tie up our cash flow for years."

Brunelli sucked air between his teeth. "Here we go again. *It's too costly. Our stock price is dropping. It's not good for the cash flow.*" He mocked Arellano and lowered his chin. "What does it take to get a budget increase?"

Arellano's eyes twitched for a second. "A solid business case."

"What does that mean?" Brunelli chuckled.

"That's enough, Brunelli," Vanderheiden said. *All you do is complain and complain.*

Everyone remained silent. Gonzalez broke it hesitantly: "Then let's deploy additional platforms to Mars and Luna."

Vanderheiden shook his head. "Once Martian Platform 4 is operational, we'll have one hundred percent transit window coverage at Luna and Mars. I don't want any idle platforms. We need to keep our budgets tight."

"What happens when the economy picks up steam and the demand outstrips our capacity?" Brunelli asked. "We need to invest *now*."

"Every line item must be justified," Vanderheiden said. "The last thing we need is Shugart gaining a seat on our board because the stock price dropped too low. We will not let them hijack this company."

Brunelli pursed his lips, and his balding forehead turned pink.

Vanderheiden looked back at Arellano and Gonzalez. *We must keep the stock price up.* He tapped his finger on the armrest. *Need more ideas.*

Brunelli's pink color faded away. "Well, I might have an idea." He glimpsed at Arellano. "Try not to shoot it down because it's...too expensive."

Arellano looked at him like she was bored. Brunelli spun up the hologram, displaying Earth. A cable extended from the surface up to thousands of kilometers above the planet. "A space elevator."

Vanderheiden's heart fluttered, but he didn't show his excitement. Brunelli's face lit up, and Vanderheiden knew his tongue was going to roll out a quick education on astrospace engineering. *He is the creative one. Does this company need that CEO?*

"A space elevator is a cable that connects from the Earth's surface to an orbital station, allowing vehicles to travel up and down without the use of rockets. It would be substantially cheaper than rockets. We could wipe out Shugart's surface-to-orbit business."

"How long would this cable be?" Vanderheiden asked.

"It would have to go up to geostationary orbit, so about 36,000 kilometers."

Gonzalez stifled a laugh, and Arellano blinked. Brunelli scowled at them.

"That's impractical." Vanderheiden shook his head, feeling deflated. *Must make calculated and disciplined decisions. Put my successor on a good footing.* "I'm not looking for a mega-construction project that'll take years to complete and blow up our financials."

Brunelli dropped his head like a bull ready to charge. "When you started this company, people told you photonic propulsion was impractical. Now, look where you are today. You got the last laugh."

He gestured at the hologram, then continued. "A space elevator would be revolutionary! People who can't afford rockets would have access to space. We would be able to fully tap the natural resources underneath the surfaces of Luna and Mars. Replenish the solar and battery farms. Accelerate expansion of nuclear energy. No more rolling blackouts. No more price gouging. It would end the Resource Crisis."

"Brunelli..." Vanderheiden whispered.

"It would lower the cost of raw materials for the zero-g manufacturing complexes. Everything built there—super-semiconductors, batteries, biomedical products, superalloys, pharmaceuticals, nanoparticles—everything would be more affordable for—"

"Brunelli!" Vanderheiden's shout silenced the room. "We can't afford this project."

"Everyone dreams of going to space!" Brunelli stood up and walked to the windows. "A space elevator would make that happen. Vanderheiden Corporation would become the company that changed the future!"

Arellano said, "We would need to see a cost estima—"

"I don't want to hear you utter the word *cost*." Brunelli swung around, pointing at her.

"Not if we bankrupt the company," Vanderheiden replied. "That would make us an easy acquisition target for Shugart. This is not the business environment to start a mega-construction project."

"Yes, it is! Yes, it is!" Brunelli stepped closer to him. "It is just like the Hoover Dam being built during the Great Depression. Material cost is low. Labor wages are dropping. *Now*...is the time."

"We aren't doing a space elevator." Vanderheiden tried to shut down the topic.

Brunelli ground his teeth and walked away to look out the window, seeing the green flatland of Houston. Clouds covered pockets of fields and forests.

Vanderheiden tossed his ball in the air. "Look, aside from the military contracts, the best we can do is protect our profit margins. I can hold the board at bay if we keep our margins high." He turned to Arellano. "Those cost cuts you proposed months ago?"

"Yes?"

"Refresh them and have them on my desk by the end of next week."

"Let's—"

Brunelli interrupted Arellano. "Let me guess...R&D budget will be the first to lose a limb."

Arellano slowly turned her head. "Yes, that is on the table. Workforce reductions, too."

Vanderheiden frowned. *She may lack charisma, but she could be the CEO who makes the tough decisions.*

"Firing employees, you mean?" Brunelli turned around and walked back to the table.

"Brunelli, allow her to scope out all the options," Vanderheiden said. "She'll give us the options, and I decide which path to take."

Brunelli stood tall and rolled his shoulders back. "You are the investors' bitch now."

All sound zapped out of the room. Both Gonzalez's and Arellano's jaws dropped.

Vanderheiden stopped tapping his rubber ball and set it down. "What did you say?" he asked with as much calmness as he could muster.

"I said...you are the investors' bitch now." Brunelli spoke slowly and more defiantly.

Vanderheiden stood up slowly, stretching his chest out and holding his head high.

"As CEO of my company, I tolerate different opinions. I accept constructive feedback." He raised his finger at Brunelli. "But I will *not* tolerate disrespect. I've dealt with your difficulties for years, but now you've crossed the line. I will have your resignation next Friday. You are no longer a candidate to be the next CEO of Vanderheiden Corporation."

"You think I will—"

"Resignation! Next Friday!"

Vanderheiden's shout frightened Arellano, and Gonzalez recoiled.

Brunelli stepped back, dropping his hands to his sides. He then marched out of the room without glancing back.

With a long sigh, Vanderheiden rested his fists on the table. *And I thought he was the one, despite being a pain in the ass.* He glanced at Arellano and Gonzalez. *Only two candidates remain.*

His hand terminal beeped a notification, reminding him of his standing Wednesday dinner with his wife and daughter. He felt the urge to skip it and stay in the Executive Chamber for the evening, fleshing out plans to pull his corporation out of financial trouble. *But I will not be the CEO who won the business wars but lost his family.*

"That's enough for today." He swept up his hand terminal. "Arellano, get me those cost-cutting measures. Gonzalez, no yellow cards. Once the earnings are public, our stock is going to drop. We need to be ready." He marched out of the black-tiled room. "It's going to get ugly."

3

THE GENERAL

The rocket hissed, cooling off after its descent to the Padre Island Military Spaceport. Dozens of launchpads lined up along the Gulf Coast. Some were silent and empty, filled with bird nests, undeterred by the stench of burnt propellant. Other launchpads held rockets swarmed by spacemen and droids. The ground crew shouted orders as the postflight procedures got underway. Droids unloaded cargo from the shuttle's belly and replaced tiles of the heat shield that had been damaged during the scorching descent through Earth's atmosphere.

"You ready, General?" a medical technician asked.

General Sinclair nodded slowly, careful not to make her head spin.

"One, two, three!" The technicians lifted her out of the seat inside the shuttle and placed her in the wheelchair on the launchpad elevator. They carried her out and then placed other spacemen in their wheelchairs.

Returning to gravity after months in weightlessness was a major shock to the body. Sinclair's limbs felt heavy, and she was barely able to move or walk. Her heart pumped hard to fight the gravity and keep the blood flowing upward. She would feel her head spinning if she made any sudden movements.

"How are you doing, General?"

"Sergeants," Sinclair spoke cautiously, afraid she would vomit. "Just get me to medical."

"Yes, ma'am."

The elevator descended, and they wheeled her across the hot tarmac toward the medical clinic. Preoccupied with her upset stomach and intense vertigo, Sinclair barely noticed the cool breeze and warm sunlight touching her pale skin.

Rolling into the clinic, the technicians lifted Sinclair, placed her on a recovery bed, and hooked her up with fluids. One spaceman vomited on the floor as technicians lifted him up, prompting nurses to assist. A nurse came by and gave Sinclair the standard cocktail of medicine and supplements for spaceflight recovery. Anti-nausea medication, muscle enhancement, mental augmentation, and calcium booster were all in the cocktail drink.

"Nurse, I need an extra dose of boosters." Sinclair took a small sip from the bottle.

"I cannot do that, ma'am. You are already near the maximum dosage for your weight."

Sinclair wanted to be sharp now. The urgent request from SPACECOM to return to Corpus Christi, Texas, was concerning. She needed her standard one week of recovery from spaceflight, but she needed to be sharp now, ready for whatever news General Abborn had to share.

"Nurse, this is my fourth deployment." The general took another sip. "I know how it works. Give them to me."

"That's a doctor's pay grade. He has to sign off on it."

"Let's save ourselves the trouble of me reporting your refusal to the doctor." Sinclair got the words out, just managing to hold the vomit in. "The meds. Now."

The nurse sighed, looking at her with contempt. She turned to the nurse on the other side of the bed. "Give it to her."

After drinking the extra dosage, Sinclair rested in her bed for a few hours, letting her body acclimate to the gravity. The bed was the most comfortable thing. Once the vertigo was manageable, Sinclair grabbed her black uniform, hobbled into a private room, and slowly changed into it.

Dressing up in Earth's full gravity was a cumbersome task. Instead of the clothes floating in midair like in space, Sinclair had to correct her instincts, forcing herself to hold the clothes so they wouldn't fall down to the floor. She put a little bit of exertion into pulling her compression leggings up, triggering some lightheadedness. She had to sit down for a minute, the leggings only halfway up her short and lean legs. After a few deep breaths, she stood slowly and pulled the compression leggings all the way up. She then put on her black uniform pants.

Adjusting the buttons on her uniform jacket, Sinclair watched herself in the mirror, seeing a petite woman with thin lips and short blonde hair. It was uncomfortable looking at the coarse scar stretching from the bottom of her neck up to the jawline on her left side.

She touched it gently and hissed, feeling the memories of the terrible day. The rail gun backfiring, killing the weapons officer. "Never again," Colonel Turunen had said. The slicing pain cutting her neck when she flew down the corridor. The colonel throwing her through the air lock, saying, "Step back, spacemen! The shuttle is full!" The *Imperator* spinning out of control, firing explosive slugs at Earth.

Sinclair withdrew her finger and rested her arms on the sink below the mirror. "None of it will be in vain," she whispered, gripping the sink hard.

She examined the two silver stars on her shoulders, and imagining two more stars made her mind burn with purpose. Once she got that fourth star and became the top military officer of the US Space Force, she would ensure the government never neglected its spacemen again. She would transform the US Space Force into a lean and ruthless war machine, unincumbered by bureaucracy and corrupted by politicians and defense contractors. That was her mission. And she intended to accomplish it at any cost.

Sinclair took a deep breath, adjusted the sleeves of her uniform, and walked out of the clinic with a slight stagger, still learning to walk again. She came to the sizzling parking lot. A sergeant, coming from a black vehicle, marched up and offered her a salute. Sinclair returned the salute.

"Ma'am, I have orders to take you to the Delta Room."

"Very well, Sergeant. Lead the way,", she said, gesturing to the car.

Cruising down the highway, Sinclair stared out the window. The large horizon was overwhelming after being cooped up in tight quarters for months. She lowered her eyes to avoid passing out. It took several minutes of alternating between looking up and down before the horizon, miles and miles of flat farmlands growing cotton and sorghum, was no longer overpowering to look at. Off in the distance, a rocket blasted off, soaring through the puffy clouds.

They arrived at the security checkpoint manned by spacemen in black uniforms and carrying assault rifles. After checking identifications, the security guards saluted Sinclair, and the gate fell to the ground.

Beyond the gate stood the Corpus Christi Space Force Base, a sprawling military complex comprised of buildings of various shapes and colors. The main administrative building stood at the center, and Sinclair couldn't decide if it was supposed to look like a rocket or a church steeple. The vehicle stopped at the recreation center, which was surrounded by statues and gardens, making it appear to belong to a royal family, not the world's most powerful military branch.

Sinclair stepped out of the car, feeling her head spin and her stomach quiver. Vertigo threatened to return with a vengeance, but the anti-nausea meds held it at bay. She grabbed the car door to balance herself, feeling the metal hot from the sunlight.

"Do you need help, General?" the sergeant asked.

Sinclair lifted her hand, dismissing him. After the sound of the vehicle sped off and faded into the distance, she slowly walked up the steps and entered the building. She had a feeling the news soon to be shared in the Delta Room would not be good.

* * *

"Can I get you anything to drink?" the bartender asked, tattoos covering both arms.

"Something easy on the stomach." Sinclair looked around the Delta Room, which was crowded with senior officers. The bartender filled up a glass with sparkling water. "Here you go, ma'am."

Sinclair grabbed the chilled glass and walked along blue walls covered with pictures dating back to the formation of the US Space Force in 2019. In the far corner of the room, she came up to the black wall with dozens of delta insignias pinned to it, a metal nameplate under each delta.

She wondered how many deltas would not be pinned to the wall if the space force had properly supplied the orbital precision bombers during the Second North Atlantic–Eurasian War.

"Never again," Sinclair whispered, looking at Colonel Turunen's nameplate.

"There she is." A heavy hand patted her back.

Sinclair experienced a split second of dizziness from the touch. With a sharp inhale through the nose, she looked over her shoulder. "General Ruiz."

"Paying your respects?" Ruiz looked at the memorial next to her, holding a glass of beer.

"No." She took a sip of water, feeling the bubbles pop in the back of her mouth. "Reminding myself why I am here."

"And what are you reminding yourself?"

Sinclair turned away from the wall, noting the dozens of generals and colonels socializing in the Delta Room. "When the next war comes, there needs be someone in this room watching out for the spacemen putting their lives in our hands. We need to be able to fight the war, not play the political game."

A set of double doors swung open, and three generals entered.

Space Chief General Abborn walked into the room, and everyone quieted down. He had a thick black-and-gray beard and skin the color of olive. His eyes were hard and tired, like he was disinterested in everything.

"I think many officers here have a genuine care for the spacemen," Ruiz whispered, leaning toward Sinclair.

"Not all of them." Sinclair watched General Maxwell follow Abborn into the room. She noted the smallest hint of a smirk on his dark-skinned face. "Many think the enlisted and junior officers are just pawns in their quest for status and power."

Ruiz walked away without comment, and everyone turned to the three generals. The last of the three to enter was General Garrett, the vice space chief. Overweight and cheeks scarred from old acne, he stood behind Abborn and crossed his arms. Sinclair knew that body language was a sign of deep, simmering frustration.

"Have a seat, Officers," Abborn said softly.

Sinclair grabbed a cushioned chair and sat down, feeling relief from the soreness in her knees and lower back. The slight vertigo from standing upright faded away.

"The Space Staff just returned from a series of congressional hearings to review the future makeup of the United States Armed Forces. After much...deliberation, the government has decided to reduce the military's budget by twenty percent."

Whispers circulated the Delta Room, and a few officers groaned.

"Settle down!" Maxwell said. Garrett gave him a side glance, his arms remaining crossed.

"With the space force having the highest budget of the six branches, we get the highest share of the cuts."

"But, sir?" Ruiz stood up. "What about the air force? Navy? Their airplanes and ships are just useless metals."

"Sit down, Ruiz." Maxwell spoke deliberately, exposing his unnaturally white teeth.

Abborn continued his announcement after Ruiz sat down. "This has forced the Space Staff to make a series of head-count reductions."

Sinclair took a quick scan around the room and noticed many of the officers served on gunships, not guided-missile destroyers. She sunk deeper in her seat, feeling a numbness crawl up her aching back.

"I am to inform you that every officer in this room will be honorable discharged, with full pensions and benefits." Abborn raised his voice a notch. "Effective at the end of this month."

An awkward silence hung over the Delta Room, nearly every officer stunned by the news. Sinclair lowered her forehead, resting it on her hand to rub away the lightheadedness. She was only two stars away from joining the Space Staff, and they just snatched it away from her because she came from gunships, not destroyers. The dream of seeing her fourth star pinned to her shoulder suddenly disappeared, replaced by the despairing thought of seeing spacecraft being destroyed and spacemen dying on the newsfeed and not being able to do anything about it. Her chest felt heavy and her breathing grew labored.

She squeezed her jaw and lifted her head, staring at Maxwell.

Ruiz blinked for a few seconds and leaned forward. "Sir, what were the criteria for selecting which senior officers to discharge?"

"Many factors were considered," Maxwell said. "This was not a decision we took lightly."

"Don't lie to us!" Sinclair shot out of her seat. "This is a purge of gunship officers."

"This is the United States," Abborn said. "We don't *purge* our servicemen."

"The gunship and their rail guns are the future of space warfare, not guided missiles."

"Not in the eyes of the government."

"I—" Sinclair stopped herself when she saw Garrett shake his head urgently. She took a breath through her nose and sat down, fingernails digging into her palms.

Ignoring the other questions asked, her mind spun over what she was going to do. She predicted war with Europe would break out during her time in service. She had to be ready for it. She was not going to fade away into retirement while thousands of spacemen went off to war under the command of incompetent generals. The *Imperator* couldn't happen again. She'd promised Turunen.

Abborn dismissed the officers, and everyone scattered off. Sinclair remained seated, stuck in her thoughts.

"Enjoy your retirement, Sinclair," Maxwell said.

Sinclair looked up to find the tall general staring down at her with a smirk. She stood up and rolled her shoulders back. "What speedboat are you going to buy? Need to spend some of the money Shugart Technologies just put into your pocket."

Maxwell's eyes widened, and he curled his lips. "I will not be accused by—"

"Walk away, Maxwell." Garrett grabbed his shoulder from behind. "I need to speak with Sinclair."

Maxwell shifted his jaw and turned to Garrett. "Don't forget what Abborn said." He walked away to speak to other officers.

"What was he talking about?" Sinclair asked Garret.

"Let's go to my office."

* * *

"This is a *fucking* purge of gunship officers!" Sinclair raised her arms after Garrett shut his office door. "How could you let this happen?"

Garrett walked past her and sat his heavy weight down on the chair. "Please sit down, Sinclair."

Sinclair shook her head. "No one else is telling me to sit down today."

Garrett chuckled and fidgeted his thumbs, swiveling his chair from side to side.

"Garrett, we had a deal." Sinclair placed her hands on her hips. "You would protect me from Abborn and Maxwell while I focused on performing my duties. You have not held up your end of the deal."

"Sinclair, all the reins have been cut. Abborn and Maxwell have the full support of the government and defense contractors, especially Shugart Technologies. I am outgunned and outflanked. Abborn is slowly filling up SPACECOM with his loyalists, pushing his challengers out."

"Then what *can* we do?"

"What matters right now is protecting those two stars pinned to your shoulder." Garrett pointed at her. "War with Europe is coming. The space force needs its best officers leading the charge, not the blockheads. I will pull every string I have and call in favors to cover you."

"Let's be honest." Sinclair stepped closer to the desk. "What strings do you have left to pull?"

Garrett didn't reply. He looked out the window behind him. A VTOL flew across the military base, low to the ground. He pulled a drawer from beneath the desk and took out a bowl of chocolate chips.

He tossed a few pieces into his mouth and turned back at Sinclair. "The war will happen, and it will expose the politically savvy generals, such as Maxwell, as incompetent, paving the way for officers like you to take the lead." He pressed his finger on the desk. "That...is what we need to prepare for."

"You are telling me to sit tight and let Abborn and Maxwell continue bulking up our fleets with destroyers and sending gunships to the scrapyards? We need to reverse course...*now*...before war breaks out. It will not matter who is leading the space force if we don't have the right combat spacecraft in orbit."

"Sinclair!" Garrett's hand turned into a fist. "What matters more: Gunships or getting those four stars?"

Sinclair grunted. She couldn't believe she had to make that kind of choice. It went against her nature. She shouldn't have to compromise her views for the stars. Not when the security of the United States was at stake.

"The four stars."

"Good." Garrett leaned back and ate another few chocolates. "That settles it. Once you get them and we have an iron grip of the space force, then we can phase out destroyers for the gunships."

Sinclair shook her head and stared out the window, looking at the many buildings. Playing the political game was foreign to her. She knew it existed, but Garrett had always taken care of it. He had kept her under his wing as he'd climbed the ranks, bringing her along and shielding her from the politics. Sinclair kept her focus on developing her strategic acumen and performing her duties well. She wanted to be ready for the next shooting war, not a political clash.

"Now...there is a way to prevent your discharge." He raised his hands, signaling for Sinclair to stay calm. "You are not going to like it, but listen."

Sinclair closed her eyes. "What is it?"

"Abborn gave me an offer: You get the honorable discharge, and I run through my last two years before mandatory retirement. Or I retire now and you remain an officer."

"Will I keep command of the Orbital Fleet gunships?" Sinclair opened her eyes.

"No, you'll be transferred to the Luna Fleet and take over as deputy fleet commander."

"Where careers go to die," Sinclair said. "My answer is no."

"Sinclair..."

"Damn Abborn and Maxwell!" Sinclair smacked her hands against the desk. "Let's blow the lid open! Expose them to the public! Year after year, war games have demonstrated gunships are more effective than destroyers."

"It's difficult explaining to senators how a hundred slugs fired from a gunship's rail gun are more likely to get past an enemy APS than a destroyer's ten guided missiles."

"Then why are we letting them dictate our strategy?"

"It's called civilian control of the military." Garrett blinked deliberately. "Mandated by law."

Sinclair pulled her hands from the desk with a sigh of annoyance.

"It won't matter anyway." Garrett waved at her. "Congress and the defense industry have Abborn and Maxwell locked in place. Give Abborn's offer serious thought. And before you make the decision, come to the war room next week. There are new developments you need to be aware of."

"Regarding Europe?"

"Yes." Garrett got up from his seat, bringing the chocolates with him. "In the meantime, I have an assignment for you."

Sinclair crossed her arms. "Let me guess...sit tight and shut up."

Garrett chuckled. "No. You need to develop your own support network inside and outside the military. Otherwise, the political vultures in both flocks will tear you apart. I know you don't like rubbing shoulders with these people, but it needs to be done."

"So, I have to play at the same level as Maxwell?"

Garrett tilted his head like a professor explaining a basic concept to his students. "Sinclair, that's how it works. Success and merits are not enough to get you to the top. Play the political game and get dirty. You'll have no regrets once you are the space chief."

"Vanderheiden Corporation didn't play it dirty, and they still won customers away from Shugart's commercial business."

"That's...a fair point," Garrett replied. "But they flipped the table over. PhotonicWay bankrupted many launch service providers."

"Creative destruction." Sinclair shrugged her shoulders.

"Speaking of Vanderheiden, you have a soccer game to go to this weekend." Garrett smiled. "With Michael Vanderheiden."

She raised an eyebrow. "What does he want to talk about?"

"Vanderheiden Corporation has no defense contracts, so he probably wants to talk about how the PhotonicWay can be leveraged by the space force. This is an opportunity to weaken Shugart's control of the military business."

"So, something good came out of that white paper I wrote on photonic propulsion."

"I still don't agree with adopting photonic propulsion, but if we can get Vanderheiden to break Shugart's grip, I'm open to it. You find out if he will do that. He broke Shugart's commercial business. I can imagine he is eager to repeat that success on the military side."

Sinclair remembered the newsfeeds talking about Vanderheiden quitting his job at Shugart Technologies to build the PhotonicWay. Speculations said he proposed the concept to the Shugart executives but was turned down. Critics of Shugart pointed to its failure to adopt photonic propulsion as a sign the company was past its prime. Congress and the Pentagon didn't seem to get the message.

Garrett checked his watch and walked around the desk. "I got a meeting with Shugart to hear their next round of excuses on why the Lampard-class gunships are behind schedule." He shook his head.

Sinclair said nothing. Garrett slapped her shoulder. "Hey, don't dwell on it. We'll get through this. Get plenty of rest. You'll need it."

Garrett ate a chocolate, walked out of the office, and slammed the door shut.

Sinclair sat motionless, processing everything that had happened today. She stared out the window, watching two vultures land on a security fence. How was she going to continue serving the space force if the gunships were being decommissioned? How could she convince Vanderheiden to fight Shugart? How was she going to continue her climb to the four stars without Garrett?

Sinclair looked at the two vultures again and thought they were staring at her.

4

THE MAGNATE

NYSE: VC 90.86 (-9.36%)

"Here are the Vanderheidens!" The waitress set down three metal trays loaded with smoked brisket, cream corn, mac 'n' cheese, baked beans, and pecan pie.

Emily grabbed a fork and ate the mac 'n' cheese, and Susann moved her pecan pie over to her daughter's tray.

"Thank you." Vanderheiden pulled out his hand terminal and wired a 100 percent tip to the waitress.

The waitress widened her eyes when she saw the notification on her pink hand terminal.

"Don't tell Rudy." Vanderheiden winked. "And don't spend it on the marketplace. Put it in a brokerage account."

"T-thank you, Mr. Vanderheiden." She stuttered the words and walked off.

Contradicting the minimalistic black-and-white interiors of the corporate headquarters, Frederick's BBQ was built out of wood and iron. The burnt smell of barbeque filled the air, and utensils clanged as the workers chopped pork and brisket. The Vanderheiden family sat at a corner table with a view of the Texas coastline, no spaceports in sight.

This is pleasant. Vanderheiden watched the pelicans fly in a straight-line formation over the waves washing up against the sand. *No shareholder complaining about stock price, company chief reporting an issue, or customer demanding to be top priority.* The aroma of smoked meat drifted into Vanderheiden's nostrils, and he picked up his fork.

"Here he comes, honey," Susann said. "Be nice."

Vanderheiden sighed. Emily looked over her shoulder, seeing the stout restaurant manager approach, and snickered after turning back to her tray.

"There's the family!" Rudy raised his hairy arms. "How's the food? Is everything good? Oh...you need a refill?" He pointed at Emily's empty glass.

"O'!" Emily spoke through a mouthful. "P'ease."

"Emily!" Susann waved at Rudy. "We can get the refills ourselves. Thank you, though."

"No, I don't mind! Anything for the Vanderheidens!"

"I insist." Susann flashed a soft smile.

"If the mother says so." Rudy bowed his head and turned to Vanderheiden. "Hey! A new shipment of Marius Hills Lager came in, straight from Luna on the PhotonicWay. You want to try it? You can taste a hint of lunar dust in it."

"No, thank you, Rudy." Vanderheiden pointed at his glass of iced water. "I'm good with what I have."

"Hey...very few people get to drink beer brewed on the moon."

"Rudy..." Vanderheiden set his fork down with a sharp click. "We've been coming here for, what? Twelve years, Rudy? Not once have we bought alcohol. We won't start today. Can we please enjoy our dinner?"

Rudy's face turned slightly pink, and his eyes flickered back and forth between Vanderheiden and his wife.

"Enjoy your dinner!" he said, then sauntered off.

"I thought he was going to make my food turn cold." Vanderheiden exhaled and shoved a piece of brisket into his mouth.

Susann finished her cream corn and wiped her heart-shaped lips with a napkin. "Everyone is struggling in this recession. Especially restaurants. Rudy knows money isn't a problem for you."

"Well, there are better ways for the restaurant to spend its money than procuring beer from Luna."

Vanderheiden ate another piece and looked to his wife, watching her eat baked beans for a moment. She was tall, nearly to his height, and tan, with short black hair. *Always beautiful.*

"Yes?" Susann noticed his stare.

"Nothing." Vanderheiden smirked and turned to Emily. Their daughter had Susann's narrow face but Vanderheiden's brown hair. "Hey...can you get off your terminal? This is one of the few nights we get to chat."

Emily opened her hands and dropped her chest, ready to protest. "I got to study the videos for the soccer game this weekend!"

"You ready for the game?" Vanderheiden asked.

Emily reached across the table, stabbed a piece of mac-n-cheese from his tray, and ate it. "I'll be ready." She smiled, showing the cheesy pasta stuck in her teeth.

Susann snorted and looked away.

"Watch your videos." Vanderheiden chuckled, shaking his head.

The family ate in silence. Vanderheiden's thoughts inevitably drifted back to his business. Before entering the restaurant, he glanced at the stock tracker and saw the VC stock price had dropped nearly 10 percent. *Damn...financial results got leaked.* He looked back outside, watching more pelicans fly over the brownish water.

"So, have you decided on the next CEO?" Susann asked.

"No." He frowned. "There isn't an ideal candidate." *It's hard to imagine someone else at the helm of Vanderheiden Corporation, the company I built.*

"Walk me through your options again." Susann gave a sharp nod.

"Gonzalez knows how to operate the PhotonicWay effectively. But he needs someone to point him in the right direction. And I don't trust him to stay sober when I'm gone."

"He's an excellent operator," she said. "How long has he stayed clean?"

"Two years...that I know of." He shrugged. "Arellano's mind only runs on financial numbers, and bean counters leading a company rarely leads to success."

"But she has been there from the beginning."

"True. And then there's Brunelli." *To no longer be at VC soon.* "He is the spirit of the company, constantly pushing us to innovate. But he is only an engineer, not a businessman. Plus, he is too volatile."

"Now we are getting somewhere." Susann tapped his arm with the back of her hand. "You were an engineer, too."

"Well...I asked for his resignation today. He went a step too far with his attitude. So, he is no longer an option."

"Oh...that's unfortunate." She gave a sad smile. "There has to be someone."

Vanderheiden took a sip of his iced water. "There is only one."

"Gabriella Scharre."

"She is the perfect candidate. She has been the board chairwoman since the start, keeping directors and shareholders off my back. We are in sync with many business decisions. No one is better than her."

"You know she won't leave Scharre Farms, right? She built that agri-tech company."

Vanderheiden stared out at the endless sea. *Like me, unable to envision myself leaving a company I built.*

"Well, who are you going to pick? Next Friday is the deadline."

He only shrugged.

"I have to ask..." Susann rested her fingers on his arms. "Is it really a hard decision? Or are you delaying the decision because, deep down, you don't want to leave?"

Vanderheiden turned to Susann. "No, I don't want to leave. PhotonicWay is my legacy."

"She is your legacy." Susann pointed at their daughter. "Companies rise and fall, but family is forever."

Vanderheiden looked at Emily, who was watching her soccer videos. The memory of her birth flooded his mind.

Twelve years ago, Susann, sweaty and exhausted, groaned in bed as the nurses worked to deliver their baby.

"And push!" the doctor shouted.

Susann grunted and yelled. Amid the commotions in the delivery room, Vanderheiden stared out the window, dreading the future. His engineering project at Shugart Technologies had just been shut down, and rumors of layoffs were circling. With his employment in question, he didn't know how he was going to support his family. He questioned his own worth.

The shrieks of a newborn filled the delivery room, and Vanderheiden turned around. A nurse wrapped the baby with brown hair in a blanket and placed her in his arms.

"It's a girl." The nurse smiled.

Vanderheiden looked down at the wailing baby, and the biggest smile grew on his face.

Emily is my legacy. Arms resting on the wooden table inside the restaurant, Vanderheiden thought about Susann's words. *My father would've laughed at that. So, she is right.*

"Let me lay it out for you," Susann said. "Pick Gonzalez if PhotonicWay remains the future of the company. Pick Arellano if you want to stabilize the business and support the shareholders. Pick Brunelli if you want the company to continue innovating. Which option do you pick?"

"The company must keep innovating," Vanderheiden replied in an instant.

"Then your decision has been made." Susann caressed his arm. "You need to fix things with Brunelli."

The light fixtures hanging from the ceiling gave out, drowning the restaurant in darkness. The orange dawn hovering over the sea created black silhouettes of people sitting at their tables. Susann and many others gasped at the sudden darkness. Vanderheiden grabbed his wife's arm and squeezed with assurance.

"Any minute now!" Rudy shouted from the kitchen in the back.

Emily's hand terminal screen illuminated her face with a blue color. She grabbed the nasal bone between her eyes and squinted her eyelids with a groan. Vanderheiden watched her with concern.

A minute later, the flights flickered back on with a struggle, brightening the customers' concerned looks. After another minute, people resumed eating and chatting.

Emily rubbed her forehead.

"Are you okay?" Susann asked.

"I've had a headache for days, and that blackout just made it ten times worse."

"Why didn't you tell me?" Susann pulled out a medical injector from her bag and selected a painkiller. "Here you go, sweetheart."

"Crazy how we have a robust space economy up there," Vanderheiden said, "but utilities are spotty down here."

"What do you expect from the government?" Susann took the injector from Emily after she consumed the medicine. "Coherent decisions?"

"They just need to decide between reopening the oil fields or pivoting toward nuclear energy. Two straightforward choices to fix the Resource Crisis."

"Please never run for a political office." Susann laughed. "It's never that simple."

"Oh...trust me. It'll never cross my mind."

"Are you Vanderheiden? The man who built the PhotonicWay?"

Vanderheiden looked up, startled because he hadn't seen the teenager approach their table. Noting his enthusiastic expression, Vanderheiden's neck tightened up as he braced himself for the usual questions. *I want to start my own company. Any tips you can share? I can't afford to travel to Luna. Do you have any discounted seats on the PhotonicWay? I want to be rich like you. What business ideas do you have?*

"We are having a family dinner." Susann shifted to the edge of her seat, closer to the teenager, and smiled. "Can you please give us some privacy?"

The teenager's bottom lip quivered, and he glanced back and forth between her and Vanderheiden for a few seconds. "Oh...sorry to bother you guys." He dropped his shoulders, disappearing into the crowded restaurant.

"Thanks," Vanderheiden said. *You just make things easier for me.* "I wasn't ready for that."

Susann winked at him. "Anyway...you should be proud of yourself for building the PhotonicWay. You've paved the way for society to tap the resources of Luna and Mars to replenish the solar and battery farms. You've done your part." She waved her hand at the restaurant crowd. "Now, other people need to step it up."

Vanderheiden knew the PhotonicWay wasn't enough. It lowered the cost of interplanetary travel, but the surface-to-orbit launches remained astronomically expensive, given photonic propulsion didn't work inside atmospheres. *But a space elevator could fix that, like Brunelli said. It could be the answer to the Resource Crisis.*

Emily got up from her seat, halting Vanderheiden's thoughts.

"I don't feel good. I need to use the restroom."

"Need me to come with you?" Susann got halfway out of her seat.

Emily shook her head and navigated between the tables toward the restrooms in the back.

"I'm glad we have her," Vanderheiden said.

Susann smiled and placed her hand on his knee under the table. "I know you had much hesitation about having a child, but I'm proud of you for being brave."

Vanderheiden felt happiness bloom in his stomach. "I didn't want to be like my father."

"You've been a great father." Susann tightened her lips together. "Especially when being a CEO for ten years. Few kids have that kind of father. Not in this world, at least."

"After what my father did, I swore I wouldn't be a successful businessman who lost his family and drowned in alcoholism." Vanderheiden wiped away a buildup of tears in his eye with a finger. "You two were very patient with me."

"I know it's tough leaving your company." Susann gave his leg a hard pat. "You'll need to find something to keep yourself occupied. Emily is going to be off to college in a few years."

"Maybe I can finally get involved in the day-to-day operations of the Houston Photonics. Become an expert in something else besides the PhotonicWay."

After chuckling, Susann leaned over his shoulder. They shared a kiss, and his lower body heated up with excitement. She pulled back with a smile Vanderheiden never tired of seeing.

Susann looked past his face and froze, her eyes widening.

"Wha..." Vanderheiden turned his head.

"Emily!"

Susann burst out of her seat and sprinted across the restaurant.

Vanderheiden twisted to his side, bewildered by her sudden panic. Then his jaw dropped.

He saw his daughter collapse into a table, sending food and drinks flying into the air, and smack her head against the concrete floor.

* * *

Vanderheiden and Susann sat in anxious silence in the doctor's cramped office. The desk in front of them was empty, except for medical papers and memos on new government policies. The shelves behind the desk had a couple mugs and crushed cans of energy drinks.

"Where the hell is the doctor?" Vanderheiden got up from his seat and looked out the grimy windows. "We've been here for hours."

"I don't want to hear you complain," Susann snapped. "I'm on the verge of a breakdown. I need *silence*."

Vanderheiden inhaled and looked down at the unkept garden outside, inspecting the plants spilling onto the concrete paths.

The door opened, and Dr. Grosso walked into the room, reviewing his hand terminal. Vanderheiden took his eyes off the ground and watched the doctor sit down. The bags under Dr. Grosso's eyes and his receding hairline made him look a decade older than he was. He scrolled through his hand terminal with a scowl. Vanderheiden wondered how many patients he'd dealt with today. *Too many*, he speculated.

The doctor finally looked up at the parents. "It took longer than expected to get approval from the board to run tests. I apologize for that."

He looked back to his hand terminal and scrolled through more pages. "I regret to inform you that your daughter"—he looked at his notes—"Emily...has Creutzfeldt-Jakob disease."

Susann gasped and grabbed Vanderheiden's arm. "I knew something was wrong when she fell down."

CJD...a degenerative brain disorder. Vanderheiden recognized the fatal disease.

"What are our next steps here?" He sat down next to Susann.

Dr. Grosso nodded. "I'll authorize prescriptions that'll help ease the symptoms. Based on the test results and the details you have shared, I estimate she has two years to live. As long as she takes the medicine, she'll be able to carry out a normal life for another twelve months before dementia, loss of movement and coordination, and psychosis set in."

Susann's mouth shuddered, hand to her face. "Are there any treatments? Anything?"

"There is a treatment called CJD-VL, but it is limited in supply, and there is a long wait list." He tapped the touchscreen of his hand terminal. "I put Emily on the list."

"Money won't be a problem." Vanderheiden waved at him. "How can we get Emily at the top of the queue?"

The doctor shook his head. "NMS manages the wait list. They determine who gets the treatment on a case-by-case basis." He paused and looked at Vanderheiden closely. "The board gives higher priority to low-income patients and people of certain ethnicities, so that doesn't play in your favor."

"You are telling me we might not be able to save our daughter because the government says we are too rich or lack the proper skin color?"

"Michael!" Susann hissed, squeezing his arm.

"It is out of my hands." The doctor shrugged. "All I can do is make the symptoms less painful for Emily and report her condition to the board. They will decide if she gets the treatment."

Vanderheiden ground his teeth.

"We'd like to see our daughter now," Susann said.

The doctor nodded and led them to Emily's room. They found their twelve-year-old daughter sitting on a hospital bed. She was watching soccer videos on her terminal, a white bandage wrapped around her head.

"Have you told her?" Susann asked.

The doctor shook his head.

Susann entered the room, and Emily greeted her with a cheerful smile. Susann grasped her daughter's hands and whispered into her ear. The girl's face turned sullen as Susann spoke.

Vanderheiden turned to the doctor. "Which company supplies the treatment?"

He checked his notes. "Valkyrie Labs."

Vanderheiden pulled out his hand terminal and looked up the contact information of the company CEO, Dr. Courtney Raymond.

"Now, if you'll excuse me, I have to go see my next patient." The doctor walked to the door.

"What about the treatment for the symptoms?"

"Just read the directions." The doctor waved the back of his hand. He walked down the hallway, turned a corner, and disappeared.

* * *

Susann strapped Emily into her seat as Vanderheiden punched in their destination on the controls of the VTOL. Soon, they were airborne, heading back to their villa southwest of Houston as the sunrise began lightening up the skyscrapers and clouds above them with a bright-orange color.

Susann and Emily sat on one side of the cabin, and Vanderheiden, the other side. He watched his ladies play a game with their hands, jousting at each other playfully. He smiled, glad Emily had her mind on something else.

Outside of her soccer games and the weekends, Vanderheiden rarely saw his daughter. Most weekdays, he left the villa before she got up and returned after she went to bed. He did usually spend a couple hours with her on the weekends, but it was never enough.

He looked out the window and saw massive crowds marching through the streets. Multiple flares reflected a neon-red color from the huge signs held by the crowd. Individuals carrying flashlights and bright flares cast giant shadows in all directions, creating bright-red figures. Vanderheiden wondered what this protest was about.

If Emily only had two years to live, he needed to spend every moment with her and take care of her when the loss of motor skills took over. On the other hand, Vanderheiden Corporation was struggling. He had an obligation to the shareholders, employees, and customers to keep the PhotonicWay running and profitable. People's livelihoods depended on those photonic platforms orbiting the planets. He couldn't step away until leadership continuance was secured.

He looked at Emily and his chest deflated. *An impossible choice.*

The three made it home, and Susann put Emily to bed. Vanderheiden retired to his office and closed the door. One side of his office was a floor-to-ceiling window, giving him a full view of the lake with its small pier behind their villa. He sat down in his chair behind the glass desk covered with family pictures and called Dr. Raymond, the CEO of Valkyrie Labs.

The tone rang for several seconds. He tapped the desk with his finger. He imagined her staring at the incoming call, wondering why the founder and CEO of Vanderheiden Corporation was calling her.

The ringtone continued.

It stopped and a sharp voice spoke: "This is Dr. Raymond."

"Dr. Raymond, this is Vanderheiden. I just want to discuss one of the drugs your company sells, CJD-VL."

Silence on the other end. The seconds ticking past turned into what felt like a minute. *Need to tread carefully,* he thought, noting her hesitation.

"What would you like to know about it?" she replied.

"My family and I just got back from the hospital with the news that our twelve-year-old daughter has been diagnosed with CJD. The doctor informed me that the only treatment available, CJD-VL, is in short supply. I'm calling to get an understanding of why the drug is in short supply."

Dr. Raymond sighed. *Definitely is a sensitive topic.* "It is best if you had this conversation with your doctor."

Vanderheiden brought the hand terminal closer to his mouth. "Look…I'm not calling as a father. I'm calling as a businessman. If this supply issue is simply a capital problem, I can connect you with investors."

"It is not a capital problem."

Vanderheiden waited for her to elaborate, but her silence persisted.

"So, what is the problem?" he asked.

Another sigh came through the line. "Normally, I would not continue this conversation, but you are a businessman, so you probably can understand what I'm about to say. There are two reasons. First is the cost of production. One of the key ingredients has to be crystallized, and only zero-g manufacturing can produce that ingredient. That doesn't come cheap. Unfortunately, the finances don't allow us to increase production without dipping into negative margins."

"There is an abundance of demand out there," Vanderheiden said. "Why can't you raise the price to bring in more funds to boost production?"

"And that leads me to the second reason: price control."

"What?" he blurted out. "Price control?"

"Yes. We are already selling at the maximum price set by the NMS, and we are barely making a profit. A few years ago, this would not have been a problem."

"You are referring to the bill passed a few years ago that gave the National Medical Service more firepower?"

"That's the one. The politicians labeled the bill to lower the health-care cost and give more people access to health care. Before then, we were selling at a high price and able to gradually ramp up production. Since then, production has plateaued and our supply is limited."

"Why hasn't the NMS offered funds to expand production?"

"They don't see it as a responsible use of taxpayers' credits."

Vanderheiden rubbed his eyes. *Another government policy with good intentions bringing more harm than good.*

"I understand, Dr. Raymond. In order to supply all the CJD patients, how much does the cost of rockets need to drop?"

She chuckled. "Not sure what tricks you have up your sleeve, but if you can reduce launch service cost by fivefold, you'd make my job a lot easier!"

Vanderheiden froze. *The space elevator. Could it be the key?* As numbers spun in his head, he stared off at the sky through the window, imagining a cable connecting the ground to space. *All the challenges overcome with just one space elevator.*

"Are you there?" Dr. Raymond said.

"Yes, I am." Vanderheiden shook off his thoughts. "I've taken enough of your time. Thanks for speaking with me."

"Not a problem." She ended the call.

Vanderheiden put the terminal down and leaned back. If he could build the space elevator and make it five times cheaper than launch services, he could pull the country out of the crisis and give Valkyrie Labs the ability to produce more dosages of CJD-VL, saving his daughter.

He ground his teeth. *But the space elevator construction could bankrupt Vanderheiden Corporation.*

5

THE GENERAL

Sinclair did not want to be at the Houston Photonics Stadium right now. One week after returning to the surface, the nauseating vertigo still lingered, threatening to slam her to the ground.

The music was loud and upbeat, causing a sharp ringing in her ears, and the green strobe lights were disorienting. An obese security guard escorted her through the crowd of intoxicated fans inside the soccer stadium. Still readjusting to the smells of Earth after months of filtered air on board gunships, Sinclair covered her nose with a finger to block the reek of sweat, marijuana, and alcohol. Calling in an orbital bombardment to wipe out the obnoxious fans crossed her mind briefly.

Sinclair bumped into a tall man.

"Hey there, darlin'," he slurred. His smirk growing, he pressed his hand to the small of her back and guided his chest close to Sinclair's face. She could smell alcohol on his breath. She grabbed his shirt and drove her knee into his groin.

He yelped and dropped to one knee, spilling his drink. Spectators and the security guard turned to the noise. Sinclair stopped moving, too wobbly to get around the downed drunk. The security guard pushed the man aside with his foot and pulled Sinclair out of the way, shielding her with all his sweaty bulk.

"Get me out of here," Sinclair snapped.

His eyes widened as he shoved people aside to clear the way.

Safely out in the club and walking down a corridor, Sinclair asked, "Why the hell did you walk me through that?"

"Look, ma'am, this is the safest way to the VIP section. It's worse in other parts of the stadium."

Sinclair scratched her nose. She was ready to return to space. People on the surface seemed eager to get drunk and high and collect basic income from the government. If she ended up being discharged from the space force, she promised herself she would find a job on Luna or Mars, where she could be with spacefarers on the edge of the final frontier.

Sinclair and the security guard came up to a door flanked by two bodyguards in black suits.

"How is it going, Giovanni?" The security guard nodded.

"Fine." Giovanni pulled out a scanner from his jacket. "General Sinclair?"

"Yes."

"Please raise your arms." He gestured with his hands. He was clean-shaven with black hair and built like a soldier with a couple of kilograms of extra weight.

Sinclair cautiously raised her arms, and Giovanni waved the scanner over her body a few times. She glanced at all three men, who towered over her. In space, she would've floated above them to feel less vulnerable.

She looked at the door, and her heartbeat picked up a notch. She hoped Vanderheiden was an easy person to speak with.

"Thank you, General." Giovanni put the scanner away and opened the door.

Sinclair stepped in and was taken aback that there wasn't an entourage of people. The minimalist room was empty, except for a bar stocked with drinks and two leather chairs. The only man present sat in one of the chairs at the front with an unobstructed view of the soccer field. This was going to be a one-on-one meeting.

The objective Garrett had assigned her, a man with long brown-and-gray hair combed back, dressed in denim jeans and a leather jacket over a collared shirt, had his back toward her, reading the newsfeed on his hand terminal.

But Vanderheiden was alert. He clicked off the newsfeed, turning around with a smile. "Glad you could make it, General."

He got up with ease, marched over in two long strides, and offered his hand. "Hopefully you had little trouble getting here."

Sinclair shook his hand and felt his firm grasp. "No issues getting here. Some fans here are...rowdy. Though, it is nice getting a VIP parking spot and being escorted by security through the stadium."

"Yes, some fans get a little crazy." Shaking his head, he let out a laugh. "Personally, I don't like it, but soccer is open to everyone. Drink?"

"I'll have a bourbon." She needed something to take the edge off.

He walked over to the bar. "Unfortunately, I only serve nonalcoholic."

"A ginger ale, then."

He poured a clear sparkling liquid into two iced glasses. "You a soccer fan?" He pointed at the green field with his head.

"I am."

"Who is your team?" He handed her the glass.

"I grew up in Portland, Oregon. Would be a betrayal of my blood if I rooted for anyone else."

He inhaled sharply and sipped his drink. "That team has been a thorn in my side."

"Same for every team!" Sinclair raised her glass and took a sip. She wished for something much stronger.

Vanderheiden laughed and checked his watch. "Ah, the match is starting soon. Let's have a seat."

Both sat down, and Vanderheiden continued. "So, Portland? Tell me a bit more about yourself."

"I left Portland's cold and wet climate for the warm beaches of the Space Force Academy at Corpus Christi. After graduation, I rotated between ground units until assigned to the Orbital Fleet, and that's where I've been since." She didn't add that she no longer had an assignment given the deep budget cuts, which she suspected Vanderheiden had read about on the various newsfeeds.

The stadium gave a loud cheer at the kickoff. "What about you?" She took a sip.

"Born and raised in Houston. After studying finance and aerospace engineering, I worked at Shugart Technologies for many years."

Sinclair thought she saw a hint of disgust on his face when he mentioned Shugart.

"When I developed the concept of photonic propulsion and proposed it to the board at Shugart as a new business opportunity, they laughed it off. Present rocket technology produced enough profit for the company. Discouraged, I gave up on the idea." He raised a finger. "However, Scharre Sr., one of the board members, liked it and asked me one simple question: 'What's your net worth?'"

The ball was kicked toward the goal and flew over the bar. The crowd groaned.

"As a worker on an hourly wage, I had a two-year-old daughter and thirty to forty years before retirement after doing nothing of significant value." Vanderheiden raised his hand and formed a fist. "I wanted to build something. Leave a legacy."

He dropped the fist and took a sip of his drink. "After Scharre Sr. asked that question, I quit my job. It was a risky and somewhat irrational move. People called me crazy. My wife was concerned." He smiled. "But I was eager for the challenge. So, I gathered investors, recruited engineers, and founded Vanderheiden Corporation."

Vanderheiden chuckled. "I wish I could've seen the faces of Tsung and the other Shugart executives when we first opened the PhotonicWay between Earth and Luna."

Sinclair hesitated, thinking about how Garrett had warned her about Vanderheiden's disdain for Shugart Technologies. "Every space officer has studied General Shugart's writing on orbital-to-surface tactics. I served on one of the orbital bombardment platforms during the war."

"What General Shugart did was incredible." Vanderheiden nodded. "Don't get me wrong. After winning the war, he could've run for president, been handed a political blank check, and formed a new global order of his own. He could've been a reincarnation of George Washington or Dwight Eisenhower. Instead, he left the military and formed Shugart Technologies. That kicked off the space economy we now see today."

He shook his head. "It is sad to see the twenty years of rapid economic growth started by him ending. General Shugart would roll in his grave today if he could see what his company has become. Instead of bringing new innovations, it has become stagnant and content with obsolete technologies, depending on political connections to keep its business afloat."

Sinclair wished he would stop the small talk and get straight to the point of her being here. But she knew small talks could lead to large partnerships.

She held her tongue and let Vanderheiden continue. The crowd cursed when a player got knocked down. A yellow card was displayed, followed by cheering.

"There is a reason I invited you here today." Vanderheiden set his glass down. "My company is hurting. The economy is in a painful recession, contrary to what the government is saying. I'm searching for new business opportunities to get us out of this revenue slide."

The cheers erupted in the stadium as Houston scored its first goal. Sinclair glanced and saw players celebrating. Vanderheiden didn't react, keeping his eyes on Sinclair.

"I read your white paper advocating for the space force to transition from nuclear thermal engines to photonic propulsion. This would be an incredible business opportunity for my company. I want to understand your reasons behind that, because if we are to support the military, I need to know their exact needs." He gestured to Sinclair. "I'm hoping you can lend your expertise."

It was rare for someone to ask Sinclair to explain her advocacy for photonic propulsion. She usually got immediate pushback without a chance to elaborate.

She had *The Art of War* memorized word for word. "'Speed is the essence of war.' Photonic propulsion is faster than nuclear thrusters. Simple as that. Who can fire their weapon the quickest? Who has the faster missile? Will the active protection system react before the hostile missile reaches its target? Who has the faster software? Will the virus be able to exploit the security loophole and take weapons offline before security plugs the hole?"

Vanderheiden sat motionless, his hands pressed against each other at the fingertips. "I read the objections to military use of photonic propulsion. It's been described as taking maneuverable cars and putting them on high-speed rails that can't maneuver. The rails, the photonic platforms, would be easy targets for the enemy."

Sinclair suddenly developed respect for the businessman. He was probing for weaknesses in his own technology.

"The railroads are how the German Empire won the Franco-Prussian War and nearly World War I. Their network moved troops and equipment to battlefields more quickly. First troops get the advantage of surveying the area, placing themselves in advantageous positions, and getting rest. When the opponent arrives later, they come in fighting with their retreat options limited."

Vanderheiden nodded, but his face gave away his skepticism.

"You don't have a maneuverability issue," Sinclair said. "The issue is where you install your platforms. The photonic platforms don't have to be confined to the immediate orbit of the planets. You can build a nuclear thermal thruster-equipped spacecraft that acts as a photonic platform. It would be a mobile photonic platform."

"Intriguing." Vanderheiden's face lit up. "I'll admit that I'm biased on this. It would be lucrative if VC entered the defense industry, but I have to be careful what I sign my company up for." He leaned forward. "What happens if the space force makes photonic propulsion the backbone of its fleet and war breaks out? Wouldn't that cause the enemy to target all photonic platforms, wiping out my entire business? Not just military but also civilian. It seems better to stay out of the military business to avoid putting a target on our backs."

"You already have a target on your back," Sinclair shot back. "Targeting critical infrastructure is a common tactic. If the space force adopted photonic propulsion, we would develop ways to protect the platforms. Right now, the expenses and risk of protecting them fall on you."

Sinclair took a last big gulp of the ginger ale and set the glass down. She turned toward Vanderheiden. "Look, during peacetime, you can use legal, business, or moral excuses to avoid developing new military technology. But war with Europe is coming. When shit hits the fan, we will adopt any kind of technology that gives us an edge on the battlefield. Photonic propulsion is the future."

Vanderheiden's eyes hardened. He got up and paced the room. The stadium roared. Sinclair saw another goal from Houston. Two to zero.

Vanderheiden's hesitation annoyed her. She needed support to protect her position inside the space force. Vanderheiden and his network of businessmen and politicians would be powerful allies.

"What do you need from me?" Sinclair asked. "I doubt you invited me here just to explain how the military can use the PhotonicWay."

Vanderheiden halted his pacing and studied her for a moment. "I have an opportunity for you, General. Leave the space force and join my company. Become the leader of our military business. In that position, you could pursue defense contracts, facilitate R&D projects, assemble a private security company using photonic propulsion as its foundation, and much more. The possibilities would be endless for you."

Vanderheiden took a sharp inhale and sat down. "I need to form this business division soon, so this opportunity won't be on the table for long. The position is yours if you want to take it."

Sinclair knew she was dealing with an astute businessman who had his share of cutthroat negotiations with suppliers, bureaucrats, and customers.

"That is an interesting offer," Sinclair said. Her heart pumped faster. The space force had been everything to her. She would not leave it because incompetent rivals won the internal politics. Garrett needed her to walk out of this lounge with a plan to keep her in the space force and weaken Shugart's grip on the Pentagon. She had to tread carefully. Vanderheiden was either a businessman who knew no moral boundaries or had lines he would not cross.

"I can do more for photonic propulsion by remaining in the space force to advocate for it. The generals currently in positions of power are close to Shugart. It will take a coalition to counter their influence and transition the space force over to photonic propulsion."

Vanderheiden placed his hands back together at the fingertips. "And who would be part of this coalition?"

"You need to hire retired officers and leverage their connections inside the military to support VC. I can tell you which officers to target. You also need to develop connections inside Congress to influence defense budgets and policies. Campaign donations and shifting jobs to certain congressional districts and states are effective ways to get support."

Vanderheiden looked like he'd just seen a ghost. The stadium's cheering halted. The opposing team scored its first goal. He shook his head. "I'm fully aware of how the iron triangle works. It is called unethical lobbying, under-the-table dealing, and...on top of it all, corruption."

Sinclair was unmoved. "Look, this is how it is done today. I can't help you if you don't commit to this. Shugart Technologies is extremely effective at it. They have generals and congressional representatives under their influence. That's why many no-bid contracts are awarded to them and they manufacture more than seventy percent of the fleet's tonnage."

Vanderheiden's face turned one shade darker. Sinclair noticed her condescending tone and immediately shifted back to a diplomatic one. "Adopting photonic propulsion isn't just a simple military contract. We are talking about replacing the backbone of the space fleet and eliminating Shugart's primary source of revenue. They will leverage its network to block the transition."

Vanderheiden pointed at Sinclair's feet. "You sat there, explaining to me that photonic propulsion has the merits to be adopted by the space force. I should not have to play the political game, spend millions of credits hiring ex-military officers, and pay politicians to win the business that should be mine on merit alone." He raised a hand. "Excuse me, it's not pay. It is a bribe."

Sinclair clenched her throat, realizing he had lines he would not cross. Vanderheiden seemed to be ambitious and cunning, but honorable at the same time.

"The merits of photonic propulsion alone will not cut it," she said.

He waved his hand toward the stadium crowd. "The economy is sputtering. The unemployment rate is climbing. Those millions of credits I just mentioned, General? That's money I could spend to hire new employees to grow my business, fund a new R&D project, or expand the PhotonicWay to Saturn or Jupiter."

The stadium turned silent again. Another goal was scored, tying the game.

Sinclair felt defeated. No partnership would emerge tonight. Without outside support such as Vanderheiden's, Sinclair would be discharged from the space force, leaving all the spacemen vulnerable under the command of inept generals when war against Europe inevitably broke out.

She stood up and her head spun fast. She grabbed the chair to balance herself. Vanderheiden stared at her with a raised eyebrow.

After a few breaths, she turned to him. "Consider my offer. I can be a valuable source inside the space force for your company. Winning defense contracts will bring billions in revenue. When you choose to reconsider, contact me."

She offered her hand. "It was a pleasure meeting the man responsible for the PhotonicWay. I hope we can meet again in the future."

Vanderheiden didn't move at first, frowning. Eventually, he stood up and shook her hand. "My pleasure."

Sinclair walked herself out of the lounge and took the emergency exit stairs back to the parking garage, refusing to deal with that rowdy crowd again.

The honorable discharge lurched in her mind. She needed to protect her two stars. Taking the deputy command post at the Luna Fleet looked to be her one and only option now. It may be where careers ended, but at least she would remain in the space force.

6

THE MAGNATE

NYSE: VC 74.66 (-17.83%)

"Take down platforms!" the protest leader shouted into her megaphone.

"And power cities!" The crowd full of young people chanted around the leader.

She raised her fist. "Take down platforms!"

"And power cities!"

The protesters erupted into cheering. The leader turned around and flashed her middle finger at the gated entrance of the Vanderheiden Corporation headquarters.

Watching the crowd block the entrance from the front seat of his car, Vanderheiden frowned. *Don't they realize PhotonicWay transports much of the materials needed for the battery farms?*

The security officer walked up to the car window and knocked on it.

"Sorry about this, sir," the officer said after Vanderheiden rolled down the window. "They came out of nowhere. Police are on their way."

Behind Vanderheiden was a long convoy of cars with employees trying to reach the office buildings. A car or two would honk every minute. He was worried it would take a long time for the police to arrive. The police seemed less able to maintain order across the Greater Houston area amid the escalating protests over the recent months.

"Can you just clear them out?" he snapped. "I have meetings to attend."

"Uh...protocol dictates we take position around the manufacturing plants inside campus when these situations occur." He paused with nervousness. "Per your approval last year."

"You're right." Vanderheiden pulled away from the open window. "Just keep them off the property."

"Yes, sir." The officer glanced over at the loud crowd. "Can a photonic platform's nuclear reactor really provide enough electricity for a city?"

"Yes, photonic propulsion requires a substantial amount of power."

"Take down platforms!" The megaphone blasted.

"*And power cities!*"

The faint sound of sirens grew louder minutes later, and then red-and-blue lights flashed past Vanderheiden. Three black-and-white police cars drove up to the entrance, surrounding the crowd. Six officers dressed in riot gear stepped out and shoved the protesters with their batons.

"Clear the road!" a police car speaker announced. "Clear the road!"

After they pushed the protesters to the flanks of the entrance, a police officer waved at the long column of cars to enter. Vanderheiden pressed the controls, and the car navigated itself toward the gate.

A protester saw Vanderheiden's luxury self-driving car, and his face turned red. He took long strides toward the car and spat saliva at it.

"Fuck you, Vanderheiden!" He smacked the vehicle with his hand.

Vanderheiden leaned toward the window with clenched fists, curling his lips with disgust.

Before the protester reached the door handle, a police officer grabbed him by the collar and dragged him back. "Stay away from the vehicles!"

The protester spun to the officer.

"My fight is not with you!" He pointed at the car. "It is with them!"

Clear of the crowd, the car sped up toward the center of the office campus, where the tall black tower spiraled up like gemelli pasta.

Every day is a fight to save my company. Vanderheiden sighed.

* * *

"Sir?" the administrator said on the video call. "There is a...Tsung requesting a face-to-face meeting with you."

Tsung? The name boomed in his head. His mind raced, searching for reasons why the Shugart Technologies CEO would be at his headquarters. *Can't be a coincidence she is here the same day as the protest.*

"She's here?" Vanderheiden asked.

The administrator nodded.

"Put them in the conference room on the ground floor." Vanderheiden jumped up from his seat in the office. "I'll be there in ten minutes. Make sure security stays with them."

"Yes, sir."

Vanderheiden paced around his office, rubbing his beard. *What is she doing here? What is Shugart doing here? What—* He stopped walking and looked up at the stock price tracker on the wall monitor, seeing 74.66. An icy feeling swept across his skin. *It can't be... Not now.*

He slipped on his leather jacket, grabbed the hand terminal, and checked the locations of his company chiefs. Gonzalez was at the PhotonicWay Command Center. Brunelli was at the University of Houston, but Vanderheiden didn't need someone with an explosive personality sharing a conference room with Tsung. Only Arellano was in her office. Vanderheiden called her.

A few seconds later, she answered with video, looking away from the camera. "Rerun the numbers. I got the boss on the line here." She turned to her hand terminal. "Glad you called. I got a—"

"Arellano, what are you doing right now?"

"We are finishing up with the cost-cutting package. Should be finished by this afternoon."

"Drop what you are doing and meet me at the conference room downstairs. Now."

Arellano's face turned firm, and she glanced off-screen. "What's going on?"

"Tsung is here." Vanderheiden sucked air through his teeth. "It's happening. Shugart is ready for a takeover."

Her eyes widened for a moment. She blinked, tucked her hair behind her ear, and nodded. "I'll be there."

They arrived outside the conference room at the same time. Two security guards stood by the door. Frosted glass surrounded the meeting space and Vanderheiden could only make out two figures seated at the table inside.

"Have they been anywhere else?" Vanderheiden asked.

"No, sir." The guard shook his head. "We took them straight here."

Vanderheiden entered the room. The first thing he noticed wasn't Tsung and her excessive amount of makeup or the hairstyle that was stuck in the twentieth century. He didn't notice the lanky man with thick-rimmed glasses, either. It was the stack of papers on the table that made his stomach tighten. He noticed Arellano looking at the paper stack with concern.

"Mr. Vanderheiden, it is a great pleasure to see you." Tsung got up and walked around the table. Smiling, she offered her hand. "I appreciate you taking the time."

Vanderheiden looked at her hand, measured her face, and glanced at the stack of papers. All her words sounded forced to him. He clenched his jaw and shook her hand.

"Mrs. Tsung, what can I do for you?"

"Cheryl, please." She spoke with an easy and relaxing voice. *Too relaxing*, Vanderheiden thought. "And you must be Mrs. Arellano."

Arellano gave a small smile, and they shook hands.

"How are your husband and kids doing?" Tsung gasped with

excitement. "I heard your son made it into the Space Force Academy. Congratulations!"

"Oh, we are excited." Arellano's face beamed with pride. "A few years ago, we thought we had failed him as parents."

Vanderheiden raised an eyebrow. *Wasn't he rejected?* He looked back at Tsung with suspicion.

"Oh, don't be so hard on yourself." Tsung waved at her. "It shows that you care and—"

"Tsung, what can we do for you?" Vanderheiden cut her off.

Tsung held her mouth open, glancing back and forth between him and Arellano. "May we sit down?"

Vanderheiden nodded.

They sat down and adjusted their chairs. Vanderheiden leaned back in his, fingers interlocked, and stared at Tsung. The long-limbed man next to her adjusted his glasses, not taking his eyes off Vanderheiden.

Tsung folded her hands on the table. "Both of our companies are under great financial pressure. This recession isn't doing anyone any good. Having too many players competing in the space transportation market is a wasteful use of resources."

She pointed at herself. "Shugart Technologies holds significant control over the surface-to-orbit market and the zero-g manufacturing complexes." She pointed at Vanderheiden. "You hold a great share of the interplanetary transportation market."

She straightened her back. "Instead of fighting each other and risking the displeasure of our shareholders, let's pool our resources together and create synergies that'll raise our stock prices."

Here it comes. Vanderheiden braced himself.

Tsung smiled and nodded at the lawyer. He studied Vanderheiden through his thick-rimmed glasses before pushing the stack of papers to the other side of the table. Vanderheiden stared at the papers, smelling the fresh ink. He didn't reach out for the stack.

Tsung pointed at it. "Here is the legal framework for us to enter a merger agreement and establish a new company...Shugart-Vanderheiden Technologies."

Vanderheiden rubbed his chin, letting the silence drag out. *I won't accept the second name slot. People would soon forget my name and my legacy.*

Tsung held her forced smile for a moment. She opened her lips, but Vanderheiden interrupted her.

"You want us to merge?" He continued rubbing his chin. "Mm... why should we join you?"

I love the irony. Tsung had been the head of the military business at Shugart when Vanderheiden proposed photonic propulsion to the board. She shot down the idea immediately and sent him away, laughing along with rest of the room. He swore to make her regret it. *Now we sit at this table at the headquarters of my company.* A grin nearly broke across his face.

"Competing against each other isn't an ideal financial outcome." Tsung clasped her hands. "Together, we come out stronger. A significant advantage for your company is the tax benefits. Since the government classified Shugart Technologies as a federal contractor vital to national security, they have granted us an exemption from the higher tax rates under the Fairness Tax Act."

Arellano grabbed the stack of papers and flipped through them.

"What are the terms of the corporate governance?" Vanderheiden asked.

"Ten seats on the board. We will allocate six to Shugart and four to Vanderheiden. I will be CEO and you take chairman."

Vanderheiden didn't reply. *This is a merger in name only.* It was an acquisition designed to put Shugart on top and gradually push out the Vanderheiden players. *I'll just be a figurehead.*

"That won't fly." Vanderheiden shook his head. "You may have more revenue, but we have the higher market value. Value drives board seat allocation, not revenue."

"Don't get ahead of yourself." Tsung's smile disappeared. "We are offering similar terms to Rhine System."

"The EU won't approve that merger. We are your only option." Vanderheiden grinned and leaned forward, eyes locking on the woman he had craved wreaking vengeance on for years. "So, you've finally realized photonic propulsion works? You know your days are numbered if you don't get the technology."

He shook his head. "You shouldn't have turned me down when I made the proposal." *I want you to beg, Tsung.*

"Oh boo...you still holding that against me?" Her lips twisted. "Either you or Rhine will merge with us, leaving the other in a difficult position against the new corporation."

"Oh...I agree one of us will struggle." He pointed at Tsung. "You won't last many more years without one of us." He grabbed the documents and tossed them back to the other side of the table with a loud thud. "Here is my counteroffer: We get six seats. Shugart gets four."

"Be careful, dear. You are not in a position to negotiate like that. Shugart Technologies holds eleven percent ownership of your stocks."

A coldness flushed through Vanderheiden. *Enough for one or two board seats.* He clenched his jaw repeatedly. *Or to achieve a hostile takeover.*

"Think about it for a couple days." Tsung got up, the lawyer following her lead. "We'll be in touch."

After the Shugart executives left, Vanderheiden snatched up his hand terminal and called his chairwoman.

"Gabriella, we need to meet. Where are you?"

* * *

The receptionist opened the black door and waved her hand. "Here you go, Mr. Vanderheiden. Please let me know if I can do anything to assist you."

"Thank you." Vanderheiden stepped into the room. The receptionist's soft footsteps receded.

Like the rest of the Gravity Rehabilitation Center, the room was dark. The only source of light came from the large, clear tank filled with a thick purple fluid. Floating inside the tank was Scharre Sr., old and dark-skinned. He wore a fitted medical suit equipped with sensors, and an oxygen mask was strapped to his face, the cord connected to the top of the tank. His rhythmic breathing sent large bubbles to the top of the tank every few seconds.

Outside the tank, Gabriella stood erect with her hands behind her back. She wore a black suit, and her hair of the same color was pulled back in a bun. Both her suit and her hair blended with the dark room. Only her pale skin and glossy red lips were visible.

Both of them chuckled. Vanderheiden looked at the elderly man and his daughter-in-law. *My staunchest allies on the board. And only Scharre Sr. detests Shugart more than I do.* When Scharre Sr. left the Shugart board and sold his shares to fund Vanderheiden's start-up, Shugart had discredited him, damaging his reputation and crippling VC's ability to raise capital during its initial years.

If boosting the stock price back up to eighty will beat back Shugart, Scharre Sr. will support me. Vanderheiden stopped grinding his teeth, and his jaw muscles relaxed. *And Gabriella will get the board in line.* He inhaled and walked toward the two.

Gabriella saw Vanderheiden and covered her laugh with her slender hands. Scharre Sr. turned his body to see the new visitor.

"Ah...speak of the devil." His voice came through the tank speakers with a Southern drawl.

Gabriella cleared her throat and extended her hand. "Mr. Vanderheiden."

"Gabriella." Vanderheiden shook her hand. "So, you two talking about me?"

"We were talking about when you pitched your business plan to my wife by accident." Gabriella chuckled. "The look on your face when I said I was Gabriella."

Vanderheiden grunted.

While Scharre Sr. had built his wealth over many decades through his bank, Theodore S. Scharre Bank, by investing in space companies, Gabriella had married into the powerful family. She had taken the reins of a failing subsidiary, Scharre Farms, and transformed it into the first large-scale, self-contained farming system on Luna.

Vanderheiden turned to Scharre Sr. "How was your Luna trip?"

"The trip was smooth." He made a soothing hand gesture. "Send my regards to Gonzalez. He has been doing a good job managing the PhotonicWay."

"I'll let him know." Vanderheiden nodded.

Scharre Sr. tilted his head down and blew bubbles. "But does he have his personal issue under control?"

"He does," Vanderheiden replied firmly. "So, what brings you back to Houston?"

"Holidays are coming up!" Scharre Sr. blurted out through the speaker. "Need to get my body fully acclimated to the gravity here before I play with fourteen screaming great-grandchildren. Hence..." He spread his arms around the tank.

The most distinct thing about Scharre Sr. was his bulging eyes. People unfamiliar with him would get the impression he was furious or disturbed before realizing that was just how his eyes were. The bulging eyes, combined with the oxygen mask covering half his face, making him look intimidating from inside the tank.

"How many more days in the tank?" Vanderheiden asked.

Scharre Sr. glanced at something inside the tank. "Eighteen more hours in here before I transfer over to a thinner fluid for three days. So, four more days."

Vanderheiden had lost track of the old man's age but knew he was at least 110. However, he had the body of a seventy-year-old, so he had a good chance of hitting age 150, a goal Scharre Sr. reminded everyone of. It was a growing market for wealthy people to take extended trips to Luna to take advantage of its low gravity to reduce stress on their bodies and prolong life expectancy. Vanderheiden had doubts about the wellness practice, believing the body's grueling readjustment to Earth's gravity negated the benefits of living in low g. *But that's their choice. None of my concern.*

"What can we do for you?" Gabriella offered a look of curiosity, not displeasure. "Social calls aren't your thing."

Vanderheiden respected Gabriella's ability to spot deceptions and lies. *Glad to have her as my chairwoman.*

"Tsung came to the headquarters today, announcing Shugart's

eleven percent ownership of our company. They've proposed a merger, which we can't accept. I need your help to prop up the stock price to prevent a hostile takeover by them."

Gabriella glanced at Scharre Sr., who spoke first. "We just learned about it, too. But buying stocks just to prop up the price goes against my principles. To justify additional investment, there need to be business opportunities. What do you have in mind?" Many bubbles blew out of his mask, past his bulging eyes, and rose to the top.

Vanderheiden summarized each business opportunity the company chiefs had proposed last week, recounting Gonzalez's outer-planets expansion, Arellano's defense contracts, and Brunelli's space elevator. He recapped why he'd declined each opportunity.

"We need to ensure our foothold at the outer planets," Scharre Sr. replied. "We may incur a financial loss when deploying platforms there at first, but that will trigger economic development for those planets, bringing us financial gains years later."

He took a deep breath and blew out more bubbles. "But given the prosperity a space elevator would create, and how it could bring an end to the Resource Crisis, we should at least consider funding a research project to investigate its feasibility."

Gabriella pursed her lips with a nod. Vanderheiden winced. *Give Brunelli any budget for a space elevator, and that budget will not stay small.*

"What about the defense cargo contracts?" Gabriella asked. "Did you meet with General Sinclair? General Garrett told me he would send Sinclair in his place."

"I did chat with Sinclair." Vanderheiden shook his head. "As we already know, Shugart has those contracts locked up. The current decision-makers at the Pentagon are backed by Shugart. Garrett and Sinclair can name us the officers and politicians not yet under Shugart's influence. We would have to bride them to enter the defense industry."

A long sigh came out of the speaker. "Everywhere I turn, Shugart has its dirty fingers in something."

"What was your impression of Sinclair?" Gabriella asked.

"Don't let her initial appearances fool you. She may be short, but I could tell she was no ordinary officer. If you are advocating for radical technology in a fiercely political environment, you must have strong guts. Every time I looked in her eyes, it was like looking at a rocket nozzle firing full blast."

Gabriella nodded with a frown. "Her days are numbered. General Abborn is clearing house. Garrett and Sinclair are on top of his cleaning list."

"Shugart." Vanderheiden straightened his back. "They are pushing for a merger and speaking to our shareholders. We need to raise the stock price to thwart Tsung. Can I look to you two to prop it up and bring other investors on board?"

Gabriella glanced at Scharre Sr. in the tank, purple light reflecting off her pale face. Her father-in-law nodded. Vanderheiden looked back and forth between them, trying to read their expressions. *I will not like this.*

Turning her head to Vanderheiden, Gabriella pursed her glossy red lips. "We can help you...on one condition."

"Name it." *I know what you are going to ask.*

"Join the Luna Business Association."

Vanderheiden sighed. "There is a reason I'm not a politician. I can't tolerate the political shit. I already have my hands full running VC."

"Mr. Vanderheiden, these issues we are addressing impact you directly," Gabriella said. "The Luna Integration Act is hurting Luna. The Fairness Tax Act is raising the business tax rates everywhere. The Corporate Transparency Act is making an already difficult regulatory environment more convoluted. Even rumors of nationalization are floating around DC."

Gabriella took a few steps toward him. "Guardian Energy, Shugart Technologies, Tenet Bank...all of them back these laws. It is all part of their plan to consolidate control of their markets. We need to fight fire *with* fire." She pointed at him. "You are one of the most respected businessmen. If you joined our association, it would raise our profile and encourage others to join. We would become a counterweight to the oligarchs."

Vanderheiden looked down at his feet. *I can't let the politics distract my company.*

He raised his eyes. "You want to know why I'm well respected and not controversial?" He pointed at the ground. "I don't comment on every political issue or stir up controversy for the numbers. I am a businessman, not a political activist. I don't *need* a target on my back."

"Don't lie to yourself," Gabriella retorted. "You *are* in their crosshairs. You represent the PhotonicWay."

Vanderheiden scrunched up his nose with tension. *Another political lecture.*

"A storm is coming..." Scharre Sr. grabbed a handle inside the tank to pull him to the glass. "We are fighting for the future of mankind. We are on the brink of becoming a multi-planetary species. Low taxes, minimal regulations, stable judicial systems. The necessary recipes for long-term prosperity. We must build that for our children and their children."

Vanderheiden crossed his arms and sighed. The burden of being the CEO seemed to weigh heavier on his shoulders. Thousands of employees depended on him. Cargo worth billions flew through the PhotonicWay. Trillions depended on his company's market value. *They are my responsibility. Is it my obligation to take on this fight?*

His daughter sitting on the hospital bed flashed across his mind. *But I must be with Emily during her final days. I must be there for Susann.* Vanderheiden shook his head and uncrossed his arms, locking eyes with Scharre Sr. "I will not be involved in your political crusade."

Scharre Sr. dropped his head and pushed away from the glass.

Gabriella frowned. "You know where we stand. If you join the association, we'll prop up the stock price and hold Shugart at bay. Others that support this association might be eager to purchase stocks if it means fighting Shugart."

Vanderheiden nodded. Nobody spoke. The humming of the tank and Scharre's bubbles popping at the top were the only audible sounds in the dark room. *If this political crusade is important enough for them to risk my company, it must be serious.* Vanderheiden rubbed his hand and looked away.

Gabriella broke the silence. "So, what are you going to do now? You have no viable business opportunities, and you won't join our business association. How are you going to keep the stock price up?"

"Cost cuts," Vanderheiden answered. "Arellano has already scoped out workforce reductions, R&D budget cutbacks, and modifications to PhotonicWay scheduling to keep costs low. Boosting our profit margins will do the trick."

"That's going to divide the board," Gabriella said. "Cooper will exploit this, and I can only hold off that activist investor for so long."

"As long as I'm CEO, Cooper will not hijack *my* company," Vanderheiden countered.

"Son..." Scharre Sr. spoke in a soft and dragged-out voice. Vanderheiden's body went rigid. Scharre Sr. had only given Vanderheiden harsh criticism a few times in his life. All those conversations started with that distinct *Son...*

"Yes?" Vanderheiden tried to sound confident, but his body felt unnaturally stiff.

"Remember the promise you made to me if cost-cutting became your top priority?"

"That I would resign as CEO?"

"Yes, son. Creating value for society is more virtuous than creating wealth for oneself."

Would they truly let the Shugart merger happen when I'm about to retire? Vanderheiden felt the fear manifest in his mind. *I am going to lose my company.* Next came the burning heartbreak. *And be powerless to save Emily.*

7

THE GENERAL

After the two soldiers in black tactical armor and holding assault rifles scanned Sinclair, she entered the war room. It was an enormous concrete room with metal foam beams running across the ceiling. Large strategic maps covered one side of the room, displaying the positions of military spacecraft and probes. The largest map was of the solar system, with many blue dots hovering around Earth, Luna, and Mars. A handful of dots were close to Jupiter and Saturn. At the center of the room was a large circular table, able to seat twenty people.

Sinclair took long strides across the shiny black floor, which mirrored everything above, making the room look twice its size. Two weeks after returning to the surface, the threat of vertigo would persist between her ears but never consume her. A few generals sat at the table, while others stood, carrying out conversations. The voices echoing off the concrete made the room loud.

One by one, the heads turned to Sinclair, and the conversations died down.

"What is she doing here?" one whispered.

All the eyes staring at Sinclair made her skin crawl. She forced herself to maintain her pace as she got closer to the table.

Maxwell turned around to see why the room had suddenly gone quiet. He saw Sinclair and set his hand terminal down so hard that the crack of the black cover on the table sounded like a gunshot.

"What are you doing here?" Maxwell walked toward her. "You are not part of this meeting."

"I'm here to assist the vice chief." Sinclair didn't stop walking.

Maxwell sidestepped in front of her. She wished she was tall and heavy enough to bump into him and knock him down. Instead, she was forced to halt. Sinclair's eyes met Maxwell's, and her mouth tightened.

"You are to leave at once," he demanded.

Sinclair didn't move, keeping her hard stare on him. She caught a whiff of his coconut cologne, the same one he'd worn at the academy. She held back the bile taste of vomit.

He leaned in closer. "Don't make this difficult."

She took her eyes off him and walked around him.

Maxwell grabbed her elbow with a hard grip. The memory of him slapping her hand terminal and bag out of her hand at the academy screeched in her mind. A primal anger deep in her chest turned hot, and she smacked Maxwell's hand away. For a split second, she clenched her fist and imagined smashing her knuckles into Maxwell's cheek and destroying his glamorously white teeth.

Maxwell's voice boomed across the room, bouncing off the concrete ceiling. "General Sinclair, I am ordering you to—"

"Maxwell...stand down." Abborn walked into the war room. "General Sinclair is part of this meeting."

Maxwell spun his head to Abborn and back to Sinclair. He stepped back, straightened his posture, tugged his sleeves, and sat down at the table. Sinclair took a seat next to Garrett's.

Abborn walked to the table. He seemed disinterested whenever Sinclair saw him, and she figured the old veteran was burnt out and ready for retirement. But she then remembered how Garrett had told her he'd taken control of the congressional hearings when they were in DC.

Garrett entered the room, sat down next to Sinclair, and winked at her. She could tell he was exhausted but trying to put on a good show.

"You are late," she whispered.

"I am the vice chief. I run on my own timeline. Plus...I figured you could handle Maxwell."

Sinclair smirked, and they both looked across the table at Maxwell. Reviewing his hand terminal now, he stood motionless like a statue. His cheek twitched, and Sinclair knew he was seething on the inside. She still searched for the right button to press to make him explode. She had to give him credit for his emotional fitness. But with Garrett retiring soon, she shuddered at the thought of Maxwell taking over as the vice space chief.

She looked around the table for colleagues she was well acquainted with. But the more generals she looked at, the deeper her heart sank. A few years ago, SPACECOM had an even split between gunship and destroyer advocates. Now, Abborn's loyalists, all officers of destroyers, dominated the table, leaving Garrett as one of the last gunship officers remaining.

Abborn spoke with General Fassbinder, the newly appointed Mars Fleet commander, for a few minutes before sitting down and kicking off the meeting. He stated the names of each officer in the war room for documentation. All the major commands were present in the room: Ground, Orbital, Mars, Special Operations, Reserve, R&D, and Materials. General Fosvik of the Luna Fleet wasn't physically present in the room, calling in virtually from Luna.

Watching Abborn, Sinclair thought about the deal he'd offered Garrett. Either Garrett retired immediately and Sinclair became deputy commander of the Luna Fleet, or Sinclair was discharged and Garrett remained vice chief for two more years until his mandatory retirement. Sinclair needed to decide before this meeting ended.

"General Maxwell," Abborn said, "let's go over the EU intelligence reports."

Maxwell stood up, and various satellite images came on the hologram. The lights in the large room dimmed, and the hologram turned everyone's face blue.

"We have been observing a higher cadence of launch activities at Baikonur and Sutherland." Maxwell flipped through various images. "The launches have been a mixture of their new destroyers, tankers, and cargo vessels contributing to the growing number of EU military assets in low earth orbit." He switched to telescopic images of the vessels in space. The sun beamed off one side of the vessels hovering above the curvature of Earth.

Sinclair leaned in closer. The propellant tankers in the images seemed strange.

"You are seeing what I'm seeing, right?" Garrett whispered.

Sinclair shook her head.

"Keep looking."

Despite the incredibly powerful nuclear-thermal thrusters, the methane tanks onboard the vessels only held approximately fifteen minutes of thrust, crippled by the stubborn laws of gravity. A vessel's maneuvering options were limited by how much propellant it held. In war game simulations, it was common for officers to spend half their time conducting refueling operations.

Sinclair frequently woke up from nightmares of being on board a gunship empty on propellant, at the mercy of an incoming missile. Sometimes a quick two-second burn could be the difference between a direct hit and missing a missile by kilometers.

Maxwell pointed at the hologram. "These series of launches appear to be aimed at bulking up their fleet for low-earth-orbit operations."

Sinclair shook her head. While other generals raised questions and added comments, she studied the images. The size and shape of the propellant tankers were different. She ran calculations on the amount of propellant relative to the number of EU vessels in orbit, and she found it to be an excessive amount for low-earth-orbit operations.

The implications suddenly hit her, and she suppressed the urge to panic. She sat higher in her seat, looking around to see if other generals had similar thoughts. Nobody seemed alarmed.

She typed a note on her hand terminal and slid it to Garrett.

THEY ARE TARGETING LUNA/MARS.

Garrett looked at her and gave one slow nod. She typed again.

THAT'S WHY YOU WANT ME AT LUNA.

He looked at her again and nodded again. Sinclair leaned back in her seat, staring at the telescopic images.

Traveling to Luna and Mars required roughly the same amount of propellant. In space travel, distance didn't matter. It mattered how much delta-v was required to accelerate and escape Earth's gravity well and decelerate to enter Mars or Luna orbit. Traveling through space at a steady speed burned no propellant.

"The Orbital Fleet is at risk here." Maxwell turned to Fassbinder. "We need to shift more assets to low earth orbit to counter these moves."

"What?" Fassbinder turned his palms up. "I just took over Mars, and I'm already fighting to keep my vessels?" He glanced at Abborn. "No, Mars Fleet can't give away any more destroyers or gunships. We are already stretched and have no reserves."

Fassbinder pointed at Maxwell and the commander of ground units. "You two have enough assets to support each other. Mars Fleet has none of that. I will not give up my vessels."

"But look at the number of vessels the EU is putting in orbit!" Maxwell pointed at the hologram.

"What if we are looking at this wrong?" Garrett put his elbows on the table. Multiple faces turned to him. "If you look at the amount of propellant they are putting up, it exceeds the delta-v requirement of low-earth-orbit operations. What if they are targeting Luna or Mars?"

"They wouldn't challenge Luna." Maxwell scoffed. "That would violate the Marseilles Agreement."

"Not if they sense weakness." Garrett stood up and walked toward the strategic maps on the wall. He was a small figure standing under the large maps. "Look...the Orbital Fleet is already the best-equipped fleet out here. Luna and Mars are vulnerable. They are ill-equipped and under-supplied. We need to bulk them up."

"Defending low earth orbit is paramount." Maxwell pressed his fist against the table. "We can't risk it."

"Luna is also paramount." Sinclair pointed at the map. "LEO might be where the space economy revolves. But where do the raw materials come from? Luna. What is the vital logistics hub between Earth and the rest of the solar system? Luna. Which celestial body has the highest number of civilians beyond Earth? Luna." She tapped her finger on the table. "Don't neglect the moon!"

Garrett walked back to the table, looking at Maxwell. "If you want more destroyers in your fleet, can you lend Luna and Mars your gunships? Those fleets are in greater need of them."

"I don't want gunships." Fassbinder looked to Garrett with disgust.

Maxwell shook his head. "No, we'll be docking those gunships so I can transfer the spacemen over to the new destroyers Shugart will deliver soon."

"So, we just...leave those gunships unattended?" Garrett asked.

"Well, if we were hitting the recruitment quotas"—Maxwell glanced at the general in charge of personnel management—"we wouldn't be having a conversation."

"Then we push our spacemen to the limit." Garrett pointed to him. "Look...Shugart listens to you. The Lampard-class gunships they are building would require fewer spacemen to operate. Can you pressure them to speed up their manufacturing schedule? They are years overdue, and I'm sick of seeing them drag their feet."

"They aren't dragging their feet. They explained to you last week why they are behind schedule. The new rail-gun design is more complicated than expected."

Sinclair looked at Garrett, wanting him to put Maxwell in his place.

"What they explained and what the truth is are two different things. They are not committing resources to the project they are obligated to commit." Garrett emphasized the words. "They are putting the *national security* of this country at risk because they want more revenue for these gunships from the contract extensions we keep granting them!"

"If you had the balls to say that, you would've said that to the faces of the men and women at Shugart!" Maxwell barred his teeth. "You don't disrespect the people paramount to—"

"Enough." Abborn brought sudden silence to the war room. He turned to Maxwell. "You will tell Shugart to speed up the gunships. You will issue them an ultimatum, and I will be on that call with you. If they don't deliver on their current schedule, we will confiscate their gunships and transfer the contract to their competitors."

Maxwell scratched behind his ear.

Shifting his eyes to Garrett, Abborn lowered his head. "The new destroyers get priority on the extra manpower. Any extra we can spare will be assigned to the new gunships and transferred to Luna and Mars. Two per fleet."

Abborn pulled up his hand terminal, setting it for the next topic of the meeting. Everyone complied except Sinclair.

"By extra spacemen, you mean subpar ones?" Sinclair asked. Garrett kicked her leg.

"You want those gunships or not?" Abborn's weary eyes fell on her.

Sinclair leaned back, not giving a response.

Abborn looked for other generals to speak. All stayed silent. The strategy session rolled on for another hour. They reviewed the latest R&D projects, such as the next-generation nuclear-thermal thrusters and improved rail guns for gunships.

They picked apart the numbers around the recruitment difficulties, but to Sinclair's annoyance, no one seemed to understand that civilians could make more money registering for basic income instead of serving in the military. The new training program for the special operators, called Raiders, was evaluated. As the minutes went by, Sinclair's back ached more, pleading for her to lie down in a bed.

They reviewed intelligence reports on South Asia. After the Second North Atlantic–Eurasian War decades ago, China was broken up into multiple nations to limit its military power, but fierce nationalism was spreading and talk of revenge against the West was increasing. Leaders were nervous these states could reunite and turn into a formidable military power able to challenge the United States.

General Fassbinder shared the patrolling patterns he wanted to carry out. Sinclair scrolled through the images of the EU fleet. She ran the calculations multiple times, changing the numbers of propellant tankers, how much propellant each one held, how many combat vessels were in orbit. Her calculations came to similar conclusions. This wasn't a low-earth-orbit operation the EU was prepping for.

Sinclair pulled up the list of vessels making up the Luna Fleet, and she didn't like what she saw. It comprised only two destroyers, one gunship, a spacecraft carrier, a full squadron of Raiders, and a handful of shuttles. The US Orbital Fleet and the EU Fifth Fleet cruising in Earth's orbit each had two to three times the Luna Fleet's numbers.

Sinclair took her eyes off her hand terminal and looked at Garrett. His arms were crossed, and his acne-scarred face held a slight frown. What would happen to him if she took over Luna deputy command, and they removed him from the vice chief position?

She interlocked her fingers and looked up, tracing the metal foam beams running across the high concrete ceiling toward the large maps. Looking at Luna, she tapped her thumbs multiple times for a long moment, staring at the blue lines outlining the moon on the wall. She turned around to face the table, her decision made.

After the session ended, Garrett and Sinclair got up at the same time. Sinclair's knees creaked against the gravity.

"Garrett, I'll take deputy at Luna." Sinclair turned to him.

Garrett stopped packing his hand terminal and paper documents and glanced at her.

"The Luna fleet isn't ready for war," Sinclair added. "I must go there and get the fleet ready. We *must* not lose the moon."

She looked at Maxwell, who seemed to be having a pleasant conversation with another general. "I don't trust anyone."

"Good." Garrett carefully slid his hand terminal and papers into his bag. "I'll inform Abborn."

He walked around the table and approached Abborn from

behind. The space chief was in conversation with General Kramer, head of special operations. Garrett whispered to him, and Abborn leaned in closer. Abborn raised his eyes to Sinclair, said something to Kramer, and walked around the large table toward her.

"Thank you for accepting the Luna deputy command, General Sinclair. Report to Padre Island for launch tomorrow morning at 0930 hours."

* * *

It was hazy the next morning in the aftermath of light rain. Sinclair woke up, brewed light roast coffee, and poured it into her thermos.

Since she would not return for at least a year, she powered down everything in her house and threw out her food. Orbital Fleet deployments typically lasted eight to twelve months to minimize health hazards from lack of gravity. Assignments at Luna ranged from one to three years because spacemen had access to artificial gravity rings and the low-gravity environment on the lunar surface, which mitigated the health hazards.

It was all about balancing the spacemen's health and the cost of rocket launches. Liftoffs from Earth, because of its strong gravity, ate up a huge chunk of the space force's budget and were always a hot topic inside congressional committees.

Sinclair dressed up in her black combat uniform, grabbed her bag and thermos, and drove to the Padre Island Military Spaceport. She went to the preparation room and suited up for the flight. Eleven other spacemen were joining the trip to the Craven spacedock orbiting four hundred kilometers above them.

After preparations were complete, the twelve spacemen left the room and walked across the bridge to enter the shuttle. The shuttle, sitting on top of a medium-size rocket, had a matte-black bullet-shaped chassis. The rocket was fueled up with liquid methane, so ice patches, steaming under the scorching morning sunlight, had already formed on the outside of the rocket.

Before Sinclair stepped inside to be strapped down and prepped for the g-forces three times the Earth's gravity when the rocket propelled the shuttle beyond the stratosphere of Earth, she took a long look at the shoreline.

White pelicans flew over the dark-blue water that washed across the light-brown sand of Padre Island. Being deployed in space for extensive periods of time and only seeing black skies, countless stars, and the boring gray modules of spacecraft made Earth breathtaking to look at.

She took a deep breath. When she returned to Earth, she hoped it would be to a safer Earth.

Sinclair stepped into the shuttle. An hour later, the nuclear-thermal engines ignited, pressing an acceleration of three g into Sinclair's chest. Propelling itself through Earth's thick atmosphere, the shuttle shook violently and her teeth vibrated. Outside the small windows, the light-blue sky rapidly turned darker and darker until, minutes later, it was black. The engines shut down, the vibration stopped, and Sinclair floated in her seat, held down by the harness. The aching in her back disappeared.

8

THE MAGNATE

NYSE: VC 75.08 (+0.56 %)

Vanderheiden stopped spinning the bike and felt the muscles burn deep in his thighs. *Today is the day.* He let out a deep exhale, dreading the board meeting to vote on the Shugart merger. *And deciding the future of my company.* He hopped off the stationary bike and powered it down. He picked up his hand terminal and saw an unread message from Gabriella. He hovered his finger over to open the message and paused. *I just need twenty minutes with my family.* He set the device down and walked to the kitchen.

He smelled bacon as Susann set the crispy meat on a plate next to scrambled eggs and turned to pour the pancake batter. Vanderheiden admired the fit of Susann's exercise clothes over her slim body and her black hair tied back in a ponytail.

Emily sat at the table, watching a replay of her club soccer team's game the night before. He kissed the top of Emily's head and stroked her brown hair.

"Good morning, Emily."

"Good morning, Dad!" She looked up with a smile.

"How are things going at school?"

"Not bad. It keeps me distracted from my..." She paused for a moment, seeming to remember she had a serious medical issue. Trying to keep the mood light, Vanderheiden held his smile.

She looked back up. "I have that essay I need to finish this weekend. Are you still able to help me with it?"

His heart sank. *I don't have the time.* His company was on track for a third consecutive quarter of revenue drop and missing its profit target. The stock price had tanked over the month. Shugart Technologies was on the move to take over his company. Each day, his position as CEO of Vanderheiden Corporation felt less secure. *My company is my only means to get Emily the life-saving treatment she needs.*

"I have a busy Friday, and I don't know how this weekend will be." He pulled the chair out, screeching against the floor, and sat down. *But I promised.* "Remind me what the assignment is again."

"I have to argue for or against the Luna Integration Act."

"Ah!" Vanderheiden smiled and rubbed his palms together. "You'll crush it because you've got the smartest man in the space industry sitting next to you."

Emily giggled when Vanderheiden tapped his forehead with his finger.

"How about this? I'll give you a couple starting points, and you write a first draft around those." Vanderheiden extended his fist. "Deal?"

"Deal!" She gave him a fist bump and pulled up a word-processing app.

"Luna Integration Act." Vanderheiden leaned back and tapped the table with his fingers. "Passed in 2094." He grunted. "Wow...seven years ago. Before it was passed, Luna was a special economic zone controlled by the US." He watched Emily type on her hand terminal.

"Because of the low taxes, lack of tariffs, and minimal regulations the special status provided, the Luna economy thrived. Mining colonies and manufacturing cities rose to support the zero-g manufacturing industry. We built much of the businesses and infrastructures during this time. But—"

"Like the PhotonicWay?"

"Yes." Vanderheiden beamed. "However, that changed when this act was passed. It revoked the moon's special status and pulled it into the greater economic regime of the United States. Now, it has to pay tariffs and adhere to...a lot of regulations. Forty percent tax rates are the norm." He leaned his head across the table. "Want to guess what happened to Luna?"

"The"—Emily looked around the ceiling—"economy shrank?"

"Yes. Also, fewer jobs led to a rise in crime." He wiped sweat off his forehead and stood up. "Start with that and come back to me tomorrow with four pages written."

"Got it!"

Vanderheiden walked over to the stainless steel kitchen and approached Susann from behind. His stomach grumbled at the warm smell of the pancakes she took off the griddle.

"Good morning." He kissed her cheek.

She turned her head, giving him a small smile. "Good morning." But her eyes didn't smile.

Vanderheiden pulled his face back, looking at her for a moment. He nodded with unease, took two of the plates, walked back to the table, and set a plate in front of Emily before setting his down. He drizzled maple syrup on his pancakes, spread soft Irish butter, and took a big bite. His eager stomach would have to wait while he chewed and swallowed.

Susann sat down and took a sip of her water. Emily typed on her hand terminal. Vanderheiden munched on his big bites of pancake without a word, glancing at Susann occasionally.

After his last bite, Vanderheiden brewed coffee. Emily finished and left the kitchen to prepare for school. He returned to the table with coffee mug in hand, spreading its aroma across the room.

"Susann, what's going on?"

"Are you trying to avoid us?" Susann took a bite of the turkey bacon.

"Am I trying to avoid...?" He blinked. "No. Where is this coming from?"

"You are spending more time at VC and taking many late-night calls in your office." She rested her hand on Vanderheiden's arm. "You can't avoid the inevitable."

"You mean our daughter's condition?" He set his mug down on the table. "Of course, I'm not trying to avoid us. Look...things are getting difficult at VC. Our financials aren't good. The board is uneasy. Shugart is pushing for a merger. And the Scharre—"

"It doesn't matter." Susann stood up and took the plates to the kitchen sink. "You're also a father. I know we agreed I would do the heavy lifting with raising our daughter"—she turned the water faucet on and looked at him as she washed the dishes—"but this time is different. This is not the time to focus on VC. Your daughter needs you.

"Her days are numbered, Michael. She might not be here next year." Water splashed on the counter when she threw the plates into the sink. "Today is Friday. Have you decided who will succeed you as CEO?"

He shook his head. "Board meeting is happening today, and the Shugart merger will probably be approved."

"And?" Susann leaned her chest over the sink.

"That means I have to stay on as chairman for two years."

"I need you, Michael." She pointed up. "*She*...needs you."

"Susann, I'm not trying to avoid this. I love our daughter, but—"

"But?" Her face reddened.

"But...Vanderheiden Corporation needs me as well. It's the only way I can get the treat—"

"Michael, she is dying!" She smacked the counter with her wet palm, sending droplets of soaped water everywhere.

"You don't think I *know* that?" Vanderheiden shot out of his seat.

A soft voice spoke from behind him. "Hey, guys...?"

The parents turned their heads, jaws slack. Emily stood at the kitchen entrance, holding her schoolbag. The silence grew heavier each second no one spoke.

"I'm...I'm ready to go," she mumbled.

Susann huffed, dried her hands off, and left the kitchen.

Emily walked to the front door. "Mom, I can go to school by myself."

"No, not with your seizures happening."

Vanderheiden got up, grabbing his coffee, and followed them outside.

Emily walked down the brick steps. Vanderheiden gently closed his fingers around his wife's arm, allowing Emily to continue walking to the car.

"Susann, we promised to never leave each other on bad terms."

She raised her eyes and locked them with his for a few seconds. Her cheek twitched and then she planted a firm kiss on his lips. She entered the car and slammed the door.

The vehicle roared to life and drove off, Emily waving hesitantly. He smiled and waved back, trying to appear happy.

Once the engine was out of his earshot, Vanderheiden pulled up Gabriella's message:

> SENIOR AND I DON'T LIKE IT BUT WE'LL BE VOTING IN FAVOR OF THE MERGER AT THE BOARD MEETING TODAY.

"Damn it," Vanderheiden cursed under his breath.

* * *

The deep mist hung low in the air and the heavy fog scattered the sun's beam as he rode down the isolated road. Unable to concentrate, Vanderheiden stared out of the window and caught glimpses of many trees flying by, with the sun flickering behind them.

Susann's question repeated in his head: "Are you trying to avoid us?" He wouldn't forgive himself if he spent more time at Shugart-Vanderheiden Technologies during Emily's dwindling days. But he also wouldn't forgive himself if he let his company collapse under his watch. *What do I do?*

Even if he stopped the merger, he struggled to imagine stepping away and VC still running smoothly. None of the company chiefs were ideal successors, and Gabriella would never leave the Scharre family's conglomerate.

Vanderheiden sighed. He could just accept the Shugart merger, avoid the chairman position, cash in on his stocks, and leave the problems to someone else. *It has been a great run. But I'm tired.* Life in retirement felt wonderful. But the thought of Tsung running the PhotonicWay made him nauseous.

The car turned onto a busy road and stopped at a red light. A handful of beggars walked up the street, eyeing each car for a second. A few years ago, beggars were nonexistent in this part of Greater Houston. Now, they were at every major intersection. Vanderheiden looked around and saw a convenience store boarded up with graffiti painted over the wooden panels.

The light turned green, and the car accelerated. The beggars walked back down the street, heads hanging down. Vanderheiden rode by the church he and Susann had attended before VC took over his life. There was a food line extending out into the parking lot, with a police car parked close by. He imagined former employees standing in those lines. He knew it would happen if he went forward with the workforce reduction Arellano was calculating. The helplessness he felt made his chest grow hollow.

Vanderheiden looked up at the sky roof and imagined the thick cable of the Earth Space Elevator stretching through the clouds. *But what if it could work? It would be an economic miracle. Instead of people lining up for food, they would line up for the space elevator to seek prosperity in space.*

Space elevators would put Shugart out of business. The Resource Crisis would come to an end with cheap access to the mining fields of Luna and Mars. It would become the pillar of a new space age. *I would secure my legacy.* The emptiness in his chest gave way to a burning fire, arms and legs tingling with energy. Valkyrie Labs could mass-produce the treatment for Creutzfeldt-Jakob disease. *And I would save Emily.*

* * *

Brunelli stood by the office door, holding a sheet of paper in his hand. Vanderheiden walked past him swiftly and opened the door. "Inside. Now."

Vanderheiden set his hand terminal and thermos down on the desk and checked the time. *Three hours and forty-five minutes.* He blew a sharp breath and rested his hands on his hips.

Brunelli walked in slowly, taking each step like he was approaching a sleeping bear. Vanderheiden glanced at him.

"Here is my resignation paper." Brunelli handed the paper over.

"What?" Vanderheiden pulled his chin back. "Damn...give me that!"

He snatched it from Brunelli's hand, tore it into four pieces, and threw it in the garbage bin.

"Sit down." He took off his leather jacket and grabbed his red rubber ball.

Brunelli looked at Vanderheiden with a mix of confusion and concern. He sat down like the chair was made of broken glass. "What's going on?"

Vanderheiden licked his lips. "I have a board meeting in"—he checked his watch—"three hours and forty-four minutes that will decide the future of this company."

"The Shugart merger." Brunelli crossed his arms.

"Yes. The board is going to approve it." Vanderheiden caressed the rubber ball, staring at the chief technology officer. "I'm going to propose the space elevator...with one key change."

"Okay..." Brunelli's lips moved like he was about to smile but didn't. "What do you have in mind?"

"Call in your engineers." He powered on the engineering application on the hologram. "We need to flesh this out before noon."

* * *

Gabriella knocked the table with her knuckles. "We're starting the meeting."

Vanderheiden was already seated, watching the directors slowly make their way to the long table stretching across the Executive Chamber. Some looked deeply concerned about the prospect of merging with Shugart.

As the company chairwoman, Gabriella sat at the head of the table. Vanderheiden and Scharre Sr. flanked her. The nine other board members eventually sat down after Gabriella knocked the table again.

Cooper, the notorious activist investor from Cooper Capital, slid into his seat last, tossing back his long ginger hair. He looked around the room with a smirk, his cleft chin up like he owned the place.

Too cocky. Vanderheiden clenched his jaw.

Gabriella stood up and narrowed her gaze on the employees sitting in the back of the room. "For the record, Brunelli and his engineering team are present in the room." She looked down at Vanderheiden. "Care to elaborate?"

"I have a major project that requires the board's approval."

"Very well." Gabriella nodded. "Let's begin. The only item on the agenda is the merger proposed by Shugart Technologies. We will need to—"

"Just put it to a vote already." Cooper opened his arms and looked around the table. He spoke with a deep Scottish accent. "We've had time to review the framework proposed by Shugart. We all know where we stand on the proposal."

Gabriella blinked like she was amused by Cooper's interruption. "Despite the compelling offer, we need to discuss it first as a board." She smiled. "We will hear each director's take on it."

"We know what the decision will ultimately be. Let's not waste time. I've got other investments to go monitor."

Vanderheiden scowled. *Let's not waste time?*

"You are one of twelve directors on this board." Gabriella dropped her smile. "You will spare the time to discuss."

Cooper scoffed and pressed his back into the seat. Scharre Sr. shook his head, eyes bulging.

"I'll go first." Vanderheiden pressed his finger down. "I founded this company to be anti-Shugart. They are complacent. They have a bloated bureaucracy. Government contracts prop them up. Joining them is admitting defeat."

"It's a compelling offer," Cooper said. "A premium on top of our stock price. It is not a defeat if the shareholders come out richer."

"What about our customers?" Scharre Sr. swiveled his seat toward the activist investor. "Our employees?"

"What about them?"

"Shugart only wants the PhotonicWay. Once we merge, they will strip VC down to the bones, laying off employees and weakening our operations, which will hurt the customers."

"That's business." Cooper waved his hand like a bug was bothering him. "Vanderheiden here is about to propose a fresh round of cost cuts. How is that any different?"

"It is not cost cuts I'll be proposing," Vanderheiden countered.

"Then what do you propose?" Gabriella sat down and interlaced her fingers. "We must consider this offer."

"You will not accept Shugart as a—"

"Vanderheiden..." Scharre Sr. cut him off. "If you want the board to turn down the merger, we need a viable alternative. Do you have one to share?"

Vanderheiden looked around the table as all eleven directors stared at him.

"I do." He stood up with a frown. "Brunelli."

Vanderheiden pressed the touchscreen of his hand terminal. The ceiling glass darkened, the lights dimmed, and a blue hologram of Earth came up, stretching from one end of the table to the other. The directors glanced at each other with heightened curiosity.

During the distraction, Vanderheiden privately messaged Gabriella and Scharre Sr.

> I'LL JOIN THE LUNA BUSINESS ASSOCIATION IF YOU SUPPORT ME.

Both got the message and looked up at him with inquisitive looks. *Yes, you know what I'm proposing.*

Vanderheiden kicked off his pitch. "Despite our market dominance of interplanetary transportation, we remain at the mercy of the launch providers who control the surface-to-orbit market like"—Vanderheiden scoffed—"Shugart. This project will break that dominance and leave Shugart in shambles."

He tapped his hand terminal, and a long cable stretched from Earth to its geostationary orbit on the hologram. "We will build a space elevator on Earth, offering a cheaper alternative to rockets."

"A space elevator?" Cooper chuckled and looked side to side. "That's science fiction."

Vanderheiden ignored him and turned to Brunelli. "Please explain how it works."

Brunelli stepped forward, rolled his shoulders back, and cracked his neck. He pointed at the hologram with a cursor. "One end of the cable would be anchored to Earth's surface along the equator to take full advantage of the planet's rotation. The other end of the cable would reach over 35,000 kilometers beyond geostationary orbit. The combination of Earth's centrifugal force from its rotation pulling the cable up and the gravity pulling it down allows the cable to remain erect and stable in a single position over Earth."

Scharre Sr. squinted his eyes. "So, it is like an athlete performing a hammer throw?"

"Yes, great analogy." Brunelli pointed at him. "To throw the hammer ball, the athlete, like Earth, has to rotate his body to move the ball in a circular motion. As long as the athlete keeps rotating at the appropriate velocity and holding the hammer ball in front of him, the hammer ball will continuously rotate parallel to the ground."

The hologram displayed shipping containers sliding up and down the cable. "Containers attached to the cable would ascend and descend the space elevator, providing a substantially cheaper way to traverse between the surface and orbit than rockets."

Brunelli took a deep breath. "We need a material that is light enough to construct and deploy but strong enough to handle the immense stress placed on the cable. Carbon nanotube is the only feasible material, but it can't be mass-produced. So, an Earth space elevator is impossible right now."

Vanderheiden took over. "Instead of Earth, we start at Luna."

"But what about Shugart—"

"Let them finish," Gabriella snapped at Cooper.

The hologram morphed into Luna with a space elevator cable stretching over 56,000 kilometers from the surface. Vanderheiden walked along the side of the table. "A Luna space elevator would be an excellent pilot program before attempting Earth."

He raised two fingers. "One, there is already an abundance of economic activity on Luna. The return on investment would be immediate. Two, the moon's gravity is much weaker. Sixteen percent of Earth's. That changes the material requirement. Titanium can be used, and Luna has plenty of it."

Vanderheiden walked behind Cooper's seat, speaking over Cooper's head. "When the Luna Space Elevator is built, we use it to enable the mass production of carbon nanotube, the missing ingredient to Earth's space elevator. The Luna Space Elevator is the key to it all." *And to saving Emily.*

"How long would it take to construct this elevator?" Cooper twisted his head.

"Luna will take approximately two years," Brunelli answered.

"And the cost?" Gabriella inquired.

Vanderheiden pressed his tongue to the roof of his mouth. *Here it comes.* "Forty billion credits."

A collective groan echoed around the room. Directors rubbed their faces, shook their heads, or whispered to each other. Gabriella blinked away her disbelief and scanned the room carefully. Vanderheiden imagined her measuring the level of support this project had. Scharre Sr. rubbed his cheek slowly, looking at no one. *No immediate pushback. That's good.*

"I'm sorry..." Cooper chuckled. "I'll take Shugart's offer over this pipe dream. A, what, 56,000-kilometer cable... That's impossible."

Vanderheiden rested his hand on Cooper's shoulder and squeezed gently. "That's what people said about PhotonicWay." He let go.

He waved his hand at the large hologram. "Imagine the revenue we would generate from this. No longer will our solar and battery farms be short of lithium or titanium. No more rolling blackouts. Once we bridge space with Earth, mankind will truly become a multi-planetary species." He shook his fist. "And Vanderheiden Corporation would be at the center of it all. They would remember us for generations!"

Scharre Sr. smiled like a father proud of his son. Gabriella stared at the hologram. Vanderheiden noticed many of the directors looked at the two, waiting for their response.

"Let me put it another way." Scharre Sr. leaned forward slowly, eyes bulging. "The board must choose either the Luna Space Elevator or Shugart. Shugart will never do this project. It'll wipe out their surface-to-orbit business, cannibalizing itself."

"This is just a far-fetched dream!" Cooper looked around with slight panic. "Vanderheiden...we know his history with Shugart. His judgment is clouded. He is just desperate! We must protect our shareholders. Let's vote on this now."

Vanderheiden crossed his arms. *You are correct. I am desperate, like I was before we launched PhotonicWay.*

Gabriella shot her eyes at Cooper. "You want your vote?" She pressed on the table and stood up. "You'll have your vote." She swallowed and raised her hand. "All in favor of the Luna Space Elevator?"

Scharre Sr. smirked and raised his hand slowly, swinging his gaze around the table. Many eyes, mirroring the blue hologram, flickered side to side. Vanderheiden raised his hand and nodded at Gabriella. She nodded in response.

One by one, five other directors raised their hands. Cooper's mouth curled downward in disgust. Brunelli pumped a fist in the air, lifting himself partially out of his chair, but restrained himself from jumping and hollering. The other engineers shook each other's hands in mutual congratulations.

Gabriella announced, like a judge in the courtroom, "The board votes eight to four in favor of the Luna Space Elevator. All in favor of advancing talks with Shugart?"

Cooper and the three other directors raised their hands.

"The board votes eight to four against advancing talks with

Shugart." Gabriella typed on her hand terminal for a moment. "That concludes today's board meeting."

Vanderheiden approached Cooper from behind and whispered, "This is still my company. Step aside and enjoy the ride."

"Go fuck yourself," Cooper said. "This isn't over."

Vanderheiden slapped Cooper's shoulder hard and walked back to his seat. Cooper grumbled and left the room, leaving behind a spinning chair.

The glass ceiling cleared up, and the lights returned to normal brightness.

"Well done, Vanderheiden." One director shook hands with him.

"Keep us informed," another said.

Directors and employees trickled out of the room slowly until only Vanderheiden, Scharre Sr., and Gabriella remained.

"Pressure is on," Gabriella said. "You need to move fast. Once the project cost appears in our financials, our stock price will decline. As long as the board backs us, we are okay. But the shareholder pressure will eventually break each director one by one if this project drags out."

"We have to keep this under wrap," Scharre Sr. said. "We don't want the government or Shugart catching a whiff of this."

"Thanks for changing your votes," Vanderheiden said.

"Don't thank me." Gabriella tightened her lips to a red line. "Build the Luna Space Elevator. And quickly."

9

THE GENERAL

"All hands," Colonel Barrows announced. "Initiating lunar orbital insertion in T minus two minutes."

Earth rotated inside the blackness of space on the monitors of the USSV *Wyoming*'s operations deck. Floating above the command console, Sinclair found the spinning globe soothing to stare at. To prevent one side from heating up with the exposure to the sun, the gunship was on the barbeque roll maneuver. This made the blue-and-green planet appear to spin like a steady wind turbine.

It was noisy inside the cabin, fans and pumps running nonstop to maintain comfortable conditions. Sinclair felt good with the weightlessness. She wasn't taking any anti-nausea medicine, given her body hadn't had the time to re-acclimate to Earth's full gravity. This felt like her natural habitat.

"T minus thirty seconds," Barrows said. The colonel, with a flattop haircut and baby-shaped face, exhibited deep concentration as he focused on the navigation hologram hovering above his console.

Sinclair nudged off the ceiling and strapped into her command seat. Despite serving in the space force for nearly thirty years, this was her first time going beyond low earth orbit. Her throat was tight from both the excitement of traveling to a different part of the solar system and the awareness of traveling far away from the only planet humans lived and breathed on. The half-meter-thick armored hull of the *Wyoming* was all that stood between her and a gruesome death in the vacuum.

Sinclair looked at the engine cameras on the rear end of the gunship, seeing Luna grow larger. Unlike the scenic blend of blue and green Earth gave off, Luna was starkly black and gray. Its many craters were easy to spot.

"T minus ten...five, four, three, two, one...mark."

Sinclair felt the soft hum of the nuclear thermal engines shudder the deck, vibrating through her whole body. The floor shook, pushing all crew members into their seats as the g-force climbed to three g. Sinclair clenched the armrests of her seat, not pleased to be back in strong gravity. Minute after minute, Luna took over half the tactical display as the spacecraft decelerated. The craters grew more visible.

"Approaching main engine cutoff. T minus ten...five, four, three, two, one...mark."

The vibrations stopped, and the gravity disappeared.

"Nice and smooth." Chief Engineer Cavalieri extended her tattooed arm out with a thumb up. "Thank you for not sending us to Mars."

Barrows grunted. "A *Nevada* will not be done under my watch."

Cavalieri tapped a button on the engineering console. "It isn't always the navigator's fault for botching a lunar orbital insertion. I heard the *Nevada*'s maneuvering thrusters are—"

"Anything that happens on the gunship is the commander's responsibility," Barrows interrupted.

"There is only so much responsibility you can give a commander. The maintenance crews at the Craven spacedock are under pressure and forced to cut corners to stay on schedule. I've been there myself."

"We are on the brink of war with Europe." Barrows pointed at the continent on the hologram. "Everyone is under pressure."

Sinclair ignored their squabble and stared at Luna. The weight of responsibility for defending it grew heavier on her shoulder the closer the *Wyoming* got to the moon. Sinclair looked around the small cabin, observing the two officers. Sinclair attempted to surround herself with officers just as competent or even more than she was. Despite the heavy burden of being the deputy fleet commander, Sinclair felt some reassurance because she was inside the gunship's operations deck with a crew she trusted, officers she was willing to give the command of a spacecraft to without hesitation.

"We need to ask her..." Cavalieri whispered to Barrows.

"Ask me what?" Sinclair replied.

"General, do you know what kind of shape the Luna Fleet is in?" Barrows asked.

Sinclair unclipped from her harness. "I would expect things to be in good shape with Fosvik as fleet commander."

Barrows glanced at Cavalieri and nodded.

"We're asking because we've heard rumors." Cavalieri moved her long-braided ponytail to her other shoulder.

"What did you two hear?"

"That things aren't in good shape. Drugs are rampant. Officers abuse the spacemen. The vessels are in disrepair." Cavalieri licked her lips. "We also heard the fleet commander is...useless."

"Those officers need to watch their words," Barrows said.

"General Fosvik?" Sinclair asked.

Cavalieri nodded.

Eyebrows drawing together, Sinclair eyed each of her subordinates, questioning their report. "We'll see for ourselves when we dock the *Decatur*."

"And we will remind the spacemen of their duty if the rumors are true." Barrows got on the comms. "*Decatur*, this is *Wyoming*. We are in lunar orbit, altitude of eighty-one kilometers. Requesting permission to dock. Over."

"*Wyoming*, this is *Decatur*," the traffic controller replied. "Permission granted. Welcome to Luna. We are glad to have you here. Over and out."

The *Wyoming* entered orbit around Luna and circled the moon multiple times, shifting its velocity and altitude to match the *Decatur*.

The spacecraft carrier of the Luna Fleet, a quarter-kilometer-long behemoth, shaped like a cylinder, appeared on their displays. Two artificial gravity rings spun around the front, while the docking ports able to hold eight vessels were at the center.

Sinclair reviewed the *Decatur* schematics, seeing it armed only with the active protection system, or APS, comprising lasers and pellet-firing turrets placed along the carrier's cargo space, liquid methane tanks, and engineering modules. One nuclear thermal engine was attached to the spacecraft's back end.

Sinclair pulled herself closer to the monitors. "Barrows, hold our distance from the *Decatur*. Perform a three-hundred-sixty-degree rotation around the carrier for a visual inspection."

"Roger that. Holding distance and starting rotation around the *Decatur*."

Six vessels were docked with the carrier. Three were cylinder-shaped shuttles, and the heat shields showed signs of wear and tear. Not an issue when traveling through Luna's lack of atmosphere. However, Sinclair doubted the heat shield would hold up against a scorching atmospheric reentry down to Earth.

The two assault craft assigned to the Raiders were in better shape. They were like shuttles but equipped with thicker hulls, armed with a short-barrel rail gun, and could latch onto a hostile spacecraft and blow holes into its hull.

The last vessel docked to the *Decatur* was the *Oregon*, a gunship with the same narrow cone matte-black chassis design as the *Wyoming*. Sinclair tightened her lips. The gunship shouldn't be chained to the carrier.

She noted on the hologram map that the two guided missile destroyers, the *Rhode Island* and the *Delaware*, were on the opposite side of the moon. Sinclair believed the best use of destroyers and their guided missiles was maintaining a defensive perimeter around the fleet, not spearheading the fleet's offense. The gunships should venture out on their own and wreak havoc on the enemy with their rail guns.

Sinclair pushed away from the monitors. "Barrows, resume docking."

"Resuming docking." Barrows punched in commands on his station.

Sinclair checked the navigation chart and grew concerned when she saw no tankers orbiting Luna. A military fleet stranded in its current position due to a lack of propellant reserves was at the mercy of the enemy. Sinclair swore to herself that she wouldn't lose the moon over a shortage of propellant.

The *Decatur* extended its docking mechanism to the lower half of the gunship's hull, where its docking port was located. A slight bump echoed when the contact was made.

"Barrows, take watch." Sinclair glided to the exit. "Cavalieri, with me."

The two officers floated through the tunnel of the docking arm. After the air pressure balanced, the hatch on the *Decatur* opened, and a strong odor of sweat and recycled air blew into the tunnel.

Floating on the other side of the air lock was Lieutenant Colonel Fabian, the *Decatur*'s commander and de facto third-in-command of the fleet. He and the two spacemen accompanying him were positioned upside down relative to Sinclair. Their cheeks appeared puffy, and their arms floated near their shoulders in the weightlessness. Sinclair spun herself to align with them.

"Welcome to the *Decatur*, General." Fabian saluted, as did the spacemen flanking him. "Glad to have you on board."

Sinclair returned the salute. "At ease, spacemen."

She glanced up and down the white-paneled interior tunnel of the carrier. Eight air-lock hatches surrounded them. The air circulation sounded heavy, like someone struggling to breathe. A light fixture or two flickered.

She frowned and cracked a knuckle. "I will perform a full inspection of the *Decatur*."

* * *

The hours-long inspection of the spacecraft carrier only put Sinclair in a sourer mood.

Feeling the soft vibration of the shuttle descending to the lunar surface, Sinclair thought about how the circumstances had killed any excitement she'd felt about setting foot on a different planetary body. The poor conditions and low morale on the *Decatur*, just as Cavalieri had described, were lodged in her mind. She needed to know if the conditions on the ground were just as bad as on the *Decatur*. What would Fosvik's response be when she raised the issues?

In the Sinus Aestuum region on Luna's near side, several kilometers north of the equator, the Aestuum Space Force Base was difficult to find at first. Much of the complex was underground for protection against radiation, meteoroids, and orbital bombardments. However, once the spaceports and anti-orbital batteries encircling the base were spotted, the broken regolith soil on top of the underground complex was easy to trace. Or someone could simply pull up thermal optics and see the base's spiderweb pattern.

General Sinclair and other spacemen were strapped to their seats, organized across multiple rows and levels. She looked at the monitors again and, to the north of the ground base, saw the rugged mountain range and a deep-impact crater looking like a perfect circle.

The engines fired, and the crater disappeared over the horizon, but the peaks of the mountain range were still visible. At touchdown, the shuttle's engines kicked up lunar dust, which took a long time to settle back to the ground. The launchpad slowly descended underground, red strobe lights flashing inside the silo. After it touched the bottom of the well, the surface hatch sealed shut, the air pressure cycled, and the strobe lights turned green.

Sinclair unbuckled her harness. The gravity was weak enough that she let herself drop to each ladder rung bolted into the hull down to the air lock. A walkway extended out to the shuttle, and everyone disembarked. Sinclair looked up and noticed one of the shuttle's heat shield panels was barely hanging onto the hull.

After grabbing her bag, she headed into the poorly lit tunnel. Walking felt awkward. Like she had done millions of times back on Earth, she would raise her leg to bring her foot forward and let the gravity pull it down. But the gravity was too weak to make it work, and she found herself just hanging her leg in the air, waiting for it to drop, before she remembered she had to pull it down herself.

She knew the bunny-hop movement was the best way to traverse on foot, but she would hit her head on the ceiling if she did that and embarrass herself on the first day. She stuck with the regular walking motion and grew more irritated as she progressed through the tunnel, wishing she could move faster.

After navigating through many tunnels connecting the ground base's underground domes, Sinclair walked through recreation. Each dome was dedicated to a specific function, such as the command center, crew quarters, armory, power station, and medical bay. The power station, holding multiple nuclear reactors, was far away from the other domes for safety reasons. The conditions of the Aestuum Space Force Base looked decent. Maybe it was because Fosvik was present on the ground.

She heard a shout coming from a room down the corridor: "*Drink!*"

Sinclair pulled her shoulders back with a sharp inhale through her nose. She walked through the tunnel toward the room.

"Fireball explosion! Drinnnnnk!"

Multiple people laughed. "*Drink!*"

Sinclair looked into the room and found multiple spacemen watching a space movie released decades ago. She recognized the drinking game. And admitted it was fun.

On the screen, a pilot hopped onto a spacecraft resembling an airplane.

"*Drink!*" A few spacemen shook their heads hard.

A flashy action scene was playing on the monitor, and multiple spacecraft flew within a few meters of each other, firing bolts.

"*Drink! Drink! Drink!*" Laughter echoed throughout the room. No such thing as close-quarter combat in space.

Minutes later, a stealth fighter appeared. The room roared. "*Finish your drinks!*"

The laws of thermodynamics made stealth in space impossible.

Every spacecraft was visible. It was the golden rule of the drinking game.

Sinclair shook her head and wanted to punch herself for losing focus. Nostrils flared and cheeks hot, she looked at the officers with frustration. She remembered the drunk lieutenant sleeping during watch duty in the *Oregon* gunship and the many spacemen in the medical bay for questionable reasons, likely trying to stay off duty. Maybe the drinking game was to relieve the bottled-up pressure.

"General," a hoarse voice said from behind her.

Sinclair turned and saw a tall, dark-skinned man with colonel insignias on his shoulders and wearing a black-and-gray-camouflage uniform, the space force special operators' trademark.

"Colonel Dressler." Sinclair addressed the commander of the Raiders Squadron 3 stationed at Luna.

"It's been a while, ma'am." Dressler approached her, offering his hand.

Sinclair glanced at his hand and raised her chin. "You will salute a superior officer."

He held his gaze at the general for a moment. An eye muscle in his face twitched. He stepped back and saluted.

Sinclair returned the salute. She tried to make sure his legendary status didn't intimidate her. He was one of the Raiders who assaulted Murray Station during the hostage crisis years ago. It got bloody. Twenty-three of the forty Raiders killed and over a dozen hostages perished. Only three European terrorists survived.

"I still remember our conversation at Kodiak," Sinclair said.

"Yes, I came to Luna at your command."

"How is Squadron 3 doing?"

"We are locked and loaded, ready for action." He dropped his head. "Have you seen the rest of the fleet?"

"I have."

Dressler nodded and looked at the drinking officers in the room. "I don't think I have to tell you how bad of a situation we're in."

Sinclair saw Dressler had assessed her by the first sentences spoken to him. He jumped off the deep end by giving her his own assessment of their dire situation.

"Speak freely, Colonel."

He cleared his throat, but the hoarse voice didn't disappear. "This fleet is in unacceptable conditions and in need of a serious overhaul and crew rotation." He pointed his chin toward the drinking officers. "I fear the Raiders are the only effective line of defense here. There are only so many spacecraft we can assault before the casualty rate depletes my platoons."

"You are reporting the fleet to be combat ineffective," Sinclair said.

"Yes. The officers either aren't holding their spacemen accountable or cannot. Our procurement and logistics are incompetent. My men have to fight tooth and nail to get the supplies."

"I understand." Sinclair wanted to say they would make changes or offer hope that things would get better, but she didn't know if she could deliver on that yet.

"All this happened under Fosvik's watch." His face displayed disgust. "Will you be different?"

Chills spread under Sinclair's skin. "Fosvik is the fleet commander." She bared her teeth. "You *will* show respect."

Dressler was unmoved. "Will you be replacing Fosvik as fleet commander?"

"No, I'm the deputy."

"I see."

"I need to report to the fleet commander." Sinclair walked past him. "We'll talk again."

* * *

Outside the command center, Sinclair rubbed her neck. The cold air flowing over the skin of her face was comforting. She paced around the corridor, unable to stand still. Poor discipline was expected, but not at the scale that it was infecting the entire fleet. Could she really turn things around?

Her stomach felt uneasy. She couldn't tell if it was her body's reaction to the low-g environment or nervousness at the thought of meeting Fosvik. She wanted to give him a tongue-lashing for his gross negligence of the Luna Fleet but reminded herself to exercise caution.

She took a deep breath and walked through the opened hatch. It was idle inside the command center, many workstations empty. If the command center was at full capacity, at least ten officers would be in the room, especially with the EU's saber rattling. A staff officer walked across the room to the command console, where General Fosvik stood, hovering over something. The staff officer showed her hand terminal, they exchanged a few words, and the conversation ended with Fosvik waving the staff officer away with his hand.

Sinclair set her bag down, walked over to the opposite side of the command console, and saluted. "General Sinclair, reporting for duty."

Fosvik was slim with brown hair and a thick mustache. A monitor next to him played the newsfeed reporting delays on payments for US Treasury bonds. His green eyes shot up from his hand terminal lying on the console. He stared at her for a moment before returning the salute. Sinclair dropped her hand and stood at attention. Four stars were pinned to Fosvik's shoulder, the number of stars required to command a fleet.

"At ease, General." Fosvik returned to his hand terminal. She remained silent at her spot. She couldn't tell what he was reading, but it didn't appear to be military documents.

Sinclair rubbed her fingers behind her back. She didn't like officers forcing their direct reports to remain silent. It was a waste of time. She could've spent these moments talking to Cavalieri about how to fix the fleet, consulting with Barrows on rotating the gunship crews and replenishing the low stockpile of anti-orbital missiles, or speaking with the mess hall officers about improving the food supply. She chewed her bottom lip.

Fosvik turned off his hand terminal. "General, what is your initial impression of the Luna Fleet?"

Sinclair gulped. She could either lie about the fleet's combat readiness and stroke Fosvik's ego or be honest and risk getting on his bad side. This assignment was the last string preventing her discharge from the US Space Force. But honesty was required if they were to get this fleet back in shape. Luna would not fall under her watch.

"We have an abundance of issues. The *Decatur*'s systems are overdue for maintenance. The shuttles' heat shields need to be replaced. The *Oregon* engines require an overhaul. We are critically short on propellant. The morale of the crew is low. Many units are overdue for rotation back to Earth. We need a fresh crew." She took a deep breath. "The Luna Fleet is combat ineffective."

Fosvik's face didn't change as Sinclair spoke. He stared at her, and Sinclair's chest tightened, thinking she made the wrong decision.

He took his eyes off her and walked around the console. "It appears your reputation accurately reflects you." His mustache moved when he spoke. "Yes, everything you said is true."

He spun on his heels on the lunarcrete floor toward Sinclair. "But don't let your experience in the Orbital Fleet set the expectations here. At Luna, everything is different. We get insufficient support from SPACECOM. We have to fight for scraps while Ground and Orbital get special servings." He waved his arm around the command center. "This is the reality we face."

"But this reality is combat ineffective." Sinclair hesitated. "How is that acceptable?"

Fosvik raised a finger. "My fleet will defend the moon when called upon."

She wanted to disagree, saying they were easy targets for EU destroyers. "There are three urgent problems we need to solve."

"Which are?"

She brought her hand forward and raised one finger. "Our propellant reserves. We are at thirty-seven percent capacity, far below operational requirements. Mars Fleet needs to return our tanker."

"General Fassbinder had a more urgent need for the tanker," Fosvik said. "Unlike Luna, there are EU vessels patrolling Mars."

"Fine. What if we lend him a destroyer in exchange for a tanker and a gunship?"

Fosvik spoke in a low tone. "General Sinclair, as long as I am commander of this fleet, destroyers will lead the way, not gunships."

Still holding one finger, Sinclair kept her eyes on Fosvik. She wondered if she could get Garrett to force him to utilize the gunships. But he wasn't the vice chief anymore. She was on her own.

"Second problem." Sinclair extended another finger. "We need to conduct more patrols. Having gunships docked idly to the *Decatur* is letting our spacemen get rusty. We need to carry out war games to boost our readiness."

"Negative. Budget and fuel constraints make that impossible."

Sinclair wondered how he'd gotten four stars. "Then let's rotate the crews. We need a fresh set from Earth."

"SPACECOM determines the rotation, not us."

"Well, then what *can* I do, General?" She immediately regretted raising her voice.

Fosvik ignored her tone and looked at her two fingers. "You said three problems."

She dropped her hand. "The food here doesn't help morale. I suggest we change our supplier."

Fosvik smiled. "Go see what you can do there. Dismissed."

Sinclair understood she wasn't a deputy fleet commander. She was a glorified chef now.

10

THE MAGNATE

NYSE: VC 73.84 (-1.65 %)

Vanderheiden Corporation was a large company dealing with hundreds of customers and operating a complex and sensitive photonic propulsion system. Vanderheiden scrolled through messages and documents on his hand terminal, sitting on the patio with a refreshing view of the Idaho mountains, seeing all the company's accomplishments and challenges.

None of the messages made his blood boil until he came across a memo on a customer's behavior. One read through the memo had Vanderheiden leaping out of the Adirondack chair and requesting an audio connection with the Xin Chemicals CEO. *No one gets away with this.*

The ringtone sounded on the other side of the line. A strong wind made the mountains whistle.

The ringing stopped. "Hello?"

"Mr. Xin?" He smiled. "It's Vanderheiden."

"Hey!" He spoke with a slight Chinese accent. "Great news! We just launched a new demineralizer that should remove that gunpowder taste from purified water extracted from the Luna ice fields."

"Well, I'm glad to hear that." Vanderheiden flatted his hand on the patio guardrail. "I'm just checking in to see how the PhotonicWay has performed for you. Are you satisfied with our service? Any issues I should be aware of?"

"My deliveries year to date have been on schedule ninety-two percent of the time. Better than last year, but still room for improvement! That is the only issue that's come to my attention over here."

"Really?" Vanderheiden reread the memo. "Because I'm reading this report from my operators citing multiple instances of your spacecraft skipping queues to enter the PhotonicWay, disrupting traffic. First, that is an unacceptable and dangerous practice."

He read down the lines of text. "Besides that, your employees have shouted vulgar phrases at my operators. I got a 'Put me on top of the queue or suck my dick.' There was one employee who directed sexist slang at a female operator. I won't repeat what was said. 'My company delivers essential chemicals across the planets. I will refuse delivery to your platform if you don't put me next on the acceleration queue' is another one."

Vanderheiden paused. "What do you have to say about this?"

"We are a vital supplier of chemicals above Earth. Any disruption to our schedule, no matter how small, will have ripple effects across the farms, environmental systems, and water plants! We can't cut corners or handle schedule disruptions."

"So, you don't deny these events occurred?"

"It's business, Vanderheiden. My employees have deliverables to meet. They are to meet them by any means necessary."

"Yes, it's business. And business transactions come with *respect*." He curled his upper lip. "We are Vanderheiden Corporation. We carry half of the space economy on our backs. Xin Chemicals would have many more difficulties if the PhotonicWay wasn't around. We have earned the respect, don't you think?"

"You certainly have..."

Vanderheiden paced back and forth on the pinewood-built patio.

"Here is what's going to happen. You...or anybody from Xin Chemicals...will never disrespect my operators. And to ensure it doesn't happen again, I'm canceling our fifteen percent discount for your shipments, effective immediately."

"What? No, you can't—"

"I'm not done!" Vanderheiden raised a finger. "And there will be no more jumping the queue. Is that clear, Mr. Xin?"

A breath was audible on the other side of the connection. "If this is how you are going to treat me, I will take my business to Rhine System."

"That's fine." Vanderheiden smirked. *I know bluffs when I hear them.* "We have plenty of other customers."

Xin ended the call, and a tone droned from the hand terminal. After messaging the operators saying Xin Chemicals shouldn't be a problem, he walked inside and navigated down two flights of narrow stairs to the first floor.

The foyer of the chalet was built out of pinewood, and a fire burned inside the stone fireplace in the corner. Leather couches and recliners, organized in a square, encircled the wooden coffee table filled with snacks and beverages. A large window unveiled the gray mountains and pine trees of Idaho. A great setting for Vanderheiden to relax, forgetting all the stresses that had gripped him for months. For years.

Standing by the bright window, he closed his eyes. *A perfect vacation with Susann and Emily.*

Footsteps struck the wooden floor. Vanderheiden opened his eyes, washing away his dream of vacation.

"Here you go." Lawrence handed a steaming cup of espresso to Vanderheiden. His thick black beard surrounded a cheerful smile.

Vanderheiden grabbed the handle and inhaled the aroma before taking a sip of the pecan-flavored espresso. Lawrence set his small glass of amber-colored alcohol on a coaster and collapsed his tall body on the couch with a deep sigh. He checked his watch and looked out the large window. "Any day now, those two."

After a second sip of his espresso, Vanderheiden looked around the foyer, wondering how many would show up for the Luna Business Association meeting. *How many will invest in my company?* Despite the board approving the Luna Space Elevator and rejecting Shugart, Vanderheiden needed to strengthen his hand against Cooper. *The more shareholders in my corner, the better.*

"Beautiful chalet." Vanderheiden nodded. "But...do you need four floors?"

"Ha!" Lawrence threw his shiny black hair back. "With regret, none of the rooms have been fully occupied at once, but I've closed many deals, so it's given me money back."

Despite their friendship going all the way back to the first contract signed between Vanderheiden Corporation and Lawrence Resources, Vanderheiden thought of the many contradictions between the two. Vanderheiden built his company, and Lawrence inherited his. Vanderheiden ran his company with a heavy-handed approach, putting nearly eighty hours a week into the business and spending the off-hours with his family. Lawrence ran his manufacturing company with a light touch, delegating responsibilities while rubbing shoulders with celebrities and politicians at lavish parties.

Vanderheiden looked at Lawrence more closely and noticed his waist was thicker. "How are things at Lawrence Resources?"

"Not good." Lawrence slouched into his couch and took a sip. "Revenue's down twenty-four percent. With this recession, customers are cutting back on new projects, so our manufacturing lines are idle. Blackburn Materials is poaching employees." He drank a bigger sip. "Fat Blackburn..."

"Well..." Vanderheiden sat down on the leather chair and whispered, "I have a project that might help you out."

"We are in the middle of nowhere!" Lawrence waved at the tall pines through the window, obscuring the gray mountains and creating long shadows across the green pasture.

Vanderheiden blinked and then relaxed his shoulders. "We are beginning preparations to build a space elevator at Luna that'll transport cargo and passengers between the surface and medium luna orbit. 56,000-kilometer-long cable made of titanium."

Lawrence pressed his eyebrows together. "You know a space elevator is impossible, right?"

"Try me."

Lawrence uncrossed his legs. "Will my company get the contract?"

"We will approach Blackburn, too, but you are the incumbent. Do you think you can supply it?"

"Come on, man." Lawrence frowned. "Blackburn?"

"You may be my best friend, but I'm betting my entire company here."

"But I'm sure we can accommodate. We've been cutting back on our resources to get through this—"

"I *need* you to accommodate." Vanderheiden pointed his finger. "Billions of credits are on the line. Can you deliver?"

Lawrence thought for a moment and then smiled. "I'll check with my managers. We would have to increase production."

"Understood. Let's meet and lay down a contract." He leaned back in his chair before jerking forward. "And do not disclose this project to anyone else. I don't need the government or Shugart hearing about this."

"Hey..." Lawrence shrugged to show the small offense taken. "It's me you are talking to."

They sat for several minutes in silence, watching the trees breathe with the wind and flames breaking down the logs in the fireplace, while the mountains remained immobile. Vanderheiden's irritation grew. *Where the hell is everyone?*

He got up and brewed another espresso. As the machine poured hot brown liquid into his mug, he heard jet engines outside.

"Ah! That must be them." Lawrence walked to the front door.

Vanderheiden grabbed the mug and turned to the entrance. He glimpsed the VTOL before Gabriella came through the front door, wearing her black jacket and black pants.

"Vanderheiden." She extended her hand with a sharp nod.

"Gabriella." Vanderheiden smiled and shook her hand.

"Did you see my company's announcement?" She smiled without exposing her teeth. "We developed a new strain of yeast that should increase the farming yield by forty-two percent. Our farms will have more mass for you to transport soon."

"Another step toward building Luna's own breadbasket."

"Exactly." She walked over to the coffee table, hands behind her back. "Now, where is that blueberry muffin Lawrence was hyping up?"

Scharre Sr. limped through the door, struggling to carry his suitcase.

"Can I take your luggage? Get you something to drink?" Lawrence followed Scharre Sr., carrying Gabriella's bag.

"No, son. I can carry my damn luggage, choose my room, and pour myself a drink!" Scharre Sr. grunted, pulling the suitcase up the wooden steps. "I may be old, but I can still handle my shit!" He nodded at Vanderheiden. "Good afternoon."

"Good afternoon." Vanderheiden smiled.

A few minutes later, Scharre Sr. came downstairs, breathing heavy. He grabbed tea and sat down. Gabriella munched on a blueberry muffin.

"Alrighty..." Lawrence clapped his hands. "Let's get down to business."

Vanderheiden looked around the foyer. "This is everyone?"

Lawrence waved his arms wide. "This is the Luna Business Association."

"Only four of us?"

"'His is e'eryone." Gabriella spoke with her mouth full of muffin.

You've got to be kidding me. "The legal roadblocks we dealt with before launching PhotonicWay nearly bankrupted VC. We are going to be facing the same problem when we build the Luna Space Elevator." He glanced at Gabriella and Scharre Sr. "Lawrence has been informed."

Gabriella and Scharre Sr. relaxed. Vanderheiden turned to Lawrence. "I need political protection. And the Luna Business Association only has four members?"

"I was there, son." Scharre Sr. sipped his tea. "That's why we started Luna Business Association."

"Look!" Lawrence shook his head. "We have bigger problems to address first... The Corporate Transparency Act. This act is...unconstitutional! How the hell did it become law so quickly?"

Vanderheiden clenched his teeth in annoyance at Lawrence changing the topic. He walked over, sat down on the recliner, and forced himself to listen. *If this day turns out to be a waste...*

"Something is off about this act." Scharre Sr. traced the top of his mug with a finger. "Two weeks ago, Congress informs the public it is being considered. Suddenly, it passes a week later and gets signed off by President Barbour?"

Gabriella took her last bite of the muffin and wiped her mouth and fingers with a napkin. "The bill is over five hundred pages, forcing publicly traded companies to disclose all major expenses." She chuckled in disbelief. "That kind of law doesn't need five hundred pages."

"Because eighty percent of the pages are unrelated to that!" Lawrence pulled out his hand terminal. "You got one section allocating one hundred million credits to this...charity I don't recognize. Another one expands a South Carolina wildlife reservation."

"Well, that cancels someone's spaceport construction plans." Scharre Sr. clicked his tongue. "Some things never change in Washington."

"Despite being over five hundred pages," Gabriella said, "the lawmakers haven't made it clear what they consider a major expense. Does this mean I have to disclose the salary of every employee at my company?" She gestured at Vanderheiden's mug. "Or do I have to go deeper and disclose every cup of coffee purchased?"

"Excellent point!" Lawrence slurred, pointing at her. "This law doesn't just impact companies. Salaries of individuals could be disclosed. That's a talking point to turn the public against the law."

Scharre Sr. waved his hand at Lawrence. "Then the SEC will just announce salaries are exempt. They have discretionary power."

Lawrence leaned back and exhaled like he was feeling the alcohol in his head.

After watching Lawrence with concern, Vanderheiden set his empty mug on the table. "My company has projects, such as the space elevator, I do not need to have disclosed to the public. I have a competitive advantage I need to protect."

"It isn't just our companies that are at risk here," Scharre Sr. said. "This kind of law will cripple public companies. It'll discourage private companies from going public, cutting them off from many investors. That's less economic growth and fewer jobs created."

"And encourage companies to move overseas," Lawrence added. "I mean...what was the motivation behind this law?"

"What about the Fairness Tax Act?" Vanderheiden asked. "That's a bigger problem for us."

Lawrence shot from his seat and stumbled over to the window. Vanderheiden noticed a distressed look on his face. Gabriella brought her eyes back down, and Scharre Sr. stared at the fireplace.

"This law is going to be pretty bad," Vanderheiden said. "They are raising the tax rate for all the brackets. If this law passes, VC is going to be paying forty-five percent." He spread his arms out with force. "That'll effectively halt the space elevator construction."

"And any transactions on Luna or Mars will have an extra five points on the tax rate." Lawrence didn't turn away from the window. "What's next? Nationalization of our companies?" He chuckled.

"That's not funny." Gabriella jerked her head toward him. "Rumors of that are going around."

"I will not let them take my company," Vanderheiden said.

"That wouldn't happen." Scharre Sr. shook his head in disbelief. "It goes against the spirit of this nation."

"You are stuck in the past." Gabriella looked around the foyer. "We need to expand our group. Have more eyes and ears around Washington. We need to strengthen our influence over the government to stop this."

Lawrence turned away from the window. "With Vanderheiden on board, we should be able to grow our numbers. We need to recruit... hard!"

Gabriella sighed. "It is time to bring Blackburn on board."

"You, too?" Lawrence looked back and forth between Vanderheiden and Gabriella. "You want Fat Blackburn here?"

"He may be a competitor of yours," Gabriella replied, "but he is a vital part of the Luna industrial base. His voice carries weight."

"He cannot be trusted!" Lawrence swung his finger down, flinching his neck muscles. "We compete in the same market, manufacture the same materials, but his company generates more profit than mine. He is doing something at Phantom Torch he doesn't want others to see." He raised his unsteady finger. "Mark my words...being associated with him will not end well."

"We need him," Gabriella replied. "Until I see evidence of the supposed criminal activity, Scharre Bank will continue financing his plants." She pressed her fingertips together. "I also suggest Xin."

Vanderheiden chuckled as his mind replayed the memory of him scolding Xin.

"Something to add?" Gabriella raised an eyebrow.

Vanderheiden inhaled. "We aren't on good terms right now."

"Fix it." Gabriella looked away. "He is the largest chemical manufacturer off Earth and supplies the bulk of fertilizers needed for my farms."

Vanderheiden shook his head. *Well, he isn't getting an apology from me.* "We'll need someone from the pharmaceutical field. Dr. Raymond from Valkyrie Labs. They manufacture the drug to treat Creutzfeldt-Jakob."

"How is Emily doing?" Scharre Sr.'s face softened.

Vanderheiden shifted his jaw from side to side. "Doctor gave her two years."

"But...what about the treatment?"

"Short supply, and Emily's at the bottom of NMS's queue."

Scharre Sr. winced. "Goddamn government."

Quick to change the subject, Vanderheiden said, "How will we take down these laws if we expand?"

Gabriella turned to her father-in-law. "We need to talk about our lobbyists."

"You have to give them time." Scharre Sr. pushed his palms out. "The federal government is a disfigured labyrinth. We can't change things overnight."

"Either that," Gabriella said, "or they are just abusing that excuse and pocketing our money."

"Lobbyists will not work." Vanderheiden stood and walked in front of the fireplace, thinking of his conversation with Sinclair about entering the defense industry. "We do campaign donations. We donate to lawmakers holding key positions on the committees. Encourage them to take our side."

Lawrence glanced at Scharre Sr. "I told you two we needed to do campaign donations, not lobbying."

Scharre Sr. stared at Vanderheiden, not moving a muscle, and eyes bulging. "If we do that, we've just become another special interest group. We swore to do this for the benefit of all Luna businesses."

"I don't care," Vanderheiden countered. "I will build the Luna Space Elevator. The government must stay off my back."

"Son..." Scharre Sr. stood up from his couch. "We have too many problems today because special interest groups hijacked this country."

"Do you want to stay clean or do you want the damn space elevator?" Vanderheiden shrugged. "I've already made my choice." *A little dirt won't hurt if the end justifies it.*

"Don't go down that path. Your pursuit of legacy will burn too many people." Scharre Sr. came over and rested his hand softly on Vanderheiden's shoulder. "Don't abuse your position."

Vanderheiden patted the old man's hand. *You may be my mentor, but I can still say no.*

"Where are your balls, Scharre Sr.?" Lawrence took an unsteady step toward the old man.

Vanderheiden swung his head toward his drunk friend. *Damn it, Lawrence. Pull yourself together.*

Scharre Sr. narrowed his eyes. "Choose your next words carefully, young man. My bank just offered you a restructuring package last week. I could withdraw it."

"Sorry..." Lawrence wobbled toward him. "I'm sorry..."

Scharre Sr. scoffed and walked away.

"When Blackburn, Xin, and Dr. Raymond join us, then we will decide." Gabriella raised her voice. "Deal?"

The three gentlemen nodded their heads.

"Good." Gabriella grabbed a second muffin. "Because I can't argue with you three when I'm hungry."

11

THE GENERAL

Sergeant Espinoza, the lanky mess hall chef, munched on a slice of bread and nodded with satisfaction. "I have to say...this is some of the best I've eaten in a while."

"So, they make the bread and rice from yeast?" Lieutenant Colonel Fabian asked.

General Sinclair nodded. "Scharre Farms has an algae-based closed ecological system at their yeast farms."

The spacemen stood in front of three containers laid on a table in the *Decatur* mess hall. Each container had the green S-shaped logo of Scharre Farms. Inside one of the artificial rings, Luna flashed in the small window every minute.

"Yeast only lives off air, so Scharre Farms grows yeast in the same environment as the tomatoes, blueberries, and cucumbers we tasted in the first container." Sinclair tapped the second container. "So that's the yeast group. We'll start with bread and rice."

"Will Scharre Farms be able to maintain a consistent delivery schedule?" Fabian asked. "Ever since the PT sessions restarted, spacemen have been eating more."

A couple weeks ago, Sinclair issued the order for mandatory physical training daily to counter the side effects of long-term space deployment. Being cooped up in tight quarters and physically idle for extended periods of time took its toll on the spacemen's well-being. Colonel Dressler has led some of the PT sessions, to the dismay of many.

"Scharre will begin expanding their facilities to support our demand," Sinclair said. "We are still getting food supply from Corpus Christi, but at a lesser frequency, so we have an alternative supply line if Scharre falls behind schedule."

Sinclair moved to the last container. "Now...the meat container."

They opened the container, seeing moist meat with a reddish-brown color. The meat was cut in various shapes, such as bite-size cubes, sausage links, and patties. The container was split between mild and spicy flavor.

"What kind of meat is this?" the lanky chef asked.

Sinclair's straight face nearly gave away a grin. "Take a bite first."

He grabbed a reddish cube and took a small bite. "Mm...salty and moist." He ate the rest of the cube. "I like it. What is it?"

"Cows, chicken, and fish are the most common meat source, but they have a low meat production yield. The meat accounts for roughly forty percent of an average cow's weight. That's useless mass, which we don't tolerate in space."

Her grin finally surfaced. "What animal can you think of that has consumable meat accounting for eighty percent of its weight?"

The chef squinted his eyes and looked side to side. Fabian's face was blank for a moment. Suddenly, as if he'd heard the funniest joke, he snickered, covering his mouth with a fist.

"Wha-what? *What?*" the chef asked. He grabbed another cube and scrutinized it.

"The animal is called *Blattella germanica*." Sinclair's smile stretched across her face. "Cockroaches."

The chef's face turned white, and all his facial muscles gave out. Fabian let out a loud roar.

"What the *fuck*?" Espinoza held the meat cube like it was radioactive. "I'm eating *cockroaches*?"

"Settle down, Sergeant," Sinclair said. The tactical armband strapped to her forearm buzzed with a message.

"Sorry, General...b-but *cockroaches*?"

"Here...let me have a bite." Fabian grabbed a cube. "Mm... Mm... Not bad."

Sinclair tapped the three containers. "This is the new food supply for our fleet. I wouldn't reveal it is cockroaches for a couple weeks." She winked. "Let them taste it first."

"Yes, ma'am," both replied.

Sinclair walked out of the mess hall. She heard the conversation resume.

"Oh shit...is that a cockroach leg?" Espinoza whispered.

"Nah...your mind is playing tricks on you."

"I swear...that's a leg."

Exiting the artificial ring, Sinclair glided down the narrow white passageway back to the central chassis. She raised her tactical armband and read the message on the screen curving over her arm.

> GENERAL SINCLAIR, I ACCEPTED THESE TERMS. ONCE YOU REPLY WITH AGREEMENT, I'LL PREP THE NEVADA GUNSHIP AND TANKER FOR TRANSIT TO LUNA. REPLY ASAP. GENERAL FASSBINDER.

Sinclair closed the message and entered the *Decatur* command deck. Barrows and Cavalieri watched the large monitors that displayed circles of different colors around Luna, marking the orbits of the vessels. Barrows had a wide sneer on his face, like everything on the monitors was offensive to him. One arm tucked across her armpit, Cavalieri had her other hand resting on her cheek. Sinclair tried to think of a time she'd seen the two in such a sour mood, but her mind drew a blank.

The two circles on the monitors intersected above Luna's north pole as two opposing vessels were about to cross paths.

"Let's see if they finish it this time," Cavalieri said with a sarcastic tone.

Barrows shook his head. "We're ending this simulation if nothing happens."

Cavalieri glanced at him.

Comm chatter inside the *Oregon* picked up. "Get the rail gun prepped and the engine spun up," Lieutenant Olsen said. "Here comes the *Barcelona*."

"Yes, ma'am," Engineer Weaver said.

But instead of the main engines firing, maneuvering thrusters on the starboard side burned. Barrows's hands shot up in disgust.

"Damn it, Chief," Captain Audubon said. "The main engine...not maneuvering!"

"Get it ready!" Olsen snapped. "We are off course!"

"Main engine is hot and ready!" Weaver said.

"We aren't close enough. Initiating burn!"

"No! Abort the burn!" Audubon said.

"And this simulation is chalked..." Cavalieri wrote notes on her hand terminal.

"Olsen, you are raising our altitude!" Audubon pointed at his console. "We are going to miss the target!"

"Shut up!"

Barrows jabbed his finger on his console. Fat red letters flashed on the monitors.

SIMULATION TERMINATED.

A collective groan came through the comm. Barrows scoffed and pushed away from the console, letting himself drift off.

"Let's put Olsen and Audubon on *potential*." Cavalieri typed her notes. "Weaver...going to *relegate*."

"No." Barrows swung his head over his shoulder. "Put Olsen on *relegate*."

"Really?" Cavalieri looked across the deck. "You think she is a lost cause?"

"Yes," he said sharply. "She has no grasp of orbital mechanics. I don't trust anyone in combat who doesn't understand it." He pointed at the roster list on Cavalieri's hand terminal.

"Audubon understands it. His tactical skills just need to be refined."

"Well, she fired the thrusters to close the distance but inadvertently raised her altitude, losing orbital velocity." Cavalieri exhaled. "Putting Olsen on *relegate*."

Proficient spacemen had a good grasp of orbital mechanics. When orbiting a planet, a spacecraft could raise its orbital velocity by lowering the altitude. The other way around, raise altitude to lower velocity. Because of that, navigators had to ignite the thrusters in the right direction depending on their intentions. Try to gain velocity and the thrusters fire in the wrong direction, and the altitude of the vessel could unintentionally be raised, resulting in lower velocity.

Sinclair leaned over Cavalieri's shoulder to see what the two were calling the PPR List. "Explain to me again the difference between *promote*, *potential*, and *relegate*."

"Anyone on *promote* is competent and should be placed in combat positions immediately," Cavalieri replied.

Sinclair frowned at the less than a dozen names under *promote*.

"Spacemen on *potential* are opportunities for improvement. Some are trained for destroyers. Others"—Barrows shook his head—"just need to sober up."

The *potential* list was the longest of the three, with over fifty names. After several weeks with the fleet, that count didn't surprise her. "And *relegate*?"

"I don't trust them." Barrows waved his hand in a cutting motion. "They are a liability to this fleet. Give them nonessential tasks or leave them at the ground base until we can rotate them off this fleet."

"Do anything of them have a glimmer of hope? This fleet would be critically undermanned if we removed *relegates*."

"Anybody with hope was placed on *potential*," Cavalieri said.

"Alright, transfer all *relegates* to the ground base. I'll find them something to do. We will be undermanned, so we need to operate in skeleton crews. Put together a roster proposal and I'll review it."

"Yes, ma'am," both replied.

After a moment, Cavalieri turned to Sinclair. "The exterior hull of the *Wyoming* has been fully refurbished. But until we replenish our inventory, I can't work on the orbital shuttles."

"We are still having supply problems?"

"The customs backlog and protests at Marius Hills are choking our supply." Cavalieri pointed at a monitor playing the newsfeed. "I see orders just sitting in warehouses, waiting to be shipped up to us."

Sinclair glanced at the newsfeed. A large group of Lunarians crammed inside an atrium were shouting. The protests seemed peaceful but heated. Issues seemed to never go away. They struck one problem down, but another emerged. Sinclair took a moment to collect her thoughts, careful not to curse in frustration. She wondered when the fleet would finally turn combat effective.

"Can't we transport the cargo ourselves?" she asked the engineer.

"Negative. Only the contractors have the vessels large enough to ship these containers."

"The Craven should have a heavy transporter to spare." Sinclair placed a call on her tactical armband. "Need to speak with our commander."

After the ringtone lasted a minute, General Fosvik answered with annoyance. "Yes?"

"General, got two matters I need to run by you. We have run all of our combat crews through simulations, and nearly half of them showed poor results. Many are ill-trained, and others are simply burnt out."

"And?" He glanced at something off-screen.

Sinclair forced herself not to shout at him. "We need to send them back to Earth and get a fresh crew. I can't raise our fleet's readiness without—"

"General Sinclair, SPACECOM makes the manpower decisions."

Sinclair expected that response. "If we can't get a fresh crew, what about a tanker? Having weak crews and little propellant makes our vessels metal buckets that don't shoot back."

"Do not call my vessels *metal buckets*, General."

Barrows rubbed his eyes, hiding his frustration.

"Will you get me a tanker?" Sinclair asked. "Just one?"

"General Fassbinder and his Mars Fleet had an urgent need for it. Decision is final and issue is closed." Fosvik raised his hand terminal close to his face. "Don't bring it up again."

Sinclair blinked a few times. If Fassbinder said he would trade a gunship and tanker for one of the Luna Fleet's destroyers, one general was lying.

Sinclair's silence prompted Fosvik to speak. "And the second matter?"

"Chief Cavalieri has reported the materials needed for fleet refurbishment are held up at Marius Hills Spaceport, citing customs delays and disruptions from the protests. We need a heavy transporter from Craven to be shifted to Luna to get the supplies moving."

"Negative. I got a quicker solution." Fosvik issued a connection request to Dressler.

"Dressler here." The colonel's hard face materialized on the screen.

"Colonel, we got containers held up at Marius Hills Spaceport again," Fosvik said. "Send a fire team down and get that supply moving. Confiscate it if you need to. I will not have the security of this fleet compromised by those damn protesters."

"Yes, sir."

Sinclair's lips parted but said nothing. She glanced at Cavalieri. "Sir, I want the supply just as much as you do, but we have to do it the right way. Lunarians are already agitated right now. Showing up with guns will escalate the situation. They are essential suppliers for this fleet, and we can't tarnish that relationship."

"We have a moon to defend. I don't care about their feelings. Get it done, Dressler."

"Yes, sir," the hoarse voice replied again.

Fosvik ended the call. Sinclair stared at the blank screen for a minute.

"Shit is about to hit the thrusters," Cavalieri muttered.

"What happens to the next batch if we confiscate these?" Barrows asked.

"I wouldn't build the materials if I were them," Cavalieri answered.

Sinclair broke her silence. "Chief, head down to Marius Hills with the Raiders. Make sure everyone keeps their heads cool."

"Yes, ma'am."

Sinclair turned to Barrows. She thought hard about what she was going to do next. She already decided but wasn't sure if she was ready to face the consequences. Hesitation during combat could mean death. She told herself to decide and carry it out quickly.

"Put together the best destroyer crew from the *relegate* list and transfer them to the *Delaware*."

"Ma'am?" Barrows raised an eyebrow. "We recommend *relegates* to be grounded."

"Just get it done." Sinclair glided out of the command deck.

She pulled up Fassbinder's message and replied.

> GENERAL FASSBINDER, I ACCEPT OUR ARRANGEMENT. I'LL PREP THE DELAWARE FOR A HARD BURN TOWARD MARS. GENERAL SINCLAIR.

She had broken probably a dozen regulations and laws by carrying out this action, but she was desperate. Luna would not fall under her watch.

12

THE MAGNATE

NYSE: VC 72.61 (-1.67%)

"Estimated arrival time to PhotonicWay in T minus five minutes," the spacecraft system announced.

Vanderheiden pressed his shoulder against the window and stared at the edge of Earth outlined by a thin, fuzzy line separating the planet's bright white glow from the black space. *Earth is beautiful.*

He felt a slight disruption in the airflow inside his private stall, like someone floating past him. He turned just in time to feel Brunelli slap his shoulder.

"How does it feel to be back in space?" Brunelli smiled. The planet's brightness lit up his leathery face and receding hairline.

"You see that fuzzy line just above the surface?" Vanderheiden leaned closer to the window and pointed with his finger. "That's our atmosphere. The survival of life on Earth depends on it."

"Becoming a romantic?"

Vanderheiden waved his hand.

Brunelli pulled himself into the stall. "You ready to scrutinize the suppliers and scout out an anchor site?"

"You know I'm just as eager as you are to build the space elevator.

This could be a new beginning for our company"—he looked away—"or the seeds of our downfall."

"It won't be our downfall."

"We need to move fast." Vanderheiden clenched his fist. "Be ruthless. Once the construction begins and the heavy cost eats into our profit, our stock price will take a beating. We can't let Cooper and other directors who oppose the space elevator gain traction inside the boardroom."

He looked closely at Brunelli. "If something is to take five days to complete, get it done in three. That's the urgency we need."

"We have not done before this." Brunelli crossed his arms. "We can't rush a mega-construction project of this scale."

"I've thrown my full support behind this project. I ask that you return the favor in my fight to keep the board on our side."

Brunelli's jaw shifted sideways, hesitating.

"Do you want Cooper to control the board, Brunelli?"

"Hell no!" Brunelli replied like someone had shocked him in the back.

"Then we need to move fast. The key is building the 56,000-kilometer-long titanium cable. Once we have cable and begin building the elevator, I'll announce the project to the public. The stock price will rise, killing any chance of Shugart's hostile takeover." He leaned toward Brunelli. "And Cooper wouldn't be able to stop us."

Brunelli nodded. "If you'll give us that budget, we'll deliver the schedule you are looking for."

"That is my intention." Vanderheiden rubbed his chin. "We can hold off Shugart for two, maybe three, quarters. Can you get the cable built by then?"

"We'll get it done." Brunelli stared at him for a moment. "Vanderheiden...I just want to say thank you for having faith in me."

Vanderheiden nodded. *You must make it work.*

"I will admit"—Brunelli paused—"that I thought I lost you for good over these past few weeks. I thought Friday was going to be my last day."

Vanderheiden moved his lips for a moment. "I did lose confidence in you."

Brunelli pulled his head back. "What changed?"

Vanderheiden looked over Brunelli's shoulder to see the engineers in the back of the cabin reviewing holographic schematics of space elevator cable and surface anchor.

"I cherished the earlier years where we had an ambitious vision and made bold moves." He shrugged his shoulders. "But these past few years of just milking the cash cow was...what's the word"—he spun his hands in the air—"annoying and unfulfilling. Shugart seeking to merge was a wake-up call. We turned complacent, just like Shugart."

He narrowed his gaze at Brunelli. "I was sick of being the investors' bitch."

Brunelli roared with laughter. "There's the man I remember!"

The spacecraft beeped. "Estimated arrival time to PhotonicWay in T minus one minute. Please secure all personal belongings and strap yourself in your seat."

Brunelli left the stall and told the engineers to return to their seats.

Several kilometers away from the spacecraft was Rubicon, the largest zero-g manufacturing complex in the solar system. The complex was a behemoth, with many modules shaped into octagon or square tubes connected by a convoluted matrix of struts and cables. On top of the complex were the inbound docks, where spacecraft unloaded raw materials extracted from Luna and Mars. On the bottom end were the outbound docks, to drop the refined goods to Earth. Three massive artificial gravity rings spun around the center of the complex. "SHUGART" was printed in big blue letters on all three rings against the exterior hull's white paint.

Vanderheiden looked closely at the spacecraft docked to the inbound docks and smiled, seeing most of the spacecraft equipped with photonic engines. For centuries, mankind had dreamed of colonizing the solar system, but there was never an economy to sustain it. That changed decades ago when General Shugart, hero of the Second North Atlantic–Eurasian War, teamed up with investors to use space's greatest value, its weightlessness, and laid the foundation of the Rubicon. Now Rubicon and other zero-g manufacturing complexes produced a hundred billion credits' worth of goods, such as super-semiconductors, pharmaceuticals, super-batteries, metal foam, and nanotech.

"Earth Platform 1 in sight," the spacecraft announced. "Acceleration in five minutes. Please remain in your seats."

Vanderheiden tightened his seat belts and strained to see the photonic platform through his window. He could only see out the port side of the spacecraft, but he saw the edge of the platform. He hadn't seen a photonic platform in orbit in years, and his heart pumped with excitement.

Thrusters firing, the spacecraft shuddered, positioned itself parallel to the photonic platform, and drifted along it. Only the bottom of the structure, which held crew modules, was visible. The thrusters burst a few times, sending the spacecraft up toward the front. At the center of the platform were the four modular nuclear reactors, manufactured by Vanderheiden Corporation, powering the photonic platform. Each nuclear reactor was worth millions and could power thousands of homes or a city.

The spacecraft climbed, the nuclear reactors disappeared from the window, and the formidable photonic beam drifted into view. The long rectangular barrel measured in at 104 meters long. VC managed eight platforms orbiting Earth, four at Luna, and three at Mars.

Vanderheiden grinned. *My legacy.*

The photonic beam disappeared. Thrusters fired again, jerking Vanderheiden to his right side. The spacecraft moved leftward to place its engine above the photonic beam, and the thrusters fired again, bringing the spacecraft to idle. The tip of the photonic beam was directly behind the spacecraft.

A few minutes later, the announcement came: "Acceleration commencing in five, four, three, two, one. Launch ignition."

The photonic engine spun up, creating a hum inside the cabin, and billions of particles fired from the photonic beam into the spacecraft's engine, ignited its main thruster, and generated speed. The g-force gently pushed Vanderheiden into his seat, and then forcefully. The hum grew louder as the number of particles flowing through the engine grew exponentially. He looked out the window, and Earth seemed to drop underneath him, creating a disorienting sensation for a moment like he was drifting off into deep space with no chance of returning home.

In theory, photonic propulsion could push a spacecraft to a velocity close to 10 percent the speed of light. However, laser dilation prevented that. The farther the spacecraft was from the platform, the more the number of particles the photonic engine caught declined, generating less acceleration. Vanderheiden always gave the analogy of someone pointing a flashlight at the wall. When they stepped away from the wall, the diameter of the light expanded but the density of the particles declined, reducing the brightness.

The acceleration was at two g, vibrating Vanderheiden's seat with a pleasant hum. He couldn't see Earth anymore, but there was still a hint of white glow off the corner of his window.

The acceleration continued for three hours, laser dilation causing the acceleration to dwindle down.

"Photonic engine cutoff," the spacecraft announced, and the g-force fizzled out.

After half a day traveling through cislunar space, the spacecraft flipped to point its photonic engine at Luna. The hum started, and the g-force climbed as the platform thousands of kilometers away fired its photonic beams at the spacecraft. Vanderheiden couldn't see Luna, only the black sky. Hours later, the deceleration stopped and the weightlessness returned.

Vanderheiden saw Luna now, noting there was no fuzzy line hugging the celestial body because of its lack of atmosphere. Just a big gray orb surrounded by black. He saw the shadows of the many hills and craters, a stark contrast to the light-gray regolith soil.

After orbiting the moon multiple times, the altitude dropping with each lap, Marius Hills became visible to the naked eye. The largest city on Luna was located inside a large lava tube in Oceanus

Procellarum. Many launchpads, industrial plants, and white domes illuminated by strobe lights and telecom equipment surrounded the more than a hundred-meter-wide hole, exposing the lava tube. Paved and unpaved roads scattered out in all directions like tree branches from the surface hole.

"Touchdown in T minus two minutes," the announcement cautioned.

Inside the hole was the lava tube, roughly eighty meters below the surface and over eight hundred meters wide in the interior, offering radiation protection and cooler temperatures. The lava tube was accessible via elevators from the hole on the top or underground tunnels bored into the interior.

"T minus thirty seconds."

The spacecraft dropped fast toward a launchpad, and Vanderheiden felt himself float in his seat, harness pressing down on his shoulders. The engine ignited, and hard deceleration kicked Vanderheiden in the ass. He held his harness tightly for the shaky descent.

"T minus fifteen seconds."

Vanderheiden took a deep breath, bracing himself for the brutish and unforgiving environment. *Time to build a space elevator.*

"T minus five, four, three, two, one...touchdown."

* * *

"It was like talking to a brick wall with the Lawrence team," Brunelli yelled over the crowd.

Vanderheiden nodded, squeezing himself through the incessant torrent of people. A constant flow of beeping droids, rolling carts, and people flowed through the narrow tunnel hugged by lunarcrete walls. The two men walked briskly, trying to reach the inner loop's exit from Marius Hills City and transfer over to the outer loop to arrive at the garages.

Vanderheiden pulled out his hand terminal and typed a message.

LAWRENCE, I DON'T SENSE ANY URGENCY
FROM YOUR COMPANY TO WIN THIS CONTRACT.
THIS SPACE ELEVATOR IS PARAMOUNT TO VC.

They walked underneath a banner of Lawrence Resources, displaying many small squares of different colors overlapping each other, next to the company name in white letters against a silver background. There was a strong human odor, a sign of overcrowding or the need for better environmental systems. Every other light fixture was turned off, and people spoke in hushed voices.

His hand terminal pinged.

I'M UNDER THE IMPRESSION WE ARE THE
INCUMBENT FOR THIS CONTRACT. YOU'LL HAVE
FULL DEDICATION FROM MY TEAM ONCE YOU
AWARD US THE BUSINESS.

Vanderheiden stopped walking and stepped to the side to avoid the crowd. Brunelli stood next to him, examining the human traffic. With each letter he typed, Vanderheiden pressed his hand terminal harder.

I WANT MORE URGENCY AND BETTER
COLLABORATION NEXT TIME OR I'LL HAVE TO
TAKE MY BUSINESS TO BLACKBURN. THIS IS
THE LUNA SPACE ELEVATOR WE ARE TALKING
ABOUT IT.

Two booming voices were heard across the tunnel. Vanderheiden and Brunelli saw a pair of men standing in front of each other, one clenching his fists and the other crossing his arms with a grin.

"That was my contract! I have a family back home I need to feed!"

"Well, don't forget birth control next time!" The other laughed and glanced over his shoulder to the crowd.

A fist flew into the smirking face, causing him to stagger back in an awkward motion in the low gravity. He rubbed his cheek, bared his bloodied teeth, and tackled his attacker to the ground. The arms and legs turned into a blur and became an entanglement. People from the crowd jumped in to pull the two fighting men apart.

"Stop it!" A gray-bearded and bald man stepped between the two. "Stop it!"

He glanced between the two men and waited until he knew he had their attention.

"Now...things aren't the way they used to be! It isn't like the old days when there was work for everyone. Times have changed!"

"I'll have the president's head for these tariffs!" someone yelled, and the crowd cheered.

"It's not just that." The bearded man nodded. "The government is trying to raise taxes on us...again!" He clenched his fist tightly like he was grabbing a rope. "They are *squeezing* us!"

The crowd gave affirmative shouts. "Fuck Barbour!"

The bearded man smiled. "So, remember that during the next election."

"Fuck that, Logan! I'm not waiting for the next election!"

Vanderheiden whispered to Brunelli, "Let's get out of here."

They arrived at the garage front office, spoke to an agent, filled out paperwork, and walked through the side door toward the garages. Inside Air Lock Seven, the heavy all-terrain vehicle, standing on four gigantic wheels, had a pressurized cabin big enough to fit eight people and cargo space to fit all the geoengineering equipment. Everyone strapped on their space suits and boarded the H-ATV.

Brunelli took the driver's seat and punched in commands. The inner hatch closed and yellow lights flashed, the air lock flushing out pressurized air. After the lights turned green, the door rose and the H-ATV rolled onto the road, hugging the interior edge of the lava tube.

Vanderheiden watched Marius Hills City come into full view through his reinforced window. It was an underground city built inside a large cave. Spotlights and windows highlighted the domes of various sizes. The sunlight lit up only a corner of the enormous lava tube. Dozens of struts built out of steel foam were placed across the cave to strengthen the integrity of the enclosure.

The window went dark as the H-ATV drove through the tunnel, up the ramp to the surface. They reached the outer hatch and watched it rise from the ground, exposing an unpaved road running over the chalky and uneven surface littered with pockets of craters.

"Hang on!" Bruce laughed and floored the accelerator.

* * *

From the windows of the conference room, Vanderheiden watched excavators tear the ashen ground apart for samarium. Dump trucks carried loads of the rare earth metal out of the giant quarry, heading east toward Marius Hills for transport to low earth orbit and supply the zero-g manufacturing complexes building nuclear reactor control rods, magnets, and batteries. Instead of heading east, Vanderheiden imagined the trucks heading south toward the Luna Space Elevator to rise off-world. *At a fraction of a rocket's cost.*

Turning his eyes away from the window overlooking the quarry, Vanderheiden looked across the table at Blackburn. His company's logo, an animated ball of black fire on a yellow background, covered the entire wall behind the bald and burly businessman. *Fat Blackburn, according to Lawrence.* Vanderheiden ignored the man's intense stare and tapped his hand terminal.

"Lawrence's price is significantly less than yours."

"That doesn't surprise me." Blackburn held his stare. "Lawrence already has the infrastructure to support your large volume. This volume you are requesting is beyond our capacity."

He activated a hologram of his factory layout, suspended over the table. "We need additional funds to expand our infrastructure and install state-of-the-art equipment to support the volume of titanium required to build the space elevator cable."

"And why should we pay for that?" Brunelli replied.

Blackburn leaned forward and pointed out the window with his fat finger. "We have direct access to the mines, allowing us to ensure we supply the highest quality titanium to you. Lawrence has no control over their mines." He scowled with his thick lips. "It would be a shame if the entire space elevator fell because they manufactured one link of the cable with inferior titanium."

"How can we ensure you are giving us high-quality materials?" Brunelli asked.

Blackburn opened his hands. "You are welcome to have an inspector stationed here."

Vanderheiden and Brunelli glanced at each other. *Lawrence never offered that.*

Blackburn smiled. Vanderheiden was unable to tell if he was trying to charm or intimidate.

"Look, I want to start this business partnership with honesty and transparency," Blackburn said. "The additional capacity and state-of-the-art assembly line will remain dedicated to VC when you build more space elevators."

"More space elevators?" Vanderheiden narrowed his eyebrows.

"I'm ambitious like you." Blackburn smiled. "I wouldn't be content with just a space elevator at Luna. Earth is your endgame."

Vanderheiden tapped the table rhythmically with his fingers. *Any more concessions from you?*

Blackburn pointed at Vanderheiden and Brunelli. "If Vanderheiden Corporation is investing heavily in this endeavor, I want to be a part of it. A space elevator will change Luna. We can be the businessmen who solved Earth's Resource Crisis."

Blackburn's large size seemed to magnify the passionate energy Vanderheiden felt from him. He sighed and took a sip of water. There was a hint of gunpowder in it. He clicked his tongue.

"Look, Blackburn. We love the enthusiasm. But"—Vanderheiden shook his head—"the price is just too high. If you dropped it by twenty points, you would be a serious contender for this contract."

Blackburn held an inquisitive stare at him for a minute.

"I can drop five points," he replied.

Vanderheiden and Brunelli eyed each other, nodded, and stood up to leave. *Never negotiate unless you are willing to walk away.* "That won't be enough for us."

Blackburn's big lips pressed together with disappointment and his face turned a darker shade of red. Vanderheiden hesitated, worried the big man was going to blow up with rage. Instead, Blackburn stood up and offered his hand. "I understand. That's how business is. My door is always open."

Brunelli shook his hand first. Vanderheiden shook his hand next. "Do I have your word that you will adhere to absolute secrecy regarding this project?"

"You have my word." Blackburn lowered his head, showing more light reflecting off his bald top.

Vanderheiden smiled and tried to pull his hand away, but Blackburn didn't let go.

"The last thing you need is the crooked bureaucrats back on Earth choking you with regulations. They have no business telling us how to run things up here. Luna needs this elevator." Blackburn tightened his grip, and Vanderheiden felt his fingers go numb.

"I *need* this elevator," Blackburn said.

* * *

After restocking on food and drinks, complimentary of Blackburn Materials, the VC team departed from Phantom Torch, a yellow flaming orb painted across the top of the main dome. They drove by a convoy of dump trucks and reached the main road. Instead of turning west back to Marius Hills City, they turned south.

The potential anchor site was in Sinus Medii, the centermost point of Luna's nearside, making it the moon's closest point to Earth. That made it the ideal spot for the anchor because the space elevator needed to point directly toward Earth for the extra gravity pull. Vanderheiden hoped the engineers' survey came back positive, proving the ground was sturdy enough to hold the surface anchor.

"We should give the contract to Blackburn." Brunelli held a tight grip on the steering wheel.

"Blackburn?" Vanderheiden kept his eyes fixed through the narrow window, watching the lunar soil roll by. "That'll just blow up our budget."

"We need the best supplier, not the cheapest."

"Look, I see how Blackburn is more eager and collaborative. But I don't know him. I don't trust him." Vanderheiden rubbed his hand, still feeling sore from the tight handshake. "I have a relationship with Lawrence, and that gives me more leverage. Lawrence Resources has the scale and experience we need."

Brunelli slowed the H-ATV down and drove it off the road down a steep ramp. No paved roads were connected to Sinus Medii, so they would have to traverse the treacherous surface like a safari. The gigantic wheels kicked up dust, and the cabin shook against the bumpy surface.

"Why don't you trust Blackburn?" Brunelli asked.

"If Lawrence doesn't trust him, there's a good reason."

Brunelli scoffed. "Or he just doesn't like Blackburn taking away his market share."

Vanderheiden didn't reply.

"Blackburn should get the contract," Brunelli said. "They are nimbler and more eager to support us. We would instantly become their biggest customer, making us their top priority. We would just be one of many customers on Lawrence's spreadsheet."

Vanderheiden jerked his head. "This project is too important for us to try out a different supplier. Lawrence Resources has been a key supplier for years."

"Then why did we approach Blackburn in the first place?"

"I hoped they would offer a lower price that I could use as leverage against Lawrence."

Brunelli's mouth moved for a few seconds before snapping shut, ending the conversation.

* * *

Brunelli kicked the brake pedal and shut down the engine. "We are here."

After everyone got inside their bulky space suits and spherical helmets, the H-ATV depressurized. The door opened, and Vanderheiden pulled his body through the threshold, seeing the flatland, kilometers of nothing but white-gray dust with small pockets of craters.

The engineers stepped out of the H-ATV after him and went straight to work, unloading all the geoengineering probes and equipment. Brunelli helped them set up the driller to collect underground soil samples, install seismometers, and spin up the spectrometer.

Vanderheiden stood out of the engineers' path and spent the time walking around, watching his heavy boots sink into the dusty ground. Ever since they arrived at Marius Hills City, they'd only walked on lunarcrete and paved roads. A common saying on Luna was no one truly touched the moon Luna until they stepped on the regolith soil in its natural form. The lunar regolith soil was soft and hard, like a thick layer of chalky powder on top of rocks. He strolled around the area, leaving behind footprints in the regolith, with no wind to blow it away. He walked briskly to shake off his worry that the results would come back negative. If negative, the only other place they could build the surface anchor was on the opposite side of Luna, in the mountainous region, where construction would be an impossible task. *And the dream would be dead before it began.*

Despite being in his space suit, Vanderheiden felt exposed, realizing a few layers of clothes and a helmet were all that stood between him and the dangerous vacuum. Other than the comm chatter, the only thing he heard was his breathing. Looking up through his visor, he saw the sun, a small, bright orb surrounded by darkness. He looked higher up and saw Earth standing directly above them like a giant eye staring down.

Being surrounded by nothing but kilometers of dust gave Vanderheiden chills at first, which changed to a feeling of freedom. No journalist or social warrior scrutinizing every move he made. No bureaucrat or politician erecting legal obstacles against him. No investor lurking around, probing for weaknesses, demanding better returns. He looked around and found none of the things he hated in life. *This is what I want...a simple life.*

Vanderheiden frowned. *I must bring my time at VC to an end, eventually.* It sounded nice being able to wake up and have a pleasant breakfast with his wife and daughter without checking his messages for urgent issues. He winced when he remembered Emily only had two years to live, leaving just Susann and him at the breakfast table. *Would we ever recover from that?*

He looked back up at Earth. *After the Luna Space Elevator, we must build the Earth Space Elevator.* He thought about Susann and Emily. *And then I'll leave VC. I promise.*

After a few hours of work, Brunelli powered down his equipment.

"What's the assessment?" Vanderheiden hopped back to the group of engineers.

Brunelli raised his sun visor and smiled. "This location has the green light!"

Cheers erupted on the comms, and everyone exchanged high fives and handshakes.

It's going to happen. Vanderheiden smiled and curled in his finger, feeling the rubber grips inside the gloves. *We will build the Luna Space Elevator.*

* * *

"Air-lock hatch for passenger flight 34 in service to Rubicon will close in fifteen minutes," the PA system announced.

"That's us." Vanderheiden picked up his bag. "Let's go."

His body still ached from walking around in a bulky space suit that fought every movement he made. If he blinked for too long, he would fall asleep. He looked at everyone else, seeing the same exhaustion on their faces.

Marius Hills Spaceport, a few kilometers north of Marius Hills City, was one massive dome holding six air locks connecting to the many launchpads surrounding the dome. Some air locks were small enough for passengers and others big enough for shipping containers. The lobby was one large open space, filled with many people and containers.

Near one of the large air locks, a few contractors and US Space

Force soldiers spoke in a heated argument next to multiple containers strapped together. A crowd of Lunarians grew around them.

"If you will *listen* to me, I'm ready to transfer the cargo to your fleet." The contractor pointed at a customs agent sitting inside the booth next to the air lock. "I just don't have the funds to pay the customs fees!"

One soldier, dressed in black-and-gray armor and carrying an assault rifle, grabbed the contractor by the collar. "Get on the ship and spin up the engine!"

A female officer built like a runner with red-and-black tattoos covering her lean arms slapped the soldier's chest armor. "Stand down, Sergeant."

"You don't command the Raiders, Chief Cavalieri," the sergeant replied.

"Stand down! Let him go!"

Cavalieri jabbed a finger in the sergeant's face, whispered something, and then shoved him away. She turned to the contractor and gently pulled him away from the soldiers with a smiling nod.

"*Leave! Leave! Leave!*" the crowd started chanting.

"We need to leave," Brunelli whispered. Vanderheiden shook his head.

Cavalieri and the contractor spoke into each person's ear to make themselves heard over the loud chants.

"*No more taxes! No more taxes! No more taxes!*"

Cavalieri grasped the contractor's shoulder and pointed at the wide-eyed customs agent standing inside the glass booth. The contractor nodded more urgently as each second went by. The chief engineer slapped the contractor's shoulder, walked over to the nervous agent, and conversed with her.

"*Leave! Leave! Leave!*"

The contractor patted the air with his hands in a futile effort to calm down the Lunarians.

The customs agent relaxed her shoulders and nodded as Cavalieri spoke with her. The chief engineer pulled her hand terminal out and transferred something to the lady. She made a last nod and typed in commands on the booth console.

"A goddamn bribe!" someone yelled. "I'll have the head of that bloodsucking bitch!"

Angry roars erupted from the crowd, and the customs agent winced. Cavalieri walked away and spun her finger in the air. The soldiers fell back to the air lock with the contractor. A few Lunarians got closer to the booth, but the Raiders paused their retreat, taking a few steps forward. The customs agent fled the booth and exited the lobby, walking as fast as possible without running.

"*No more taxes! No more taxes! No more taxes!*" The chant grew louder.

The contractor strapped on his helmet and exited through the air lock, the chief engineer and the soldiers behind him.

"You think we fear you?" A man in a yellow coverall jogged toward the air lock, arms raised. "Don't expect it to be this easy next time you try to take our containers!"

"Oh really?" A soldier pulled out a baton from his belt and charged the man. "Looks like someone needs a lesson!"

The man jerked back and tripped, falling to the ground.

Baton raised in the air, the Raider stood over the whimpering Lunarian and laughed.

Cavalieri spun around. "Corporal!"

The baton came down and hit the Lunarian in the shoulder.

"You think you can threaten the Raiders?" The baton came down again. "The *fucking* Raiders!"

The crowd turned quiet and stepped away from the Raider.

"Help!" The man in yellow coverall squealed after a third strike hit his neck.

The sergeant grabbed the Raider by the collar and dragged him back to the air lock. "Stand down, Corporal!"

The aggravated soldiers walked into the air lock, and the hatch sealed shut.

Logan, the bearded man Vanderheiden had seen a few days before, walked to the victim lying on the ground. "You okay, Vlad?"

"No..." Vlad moaned and raised his bruised arm. "That bastard broke it."

"Get him to the clinic!" Logan shouted. Two men pulled Vlad up, and the three disappeared into the tunnel back to the city.

Logan stood up, walked to the closed air lock, and turned to the crowd.

"They don't own us!" he shouted, spit coming out of his mouth.

A few people cheered.

"Remember this day!" He spun around and pointed at the air lock. "Next time they try to confiscate what is ours, we will fight!"

"Air-lock hatch for passenger flight 34 in service to Rubicon will close in five minutes. This is your last call," the PA system broadcasted.

"Let's go!" Brunelli hissed through his teeth. Vanderheiden reluctantly followed him and the rest of the engineers to their assigned air lock.

Before entering the air lock, he turned around and scanned around the lobby, seeing many Lunarians with ravenous looks, like they were seeking a fight. Vanderheiden felt his heart drop. *It's a powder keg here.*

13

THE GENERAL

Sinclair glided into the *Decatur* command deck and found Lieutenant Colonel Fabian and two spacemen monitoring space traffic.

"General." All three spacemen manning the deck acknowledged her.

"As you were." Sinclair reviewed the hologram, visualizing the complex web of space traffic between Earth and Luna.

The *Nevada* gunship and the propellant tanker, promised by General Fassbinder, were two weeks out. Soon, the Luna Fleet would have a third gunship, making Sinclair less anxious about the fleet's ability to defend the moon.

There was a nonmilitary icon on the hologram, heading toward the *Decatur*. "We got a civilian spacecraft inbound?"

"Yes, ma'am." Fabian glanced at his console. "It's on the manifest. We are monitoring its approach. Orders direct from General Fosvik."

"Hmm." Sinclair pulled herself out of the command deck. "Carry on."

She floated down the narrow tunnel toward the docks and entered the *Wyoming*. She found Chief Cavalieri in the navigation seat.

"How was the patrol, Chief?" Sinclair hovered near the cushioned ceiling, looking down at her.

"We are taking baby steps, ma'am. Colonel Barrows is debriefing the gunship crew."

"I hope he isn't yelling his head off."

"He is getting better." Cavalieri smiled and pointed at the monitors. "Got a crew outside working on the main engines. We found a way to prolong their life cycles without sending the *Wyoming* back to the Craven spacedock."

"Got it." Sinclair pushed off the ceiling to get closer to the monitors. "How are the gunship crews coming along? Are they ready for combat?"

"They are slowly turning into a somewhat competent fighting force. Each day, we take two steps forward and one step back. We just need more time."

Even if the gunship crews were ready, shortages of materials and propellant were the bigger problems. The escalating anti-government protests on Luna shut down and delayed many deliveries to the fleet. Sinclair wondered if they were going to have to bribe their suppliers, like Cavalieri did at Marius Hills, or send more Raiders to force materials to move again.

"Are any of the crews coming to their shifts intoxicated?" Sinclair asked.

Cavalieri shrugged. "Not for weeks."

"Good."

"When the *Nevada* arrives, we will get busy." The chief engineer smiled, her freckles moving on her cheeks. "We'll have many more war-game scenarios to throw at the crews with three gunships." She chuckled. "Barrows has some dirty tricks ready."

Sinclair smiled. "Run the current *Nevada* crew through a few war games. We may have to swap them out if they aren't in good shape. Have a replacement crew ready."

"Yes, ma'am."

Sinclair's tactical armband pinged with a message from Fosvik.

REPORT TO THE COMMAND DECK ASAP.

Sinclair raised an eyebrow, surprised he was on the *Decatur*. She was tempted to ignore the message for a moment, but her instincts already had her flying out of the deck.

"Ma'am!" Cavalieri shouted over her shoulder.

"Yes?"

"I don't know how much shit you are dealing with, but things will get better." She nodded. "I know it."

Sinclair thought for a moment. "Thank you, Chief."

* * *

The three spacemen were at their stations, seemingly uncomfortable. She scanned the command deck and found Fosvik in the back corner, stroking his mustache with nervousness.

"General." Sinclair floated toward him.

"Good, you are here." Fosvik looked at a screen showing the civilian spacecraft docking the *Decatur*. "They have arrived."

"Who?"

With a stern look, he signaled for her to follow.

They went down to the air-lock module. A few spacemen surrounded the air lock the civilian spacecraft docked to. The hatch slid open.

A woman, uncertain with all her movements, came through the opened hatch first.

"Someone take my bag!" She awkwardly tossed her large duffel bag at the spacemen. One of them caught it with ease.

"Welcome aboard," Fosvik said.

"Larson." She shook hands with the two generals. Sinclair lost track of who held what positions in the Barbour administration, but she believed the woman with long, dark amber hair and freckled cheeks was Secretary of Commerce.

Two business executives came out of the air lock, holding onto their bags. They avoided eye contact with Larson.

"Welcome to the *Decatur*." Sinclair extended her hand to the other two. "General Sinclair."

"Lawrence. Founder and chief executive officer, Lawrence Resources." The dark-bearded man tightly shook her hand.

"Hi...Amanda Castlereagh. Castlereagh Manufacturing." The woman with ginger hair smiled eagerly and tried to nod but ended up bowing in the weightlessness.

Two business leaders stuck in a spacecraft with Larson? Sinclair would've enjoyed eavesdropping on that conversation.

"Need somewhere private to talk." Larson looked around. Fosvik nodded and gestured down the corridor toward the rings.

All five went to the officers' quarters filled with tables and boxes of rations, and Sinclair shut the hatch. Larson floated on one side of the room, facing the two businessmen on the other side. Sinclair and Fosvik hovered between the two groups.

Sinclair saw red blotches above Lawrence's black beard and recognized the alcoholism. Garrett had the same facial redness leading up to the intoxicated episode at the Delta Room years ago that would've led to his dishonorable discharge if Sinclair hadn't pulled him out of the room before he could cause more trouble.

Fosvik spoke first. "I was told less than twenty-four hours ago that I should expect your arrival and act as your host." He turned to Larson. "Care to explain the nature of your visit?"

"I'm here to settle the strikes on Luna. I need you to—"

"Let me correct you...again." Lawrence angled his head forward. "These are protests against the policies of *your* administration, not strikes against our companies."

"I'm not sure why you believe the policies are the problem. These workers are receiving slave wages, and conditions at your facilities are poor. If you treated them well, we wouldn't be having this problem." Larson gave a mocking smile.

"Ms. Larson, that was never a problem until your government stripped away the special economic zone. Throwing taxes, regulations, and price controls at us doesn't help."

"Someone's got to keep the lights on and the roads paved."

"We do that ourselves," Lawrence said.

"You are negotiating with the workers, not the government." Larson pointed at him. "Public policy is *not* up for debate."

Lawrence turned to Castlereagh. "It is like talking to a wall here."

All three started talking over each other, voices turning hostile. Sinclair glanced back and forth between Fosvik and the bickering three, expecting the general to step in. But Fosvik said nothing.

"Enough!" Sinclair's shout bounced off the walls and silenced the arguments. "Mr. Lawrence and Ms. Castlereagh, you are unwilling to raise wages and bring the workers back into your workforce. Ms. Larson—"

"We *can't* afford raises, ma'am," Lawrence replied. "Not in this economic environment." He glanced at Larson.

"Then what will you do?" Sinclair asked.

"Wait it out," Castlereagh replied. "All recessions end."

"Wait it out?" Sinclair kicked back to hover closer to the two business executives. "Here is my problem with that, Castlereagh. As long as production delays continue, they compromise the security of Luna because the space force depends on materials delivered by you."

"By the space force, you mean the government?" Lawrence grinned at the secretary. "Ah...so, you have a stake in these negotiations. Therefore, public policy *is* up for debate." He crossed his arms. "Reimpose Luna's special economic zone status, and the production problems will disappear."

"The taxes and regulations are necessary." Larson shrugged. "You are a business. Deal with it."

Lawrence barreled his chest out. "You watch your—"

"*Enough!*" Sinclair turned to the secretary. "Larson, you say your administration is not interested in policy changes. What are your next steps, then?"

Larson considered her response. "If you do not help the workers, my administration will take drastic steps to protect them."

"Define drastic steps...?" Lawrence asked with a tone of suspicion.

"Do what I tell you to do, and we won't have to talk about that."

"You can't tell us what to do!" Lawrence jabbed his finger at her.

"We are a private company. We answer to our shareholders, not the government!"

"Not for long."

"What does that mean? You are going to confiscate our companies? Huh?"

Larson sneered and carefully pulled out her hand terminal. "Here is an executive order signed by President Barbour. The Commerce Department is authorized by the National Security Act to confiscate assets deemed vital to national security." She pointed at Sinclair. "As explained by the general here, the economic disruptions compromise the Luna Fleet."

Lawrence chuckled and glanced at Sinclair.

Larson put her hand terminal away. "So, unless you get the workers back at their jobs and turn the manufacturing lines back on, General Fosvik will be ordered by the Joint Chiefs to deploy forces, take control of Marius Hills City, and restart production."

"Jesus Christ..." Castlereagh whispered, raising a hand to the back of her neck.

Lawrence held his stare on Sinclair. She couldn't tell if it was hatred or a plea for help.

"So, all three of us are going to go down there and explain the situation to the workers." Larson turned to the fleet commander. "General Fosvik and the Luna Fleet will be on standby."

"This is not right." Lawrence took his eyes off Sinclair. "We built Luna, not you. You can't take it away from us!"

"Nothing is stopping us."

"Oh!" Lawrence widened his eyes. "We'll see about that."

Fosvik cleared his throat. "Things are heated down there. Do you need Raiders to escort you?"

"No, I already have contractors with me. Former special forces."

Larson and the two business leaders left the quarters and were escorted to the shuttle for the descent to Marius Hills City.

"I don't have a good feeling about this." Fosvik stroked his mustache.

Sinclair cracked a knuckle. "Neither do I."

14

THE MAGNATE

NYSE: VC 70.90 (-2.36%)

The car dashboard chirped, and Vanderheiden forced his eyelids open, feeling his eyes roll forward. Pulling his head off the headrest, he looked left and right, struggling to understand where he was. He glanced at the hand terminal on the seat next to him and looked out the window at the hospital entrance. People strolled in and out under the rusty white "Hospital" sign, the letter *L* missing a corner.

Vanderheiden rubbed his eyes, stepped out of the vehicle, and instructed it to go park. He watched the tires roll over and crush tear-gas shells and paper signs. Four police cars were parked around the hospital, with police officers holding thousand-yard stares and arms crossed. *Riots must've been violent last night.*

Walking through the entrance, Vanderheiden came to the visitor's desk and signed himself in. After taking a sip of her energy drink, the desk nurse told him to head to the third floor. Vanderheiden went to the elevator, pressed the button, and watched the green numbers of the floor indicator count down.

"What do you mean the board rejected my request?"

Vanderheiden looked to his side and saw an old woman with shaking arms speaking with an NMS agent sitting inside a glass booth.

The agent spoke in a flat voice, eyes drooping. "Mrs. Peaty, your past offenses in purchasing medications off the black market were noted as the deciding factor."

The elevator beeped and the doors slid open. Vanderheiden stepped inside, still listening.

"Because you are always short on supply!" She jabbed her finger at the glass, hand quivering. "If you understand how much pain I have to deal with—"

The doors closed, and Vanderheiden felt the extra weight in his knees as the elevator ascended.

"That damn board..." he muttered.

He wished he could transfer Emily to a different hospital. The quality of care here was lacking. But every hospital was managed by the government, so it wouldn't make a difference. He couldn't go to a private practice because they were outlawed. *All in the name of bringing health care to all.*

His hand terminal beeped. Vanderheiden opened Gonzalez's message and groaned with annoyance.

> WRIGHT-TAKAHASHI'S DAWNBREAKER MISSED
> ITS LUNA-INBOUND DECELERATION WINDOW
> AND IS LOOKING AT A 5-MONTH ELLIPTICAL
> ORBIT BEFORE RETURNING TO EARTH.

He opened a draft message to reply but then turned the screen off. *I can't. Not right now.*

The elevator slid open. He walked down the hallway and entered Emily's room. Pale and sweaty, Emily was asleep in her bed, an intravenous line attached to her arm and an automated injection device behind her bed. An unfinished meal lay on the table next to her. Susann leaned against the window, staring at their daughter. The rising sun lit up half of her face. He saw her messy ponytail, an unusual hairstyle for his wife.

Vanderheiden walked over and kissed Susann on the cheek. "How is she doing?"

His hand terminal beeped.

"She had pneumonia." Susann rubbed her forehead. "Dr. Grosso said this is to be expected, given the disease is disrupting her coughing reflex. She should make a recovery in a day or two, then she'll be discharged."

Past Susann's head, Vanderheiden saw protesters massing down on the street below like ants surrounding a bread crumb. He turned away from the window, dropped to one knee next to the bed, and grabbed Emily's hand. It was warm and moist. He kissed her forehead and rubbed it. She muttered something but kept her eyes closed. The injection device chirped, and clear fluids rushed into Emily's arm.

I want to be here every minute. He shut his eyes. *But just too much is happening.*

His hand terminal gave two urgent beeps. He stepped away from the bed and opened the message from Brunelli.

> LAWRENCE DELAYED THEIR TITANIUM SHIPMENT AGAIN. BLAMING THE PROTESTS. 8 WEEKS BEHIND SCHEDULE NOW. I NEED LAWRENCE TO GET THEIR SHIT TOGETHER. WE'VE ONLY BUILT 13% OF THE CABLE.

Vanderheiden raised his hand terminal, ready to slam it down to the ground. He lowered it slowly and squeezed his nasal bridge with his fingers. He opened his eyes and reread Brunelli's scathing report. Not even a few months into the project, and the space elevator cable had run into trouble. *Those damn Luna protests.* He massaged his sore jaw muscles. *Need to put Lawrence's feet to the burner.*

"Is everything okay?" Susann asked, still watching Emily.

"Just another day." He shook his head.

"Are you going to be able to take leave from the company soon?"

"No, not anytime soon."

Her voice grew exasperated. "Can't any of your company chiefs handle being interim CEO in your absence?"

"Susann...I'm betting the entire company on the Luna Space Elevator, and nothing is going right with the construction. I can't *step* away."

"Michael...I know what you are dealing with." Susann turned to him. "But your daughter needs you. The staff here is awful. Dr. Grosso barely checks on her."

"What do you want me to do?" He crossed his arms and widened his feet.

"I'm on the verge of a breakdown here." Her lips quivered. "The other day, I was on the phone...*screaming*...at the agent to get Emily higher on the queue list for the treatment." She rubbed her face. "I just need you with me. By my side."

"Come here." He sat down next to her and embraced her shoulders.

Susann fell into his arms and heaved for a few breaths.

"What can I do?" He rubbed her back. "Just tell me."

"Get Emily on top of the queue."

"How can I do that?"

"Use your team of lawyers to cut through the red tape."

He shook his head. "VC is in space transportation, not health care."

Susann pulled back her head and locked eyes with him. "Surely, you know someone with connections to NMS!"

Vanderheiden didn't reply. *Maybe Dr. Raymond?*

His hand terminal buzzed with a connection request.

"I have to take this." He sighed. "Arellano only calls if it's urgent."

Susann scoffed and turned away.

He answered. "Speak."

"I know you are at the hospital, but VC needs a press release today, countering Cooper's public statement." Arellano tried to sound sympathetic. "I wouldn't be calling you if it weren't important."

"What public statement?"

"You haven't seen it?" Arellano replied. "Okay...in summary, he is calling for leadership change. This section of the letter summarizes it: 'The declining net income and lack of explanation from Vanderheiden and the C-suite raises questions about their ability to navigate through the difficult business environment and alludes to lack of vision.'"

"What!" he shouted.

"Gabriella is already here, asking for you." Arellano stumbled over her next words. "Sir...the longer we stay silent, the less confidence the shareholders have in us and the more willing they are to cooperate with Cooper. The Luna Space Elevator is first on Cooper's chopping block."

He sighed. "Work with Gabriela on a public statement draft. I'll be there in an hour."

"Sir—"

He ended the call and ground his teeth. *This fucking day...*

"Dad?" Emily whispered.

Vanderheiden spun around. "Did I wake you up?"

Emily nodded slowly.

He leaned over and kissed her forehead. "How are you feeling today?"

"Everything hurts." Emily lifted her eyebrows and widened her eyes, trying to wake up.

"Hang in there." He stroked her sweat-soaked hair. "You'll be out of here in a few days."

Emily tried to speak, but her jaw jerked open rapidly three times and her head finished off with a quick twist to the side.

Susann muffled a gasp with her hand. Vanderheiden smiled to hide his unease. *The involuntary movements are starting.*

Emily asked after the twitching stopped, "Can you help me with another essay?"

"What's the topic?"

"The consequences of the Marseilles Agreement signed by the US and the EU after the war and how the article requiring EU to give up claims to Luna hindered the development of its space economy."

"Listen..." He patted her arm. "We'll talk to the school about pausing your assignments. You need to focus on getting better."

His hand terminal beeped. "I have to go. Get your rest. Something urgent has come up."

Emily nodded and closed her eyes. Vanderheiden stood up and walked toward the door.

"I see where your priorities are," Susann said.

"What do you mean?" He stopped.

Susann didn't look at him. Her eyelids fluttered, watching Emily.

"Susann..." He pursed his lips. He hated seeing them go separate ways on bitter terms. *We promised to never do that.* But he feared there were no words that could fix the difficult times they were experiencing. He left the room.

He instructed his car to pick him up. After taking the elevator down, he walked through the lobby, eyes on the red-and-blue strobe lights visible through the entrance's glass door. He stepped outside and saw a crowd of angry faces and handheld posters. The smell of burnt flares was evident, and a hint of tear gas stung his eyes.

Vanderheiden changed his car's pickup location and walked briskly around to the other side of the hospital, trying to avoid the crowd's attention. He navigated through a garden filled with flowers and bushes darkened by the hospital's large shadow.

From the corner of his eye, he saw two men wearing motorcycle helmets and heavy coats walking toward him. Alarms rang in his head. *Heavy coats and helmets in Houston?* Vanderheiden picked up his pace.

The two walked faster. Vanderheiden burst into a sprint, leather shoes smacking against the brick walkway.

"Damn it!" one of them cursed behind him.

He hurdled over a low hedge and nearly lost his balance after his foot caught on one of the bushes. He glanced back, seeing the two running with fists clenched. In the crowd on the street, a flare lit up, turning the two men into black silhouettes.

He ran down many concrete steps and past several trees. His car came into view, and Vanderheiden sprinted harder. He heard heavy steps behind him match his cadence.

"Don't let him get away!" one of them shouted.

He bumped into his car, pulled the door open, and slammed it shut after he got in. One of his chasers slapped his hands on the glass.

"Mr. Vanderheiden!" His scream was muffled. "Your day of reckoning is coming!"

Vanderheiden punched the dashboard for the car to speed off and a spinning circle flashed on the screen. The second chaser circled to the other side, pulled out a baton, and swung at the window.

Vanderheiden jerked away from the window, covering his face. He heard a loud thump. He took a quick peek, seeing the attacker pull the baton back for another swing.

The car sped off, acceleration pressing Vanderheiden into his leather seat. He looked behind him, his quick breaths fogging the cracked window. He saw the two attackers standing in the street panting, turning smaller as the car zoomed away.

15

THE GENERAL

"Look at the size of that crowd." Lieutenant Colonel Fabian pulled up live security footage of the Marius Hills Spaceport atrium.

Everyone on the *Decatur*'s command deck stared at the screen, and Sinclair admired the hundreds of Lunarians being able to squeeze into the cramped lobby. Countless fists waved in the air, creating a turbulent sea of humans. A green laser blinded the camera every few seconds.

Sinclair wondered how long before the environmental system overloaded and crapped out. That would be an easy way to neutralize the protest. She glanced at Colonel Dressler floating next to her, his eyes locked on the screen, clearly weighing his tactical options to take down the protesters. The thought of Raiders gunning down protesters made her lungs tighten.

Fabian turned away from the console and handed a headset to General Fosvik. "I've got Larson on the line, sir."

"Put her on speaker." Fosvik's eyes darted back and forth as he stroked his mustache.

The main screen covering the back of the command deck switched to the spaceport control room, overcrowded with dozens of federal employees. Some remained at their workstations, managing traffic in and out of the spaceport. Others looked around with terrified faces, overwhelmed by the volatile situation.

Fabian nodded at Fosvik. Sinclair drifted closer to hear the audio.

"Larson"—Fosvik cleared his throat—"are you reading us?"

Larson paced along the workstations, holding a headset to her ear. Lawrence and Castlereagh stood at the other corner of the room, staring at the raucous crowd outside. Larson's lips moved on the footage, and a second later, her voice came through the command deck.

"I can hear you, Fosvik." She looked up at the security camera. "What do you need?"

"How is it going down there? Do you need help?"

Larson shook her head. "No, we are fine down here. The workers are riled up. They just need time to cool off." She pointed at the camera. "I don't want soldiers showing up and igniting it into a riot."

"Understood, Larson."

"General," Dressler said, "that spaceport is a vital supply hub for our fleet. We need to put boots on the ground and maintain security." He gestured at the screen. "We can't lose it."

Fosvik looked back and forth between Dressler and the main screen. Larson's lips moved, her voice following the time delay. "My contractors have it under control."

The four contractors in civilian clothes and armed with carbines stood in a line outside the control room, facing the crowd with their backs against the reinforced glass.

Colonel Dressler coasted over to Fabian and tapped his shoulder, pointing at a video feed of the contractors. Fabian switched the video back to the lobby. Dressler shook his head after looking closer. "They are just about ready to pull their triggers. I know that team leader."

"You know him?" Sinclair asked.

"Alvarado." He glanced at Sinclair. "There is a reason the Raiders discharged him." He turned to Fosvik. "General...I suggest we spin up a Raider platoon and deploy them to the spaceport. We'll take control of it."

"For the record"—Sinclair raised her voice, close to Fosvik's ear—

"I advise against deploying the Raiders. We are the military, not the police force. Have private security from Copernicus Quarter come to Marius Hills."

"We don't have the time!" Dressler swung back to Sinclair.

Larson sharpened her voice. "Keep your soldiers at bay, Fosvik."

"Negative, Dressler," Fosvik replied. "We don't need to instigate a riot."

Dressler started replying, "With all due respect—"

"We are the military, not the federal police." Fosvik waved his arm. "We will not engage in a domestic political issue."

"It will become a military matter if they shut down the spaceport," Dressler replied.

"I am needed elsewhere," Larson interrupted. "I'll call Copernicus. We'll stay in touch." She pulled her headset off.

"Keep monitoring the situation, Colonel." Fosvik looked down at Fabian. "Updates every thirty minutes."

"Yes, sir," Fabian replied.

Fosvik made his way to the exit, and Dressler cut into his path. "Sir...we must deploy my Raiders. Marius Hills looks ready to blow up at any point."

"How long have I been here, Colonel?" Fosvik lowered his chin, eyes locked on Dressler.

Dressler raised his head, looking down his nose at the general. "Three years, sir."

"Right," Fosvik said. "This isn't the first protest on Luna I've seen. And it won't be the last. Things will cool down eventually."

Sinclair moved between the two men. "At least put Raiders on standby for deployment. Deploy them if things blow up."

Fosvik glanced at Dressler and nodded. "Spin them up, then."

"Roger that." Dressler raised his tactical armband. "I'll get Kraken Platoon ready."

Sinclair heard a higher pitch in his hoarse voice. After Fosvik glided out of the command deck, Sinclair followed Dressler to the second habitat ring, where the Raiders were quartered. After entering the habitat ring and returning to artificial gravity, Sinclair walked through multiple modules. She heard commotion as she got close to the Raiders section.

"Whoo!"

"Let's go! Let's go!"

Many Raiders, surrounded by exercise equipment, cheered. They were diverse in size, shape, and skin tone. One thing they all had in common was a patch with a blue sea monster strapped to their left shoulder.

One Raider saw her. "General on deck!" All snapped their arms and legs together.

"At ease." Sinclair walked toward the special operators. The cheering resumed, but more subtly.

The prep room was packed with combat space suits and racks holding the RG-79 recoilless assault rifles, rocket-propelled grenades, drones, body armor, and flash grenades. Twenty Raiders, with the help of comrades, struggled into their skintight space suits. Preparation for combat in space was a cumbersome task. Raiders had to go through prebreathing and strap into their combat space suits, a complex task requiring multiple people to assist. When they strapped into the assault craft, it went through a long preflight checklist.

Dressler bent over each Raider and whispered into their ears. He slapped their shoulders afterward. Other Raiders pulled the assault rifles from the racks, cleaning and checking the firing mechanisms. After speaking to the last Raider, Dressler stood next to Sinclair.

"The Raiders ready?" Sinclair whispered.

"Yes, ma'am." Dressler nodded. "Captain Brawner has combat experience, so they have a seasoned officer leading them."

"The Murray Station?"

"Yes, ma'am. He was a squad leader. Held himself well."

The Raiders experienced the toughest training compared to other special forces. Instructors would put the candidates in a low-pressure environment without prebreathing, giving them the bends, and have them conduct drills to test their pain tolerance. Space was a volatile environment. One moment, they could exchange gunfire with the enemy in gravity. The next moment, they could be engaged in melee combat in weightlessness, surrounded by debris flying like bullets.

"These are civilians complaining about government policy, or poor working conditions, depending on who you talk to," Sinclair said. "These aren't heavily armed terrorists. Minimize the use of force if you have to engage."

Dressler held his silence for a few seconds. "They gave me the order to minimize collateral damage before we assaulted Murray Station. Lost twenty-three Raiders and over a dozen hostages."

"Marius Hills City is essential to our fleet. We can't put it at risk."

"We lost many lives that day because that order tied our hands." He lowered his voice. "I don't like—"

"Colonel Dressler, both of us are combat officers. I *know* what it means to be ordered to minimize collateral damage."

Dressler looked away from her. "Yes, ma'am."

Some Raiders digested anti-nausea and hyper-focus supplements. Others were now strapping on composite armor plates and slipping tactical equipment into their pouches. One Raider had lined up their headgear in two rows of ten, dome helmets equipped with a tactical display, and cleaned them down. One by one, they handed each Raider their recoilless assault rifle.

"Why are you against deploying the Raiders?" Dressler asked.

Sinclair clenched her jaw muscles. "There is a reason we separate the military and police. The police enforce the law and maintain order. Citizens are never their enemy. The military is a killing machine designed to cripple and destroy its adversary. Its own civilians should not be the targets."

"But this is Luna," Dressler replied. "We are outside the normal bounds of law. It is the frontier."

"Europe is the enemy here, not the Lunarians."

"And we must keep Marius Hills under our control if we are to fight Europe."

Sinclair's tactical armband beeped, and she answered the connection request.

"General, you better get back here." Fabian's face came on the screen. "Looks like Larson is going out to the lobby."

Sinclair and Dressler scrambled back to the command deck. On the screen, Larson talked to Lawrence and Castlereagh. She pressed her index finger and thumb together, swaying them at Lawrence like a lecturing professor. Lawrence shrugged and waved his hands from Larson to the crowd. Castlereagh remained unmoving, watching the two argue.

"Can we get audio?" Sinclair asked.

"Negative, ma'am." Fabian shook his head. "Someone cut us off."

Larson moved toward the door and opened the door. The two business executives reluctantly followed her.

Tightness gripped Sinclair's throat, watching them leave the safety of the control room and face the crowd, which seemed to have grown thicker.

The wave of hands settled down when Larson walked into the lobby. The contractors lined up with her, two at each side. Unable to get audio, Sinclair could only speculate about her words. For a few minutes, Larson spoke, her arms jerking. Twice, protesters turned their heads to each other.

"What's going on?" Fosvik entered the command deck.

"Larson's speaking to the crowd," Sinclair replied.

"And that's why I'm here?" He turned his palms out.

"Let's just watch," Sinclair snapped.

Larson's arm waving dragged on for minutes, and Sinclair drifted her focus to the orbital map, noting the *Decatur*'s position relative to Marius Hills City.

"Oh..." Fabian muttered.

Sinclair missed it. She looked back at the main screen. It was like the security footage had jumped a few minutes forward. Lunarians yelled, their mouths square with anger and frustration, pointing fingers at Larson. The contractors spread their legs out and pressed the carbines to their shoulders. Larson must've said something that had instantly turned the crowd hostile.

"Retreat..." Dressler whispered like he was talking to the contractors.

A bottle flew and smashed into the reinforced glass behind the contractors. Everyone took an uncertain step back toward the control room, heads spinning to find the person who threw it. One bottle thrown turned into five, agitating the contractors and prompting them to raise their carbines and point them at the feet of the crowd. Five turned into a storm of bottles, wrenches, and food.

Larson waved for everyone to move back into the control room. The contractors ignored her, took two steps forward, and raised their carbines. Sinclair's chest went hollow, having seen this motion many times at firing ranges.

The muzzles sparked, and many Lunarians in the front row fell in a cloud of blood. The rest scattered away from the gunfire, pushing and tripping over each other. Larson and Castlereagh fell to the ground and curled up behind the contractors. Lawrence froze, watching the torrent of gunfire in shock. The gunfire was only a brief second, but it dragged out like a minute for Sinclair.

The crowd came to a standstill, and the contractors glanced at each other, lips quivering.

"Move it!" Dressler hissed.

A tight flash ignited from a corner of the lobby. A contractor jerked and looked down with confusion, seeing dark liquid spill out of his chest. He collapsed, knee hitting the ground covered in a thick pool of blood.

"Let me send Kraken!" Dressler said to Fosvik.

Pockets of gunfire flashed from the crowd. Metallic debris popped off the ground around the contractors. Bullets cracked the reinforced glass. People inside the control room hide behind the workstations. The contractors returned fire, spraying bullets everywhere.

"The protesters are armed!" Dressler grabbed slack-jawed Fosvik and shook him. "Give me the order!"

"Get off him!" Sinclair shouted, grabbing Dressler's shoulder.

Larson and Castlereagh scrambled for the door. Lawrence made it halfway before grabbing his neck with both hands and falling to the ground. Castlereagh shouted, clutched his shirt, and dragged him into the control room with a struggle.

The contractors walked backward into the control room, firing at the crowd. Another contractor went down, slamming face-first into the ground. The last two made it into the control room and barricaded the door with chairs and tables.

"General!" Sinclair barked, her lungs feeling like they had nearly ruptured.

Fosvik blinked, and blood returned to his pale face. "D-deploy the Raiders!"

Dressler turned to Fabian. "Are we in position for orbital descent?"

"Negative. Eleven minutes."

Dressler sighed. The protesters cursed at the control room, banged on the reinforced glass, and smashed a sledgehammer into the barricaded door. Shoving matches and fistfights broke out in the lobby under the smokey haze of the gunfire. People surrounded bodies lying on the ground, unmoving.

Inside the control room, Castlereagh clutched with both her hands a gunshot wound squirting blood from Lawrence's neck, a pool of dark-red fluid expanding underneath his body. Larson paced around the crowded room, rubbing her neck. Lawrence eventually stopped moving, staring at the ceiling. Castlereagh's back went slack, and she rested her bloodied hands on her knees, staring at him.

Watching the orbital map and the growing panic in the control room, Sinclair hated the helplessness. The urge to grab an assault rifle, drop to the spaceport, and restore order clutched at her mind. She came to the moon, ready to whip the Luna Fleet into proper war readiness and prepare for an inevitable clash with Europe. Being faced with domestic violence came as an incomprehensible shock to her. She didn't want the war machine she was patching together to be used against Lunarians. It wasn't right.

After a long ten minutes went by, Dressler spoke the words Sinclair waited for.

"*AC-3A* disengaged and inbound to Marius Hills."

On the docking-port camera, the assault craft, with heavily

armored hulls and wings on each side sides, undocked from its port and dropped out of the camera's view. Twenty videos, from the headcams of each Raider, appeared on the main screen. They checked their gears, exchanged orders, and offered encouragements.

Sinclair saw a strange movement in the lobby. She looked closer, and it took her a moment to process what was happening. Four men were prying the barricaded door open with heavy equipment.

"They are about to breach the control room," Fabian said.

"Kraken is moving as fast as they can," Dressler reported. "ETA ten minutes."

Fosvik's breath was shallow and his skin turned pale again.

The barricaded door blew open, and the contractors, crouching behind workstations, opened fire. Multiple protesters fell to the ground. Others returned fire, and the contractors crumbled to the ground.

A swarm of angry protesters swarmed the control room. One protester swung a blunt weapon at Larson. Her head snapped back, and she fell to the ground. They beat others amid the unfolding carnage and blood spilling. There was no audio from the feed, but Sinclair heard the screaming in her mind.

On the *AC-3A* exterior camera, the bright-gray surface, riddled with craters, grew larger as the assault craft descended. Dressler got on the channel. "Kraken-1, be advised: Tangos have seized the control room."

"Roger that, *Decatur*." Captain Brawner hand-signaled his acknowledgment.

Protesters turned to the workstations in the control room. Many pointed at the screen, and arguments broke out among the protesters. Some waved their hands, signaling for everyone to stop. Others nodded and clenched their fists. Sinclair assumed they now saw the assault craft's descent.

Minutes later, Fabian counted down. "One hundred meters...fifty meters...ten meters."

The assault craft's engines fired, kicking up lunar dust, and it landed two hundred meters from the spaceport.

"Move! Move!" Brawner shouted.

"Keep it tight, brothers!" a squad leader followed up.

The Raiders exited the craft in rapid fashion. The spaceport's large gray dome, surrounded by many launchpads, was visible on most headcams.

"Check your weapons and gear!"

"Deploy the drones."

"Move out!"

The Raiders activated their jetpacks and flew a few meters above the lunar surface in three separate diamond formations. Legs hanging loose below them, the soldiers aimed their assault rifles at the enormous dome.

The three squads split apart. Paladin Squad's objective was the environmental control and power systems. Viking and Samurai, led by Captain Brawner, were to breach separate air locks and assault the spaceport lobby.

The main dome got bigger as they got closer, the sun illuminating the structure and the rockets encircling it. The light-gray soil was bright enough to look like dirty snow.

"Protesters attempting to access the launchpad controls," Fabian said.

Dressler got on the comm. "Viking-2 and Samurai-3, be advised: Tangos attempting to take control of rockets. Pick up the pace. Over."

Both squad leaders acknowledged: "Pick up the pace!"

Sinclair noticed Dressler used the word *tango*, a slang term for *target* or *enemy*. She restrained herself from reminding Dressler that this was supposed to be a police action. Raiders were off the leash, and there was nothing she could do. This was Dressler's mission now.

Viking Squad reached the southern air lock first. They planted their breach-and-seal charge on the hatch and stood by for entry, weapons pointed at the charge. A minute later, the Samurai Squad arrived at the northern air lock.

"Paladin-1, give us a sitrep." Brawner called out on the comms.

"Twenty meters out," the Paladin leader replied. The headcams showed his squad approaching a smaller dome several meters away from the spaceport.

A minute later, Paladin reached the air lock, planted its breaching charges, and lined up in assault formation. Sinclair's heart pumped hard.

Sinclair watched hostile arguments among the protesters. Many raised their firearms and checked their ammunition.

"On my mark." Brawner counted down. "Three...two...one..."

Sinclair held her breath and cracked her knuckles. She closed her eyes and let go of the heavy feeling.

"Mark."

16

THE MAGNATE

NYSE: VC 63.27 (-10.76%)

Underneath the glass ceiling of the Executive Chamber, exposing the heavy clouds drifting to the north, Vanderheiden sat at the long table with a corner of his lips twisted, eyes locked on Cooper. *I would still be with my daughter if it weren't for you.*

Cooper grabbed pistachios from his bowl, tossed the green nuts into his mouth, and snapped open a soda can. Gabriella sat between the two men at the head of the table, watching them. A couple seats away, Arellano tapped her hand terminal, refreshing the stock tracker.

Vanderheiden took a deep breath. "Why did you throw us into the flame trench, Cooper?"

"Have you checked the stock?" Cooper pointed at Arellano's hand terminal. "Our costs are rising, and our shareholders are recoiling from it."

"We all knew building the Luna Space Elevator was going to be painful."

"I allocated a significant amount of my hedge fund into this company, and the stock is pulling my numbers down." Cooper thumbed over his shoulder. "I've got my own investors to worry about."

Vanderheiden cracked a few laughs and pointed at the chief financial officer. "Arellano has to oversee the balance sheet and keep the cash flow running." He referred to the speaker on the table. "Brunelli is at Marius Hills pushing Lawrence to speed up cable manufacturing." He swung his arm downward. "Gonzalez is dealing with uncooperative customers at the PhotonicWay Command Center."

Vanderheiden smacked the table with his palm and brought his chest forward, staring more closely at Cooper. "So, instead of working on those things...we are sitting here, dealing with *you* and the *fallout* from your public statement!"

"Take it down a notch," Gabriella whispered with a firm tone.

Cooper shrugged. "It all comes back to the stock price."

Vanderheiden grabbed his hand terminal, opened a copy of the public statement, and read a section out loud. "'The declining net income and lack of explanation from Vanderheiden and the C-suite raises questions about their ability to navigate through the difficult business environment and alludes to a potential lack of vision.'" He put his hand terminal down. *I will burn you for this.* "Potential *lack of vision*? That is bullshit!"

His outburst startled Arellano, and she took her eyes off the stock tracker.

Gabriella raised her voice. "Vanderheiden..."

"The Luna Space Elevator *is* the vision!" Vanderheiden jabbed his finger at Cooper. "You are committing sabotage against my company! We have legal grounds to sue you!"

"Vanderheiden!" Gabriella snapped. "That's enough!"

He held his finger up. "This corporate raider is—"

"*Enough!*"

Vanderheiden twisted his lips and swallowed. He sat back and crossed his arms.

Gabriella huffed and swiveled her chair over to the activist investor. "Cooper, the Luna Space Elevator will give you the ROI you seek. Vanderheiden and his team need all the support they can get to build it, and your public statement may have just kneecapped them."

"No, no, no..." Cooper chuckled, shaking his head. "I—"

Gabriella raised a finger, cutting him off. "I strive to lead a board of directors that is transparent with one other. That public statement was unnecessary. You need to place all of your cards on the deck." She tapped the table. "Right now. What are you trying to accomplish here?"

Cooper tossed a few pistachios into his mouth, wiped off the salt, and took a sip of his soda. "I need the stock price to recover. With this recession, investors are pulling back, putting pressure on my firm."

"The space elevator—" Vanderheiden spoke.

Gabriella shot her eyes at him. "Let him finish."

Cooper stretched his hand toward the glass wall. "Indexes are turning red. Several Treasury bills just defaulted. This company is about to have another quarter of revenue decline. We need to lock-down our financials. The space elevator project leaves us vulnerable."

"Okay." Gabriella swiveled to the other side. "Vanderheiden?"

"It is temporary," Vanderheiden replied. "Once the elevator is completed and we send traffic through it, the stock price will take care of itself."

"But how long do we need to bleed?" Cooper asked.

"Right now, it is six quarters before we open it." Vanderheiden looked at the speaker. "Brunelli?"

Brunelli's sharp voice cracked through the static. "Lawrence is having labor challenges, causing delays in production. We are tweaking the titanium refinement process to reduce headcount requirements. Once that is completed, we'll be back on schedule."

"But how realistic is eighteen months?" Cooper leaned over to the speaker. "Can Lawrence deliver?"

"The cable production is Lawrence's top priority."

"But can they do it?" Cooper stood up and walked past Gabriella toward the window, pointing at the clouds. "Because I've spoken with Lunarians, and the civil unrest up there is crippling its industrial base, especially at Marius Hills. Tensions are boiling across the moon." He turned around. "I challenge all timelines until I see the cable built."

Vanderheiden considered his answer. "Eighteen months, Cooper."

Cooper shook his head. "We need to halt the project. Its cost is tearing us up."

"No one is canceling the space elevator," Brunelli retorted. "Not when the surface anchor is under construction."

"Do you really believe a 56,000-kilometer cable will work?" Cooper squinted his eyes at Vanderheiden.

"I..." Vanderheiden lost his train of thought. *So many things could go wrong.* "Many doubted the PhotonicWay. We delivered it. We will deliver the Luna Space Elevator."

Cooper rested his hands on the back of the chair after he returned to the table. "Vanderheiden...you either halt the Luna Space Elevator and clean up the balance sheet"—he lifted his eyes—"or you merge with Shugart to spread the financial burden."

The uproar that broke out in the Executive Chamber made the words difficult to hear. Vanderheiden jumped out of his chair, shouting at Cooper. Brunelli went through a dictionary of curse words, the speaker struggling to keep up. Cooper switched between shouting at the speaker and waving off Vanderheiden. The arguments between the directors and executives in the room reached a crescendo.

Gabriella silenced the speaker, cutting off Brunelli's cursing. "Stop it! Stop it!"

"Shugart?" Vanderheiden smiled and slowly returned to his seat. "You must be joking!"

"I'm serious." Cooper nodded and sat down with a huff.

"You are directors of Vanderheiden Corporation!" Gabriella smacked the table. "Have some respect for yourselves!"

Vanderheiden shifted his jaw out. "He suggested we merge with Shugart." He asked Cooper, "Are you in league with Tsung? Huh? Did she offer you a seat on the Shugart board?"

"Cooper, don't reply," Gabriella interjected. "Both of you, be quiet."

Vanderheiden sighed, pulled out his rubber ball, and caressed it hard, imagining the ball being Cooper's face.

Gabriella ran her palm across her black hair and sighed. "I get it. Cooper...you want a higher stock price. Vanderheiden...you want your space elevator. I get it." She let out a deeper sigh. "We need to cauterize the wound...*now*. The only way to raise the stock price and keep the space elevator running is to make it public."

"Absolutely not!" Vanderheiden shot back. "When Shugart hears about it, they'll push the government to interfere with legal injunctions and regulatory delays. We can't let bureaucrats choke our construction."

"I agree with her." Arellano nodded at Gabriella. "Having that stock price boost would bring in a cash infusion and keep Shugart off our back."

Vanderheiden turned to her. "If we announce now and the cable fails, we'll look incompetent and the shareholders will revolt."

Cooper smiled and took a sip of his soda. "What if we seriously considered Shugart's offer? Bringing Shugart on board would help us shelter these financial challenges."

Vanderheiden ground his teeth. "Shugart only wants our photonic propulsion technology. They'll just mothball the space elevator because it threatens their launch services business. And then they'll strip VC down to the bone and purge our employees."

"Okay, then." Gabriella flicked her hand. "If you won't announce or consider a merger, then we need to cut costs. The stock needs to be protected."

Arellano stopped watching the stock tracker and rested her elbows on the table. "We can do a twenty to thirty percent wage cut across the company. Workforce reductions, too."

"And we are talking about it...again," Brunelli said.

"No," Vanderheiden shot back, looking at Cooper. "Every cost incurred by this company is justified. I will not cut wages. We have many challenges ahead of us, and we need our employees. The last thing we need is eroding employee loyalty."

Cooper smirked. "If cutting employees will raise the stock, then we will do it."

Vanderheiden's blood felt like it was boiling, and he squeezed his rubber ball harder. Brunelli spoke before Vanderheiden lashed out at Cooper. "Let me explain something here. Vanderheiden built this company from scratch by focusing on building innovative products, paying and training a motivated workforce, and keeping our customers satisfied. Nowhere did we cut costs on our way to growth."

"We can handle the financial burden." Vanderheiden took a deep breath. "The space elevator will put this company in an excellent position once the economy picks back up. Countless customers will knock on our door to be placed on the space elevator queue."

Cooper shot his hands up. "I don't think I am making myself clear. If you agree to these budget cuts, you will have my support and I'll withdraw my public statement."

"And if we don't?"

"Then I will follow through on my demands listed in the statement."

You are bluffing. "You don't get to push me around like that, Cooper. You are one of many shareholders. You know the damage Shugart will create. You take away the once-in-a-lifetime opportunity for us to be the first to build a space elevator." Vanderheiden rose from his seat. "*I* run this company, not you. We *will* build the space elevator."

"Choose your next words carefully, Vanderheiden," Cooper warned. "Just because you started this company doesn't mean you'll continue to run it."

Vanderheiden snapped. "You dare—"

"Both of you!" Gabriella interrupted. "Enough!" She rounded on Vanderheiden. "I support the cost cuts. Tough but necessary decision."

"I agree." Arellano nodded. "The space elevator is everything for this company now. We must finish it, whatever the sacrifices are."

"Just do it," Gabriella whispered to Vanderheiden. "Keep the cost down. Elevate the stock."

Vanderheiden clenched his fists. *Just one concession of many before I lose my company.* "Fine." He pointed at Cooper. "But I won't forget this."

Cooper shrugged, grabbed his empty bowl and soda, and headed for the door. "I'm glad my concerns are being addressed. This was a productive conversation, but I need to take my leave. Other investments require my attention."

After the door closed with a click, Vanderheiden raised his arms sideways, eyeing Gabriella and Arellano. "What the hell was that? You two?"

"You were on thin ice there." Gabriella clasped her hands on the table. "He isn't the only shareholder who's unhappy. Being inflexible is going to break you. Something had to give."

"Look...you still got your space elevator," Arellano replied.

"But what about the PhotonicWay? Cost cuts will hurt its performance." Vanderheiden shrugged. "The employees? They've fulfilled their tasks, and we are going to cut them because a few shareholders wailed?"

"Like it or not, we answer to the shareholders," Gabriella said. "We can't let our company turn divided when Shugart threatens a hostile takeover and the economy wobbles near collapse."

"You haven't appeased him." Vanderheiden pointed at her. "You've emboldened him. Before we know it, he'll be pushing to halt the construction again for extra points on the stock price."

"Vanderheiden, I am with you on the space elevator to the very end." Gabriella got up, grabbed a banana from the bar, and turned around. "But I have a board to manage. You and Brunelli need to speed up the construction. We can only survive this financial crunch for so long."

"We should reconsider Blackburn," Brunelli said. "Things are getting tense at Marius Hills, and the US military is stepping in. I haven't heard of any problems at Blackburn's facilities in Phantom Torch."

"No." Vanderheiden set his rubber ball on the table. "We are sticking with Lawrence." *I will make no more concessions today.*

17

THE GENERAL

Pressurized air and lunarcrete fragments jettisoned out of the breached air locks like a jet engine. Raiders stood clear of the rush, waiting for the venting air to subside. General Sinclair kept a close eye on the headcams of Captain Brawner and Viking Squad. Once it turned into a soft wind, the Raiders entered the holes in rapid succession. The charges resealed the hole after the special operators entered them. They recycled the air inside the air lock.

"Prepare to breach," Brawner ordered. "Three, two, one...execute, execute!"

The inner hatch opened, and Viking Squad fanned out in all directions, making sure the gray hallways were covered. Everything came to a standstill. Raiders held their defensive posture for a minute, waiting for any immediate hostiles to appear.

Sinclair cracked her knuckles, her eyes scanning through the footage from twenty headcams, digesting every piece of information she could find. She pushed down the impatient urge to jump into the monitors and shove the Raiders toward their objectives. Disliking the lack of control over the unfolding battlefield, she tried to be at peace with the helplessness.

"Move out," the Viking leader said. The squad stood up, fell into tactical formation, and sauntered deeper into the dome, toward the atrium. They navigated through rooms and corridors in a methodical fashion, switching between providing cover and moving quietly.

"Kraken-1, this is Paladin-1. Twenty-five meters from power and environmental controls. No contact with hostiles."

"Roger that, Paladin-1," Brawner replied. "Report once objective is secured."

Samurai Squad came to a halt, and all six Raiders lined up against a wall.

"Two armed tangos spotted."

"Stun rounds." Samurai leader hand-signaled. "Put them down."

Two Raiders fired their jetpacks and popped from cover, firing two stun bullets at each gunman. Both dropped and convulsed on the ground, grinding their teeth. The Raiders approached them, stripped away their guns, and tied them up with plastic straps.

"*Decatur*, Samurai-3 here. Detained two tangos armed with military-grade weapons."

"Acknowledged, Samurai-3. Proceed to objective. Stay in sync with Viking-2." Dressler muted himself and turned to Sinclair. "This is a coordinated armed insurrection."

"Stay sharp." Sinclair nodded. She glanced at Fosvik, who fidgeted with his mustache nervously.

After waving their weapons at civilians, forcing them to scatter off, Paladin Squad reached a door labeled "Power and Environmental Control." Two Raiders kneeled on both ends of the hallway, while the rest of the squad barged into the control room. Two technicians fell from their chairs, alarmed by armored space suits aiming assault rifles at their faces.

They tied the technicians down, and a Raider worked on the blinking control panels. The Paladin leader clicked on the channel. "Power and environmental secured. Ready to shut down power."

"Acknowledged, Paladin-1." Brawner gestured for Viking Squad to keep moving. "Shut down power now. Stand by for airflow cutoff. Samurai-3, sitrep. Over."

"This is Samurai-3. Balcony secured." The Raiders hid behind columns on a balcony overlooking the atrium, which was overcrowded with people. "Got visual on an abundance of targets. Spotted multiple armed tangos. Ready for overwatch."

"Roger that, Samurai-3. I see them on your headcams. Viking-2 twenty meters out from the assault point. Stand by."

"All stations, be advised: power cutoff at mark," the Paladin leader said. "Three, two, one...mark."

Everything switched to black, and then the red emergency lights lit up, turning objects and people into red shadows. The Raiders' tactical displays switched to dark vision, giving off a distorted greenish color scheme. The commotions in the atrium grew to a shrill hum.

"Kraken-1, this is Paladin-1. Standing by for airflow shutdown. Ready at your mark."

"Stand by."

Viking Squad continued its seamless transition between providing cover, moving swiftly, and ordering civilians to evacuate. Eventually, the squad leader raised his fist when the squad reached a large hatch.

"This is Viking-2. At the assault entry point."

The Raiders checked their gear, prepped stun grenades, and slapped shoulders.

"Paladin-1, cut the air now," Captain Brawner ordered.

The depressurization alarm blared, and yellow lights flashed, mixing with the red lights. The chalky-gray corridors flashed between the red and yellow darkness. It was hard for Sinclair to see what was happening. She focused on the audio. The screams and yells from the atrium grew into a panic.

"Viking-2, Samurai-3, move in." Brawner waved at the hatch. "Go! Go!"

Samurai Squad moved away from the struts and pointed RG-79s over the railings down at the lobby occupied by a swarm of red silhouettes. The commotion became muffled as the air pressure dropped. Half the crowd was falling to the ground, struggling to breathe.

The hatches slid sideways, disappearing into the wall. Viking Squad fired their jetpacks, spreading out across the southern side of the lobby, and sought cover behind lunarcrete furniture and steel foam columns.

Vague muzzle flashes popped in some headcams. Sinclair's neck tightened up.

"Contact!"

"Got three shooters!"

"No clear shot!"

"Give me targets!"

Bullets kicked up fragments around Viking Squad. The HUDs inside their tactical helmets scrambled to find targets, but the sizeable crowd scrambling away from the gunfire made everything a blur.

"Samurai-1, you got eyes on them?"

"Negative! Your left flank is clear!"

Three shooters turned into six, coming from many corners of the lobby. Raiders' tactical displays struggled to find targets. Gunfire rang across the large space and chipped at their cover, ricocheting off the steel foam. A few people jerked and fell to the ground. It felt like a hand clutched Sinclair's heart. She forced herself to breathe.

"I can't find them! They're behind civilians!"

"Samurai-1, flash-bangs!"

"Popping flash!"

They launched a volley of flash grenades across the lobby, and blinding flashes ignited the struts holding up the dome and hundreds of people. Most of the crowd dropped to the ground, covering their faces and screaming. Many had blood coming down their noses and out of their ears. The tactical displays countered the flash, bringing no harm to the Raiders. The gunfire ceased temporarily.

"Viking-2, shift left! Shift left!" Brawner jabbed his arm toward the corner of the lobby opposite the control room.

Gunfire erupted behind a thick strut. Two Raiders from the balcony opened fire at the source of the muzzle flash.

"Tango down!"

A card under Viking Squad flashed yellow on the *Decatur* command deck's main screen.

"I'm hit!"

The Raider dropped to the ground, behind no cover, and blood spilled in front of him. More gunfire snapped and bullets kicked up around him.

"Flash-bangs!"

A second wave of flash-bangs exposed the rage, agony, fear, and helplessness of the Lunarians. Anyone without a pressure suit was on the ground, gasping for air.

"Come on!" A Raider stretched out his hand toward his wounded comrade. "Come to me!"

The wounded Raider struggled up to his feet and slipped on his puddle of blood. Two bullets hit his back, knocking him flat to the hard floor.

"Fuck this!" Brawner cursed. "Samurai-3, open fire on hostiles now!"

The Raiders raised their assault rifles at the muzzle flashes. They held their triggers, and dozens of bullets roared across the atrium. Blood burst everywhere. People dropped to the ground.

"Viking-2, move across the lobby. Now!" Brawner pressed the butt of his assault rifle against his shoulder. "Take down these fuckers!"

The Raiders pushed through the lobby from two sides, shifting from cover to cover, launching flash-bangs and shooting every few seconds. Samurai maintained a violent barrage of suppressive fire. The blood, gunfire, flash-bangs, and light alarms turned the atrium into a fireworks show.

One by one, the Raiders caught each hostile off-guard and put them down. One tried to get back up, and a Raider blasted a double tap at his head, splitting the skull open.

A crowd of space suits ran toward the underground tunnel entrance to escape the atrium. Gunfire popped from the crowd.

"Open fire!"

A volley of bullets from Raiders dropped the runners.

Three Raiders formed up outside the control room.

"Breaching! Breaching!"

They stormed the room overcrowded by people and workstations. They shot all people holding weapons or blunt instruments. Stray bullets tore up workstations and screens. They shoved down unarmed people, some with bloodied faces or horrified expressions. Others lay on the ground motionless.

"Control room secured."

Brawner clicked his comm button, walking around the lobby and stepping over bodies. "Paladin-1, restore power and airflow."

"Roger that, Kraken-1. Restoring power and air pressure."

"And send four units to the lobby. Viking-2, set up a defensive perimeter around the lobby." Brawner looked up to the balcony. "Samurai-3, send three units to the ground floor and assist Viking-2. Maintain overwatch up there."

Half of Samurai Squad jumped down from the balcony and helped Viking shepherd the crowd, searching for anybody concealing a weapon.

"*Decatur*, this is Kraken-1. Marius Hills Spaceport secured. Standing by for orders."

"Stand by, Kraken-1." Dressler turned to the two generals.

Fosvik was pale as a ghost, his hands shaking.

Sinclair whispered, "General, we need to deploy another platoon to secure Marius Hills. There could be pockets of resistance outside the spaceport. We need to coordinate with private security."

Fosvik nodded with hesitation. "Sinclair, head down to Marius Hills and take command of all security units. Survey the damage. Interrogate the prisoners. Debrief the Raiders. Colonel Dressler, get all your platoons spun up."

"Roger that," Sinclair and Dressler both replied.

"I'll stay here and"—he took a deep, shaky breath—"deal with the Joint Chiefs." He clenched his hand to stop the shaking.

18

THE MAGNATE

NYSE: VC 59.88 (-5.36%)

Lawrence is dead!" Vanderheiden announced, his voice bouncing off the white tiles of Scharre Sr.'s sizeable penthouse overlooking the Potomac River. He looked up from Brunelli's message on his hand terminal and studied the stunned faces forming a semicircle around him.

Dozens of business executives and investors of the Luna Business Association responded with whispers and murmurs. Vanderheiden recognized many of the new members, coming from Castlereagh Manufacturing, Xin Chemicals, Sano Properties, Whelan Engineering, and Valkyrie Labs. How big the association had grown was impressive after only four of them met at Lawrence's chalet last year. He wished Lawrence was here to see what he had built.

Off in the corner of the penthouse, Scharre Sr. sat down in a cushioned chair, face resting in his hands. Gabriella kneeled next to him and rubbed his back, whispering into his ear.

Lawrence is dead. Vanderheiden turned away from the crowd. After a few long breaths, he looked through his faint reflection on the floor-to-ceiling window, watching the murky brown river flow by. He noticed a hint of bags under his eyes and rubbed them with his knuckles, wiping away the buildup of tears.

Vanderheiden took another deep breath and reread Brunelli's message.

> LAWRENCE'S DEATH CONFIRMED. I JUST SAW HIS BODY. SHOT IN THE NECK AND BLED TO DEATH. LAWRENCE RESOURCES IS OFFLINE. WE NEED TO SWITCH TO BLACKBURN NOW.

He knew they would have to pay a heavy premium to secure production capacity at Blackburn Materials. Considering the switch to Blackburn felt like a betrayal to his friend. With Cooper and other directors demanding that he bring costs down, Vanderheiden wondered if he should help Lawrence Resources rebuild, risking a significant delay in the space elevator construction schedule. *No...that would give Cooper or Shugart the chance to take control of the board.*

"This is the moment!" a heavy voice rang out in the expansive room and silenced the conversations.

Vanderheiden turned away from the window and saw Blackburn sauntering to the center of the penthouse under his heavy weight. His eyes burned with ambition, like he was ready to embrace the chaos.

"People..." Blackburn said, "the governments are going to use the Marius Hills Massacre as an excuse to gain new powers and strip away our rights. I promise you"—he held up a wavering finger—"the White House and Congress are discussing more ways to tax and regulate us. We must stop them!"

Blackburn raised his double chin. "I say we go public. We go public, explain our side of the story and the struggles we deal with, and issue a list of political demands!"

Gabriella stood up with alarm. "Blackburn, we weren't meant for that. We are to work with the government behind closed doors to avoid public scrutiny."

"It's not working!" Blackburn exclaimed. "It's getting worse. We must stand our ground. Take the fight public!"

Many heads nodded. Scharre Sr. lifted his face from his hands. "The last thing we need is a target on our backs. Bureaucrats will try to bring the hammer down on us." His bulging eyes were red with tears.

Dr. Raymond crossed her arms and spoke, showing a gap in her front teeth. "I already have a fragile relationship with the FDA. This publicity will not help my company."

Blackburn turned to her. "So, you'll just sit here and continue to take the beating?"

"I never said we should do nothing."

Blackburn walked to the windows and spun back to the crowd. "We need to make it known that many businesses don't support these draconian laws. It is time for the silent majority to make themselves heard. If we don't do this, the government will continue to trample over us."

Many in the room shouted affirmations. Gabriella and Scharre Sr. exchanged anxious glances. Dr. Raymond closed her eyes, shaking her head.

Chills ran down Vanderheiden's back. *The last thing I want is to become a public punching bag.*

"Alright, that is our decision," Blackburn said. "We are going—"

"Stop it right there," Gabriella snapped loudly enough to silence everyone. "Before we do this, we need to make sure the one person in this room who will get the most flak is ready."

"And who would that be?" Blackburn scowled.

Gabriella turned to Vanderheiden. "Are you ready for it? You are the face of this organization."

He locked eyes with her. The sunlight coming through the windows seemed to make all the faces staring at him turn brighter. His stomach lurched.

"Is there another option?" he asked.

Hoping for an answer from one person, instead, conversations broke out across the penthouse. Gabriella and Scharre Sr. traded words. Blackburn hissed at Dr. Raymond.

Vanderheiden knew Blackburn's point about the need to change the strategy was valid. Either their association was incompetent at closed-door discussions or they lacked the influential firepower

Tsung and other oligarchs held. *Something needs to change. If we don't change, the Luna Space Elevator is at risk. My daughter's life...is at risk.*

"Look, we need a decision here!" someone shouted over the crowd. The atrium silenced again and everyone turned back to Vanderheiden.

He looked around the penthouse. Scharre Sr. gave a slight shake of his head. Gabriella curled her lips. Blackburn didn't move a muscle, his face uncomfortable to look at.

"Fine." He sighed. "We'll do it your way, Blackburn."

* * *

The Luna Business Association discussed, debated, and argued for hours over the list of political changes to demand. Meals and drinks were served. The exhaustion finally hit Scharre Sr., and he left the atrium for a quick nap. Blackburn marched his heavy weight around the room, presenting his arguments to various members with inflexible passion.

Gabriella stood up and put the list of demands on a hologram for everyone to see. She read through the first section, summarizing the Luna Business Association's support for the victims of the Marius Hills Massacre, the scathing criticism of the military's heavy-handed response, and advocating for change in the laws governing Luna.

"Here are the legal demands as they stand," Gabriella said. "'Repeal the following laws: the Fairness Tax Act, Corporate Transparency Act, Space Homestead Act, and Luna Integration Act.'"

Scharre Sr. came back down to the main floor, taking each step down the stairs slowly. "Those demands are too aggressive. All of them risk being shot down."

Blackburn shook his head. "No, we need to shoot for the stars and hope we land on Neptune."

"Let's start with the Fairness Tax and Space Homestead Acts first," Scharre Sr. replied. "It won't be difficult to convince key representatives that the high business tax rates and the discriminatory tariffs are harmful to Luna. For Space Homestead, we just have to expose the rigged land auctions." He opened his arms. "Once we achieve success, we will build credibility, which will make the other two acts easier to repeal."

"So, we take Luna Integration off the table?" Blackburn rebuked. "Absolutely not! The price controls that favor the crony oligarchs must not stand!"

Gabriella held her hand at Blackburn and looked at her father-in-law. "Mr. Scharre, I know all of these demands won't be met. We know that reality. But the more demands we have, the more conversations and conflict among the representatives it'll generate, which is exactly what we need. We can't face a united front inside Congress."

"I have one more demand I would like to add," Alexis Castlereagh said. "I want the US government to take full responsibility for the Marius Hills Massacre. They set the oppressive conditions that led up to the protests and carried out the massacre with their own soldiers. My sister nearly died up there."

"I'm going to side with Mr. Scharre on this one," Gabriella replied. "That'll just infuriate the government, making our demands dead on arrival."

Alexis pulled out her hand terminal. "Amanda recorded a meeting she had with government officials and military officers a few weeks before Marius Hills. Lawrence, Commerce Secretary Larson, General Fosvik, and General Sinclair were part of the conversation."

A shock went up Vanderheiden's back. *Sinclair was part of the massacre?*

"Here is a part of the conversation." Alexis tapped the screen and the audio file played.

"Define drastic steps..."

"Do what I tell you to do, and we won't have to talk about that."

"You can't tell us what to do! We are a private company. We answer to our shareholders, not the government."

Vanderheiden recognized Lawrence's voice.

"Not for long."

"What do you mean by that? You are going to confiscate our companies? Huh?"

There was a momentary silence.

"Here is an executive order signed by President Barbour. Authorized by the National Security Act, the Commerce Department is authorized to confiscate assets deemed vital to national security. As indicated by the general here, the economic disruptions compromise the Luna Fleet."

Someone chuckled.

"So, unless you get the workers back on their jobs and turn the manufacturing lines back on, General Fosvik will be ordered by the Joint Chiefs to deploy forces, take control of Marius Hills City, and restart production."

"Jesus Christ..." a female voice said.

"So, all three of us are going to go down there and explain the situation to the workers. General Fosvik and the Luna Fleet will be on standby."

"This is not right. We built Luna, not you. You can't take it away from us!"

"Nothing is stopping us..."

Alexis stopped the recording. "We argued for restraint."

"We need to publish that recording!" Blackburn pointed at her hand terminal. "We need public opinion on our side. That'll weaken the government's position."

"No, we should keep this recording in our back pocket," Gabriella said. "When the government deflects blame and claims to have attempted restraint, we publicize this recording to expose their lie."

She turned back to the hologram. "All right. These are the demands we've put on the table. Do we agree with these proposals?" She scanned the room.

The atrium was silent. There was no movement for a solid minute.

"I'll sign it first," Blackburn growled.

Others followed his lead and signed the document on Gabriella's hand terminal. Some members quickly walked over to the table as if being one of the first few to sign came with special privileges. Others, such as Scharre Sr. and Dr. Raymond, did not appear eager to pick up the stylus.

One by one, people's heads turned to Vanderheiden. Knowing it was his turn, he forced his legs forward, his body stiff and unnatural as he walked toward Gabriella's hand terminal lying on the table.

He forced his fingers to grab the stylus and sign the screen. He slapped the stylus down and walked back to the window, looking at no one.

After Gabriella signed it, she turned to Scharre Sr., who sat in his cushioned chair. "Mr. Scharre?"

Scharre twisted his lips for a moment. Slowly, he got up and signed the document, hands shaking. "I hope we didn't just sign our companies' death warrants."

* * *

"Blackburn." Vanderheiden approached the large man from behind.

"Vanderheiden." Blackburn turned away from a huddle of investors and smiled, offering his large hand.

Vanderheiden shook it hard. "Let's go somewhere quiet."

"Excuse me." Blackburn nodded to the investors, his thick neck jiggling.

The two men went underneath the stairwell, away from the crowd.

Vanderheiden whispered close to Blackburn, "I need you to take over cable production for the Luna Space Elevator."

"Vanderheiden"—he smirked—"if you had asked me a few weeks ago, it would've been a simple decision."

"But?" Vanderheiden replied.

"With Marius Hills offline, many new customers are coming to me, raising bids for my production lines at Phantom Torch." He looked away and squinted his eyes. "If you can pay a high enough price, I can push customers out and give you a production line or two."

"How much are we talking?"

Blackburn scratched his neck. "24,000 credits per kilometer of the cable."

"Damn it, Blackburn!" Vanderheiden gave a violent nod. "That's twice your original offer! That's going to cost my company over a billion credits."

"I only give the lines to the highest bidder." Blackburn shrugged softly.

The price was high enough for Vanderheiden to consider sticking with Lawrence Resources. *But I can't fall behind schedule.*

"You've said it yourself," Vanderheiden said. "You need the Luna Space Elevator. Luna needs the space elevator." He crossed his arms. "I'll accept your original offer. 12,000."

Blackburn's eye twitched. "What's the cable length at right now?"

"We still have 27,600 kilometers to build."

"Lawrence"—Blackburn snickered—"only built less than half of the cable?"

Vanderheiden held his tongue. *Do not mock my dead friend.* "It is not an easy task."

"20,000 credits and give me the Earth Space Elevator."

"At that price, the board will shut down the project and you won't get any money."

Blackburn took a step closer to him. "Are you telling me there are dissenters inside your company threatening the space elevator? Should I not even consider bidding?"

"Do you want the space elevator or not?"

Blackburn studied him closely.

"16,000, and you get the Earth Space Elevator." Vanderheiden stretched out his hand for a handshake. *Take it or I'll risk it with Lawrence.*

Blackburn looked at Vanderheiden's hand and took a long examination across the penthouse, studying the Luna Business Association. He locked his eyes back on Vanderheiden.

"Deal." Blackburn grasped his hand, and an enormous smile stretched across his bushy face. "This will be the beginning of a valuable partnership."

Vanderheiden forced a smile. *For us or for you?* He couldn't put his finger on it, but he felt an unsettling vibe around Blackburn, like there was another side to him he wasn't seeing. Lawrence's death came at the worst possible moment for Vanderheiden Corporation. *And the most opportune time for Blackburn.*

19

THE GENERAL

General Sinclair walked around Marius Hills Spaceport with Chief Engineer Cavalieri in their space suits with helmets off. A soft haze shrouded the atrium, scattering the yellow emergency lights. The environmental system groaned to flush out the air reeking of blood, gunpowder, and rubbing alcohol. Near the loading docks, Raiders stood guard near hundreds of prisoners receiving aid from medical technicians, some with blank stares, others full of rage and refusing it altogether.

"This wasn't spontaneous." Sinclair kicked an expended bullet casing into a pool of blood. "This was a coordinated effort. They had been planning this."

Scattered across the floor were weapons and dozens of bodies lying in puddles of blood. Two spacemen picked up a deceased woman by her shoulders and feet and placed her on a large plastic sheet. After wrapping her up, they sealed the sheet with industrial tape, then dragged it over to the loading docks, where other bodies lay near an open cargo container ready to be packed.

Sinclair walked by the makeshift morgue. There were too many bodies to count. So many that the spacemen were forced to use plastic sheets and tape once they ran out of body bags. They saved the body bags for victims killed by gunshots or explosives. Those who died from suffocation got the plastic sheets. Sinclair sighed, wishing the Lunarians had just laid down their weapons when the Raiders showed up like they were supposed to.

Colonel Dressler finished speaking with Kraken Platoon and walked over to Sinclair. Captain Brawner sat in a chair, rubbing his forehead with a bare hand. A few Raiders were having hushed conversations behind him.

"Fifty-seven dead and counting, ma'am." Dressler reported, readjusting the strap of his recoilless assault rifle.

Cavalieri inspected a metal pipe modified into a blunt instrument on the floor. "This was supposed to be a police action, Colonel. Not a military assault."

"The terrorists were heavily armed." Dressler pointed at prisoners on their knees and in handcuffs. "My men had to protect themselves."

Cavalieri stood up, trying to match Dressler's height. "You were supposed to give them a chance to cease and desist, not cut off their air and open fire."

"Open fire?" Dressler replied. "We didn't fire the first shot."

"Fifty-seven...dead! How many—"

Dressler pointed at Cavalieri. "I will *not* have an engineer question my methods."

"Enough!" Sinclair shouted.

Cavalieri snapped her mouth shut, and Dressler pressed his lips into a thin line.

Sinclair looked at the blunt weapon in the engineer's hand. How could they have done this differently? Larson could've allowed Raiders to beef up security, but she'd refused. Fosvik and Sinclair could've sent Raiders anyway, but the businesses had not wanted military presence at their facilities. They could've let the terrorists take over the control room and let federal authorities deal with the negotiations, minimizing casualties.

"We were put in a problematic situation." Sinclair turned to the officers. "Our intelligence failed. The protesters were more determined, more militarized, than we anticipated." She looked at a dead body dressed in a space suit with three gunshot wounds and the carbine lying next to him. "Cutting off the airflow was supposed to neutralize the situation. But the shooters were ready for it."

"General—" Cavalieri twisted her head.

"Chief," Sinclair said, "return the spaceport back to normal operations. We can't let it be shut down for an extended period." She looked around at the damaged lobby. "We are going to need a quick recovery effort before it turns into a food crisis for the rest of the city."

"Yes, ma'am." Cavalieri marched off and shouted orders at her engineers.

Her hand terminal rang with an inbound call, and Sinclair slid it out of her chest pocket. The call was from Colonel Barrows, and Sinclair answered it.

Barrows gritted his teeth. "General, we've gotten urgent intelligence. The EU Fifth Fleet in low earth orbit is consolidating its units and stocking up on propellant. A trans-Lunar injection maneuver looks to be in the works."

Sinclair knew this might happen, but not this quick. "Has Fosvik been informed?"

Barrows opened his mouth but hesitated. "Yes...but he didn't believe it was a TLI maneuver they were preparing for."

"I'm heading to the command center to speak to him." She closed the connection.

Cursing, Sinclair jogged over to the air lock, Dressler following her. Her terminal beeped again, this time with a message from Abborn. She unhooked her helmet from her belt, scanning through the message at the same time. She stopped jogging and blinked.

"Damn..." She read it more slowly a second time.

"What is it, ma'am?" Dressler asked.

"Take me back to Aestuum." Sinclair snapped her helmet onto the neck seal. "Now."

* * *

The command center was the most active Sinclair had seen since she'd joined the Luna Fleet. Spacemen walked briskly or jogged between stations and spoke to others with wide eyes and sharp tones. Many colors flashed on consoles, like a disco party. Telescopic images of the European Union Fifth Fleet filled the large monitors.

At the command console, Fosvik rubbed his chin, reading something on his hand terminal. Barrows stood on the other side, hands behind his back, staring at the fleet commander with an inquisitive look. He gave Sinclair a side glance when she approached the console. Colonel Dressler entered the room and stood by the door.

"General Sinclair." Fosvik handed his hand terminal across the command console lit up with an orbital map of Earth and Luna. "I take it you've seen the report?"

Sinclair grabbed the hand terminal and read the numbers, corroborating Barrows's report. "Shall we raise fleet readiness, sir?"

"Negative. General Abborn has ordered us to stand down, urging restraint. It's just a pressure tactic to rattle us."

Sinclair read the intel report again. Two tankers and five-plus combat spacecraft in close proximity. She shook her head. Too many for a pressure tactic.

"I don't believe this is a ruse, sir." Sinclair set the hand terminal down and slid it across the orbital map. "This is the real deal here. Raise our fleet's readiness."

"What makes you say that?" Fosvik tapped the console.

"The amount of combat material being moved around is too much for it to be a ruse or training exercise." She pointed at the hand terminal. "The EU would only move that much material if they were preparing for an invasion."

"It's a ploy," Fosvik argued. "We will not react to it."

"That's no longer your call, sir."

Fosvik froze and studied Sinclair closely. Barrows pulled his head back, glancing back and forth between the two generals.

"What did you say, Sinclair?" Fosvik walked along the edge of the console toward the deputy commander.

Sinclair pulled out her hand terminal and opened Abborn's message. "Per orders from the chief of Space Operations, you are hereby relieved of command of the Luna Fleet. Effective immediately."

She holds out the terminal to General Fosvik.

"Get that fucking hand terminal out of my sight. You will not—"

"Read the message!" Sinclair jabbed the hand terminal hard against his chest.

Fosvik took a step back, nearly falling from Sinclair's blunt force. His lips twisted with rage, and his neck stiffened, turning red. Looking at the hand terminal, he snapped it out of Sinclair's hand. She stood at attention.

Fosvik's face dropped and his skin turned white after he read Abborn's message. After a few breaths, he shook his head and tossed the hand terminal onto the command console, letting it clatter against the glass.

"Stand down, Sinclair," Fosvik said, "or I will have you removed from the command center."

Sinclair scoffed. "You aren't the commander anymore." She looked over her shoulder. "Colonel Dressler, remove General Fosvik from the command center."

She heard the Raider take sharp steps toward her.

"No!" Fosvik roared. He grabbed the hand terminal and threw it at a wall monitor, leaving a small mark on the device's graphene frame. "This is *my* fleet!" He raised a shaking finger. "You... I won't forget your secret dealings with the Mars Fleet for that gunship and tanker. I know you want your war. Your glory. And I will do everything in my power to make sure you don't get it! You will not spoil my retirement. *Do you understand me?*"

Sinclair didn't flinch. War was coming, and incompetent commanders must go.

Colonel Dressler came up in between the two generals and stood firm, looking at neither officer.

"Get Sinclair out of my sight!" Fosvik shouted at the Raider, a small spit of saliva landing on his chest armor plate.

"Can I review the orders, General Sinclair?" Dressler showed his calloused palm.

Sinclair didn't move, holding her stare on Fosvik. Colonel Barrows stepped away from the command console, picked up the damaged hand terminal, and rested it on Dressler's hand.

Dressler methodically read the message and set the hand terminal on the console. "General Fosvik, please follow me." He grabbed the general's arm.

"No!" Fosvik tried to pull his arm away, but Dressler kept his grip tight.

"General Fosvik, turn over your insignias," Sinclair said firmly. "I am the interim fleet commander now."

Fosvik reached for Sinclair, but Dressler pulled him back. The two struggled into a tug-of-war. Fosvik strained to escape his tight grip. "I will take you down!" Veins popped through his neck. "*Do you hear me?* I will take you— Uff!"

Dressler slammed him to the wall and pulled the general's arms back, handcuffing him. "If you had taken good care of your spacemen," he whispered into Fosvik's ear, "I would've considered covering your six."

Fosvik groaned and slid to the ground in defeat. Sinclair bent down and unclipped the insignias from his shoulders, leaving Fosvik appearing naked and powerless. Like Dressler said, he would've been a good commander if he had put up the same kind of fight he'd just given to keep his fleet properly supplied and ensure his spacemen were cared for.

Sinclair looked at Dressler and flicked her thumb at the door. He nodded, pulled Fosvik up by the shoulders, and hauled him out of the command center.

Sinclair looked down at the pins, the metal frame feeling cold against her palm. She always imagined General Garrett clipping the fleet commander insignias on her shoulders in a grand ceremony, not stripping it away from another officer. Ever since the destruction of the *Imperator*, she'd put decades of hard work into becoming a fleet commander, a general the spacemen deserved. She thought it would feel euphoric, but the only thing she felt was a hollowness in her chest, like she hadn't earned the markings. Sinclair set the insignias down and caressed her hands along the frame of the command console.

"What are your orders, General?" Barrows came to her side, glancing at the door.

"Raise the fleet's alert status."

"You think Europe is going to make a move?"

Sinclair gestured at a wall monitor of a newsfeed covering the Marius Hills Massacre. "If they are looking for an excuse to invade, we just gave them one. Many US-EU joint ventures operate out of Marius Hills."

"In that case, ma'am," Barrows said, "we need to pull all units from Marius Hills. Our gunships and destroyers are not in combat positions. It would take us more than four days to get our fleet ready. If the EU launched now, we wouldn't be able to put up a fight."

"That's correct, Colonel." Sinclair nodded. "Head up to the *Decatur* and coordinate the effort."

"Yes, ma'am." Colonel Barrows took a step back, saluted, and sprinted out of the command center.

Sinclair looked around at each spaceman inside the command center, many staring at her, and imagined each one riddled with gunshot wounds or suffocating in a deadly vacuum like some Lunarians had at the spaceport. A nauseous feeling settled in her stomach. She had put so much work into rebuilding this fleet. It had to be for a purpose.

Sinclair unclipped her insignias, picked up Fosvik's, and clipped them to her shoulders. She grabbed up her hand terminal, opened a message, and ordered all senior officers to report to the command center.

"Now...we will do things my way, " she murmured.

20

THE MAGNATE

NYSE: VC 61.65 (+2.96%)

Vanderheiden pushed the glass door open with frustration and stepped onto the cracked sidewalks of downtown Arlington. He looked down the road, seeing the Washington Monument through a small gap between buildings, and shoved his hands into his black leather jacket. *My least favorite city.* Gabriella came up to his side, crossing the name of a major shareholder off her hand terminal.

"Goddamn..." Vanderheiden looked up behind him at the tinted windows of the office building they'd just walked out of. "How many shareholders are following Cooper's playbook now?"

"At least many of them oppose Shugart," Gabriella replied.

"I'm not worried about Shugart. It's their demands for cutting costs that threaten the Luna Space Elevator."

"It's hard enough explaining the growing cost without disclosing the project." Gabriella pulled a strand of black hair away from her face after a sharp wind blew down the street.

"Do they think I'm just going to run my own company into the ground?" He stretched his arms out. "Did they forget where the *Vanderheiden* in the company name came from?"

Gabriella chuckled and looked at her hand terminal.

The tall and bulky Giovanni stood behind them and watched pedestrians walking by and vehicles rolling up and down the street. After Vanderheiden told Susann about the two men chasing him from the hospital, she'd demanded action from the board, and Gabriella had instantly revised their contract with Giovanni's security firm, shifting to full-time personal security, despite Vanderheiden's protest.

His hand terminal chirped, and Vanderheiden opened the message from Brunelli.

> CABLE 71% COMPLETED. NOW PROJECTED TO
> BE READY IN 6 MONTHS. SURFACE ANCHOR
> INTERNAL STRUCTURE COMPLETED. NOW
> POURING LUNARCRETE AND INSTALLING
> EXTERIOR PANELS.

Vanderheiden replied with a congratulatory note and told him to keep expediting the schedule. *3,000 kilometers built in a month?* he thought. *Impressive, Blackburn...*

"Who's next?" Vanderheiden closed his hand terminal and glanced over Gabriella's shoulder at her list of shareholders.

Gabriella pointed at her screen. "Next is Avon L—"

Giovanni bumped into her, unbuttoned his jacket, and stepped in front of them, facing the road.

"What the hell, Gi—" Vanderheiden stopped, grabbing Gabriella's arm as a black SUV rolled up.

A young man with a thin mustache and an ear piercing stepped out of the vehicle. "Please get in the vehicle, Mr. Vanderheiden." He crossed his hands.

"Not so fast." Giovanni raised his hand, towering over the stranger. Vanderheiden took another step back and glanced in both directions. The passenger window slid down, and Vanderheiden recognized the slim, bald silhouette with thick glasses.

"Apologies for that, Mr. Vanderheiden," the mysterious man said. "Agent Torrez can be too blunt. May I get a few minutes of your time?"

Vanderheiden recognized the voice from many newsfeed videos.

Giovanni's head jerked back and forth between Torrez and the mysterious man inside the vehicle.

"Giovanni, it's okay." Vanderheiden placed his hand on his shoulder. "That's Senator Contador."

"I don't care." Giovanni kept his eyes locked on Torrez. "I'm going to need to see some IDs!"

His mustache curling up with a smile, Torrez pulled an identification badge out. "Capitol Police."

Giovanni nodded. Torrez put his badge away and opened the passenger door, staring at Vanderheiden. "Your vehicle can follow us."

Vanderheiden did not like unannounced meetings. *But the political labyrinth runs on informal conversations and secret meetings, not public committees.* Gabriella always told him Senator Contador ran Washington, not President Barbour. He couldn't help but let his curiosity spin in his head over what the senator wanted to discuss.

"I'll take care of Avon Lake Capital." Gabriella nodded.

Giovanni leaned into Vanderheiden's ear. "You know the drill, sir."

"Thanks." Vanderheiden got into the vehicle and discreetly started recording on his hand terminal. He crossed his legs, leaned back into the leather seat, and observed Senator Contador, noting his deep dimples and balding black hair.

"Let's go for a drive," the senator said. Agent Torrez hopped in, and the vehicle merged into the traffic. They drove over the George Mason Memorial Bridge, crossing the murky gray river.

"Thank you, Mr. Vanderheiden, for accommodating me on such short notice." Contador spoke without looking at him. "I know you are busy meeting with your shareholders. I have a pressing matter that simply couldn't wait."

Vanderheiden couldn't tell if Contador seemed annoyed by this conversation or if he was looking away to hide his nervousness. *I have leverage somewhere.*

"What can I do for you?" Vanderheiden asked.

They reached the other side of the river and drove by the white rotunda of the Thomas Jefferson Memorial. Contador turned to face his fellow passenger.

"The expansion of the space frontier has created major upheaval for the country. Civil tensions, corruption, greed, unemployment. All threaten the stability and prosperity of this great nation." Contador squinted his measuring eyes behind the spectacles. "The escalating chaos calls for certain people to step up, take the reins, and steer this country in the right direction…to a better future. You and I are men who hold significant power. We bear that responsibility."

"I've already done my part." Vanderheiden shrugged. "Just look up at the PhotonicWay."

Contador blinked a few times, his lips unmoving. The SUV circled the Washington Monument. The tall marker that seemed to reach for the white clouds drew Contador's attention.

"I want to offer you a chance to start with a clean slate."

"Why do I need a clean slate?" Vanderheiden lowered his eyebrows.

"Megacorporations have run amok, bringing corruption and breeding disorder. It is time to redirect them back toward pursuing the interests of the people."

"I could say the same about the government." Vanderheiden smiled. *Blame the corporations first before blaming yourself, huh?*

"You have disrupted the space economy, sending—"

"I have created progress." Vanderheiden raised his voice over the senator's. "Traveling to Luna has never been as cheap as now. The PhotonicWay enabled the colonization of Mars, and we'll soon touch Jupiter and Saturn. You should be thanking me, Senator, not scorning me."

The senator smiled. "You left behind a path of destruction. Many launch services have gone bankrupt, leaving their workers jobless, thanks to your destruction."

Does any politician understand basic economics? "Their technology is obsolete. You have to tear down old and obsolete institutions to pave the way for new and better ones."

"At the cost of destroying people's careers?"

"The PhotonicWay paved the way for the rapid colonization of

Luna and Mars. It's what's preventing the Resource Crisis from turning into a catastrophe."

Contador swept his hands across the cabin. "This country is in an economic crisis. People are struggling to meet their needs."

Vanderheiden tilted his head toward the senator. "Certainly, the new laws you passed contributed to that? Raising taxes? Choking us with regulations? Letting the Fed print cash without limits? Crippling Lunarians with tariffs that favor Shugart?"

Contador dropped his smile. "I am not here to debate with you, Mr. Vanderheiden. I represent the people. *You* do not. Your *list of demands* will have no influence on what happens on Capitol Hill. So, listen to me when I say I'm offering you a clean slate."

Vanderheiden looked out and saw the Second North Atlantic–Eurasian War Memorial, a giant black pyramid. A couple homeless people with shopping carts sat beneath the statues of soldiers surrounding the memorial.

"What are you offering?" Vanderheiden turned back to the senator. *I have no interest in what you have to offer.*

The senator adjusted his black jacket, smoothed his red tie, and nudged his glasses. "Space is the future of mankind. We need a space conglomerate that represents the interests of the United States and safeguards our future. Tsung is a true patriot. She has done everything this government has asked her to do. I ask for you to accept the merger framework she offered."

"Why should I give up something I built?" Vanderheiden flipped his hands open. "This is the United States...a free country."

"The days of excessive competition and wasteful uses of resources has to end. It is what has brought us to this crisis. It is time for unity... time to consolidate our industries."

"Competition, not collectivism, breeds progress."

"This is for the public good." The senator shook his head. "I ask you to do your duty as a citizen and do what the government asks you to do. If you agree to Shugart's merger, I will make sure Tsung gives you a position of influence inside the new conglomerate."

Vanderheiden found it hard to imagine Tsung accepting that

arrangement. *She'll only be satisfied seeing VC taken away from me.* His hands were resting on his jeans, and he slowly turned them into fists.

"Let me explain something here: In the years I've run VC, your government has been nothing but a hindrance. First, you tried to shut us down before our first launch. And then you raised taxes and slapped regulations on us. What makes you think you get to have a say in my company?"

"We are the government." Contador gave a nod. "Accountable to the people."

"Are you really accountable to the people?" Vanderheiden smirked. "Because from where I stand, anytime the government fails, the politicians play the blame game and stir up emotions. But people have to wait years for the next election to make changes. But, most of the time, the politicians get reelected and the failures of government continue."

"Mr. Vander—"

Vanderheiden raised his finger again. "Private companies, on the other hand, are accountable to their customers and shareholders. If we fail to meet customers' needs, they take their business elsewhere, hurting our finances. Customers don't have to wait years to make change. They can go to a different supplier the next day or hour. Shareholders can force leadership change at any time. Our existence is at risk every day. So...the way I see it, the people have more say in what companies do than governments."

He noticed the senator's face turning pink.

"You need to understand what is at stake, my friend," Contador said. "If you don't join us, you will be destroyed."

"Is that a threat? You going to shoot me like your government did at Marius Hills?"

Contador twisted in his seat toward him and smiled. "I'll add something to make this deal more attractive."

A sinking feeling pulled his heart down. *I don't like this.*

"I can bring your daughter to the top of the list," Contador said.

Time slowed down, and the sounds of car engines, birds chipping, and people shouting in the streets turned inaudible. A flash of heat swam from his face down his neck. Staring at the senator, Vanderheiden closed his jaw slowly and then ground his teeth. Time sped up as many sounds flowed through his mind.

"What did you say?"

The senator's uncomfortable smile returned. "Your daughter is sick. Creutzfeldt-Jakob disease, right?"

Vanderheiden looked at him, nostrils flared and eyes full of judgment. *You dare to extort me?*

"I can call in favors to the NMS to have your daughter moved to the top of the list if you agree to the Shugart merger."

Vanderheiden wanted to grab the senator's expensive suit and slam his fist through the senator's thick eyeglasses, knocking them off. He looked out the window to suppress the violent thought.

"Earlier, you talked about how greed and corruption were hurting this country," Vanderheiden said. *I will not bend to people like you.* "Want to know where the greed and corruption really is?" He looked back at Contador. "Look in the mirror."

Vanderheiden slapped the back of the seat in front of him. "Let me out!"

Agent Torrez pulled the vehicle to the curb, near the grass and concrete sidewalks of the Lincoln Memorial. Vanderheiden shoved the door open and stepped out without looking at Contador.

"You are making a mistake, Mr. Vanderheiden."

"Many people told me that before I started my company." Vanderheiden turned around and saw the senator leaning across the cabin, hand resting where Vanderheiden had sat. "Don't stand in my way, Senator."

"Your greed and corruption will be exposed," Contador sneered.

"This might come as a surprise to you, but many businesses run a clean shop, including mine."

"I wouldn't be so sure of that." The senator rolled up his window halfway until he forgot something. "Oh...and don't bother listening to your recording. We have a scrambler."

He smiled, and Torrez floored the accelerator.

"That bastard," Vanderheiden muttered.

Giovanni braked the SUV to a stop and got out. “Is everything okay, sir?”

“Ask me when I retire.” Vanderheiden pulled out his hand terminal and saw the audio file was corrupted. He cursed under his breath.

“What did you two talk about?” Gabriella slammed her door shut and jogged toward him, eyes firm with concern.

“The government is backing Shugart’s hostile takeover.”

“So, we could lose the company any day now?”

“Damn him. Damn them all.” Vanderheiden stroked his beard. “There is only one thing we can do.”

“And what’s that?”

Vanderheiden closed his eyes and inhaled a deep breath. *And I don’t want to.* “It’s time to make the Luna Space Elevator known to the public.”

21

THE GENERAL

All the spacemen watched Colonel Barrows scroll through the intelligence reports. General Sinclair hovered at the center of the *Decatur*'s command deck, finding herself turning to the corner Fosvik typically hovered by to gather his thoughts. Each time he wasn't there, she remembered she was the Luna Fleet commander, and the weight of responsibility grew heavier on her back. It had been weeks since they'd transferred Fosvik back to Corpus Christi for reassignment.

"The intelligence network is heating up," Barrows said. "Multiple sources confirm the Fifth Fleet is preparing for a trans-Luna injection burn. It could be any day now." The colonel crossed his arms. "Diplomacy has failed."

"You can't say that until the State Department says so." Chief Cavalieri leaned over Barrow's shoulder.

"That would mean admitting failure," Barrows replied. "Diplomacy is the State's only tool."

"This can go either way." Sinclair inspected the orbital hologram illuminated above the command console. "Many invaders in the past have used diplomacy as a cover to catch their adversaries off-guard during an invasion."

"But we have to give diplomacy a chance." Cavalieri swung her tattooed arm across the command deck. "We are talking about hundreds of lives here. Our nation doesn't have an appetite for war. Luna isn't ready."

"Don't lie to yourself, Chief," Barrows said. "Diplomacy doesn't always work."

Sinclair knew the fleet would come to Luna someday as soon as she saw the telescopic images in the war room back at Corpus Christi. Recent images now showed propellant tankers being consolidated and prepped for hard burns. If the EU intended to occupy the moon, they would need to stock up on propellant to sustain multiple burns. She hoped the movements of the Fifth Fleet were a bluff by Europe in the ongoing negotiations with the United States in response to the Marius Hills Massacre.

While she longed for peace and wanted every effort to avoid war exercised, she found the imminence of war welcoming. All her life, she had been training for it. This was her chance to prove the superiority of gunships. A chance to move past the *Imperator*.

Sinclair drifted to the large monitors. "We have to be prepared in case the negotiations are a ruse and the EU intends to invade Luna. Order all spacemen to withdraw from Marius Hills and move to their combat stations."

"But, ma'am," Cavalieri said. "We still have much more to do with the recovery effort at the spaceport."

"Lunarians have to manage on their own, Chief." Sinclair pointed at the hologram. "We have bigger problems here."

She turned to Barrows. "Position the fleet into combat formation. Make sure the gunships are in the correct positions. I need to speak with SPACEOM." She went to the comm station and requested a connection to Abborn.

After a few seconds, Maxwell's dark face emerged on the screen, and Sinclair's core tightened, disliking his smirk.

"What can I do for you, General?"

"I need to speak to General Abborn."

"He is busy right—"

"Maxwell!" Sinclair sharpened her voice. "I will speak to Abborn."

He tightened his lips and shifted his jaw side to side. The screen went black, and then Abborn appeared on the video. The skin around his gray eyes appeared to have hardened over the last few months, like he had seen more than his mind could endure.

"Speak, General Sinclair."

"Intelligence confirms the Fifth Fleet is preparing a TLI. I'm raising the alert status of the Luna Fleet. What are our next ste—"

"Negotiations are still ongoing, General. This is another pressure tactic to make us bend to their demands. I order you to hold your orbits and not give the Europeans any excuse to escalate."

"That would be a direct violation of the Marseilles Agreement if the EU military entered—"

"We violated the treaty first by shooting Europeans!" He pointed at her. "Europe is asking for blood, and it has crossed my mind to deliver you and Fosvik to them to keep the peace."

She inhaled. "Don't shift blame—"

"I sent you to the moon and forced Garrett to retire so there would be more restraint in the military. I don't need warmongers running high command. The last thing our nation needs is war. I sent you to Luna so you wouldn't cause trouble, and you *had* to stir shit up!"

"I don't control the cards that are given to me, sir. Luna was already rumbling when I got here. To ensure the EU doesn't launch their TLI, raise the Orbital Fleet's alert status and—"

"General Sinclair..." He squinted his eyes. "I order you to stand down and allow the EU fleet to enter Luna if they kick off a TLI. Negotiations will play in our favor. The EU is sending half of its fleet to the moon. That'll leave them exposed here in low earth orbit. That is the trump card we have."

A sense of paralysis gripped Sinclair's muscles. She couldn't believe what Abborn was ordering her to do. Looking around the command deck, she saw many slack faces. She tightened her lips and turned back to the space chief on the screen.

"We've already lost Luna the moment the Fifth Fleet arrives. Their fleet outnumbers us. We must strike during the TLI, when they are most vulnerable. The Orbital Fleet needs to make a TLI burn if the Fifth Fleet does. We can attack them from both directions in a pincer formation when they arrive at Luna."

Something off-screen distracted Abborn. "I don't know if I can make my orders any clearer. You are to stand down and maintain current orbital patterns."

"I will not lose the—"

He snapped his head back toward her. "Stop pushing for war! It is only bloodshed over...trivial geopolitics! I'm constantly having to tell politicians and other generals to tone it down."

Sinclair popped her knuckles one by one. "Are you ordering my fleet to give up Luna?"

Abborn grew more distracted again. "Call it what you like. It is simply the European Union entering the arena, but all swords remain sheathed."

"There are multiple troop shuttles inside the Fifth being prepped," Sinclair said. "This is not a vanguard unit. This is an occupation force. What will you do when the Fifth attacks? Our only chance is to attack at the end of their TLI, with Orbital's support."

"It will not happen."

"But what will you do if it happens?"

Abborn didn't respond for a moment. "Are my orders clear?"

Sinclair bit her lip. "You didn't answer my—"

"Are. My. Orders. Clear?"

She exhaled. "I have received your orders."

"Good." The screen went black.

Sinclair turned to Barrows. "What's the current makeup of the Fifth Fleet?"

"Five destroyers, two gunships, two propellant tankers, and a carrier with eight shuttles docked."

"The fleet commander?"

He lifted an eyebrow. "You think it is Medvedev?"

She nodded. "He would be my first pick if I were on their side."

The Luna Fleet held the moon with two destroyers and three gunships. The odds were against them but not overwhelming. The three gunships should be able to hold off the destroyers. Sinclair was more concerned about the two EU gunships. She turned furious at Shugart for not delivering the Lampard-class gunships on schedule. Having one or two of those gunships would make this much easier.

"Chief, is the tanker topped off with propellant?"

"Yes, ma'am," Cavalieri replied.

Sinclair turned to back to Barrows.

"Colonel Barrows, take command of the *Nevada*. Chief Cavalieri, you got the *Oregon*. Get the gunships prepped. Move out."

The two officers snapped into salutes and glided out of the command deck.

Sinclair turned around after watching the two leave and was taken aback by seeing every spaceman in the command deck look at her like a deer in the headlights. She guessed the possibility of death by suffocation, burned by the sunlight, frozen by the shadow, or rail-gun projectile crossed their minds. Their lives were in her hands now.

"Lieutenant Colonel Fabian," Sinclair said, "you have command of the *Decatur* and the *Rhode Island*."

"Yes, ma'am. Eh...who is commanding the *Wyoming*?"

"I am."

Multiple alerts blared, and Fabian scrambled over to the console. "General!" he exclaimed after reading the alerts. "Multiple hard burns by the Fifth Fleet detected!"

Sinclair looked at the scopes and saw white engine fumes from multiple vessels. "Start the clock."

With current acceleration and trajectory, the fleet would arrive in thirty-three hours.

The breathing of a few spacemen quickened. Many exchanged glances. Sinclair's heart was beating hard enough, she thought it would break through her rib cage. She fought to hold her composure.

"Do I need to get Abborn back on the line?" Fabian asked.

"Negative," Sinclair replied. "We're on our own."

She took a deep breath, but her strong heartbeat made it difficult. After the urge to panic faded, she opened her eyes and looked at Fabian.

"Action stations!"

The combat alarm wailed.

22

THE MAGNATE

NYSE: VC 81.55 (+32.28%)

Vanderheiden fiddled with the sheet of paper holding his speech draft, folding it back and forth in different ways, looking for something to distract himself. He examined the hundreds of people filling up the front lobby of the Vanderheiden Corporation headquarters, ranging from journalists to investors to analysts. With a podium engraved with the big white letters "VC" standing in the back of the lobby, the area looked like a large auditorium instead of the ground floor of the corporate headquarters.

Vanderheiden pulled on his collar, tight around his neck, and let out a deep exhale. *I still have a chance to turn back.* He looked over to the company chiefs and a few directors standing behind the stage with him.

Arellano had her eyes glued on the stock tracker, hoping the VC stock price would go above 160, the price they predicted would force Shugart to call off its hostile takeover. Scharre Sr. and Gabriella were having their own conversation, glancing between each other and the crowd. Cooper paced the back wall, arms crossed, and looked at no one in particular. Two of the company chiefs were missing. Brunelli was at Luna overseeing the final touches of the surface anchor construction and pushing Blackburn toward the last few hundred kilometers of cable production. Gonzalez spotted strange readings from the Luna sector at the PhotonicWay Command Center and declined to come.

Vanderheiden looked down at his folded sheet of paper. For many weeks, the country had been on edge. Both sides of the Atlantic Ocean were invoking fervent patriotism in the face of possible war, following the shooting at Marius Hills. Bills granting the government more authoritative power were being considered, breeding excitement and raising alarms. People demanded blood for the massacre of Lunarians at Marius Hills, and others fiercely defended the US Space Force. The Luna Business Association made itself public with the list of demands, garnering both an outpouring of support and waves of scathing criticism.

Vanderheiden unfolded his paper and scanned the words. *Time to splash the newsfeed with positive news. But will this announcement make the top of the newsfeed, considering everything else that's happening?*

Cane, the corporation's public relations officer, dressed in a green suit, walked up to the podium.

"Hello, everyone?" She smiled. "Yes! Everyone...please gather around." She raised her hands, gesturing for the crowd to come toward the podium like a teacher in a kindergarten class. "Gather around..."

The crowd quieted down and slowly converged toward the podium, with a mix of eagerness and caution.

She glanced over her shoulder at Vanderheiden. "Today, we have a special announcement to make, coming directly from the CEO and founder of Vanderheiden Corporation, Mr. Vanderheiden. He will gi—"

Applause interrupted her, followed by a few boos and jeers. Gabriella covered a chuckle with a fake cough.

Vanderheiden stopped fidgeting his paper. *I can't please everyone.*

Cane cleared her throat. "Mr. Vanderheiden will give a quick speech. Please…" She gave an elaborate smile. "Hold your questions until the end. Thank you!" She stepped away from the podium.

Vanderheiden walked to the podium surrounded by journalists and analysts, his footsteps hitting the floor tiles and rattling his eardrums. He unfolded the paper on the podium, pressing the bends repeatedly to flatten them out. He squinted his eyes at the spotlights, which made his skin feel hot, and small beads of sweat trickled down his forehead. He took a deep breath and scanned the crowd. The spotlights only let him see black shadows in the lobby.

Dozens of employees from the upper balconies looked down at him. Many leaned on the guardrails with small smiles. Vanderheiden guessed they were longtime employees because they knew he only gave speeches when he had a major announcement to make. A few others had their arms crossed, their eyes narrowed.

Vanderheiden flattened the speech draft again and glanced to his side, thinking about Brunelli. *He should be here, making this announcement with me.* This project was his idea. *I just rallied the troops and allocated resources toward the effort.* He picked out Cooper from the corner of his eyes. *And held corporate raiders at bay.*

After clearing his throat and rolling his shoulders back, Vanderheiden said, "I'll keep this announcement brief." He took a quiet inhale through his nose.

"When Vanderheiden Corporation was formed eleven years ago, our mission was to bring access to space to many people. We achieved great milestones by connecting Earth, Luna, and Mars with the PhotonicWay. Each time we've reached a new planet or moon, new waves of prosperity have been unleashed. We've enabled the colonization of Mars, fueled the growth of zero-g manufacturing, resupplied the solar and battery farms, holding off a catastrophic energy crisis, and allowed common people to become spacefarers."

He looked up and still only saw black shadows, unable to measure the crowd's reaction. *Just say the words.*

"Unfortunately, the cost of rockets and their launch services remain persistently high, threatening to bankrupt many people and reignite the Resource Crisis, leaving our battery and solar farms depleted of critical materials. To continue our mission, we are announcing our next major project...an effort intended to offer a substantially cheaper alternative to rockets. A cheaper way for people to reach space from the surface of Earth and Luna."

He raised his hand and pointed at the large hologram projector to his left. A large blue diagram of the Luna Space Elevator was unveiled. A few people gasped.

"For months, we have worked hard to make this a reality. I am proud to announce the Luna Space Elevator!"

Whispers fluttered across the crowd, but Vanderheiden didn't hear the applause he hoped for. *Disbelief or confusion?*

"I knew it!" someone yelled from the back with excitement.

One person clapped. Then another. A few people clapping rolled into a wave of applause. Then the entire lobby radiated with roaring applause. Vanderheiden smirked and glanced behind him to see his company chiefs and directors staring at the crowd in disbelief.

After the applause settled down, Vanderheiden searched the paper for his next words. "The space elevator is a cable that connects from the lunar surface to an orbital station, allowing vehicles, personnel, cargo, etc., to travel up and down without the use of rockets. In partnership with"—he glanced at the words *Lawrence Resources* typed on his sheet—"many Luna-based companies and the support of countless Lunarians, the space elevator will be built and fully operational in eighteen months."

He slapped the podium with pride. "Now, I will take questions."

A thunder of questions flew at him, and he couldn't catch a single one. Vanderheiden had trouble picking out the dark figures. Before he raised his finger in a random direction to pick a question, Cane stepped up to calm the crowd down, patting the air with a smile.

"Of course, we can only do one question at a time." She pointed at the front row. "Let's start with this gentleman."

"Thank you," the investment analyst said. "My knowledge of space elevators is spotty, but I do know this for a fact: space elevators have been studied for many decades, all coming to the same conclusion. It is impossible. What's different this time?"

Vanderheiden nodded. "Many factors have enabled us to pursue this project. Gravity is the biggest hurdle for any space elevator. Fortunately, Luna's gravity is weak, making this a smaller obstacle to overcome. The expansion of the Luna industrial base gave us access to the large amount of titanium required to build the elevator. Other"—Vanderheiden coughed and cleared his dry throat—"other factors, such as our large cash reserve and Luna's...relatively business-friendly environment have made this possible. Next question, please." He grabbed a bottle of water from the podium and took a sip, feeling the cold liquid soften his throat.

"The lady over there in the red shirt." Cane pointed, but Vanderheiden couldn't see where. *These damn spotlights.*

"Megaprojects, such as bridges, canals, and dams, are owned by governments due to their vast scale and importance to the economy. A space elevator would seem to fall under this category. Will the Luna Space Elevator be wholly owned by Vanderheiden Corporation, or will you pass control of it over to the US government?"

"No." A corner of Vanderheiden's upper lip twitched with irritation. "We will build the Luna Space Elevator. We will keep the Luna Space Elevator. If the US government wants it, they will have to offer a premium price large enough to satisfy the shareholders. Next question."

The crowd vibrated with whispers.

"Let me have a follow-up to—"

"Sorry, ma'am!" Cane waved at the lady in the red shirt. "We got many eager to ask questions. You over there!"

"Thank you, ma'am." Vanderheiden recognized Alexandra Greenwood's voice, the investigative journalist from the *Overseer*. He never liked her articles or her questions.

"Mr. Vanderheiden, this announcement coincides with many things. Shugart's hostile takeover bid of your company and growing pressure from the shareholders, your disclosure as a member of the Space Magnates and their publication of the list of demands, the terrible tragedy at Marius Hills, and much more. You are getting pressure from multiple—"

"Is there a question?" Vanderheiden snapped.

"Much pressure is on you, Mr. Vanderheiden. Do you have a prototype or something to prove this space elevator will work, or is this just a power play to boost the stock price and your publicity?"

Vanderheiden remained silent for a while. He clenched his jaw, drawing in a breath and puffing out his chest.

Cane leaned toward him, dropping her smile. "Want me to cover for you?"

Vanderheiden ignored her. "I'd be lying to say this company wasn't under pressure. The development of the space elevator has been underway for nearly a year now. Shugart's hostile takeover attempt certainly played a role in the timing of this announcement. But this isn't about boosting our stock price. It is about following our mission: bringing space access to all."

Alexandra shouted, "What about the Space Magnates—"

Vanderheiden raised his hand to silence her. *Am I really about to publicize my political views?* "I hope the Marius Hills Massacre demonstrates the injustice Lunarians face. I signed the list of demands because spacefarers deserve the freedom to pursue their ambitions and not be shackled by the government."

He looked at the hologram of the Luna Space Elevator spinning slowly. "If we continue down this path of granting our government more authoritative power, it will only harm the prospects of the space elevator. So, we can't do it on our own. Vanderheiden Corporation needs the support of the public. I need people to speak out, talk to their politicians, convince their friends and families, anyone, to support the list of demands and stop the government from taking away our right to pursue ambitions."

A roar of applause thundered in the lobby.

"That's right!"

"You tell them, Vanderheiden!"

If there were any jeers or boos, Vanderheiden didn't hear any.

Vanderheiden spoke into Cane's ear, speaking loud enough to be heard over the cheering. "That's all the questions I'm taking."

He walked away from the podium. With each step he took, the louder the applause grew.

"Thank you, everyone!" Cane announced. "That's all the questions we will be taking. Please monitor our press releases for a more detailed briefing. Thank you!"

Vanderheiden looked up and saw enthusiastic employees. They clapped, cheered, leaned over the guardrail, extending thumbs to Vanderheiden. He smiled and nodded at them.

Walking toward the back of the lobby, Vanderheiden grew concerned by how uneasy Arellano looked. She was always calm and cerebral, but she was looking at her stock tracker like she was about to combust spontaneously.

"Oh God! Oh my God!" Arellano was on her toes.

Gabriella smiled at Vanderheiden, almost giggling. Scharre Sr. had a satisfied smirk under his bulging eyes. Cooper seemed to be in a state of disbelief, not pacing along the wall.

"What's the stock price now?" Vanderheiden asked.

"234!" Arellano let out a whoop. "And it's still climbing!"

Vanderheiden blew out a breath. *An all-time high.* Investors must be tripping over each other to scoop up company shares.

"We did it," Vanderheiden whispered. "We've stopped Shugart."

"Yes!" Gabriella clenched her fists and hugged him.

"Well done." Cooper patted Vanderheiden's shoulder and walked away.

When Vanderheiden turned to Scharre Sr., he wore a look of concern. "I hope you know what this means, son." Senior extended his hand.

"What does it mean?" Vanderheiden grabbed it and shook.

"Now the hard work begins. You must deliver on this promise...or the shareholders will have your head."

* * *

"Ladies? I'm home." Vanderheiden walked around the villa, holding two bags of Greek food. The smell of cooked lamb and tzatziki sauce made his stomach rumble.

He hoped to surprise them with an early return home from work, something he hadn't done in a long time. After the public announcement and the stock price jump, Vanderheiden felt on top of the world, clearing his work calendar, determined not to let this feeling be spoiled by trivial business matters.

Susann messaged him.

> WE WENT OUT FOR ICE CREAM. DIDN'T REALIZE YOU'D BE HOME EARLY. SEE YOU IN 30 MINUTES.

Disappointed, Vanderheiden put the food on the kitchen counter, emptied his pockets, slipped out of his leather shoes, grabbed a chilled bottle of sparkling water, and collapsed on the couch with a sigh.

He turned on the wall monitor and started scrolling through the newsfeed. His grin grew bigger when he saw the space elevator was the top story. He selected the first video he saw, showing a news anchor with thick black hair.

"Have you imagined a cable connecting from the surface of Earth to LEO and beyond, like an elevator taking you from the first floor to the top of a skyscraper? Well...what I just described is literally called a space elevator, and Vanderheiden Corporation, the space transportation company operating the PhotonicWay, is attempting to build a space elevator on Luna. My guest here is Dr. Kiernan Kubler, a renowned astroengineer with decades of experience in space infrastructure and zero-g manufacturing. Dr. Kubler, thank you for joining us today. What is your initial response to VC's announcement? Is a space elevator possible?"

Above his oval-shaped optics, Kubler's eyebrows jumped up, like he was in disbelief. *"It's impossible, Matt. The laws of physics and the brutal reality of gravity make this space elevator concept unrealistic. I don't know what VC is thinking—"*

Vanderheiden flicked his finger sideways to switch the channel. *The opinion of a longtime consultant for Shugart is irrelevant.* A different video played, this time Alexandra Greenwood from the *Overseer* giving her report.

"I applaud Vanderheiden for taking on this challenge. But is there an ulterior motive? Is it a power play to increase his publicity? Note that a few weeks ago, this secret organization of billionaires called the Luna Business Association, also known as Space Magnates, announced their list of demands, demanding the government roll back regulations and reduce taxes to empower greedy capitalists. Now, Vanderheiden—"

Vanderheiden flicked his finger, changing the channel. He took a sip. *Space Magnates?* He wasn't sure how he felt about being called that.

He switched the channel to an amateur commentator wearing a beanie cap. *"I'm still trying to wrap my mind around this. My—my engineering background is screaming, 'A space elevator is impossible!'"* He paused, the camera light reflecting off his wide eyes. *"But this is VC we are talking about here. Vanderheiden knows what he is doing. If they say they are going to do something, they will do it. It...it's happening. We are going to ride up a space elevator!"*

Vanderheiden nodded and flicker his finger. *Samantha's Corner*, a Luna-based program he was unfamiliar with, came on. The channel's host, Samantha, freckled and slim with an olive skin tone, sat in a small room barely big enough to fit four people.

"Today, I have Logan, a warehouse operator at the pavilion, with me." She turned to a bald man with a long beard wearing a blue jumpsuit sitting next to her. Vanderheiden instantly recognized him as the person who'd broken up that fight at Marius Hills and got the crowd fired up at the spaceport after confronting the Raiders. *Hard to forget that man.* Logan leaned on the wall like he was trying to be respectful of Samantha's space.

Samantha asked, *"You've been living and working on Luna for...at least two decades, right?"*

"Yes, twenty-three years and counting, Samantha." He spoke in a gentle voice.

"Wow. I could go down a deep hole with so many questions to ask, but I

want to stay on the space elevator topic. I'll ask you a simple question: A space elevator on Luna—what does this mean for you?"

Logan chuckled and took a deep breath. *"I try not to be dramatic, but...for me, this is life-changing."*

"Seriously?" Samantha twisted her head.

Vanderheiden set his bottle down on the coffee table and leaned closer, resting his elbows on his knees.

"Yes," Logan replied firmly. *"This recession has been hard. The volume of cargo moving through my warehouse has diminished by half. On top of that, the operators of the spaceports I run my shipments through have been consolidated under Shugart."* He spoke the company's name like it was repulsive. *"And they've raised their fees. So, it has been challenging for my business."*

He tugged at the collar of his jumpsuit. *"Challenging enough that I've started selling my personal items to make ends."*

"But how does the space elevator solve that?" Samantha leaned closer.

Logan shook his head like he'd forgotten the original question and smiled. *"If what Vanderheiden says is true, that the space elevator will be a significantly cheaper alternative to rockets, which would reduce the cost of shipping my cargo significantly. So..."* He raised his fist. *"Woo! That's more money in my pocket! More trips to the pub!"*

"Yeah! Woo!" Samantha chuckled, her smile stretching her freckles.

Logan reflected her smile. *"Vanderheiden is absolutely right. The cost of rockets to escape the gravity wells of Earth and Luna makes it difficult to grow my business. With the space elevator, that should no longer be a problem. Once the space elevator is complete, I plan to move my warehouse operation near the surface anchor in Sinus Medii. Because"*—he pointed at his host—*"I want to be in the right place when the Luna economy explodes."*

"Okay...okay, so you believe this space elevator is the best thing that could happen to Luna?"

"Yes, it will be. No doubt."

"How do you think other Lunarians are reacting to it?"

"Eh"—he took a deep breath—*"let me put it this way: if this construction is successful, let's just say Vanderheiden will have found himself many loyal followers. Say what you will about businessmen and their greed. But*

he is doing something good here. Next time he is up here, I will ask how I can help."

Vanderheiden reached out for his bottle and raised it to a toast. "Thank you, Logan."

He brought the bottle to his lips and pulled his head back to drink the rest of it, a bubbling sensation draining down his throat and into his gut. He got up and walked to the kitchen for a second bottle. A call from Gonzalez rang before he got to the counter.

Vanderheiden froze, staring at the hand terminal. *He only calls in emergencies.*

He slowly set the unopened bottle, a soft click on the counter, and tapped the screen.

"Gonzalez, what's up?"

"Sir...we got a serious problem on Luna."

He stiffened his grip on the hand terminal. "What kind of problem?"

"I've got footage from the Luna platforms and readings on the map of military vessels performing hard burns and firing missiles and slugs at each other!" Gonzalez waved his hands erratically. "There is debris flying everywhere. Luna Platform 4 is offline. I can't get in touch with the crew. We are trying—"

"Gonzalez, slow down!" Vanderheiden barked. "What's happening?"

"A war is blowing up on Luna."

23

THE GENERAL

Strapped to her seat in the *Wyoming*'s operations deck, Sinclair watched the hologram and the many screens surrounding her. No matter how many times she readjusted the straps around her space suit, her chest felt constricted. Her torso muscles hardened and tensed up with each breath she drew in. The waiting game before the imminent battle was agonizing. She wanted to feel the accelerations pressing her into the seat and violent shakes from the rail-gun salvos.

"Looks like they are prepping for deceleration," Captain Audubon from navigations reported.

The hairs on Sinclair's neck stood up when all the Fifth Fleet's gray-painted spacecraft, visible through the gunship's telescopes, spun on their short axis in successive fashion, pointing their engines at Luna. The Fifth Fleet, presumed to be commanded by General Medvedev, comprised of five destroyers, two gunships, two propellant tankers, and the *Piedmont* spacecraft carrier, which held eight shuttles.

After the deceleration countdown passed under the two-minute mark, Sinclair's vision gradually turned into a dark tunnel, narrowing her focus on the engines and waiting for the engine burns to emit light.

"This is *Oregon*," Chief Engineer Cavalieri's chatter came through the fleet-wide channel. "All five destroyers and both tankers shifting to the front of the enemy fleet."

"This is *Nevada*," Colonel Barrows replied. "Confirmed. The gunships are hugging the *Piedmont*. *Wyoming*, requesting permission to target the gunships."

Sinclair scrambled for the comm button on her tactical armband. "Negative, *Nevada*. Your priority target is the tankers."

"We hoped those gunships would stick with the tankers. Those gunships are going to be a serious problem if we don't take them out now."

"Negative." She waved her hand in a cutting motion. "We'll deal with them later. Take out the tankers. We must cut down their delta-v."

"Roger that, *Wyoming*," Barrows replied.

After calculating the Fifth Fleet's estimated retro-burn timeline, the *Nevada* had performed a hard burn hours ago to put it in a wide elliptical orbit. If Barrows had timed it properly, the *Nevada* should cross the Fifth Fleet during its deceleration and be able to fire a devastating barrage of tungsten slugs into the opposing fleet's left side. If Barrows could take out the tankers and deplete the fleet's delta-v, their seven-to-four combat vessel advantage would be negated.

"Strap in!" Sinclair ordered.

She checked her seat harness and tightened it until her shoulders ached. She raised her head and scanned the oval-shaped operations deck. Captain Piazza manned the weapons station, rubbing her fingers together, close to the rail-gun controls. The lights radiating from the console made her thick freckles look black and green eyes pale. At navigations, Captain Audubon constantly flipped between cameras on his main screen, checking the orbital map and main engine statuses. Second Engineer Lamar monitored the readings from the nuclear reactor belowdecks. His tall and bulky figure made his seat appear too small for him.

Sinclair felt uncomfortable with the three new faces on the operations deck, wishing she had more training time with them. The only comfort she had was that the three were highly recommended by Barrows and Cavalieri.

Sinclair checked the hologram, seeing the *Oregon*, their propellant tanker, and the two assault craft, each loaded with Raiders hovering closely to the *Wyoming*. Multiple dots, a blend of white and blue, flashed at the corner of Sinclair's vision.

"Multiple engine burns detected from the enemy fleet," Cavalieri said.

"Roger that," Barrows replied. "Warming up the rail gun."

Sinclair stopped the retro-burn countdown clock, resting at the T minus twenty-three-seconds mark. Everything was proceeding accordingly. The *Nevada* was still on an intercept course. Her carefully orchestrated battle plan was intact. But the thought of the chaos engulfing Luna once the first shot was fired zapped away her momentary satisfaction.

The bright engine plumes got closer, traveling at approximately 9,000 kilometers per hour and decelerating. Sinclair wondered what the mood was on the *Piedmont*. Did General Medvedev expect an attack, given ongoing diplomatic efforts? But Sinclair wasn't taking the chance, not with her spacemen's lives on the line. She would never recover from being the general who lost Luna.

"Three minutes to target," Barrows stated.

Sinclair zoomed in on the telescope and saw the vanguard group, comprised of the five destroyers and two tankers, continuing to separate from the Fifth Fleet. The destroyers and tankers held their course, not reacting to the *Nevada*'s intercept. Sinclair felt a glimmer of hope in her stomach. It seemed too good to be true.

"Two minutes to target. Rail-gun targeting package is being calculated. Stand by."

Eyes locked on her rail-gun monitors, Captain Piazza rubbed her fingers near the controls, ready to fire the rail gun. Sinclair eyed her closely.

"Easy, Weapons. We got several minutes before our turn."

Piazza nodded but continued to rub her fingers. If the vanguard group, after getting damaged by the *Nevada*, continued its approach toward the equatorial orbit, the *Wyoming* and the *Oregon*, approaching directly south after passing over the north pole, would be able to hit them.

She shifted her eyes to Audubon, who appeared uneasy. He stretched out his fingers. Sinclair couldn't hear it but imagined the knuckles cracking. If the vanguard group changed course instead, her two gunships had to react immediately.

"Navigations, stand by for potential course corrections. We have to be ready for the vanguard group changing their course."

"Yes, ma'am." Audubon jerked his hands toward the joystick on his console.

"One minute," Barrows reported. "Targets zeroed in."

Heart pounding up her throat, Sinclair pulled up the *Nevada* rail-gun camera and saw seven gray dots, barely visible in the distance, with the white curve of the moon edging on the side of the camera. The rail gun aimed to the left of the dots, leading its targets.

At the orbital speed of over 4,250 kilometers per hour that the *Nevada* traveled, Barrows only had a brief window of fifteen to twenty seconds to fire on the tankers. Once the outlines of the spacecraft on the rail-gun camera became distinguishable, Barrows's voice blurted out: "Commencing fire."

The camera shook violently from the rail gun's barrage, and the dots became blurs. The rail gun fired ten-round bursts, burned its maneuvering thrusters to adjust aim, fired another burst, and repeated.

Sinclair switched to the *Wyoming* telescopes pointed at the vanguard group. No signs of debris were visible. The electromagnetic rail guns generated such substantial velocity that nothing could stop the tungsten slugs. The targeted spacecraft could only hope to dodge the slugs or for none of the vital systems to be compromised.

After three sets of bursts, Barrows announced, "No impact on target. Recalibrating target package."

Sinclair gripped her main monitor, resisting the urge to yell at Barrows to take out the tankers.

Firing their maneuvering thrusters, small white plumes flew out of the tankers, and they shifted to the side, putting the destroyers between them and the *Nevada*.

"Knock out the tankers, *Nevada*!" Sinclair smacked the armrest.

"Firing!"

The rail-gun camera wobbled against multiple bursts. The vanguard group seemed undisturbed, gently approaching Luna.

But in a successive manner, one slug after another burst through the hulls of the vessels, splashing debris everywhere. The destroyer closest to the *Nevada* turned into an ugly piece of metal, its armored hull riddled with holes. Hundreds of pieces of debris flew out the destroyer's opposite side, hurdling toward the other destroyers like scattershot and chipping them. One tanker tumbled uncontrollably, jettisoning excessive amounts of liquid methane into the vacuum, glittering in the sunlight.

"One tanker down!" Piazza shook her fist.

"Brace for spin!" Barrows ordered his crew.

The gunship flew a few kilometers beneath the hostile vessels, ceased firing, and, with a furious burn, spun around, pointing its rail gun at the targets.

"Firing!"

The volley was as destructive as the previous one. Two destroyers were hit with multiple slugs. Another destroyer seemed to receive a final slug that compromised its engine, throwing it off course and rolling down toward the surface.

Sinclair locked her eyes on the second tanker, seeing no liquid methane cloud. With a few precious seconds remaining, the *Nevada* maintained its firing, pulling farther and farther away from its targets until it was no longer visible on the rail-gun camera.

But the tanker remained intact.

"Damn it!" Barrows exclaimed on the channel after the gunship ceased firing. "*Wyoming*, be advised. One tanker and two destroyers down. Second tanker remains active."

"Copy, *Nevada*." Sinclair switched her channel to the ground units. "Artillery Unit 5-6, this is *Wyoming*. Launch all missiles against the vanguard group entering orbit. Over."

The artillery unit commander came online. "*Wyoming*, my orders were to fire these missiles against the *Piedmont* and the gunships. I only have enough missiles for one full salvo. Confirm the vanguard group is the target. Over."

Seeing on the orbital hologram the vanguard group brushing against the edge of the missiles' range, Sinclair blurted: "Confirmed! Fire! Fire!"

"Launching."

Sinclair imagined the doors of the missile cells built into the ground sliding open and a volley of missiles launching, blowing lunar dust everywhere, and hurdling toward the black sky.

Sinclair watched the large cluster of engine plumes emerging from the surface and speeding toward the vanguard group. Turning it into a duel, a handful of missiles flew out of the destroyers and sped toward the incoming salvo. A few missiles made contact, setting off explosions.

The destroyers' active protection system opened fire, and the swarm of missiles met the spacecraft. A debris cloud blossomed, growing thicker as the missiles struck the spacecraft or were destroyed by APS.

Sinclair let out a sigh, watching the carnage unfold. It was hard to see which spacecraft were hit with shards of metal, liquid methane, and bodies flying everywhere. She found it strange to feel sympathy for the young spacemen getting burned by explosions or ripped to shreds by flying debris.

Alarms blared, striking Sinclair's ear.

"Missiles inbound!" Audubon tapped in commands, arming the APS.

A dozen missiles emerged from the debris cloud and sped toward Sinclair's group.

"Two minutes to impact!"

"Raiders! Line up behind the gunships!" Sinclair inhaled sharply. "Weapons! Open fire on the missiles!"

"Firing!" Piazza jabbed her finger on the console.

Sinclair felt her body rattle from the rail gun's bursts. For what felt like several minutes, Sinclair watched the red dots slowly approaching the blue dots on the hologram, waiting for the impact to knock her sideway and see debris ripping across the operations deck.

The red dots got closer and the rail gun went full auto and the APS buzzed, firing hundreds of pellets, attempting to cripple the missiles. Sinclair clenched her jaw hard to stop her teeth from clattering from the rail gun.

"Brace for impact!" Audubon shouted once the red and blue dots overlapped.

Several pops ricocheted across the armored hull, shaking Sinclair's seat, as missile debris smashed against the gunship. The gunship's tapered hull stood a slightly better chance against debris compared to missiles and slugs. But it only took one piece of debris hitting the rail gun's barrel or the nuclear reactor to cripple the *Wyoming*.

The popping tapered to silence.

"All clear!" Audubon announced.

Sinclair loosened her straps and scanned her monitors to assess the damage.

"Status report!" Sinclair ordered on the group-wide battle channel.

"All systems nominal." Second Engineer Lamar gave Sinclair a thumbs-up, sweat covering his forehead.

Yellow and red alerts covered the *Oregon*'s status cards.

"*Wyoming*, this is *Oregon*. Multiple pieces got through our hull. We are working through the damage."

Sinclair looked at the orbital hologram, showing the dotted line of their rail-gun range rapidly approaching the vanguard group. "*Oregon*, are you still combat effective? T minus seven minutes to our attack run."

"Stand by, *Wyoming*," Cavalieri shouted. "Reboot the power grid!"

Sinclair pressed her lips together. She couldn't hold down Luna with the *Oregon* offline and the *Nevada* circling back. If she could make her attack runs against the destroyers and the tanker successful, the *Wyoming* might stand a chance against the *Piedmont* and the two gunships until the *Nevada* reentered the war zone. She cracked a knuckle and locked her eyes on the vanguard group on her monitors, seeing its debris field clearing up.

Sinclair turned to Piazza. "Weapons, status report?"

"Rail gun is fully operational." Piazza leaned close to the controls. "Analyzing target data."

"Navigations"—Sinclair twisted to the other side—"still on intercept course?"

"Yes, ma'am!" Audubon repled.

Four minutes later, Cavalieri came back on the channel. "*Wyoming*, this is *Oregon*. The power system is malfunctioning. We are unable to power up the rail gun or the APS. ETA thirty minutes to make repairs."

"Three minutes to target!" Piazza announced.

Sinclair muted herself and jerked her head toward Audubon. "Shift our position to the front of the *Oregon*!" She unmuted. "*Oregon*, are your thrusters fully operational?"

"Affirmative," Cavalieri replied.

"Stay behind the *Wyoming* during the attack run and remain inside our APS range."

"Acknowledged." Cavalieri lowered her voice. "Sorry you are on your own here, General."

Sinclair ignored her. Nothing was going right here, even before she had a chance to attack the enemy fleet. It unsettled her that the chaos was only going to get worse. Starting the fight was easy, but finishing it seemed impossible.

Five gray spots emerged on the rail-gun camera. "Opening fire in ten seconds," Piazza said.

The countdown clock soon hit zero, and the rail gun lit up with several bursts. All the slugs were well placed on the targets, creating a satisfying thick field of debris. Frozen methane engulfed the tanker. The targets seemed unable to move, likely disoriented and struggling to recover from damage dealt by the *Nevada* and the ground missiles. One destroyer fired a pathetic number of missiles, and the *Wyoming* APS immediately ripped them.

Moving quickly down the moon toward the south pole, Sinclair zoomed in on images taken during the attack run, and she couldn't find any undamaged spacecraft. But it was hard to tell which ones were still active.

"Navigations, plot for another intercept." She felt the momentum of the successful attack run carry her words. "Execute flight plan once calculated."

"Copy," Audubon replied.

The main engines fired and the gunship quivered. The *Oregon* and the two assault vessels were on their tail.

During the minutes-long course correction, Sinclair watched the *Piedmont* and the two gunships enter lunar orbit unchallenged. Sinclair found herself wishing for an extra gunship to confront them or another salvo of ground missiles to launch.

All eight shuttles undocked from the *Piedmont* and made a rapid descent for the surface, heading toward the Aestuum Space Force Base. Sinclair imagined multiple platoons of marines inside the shuttles, heavily armed and outnumbering the Raiders and security officers under Colonel Dressler's command.

"Ground Base, this is *Wyoming*. Eight enemy shuttles heading toward you."

"Roger that, *Wyoming*," Dressler replied. "We're tracking them."

Antiair rail guns stationed around the base opened fire, a mixture of slugs and pellets. A few shuttles were hit, but all their trajectories remained unchanged. Minutes later, the shuttles landed, and small, dark figures spread in two groups, approaching the ground base from two directions.

"They're all yours, Dressler," Sinclair whispered. She turned her attention to the *Piedmont* and the two gunships floating close to it.

24

THE MAGNATE

NYSE: VC 245.02 (+200.45%)

Vanderheiden rushed into the PhotonicWay Command Center, his shoulders nearly hitting the edges of the automatic doors. "Are they still shooting up there?"

"Still fighting." Gonzalez turned away from his workstation. "Two US gunships knocked out three EU destroyers and both of their tankers."

"Shit..." Vanderheiden rested his hands on his hips and watched the hologram above them displaying Luna and all spacecraft orbiting it. "What's the latest on Luna Platform 4?"

"Platform 3 has a visual on it." Nicole swiveled around in her chair, showing her thick glasses and double chin. "Hull seems intact, but there is visible damage to its comm arrays."

"Put it on the screen."

A telescope feed came up as the main screen shifted sideways. The gray T-shaped photonic platform with the VC logo painted on the photonic beam was crystal clear in the black space. Debris floated around the damaged comm arrays. *An accident or a deliberate attack?*

"Keep monitoring."

"Yes, sir." Nicole swung back to her workstation.

"So, what does this mean?" Bakker crossed his arms, glancing at the other operators. "Are we at war?"

"If this isn't war," Gonzalez replied, "then I don't know what would be considered war."

"We need to shut down all inbound traffic to Luna," Nicole said. "Protect the platforms."

"No!" Bakker pointed at the status cards on the main screen. "We got over thirty spacecraft inbound for Luna. We can't shut it down while they are in transit."

"One platform is already offline." Nicole raised her voice. "We can't risk another one!"

Vanderheiden frowned, trying to ignore the sharp argument behind him. He stared at the PhotonicWay traffic map, stretching from Earth to Mars.

"We can handle the traffic with three platforms!"

"What if a second pla—"

"Enough!" Vanderheiden shouted, his vocal cords vibrating. "I will have silence for one minute!"

The command center went silent. Slowly, soft voices resumed speaking, operators on their headsets or taking their conversation to a corner.

Vanderheiden's eyes flickered everywhere from the main screen to the hologram, his mind spinning with the abundance of information. Being inside the command center was like getting front-row seats to the violent battle. The operators could track spacecraft movement and detect any rail-gun discharge or missile launch with the telescopes and long-range sensors on each photonic platform hovering above Luna.

He looked at the status of the four platforms orbiting Luna. *We must protect the PhotonicWay.* His eyes shifted over to the list of inbound traffic. *But we can't put the spacecraft in transit at risk.* It would be a disaster for Vanderheiden Corporation.

He ran both hands through his hair and pressed them against the back of his neck. *Only bad choices here.* He ignored the many eyes looking at him. Holding a deep breath until his lungs ached, his eyes snapped open. "We're shutting down the Luna sector."

"But, sir"—Bakker raised his hand—"that'll put inbound tra—"

"I know what it means," Vanderheiden replied. "War is breaking out up there. Tough choices will need to be made. I will make the calls here and bear the burden of its consequences." He pointed at Bakker. "Now, listen to me!"

"Yes, sir."

"Have all platforms raise their altitudes above the war zone. Need to keep them above the gunfight and all the debris fields. Give them a...twenty-kilometer buffer." He walked over to Nicole. "Start the altitude corrections now."

"Got it." Nicole arched her back and typed furiously on her keyboard.

Vanderheiden turned to Gonzalez at his workstation. "Put the command center under lockdown. Order all off-duty operators to return. Stock up on food, drinks, and sleeping bags. Get plenty of it."

"Will do, boss." Gonzalez nodded and shouted for his assistant.

"Call your friends and families!" Vanderheiden raised his voice for everyone in the command center to hear. "No one is leaving until this crisis has passed."

Vanderheiden looked to Bakker. "Now...the problem you've pointed out."

"The inbound traffic?" Bakker raised his head.

"Yes, redirect all of it away from Luna."

"Er..." Bakker glanced up at the main screen. "There are many spacecraft that'll need the Luna platforms to redirect. Raising the altitudes will limit how many we can decelerate or redirect." He shook his head. "We are going to miss some."

"Yes, I know." Vanderheiden clamped his jaw. *Sacrifices will be needed.* "I need you to take point on which spacecraft we decelerate at Luna, redirect to Earth, or give no beam power at all. Coordinate with Nicole."

Bakker's eyes widened. "Which ones do we sacrifice?"

"We must prioritize the manned spacecraft. Sacrifice the

unmanned if necessary."

"Holy shit..." Bakker turned his head to the traffic map on the hologram. "Our customers won't be happy."

"No, they will not."

The command center became the greatest flurry of people Vanderheiden had ever seen in the room. Gonzalez walked from workstation to workstation, talking urgently with each operator. Nicole pounded her fingers on the keyboard hard enough that Vanderheiden thought the keyboard was going to break.

Bakker hunched over his workstation, speaking into his headset, his dreadlocks swinging side to side. "Steve...Steve! Have you shut—" Bakker groaned and rested his hand on the desk. "Stop it! *Stop it!* Have you shut down all inbound traffic from Earth?" He cursed something under his breath. "Just do it!"

Vanderheiden pulled out his hand terminal. *I shouldn't look at it.* He glanced at the stock tracker and turned off his hand terminal as soon as he saw a red negative percentage next to the VC symbol. *I didn't need to see that.*

"Look!" Gonzalez stood up behind one workstation, pointing at the hologram. "EU destroyers are burning to intercept the *Decatur* and the *Rhode Island*."

Many operators lifted their heads. Vanderheiden found it intriguing to watch each military spacecraft's movement, deciphering why it chose that orbital speed and altitude, and compare the effectiveness of guided missiles against rail guns. It was a surprise seeing the rail guns knock out many destroyers.

The hologram beeped, showing engine burns detected from the *Decatur* and the *Rhode Island*. Their trajectory lines pulled away from the EU destroyers.

"Looks like the US doesn't want this fight," Gonzalez replied.

Another beep sounded, and the EU destroyers corrected their orbital paths, back on intercept course. The *Decatur* and the *Rhode Island* replied with another burn, taking them off the intercept line. The two units went back and forth on the course corrections, setting off beeps in the command center that lasted many minutes.

"Eventually one of them is going to run out of propellant," Vanderheiden said.

After the EU destroyers burned for a tenth time, the lack of a follow-up alert from the US side caught everyone's attention.

"Did they run out of propellant?" Gonzalez asked after two minutes of silence.

"Here come the destroyers..." Bakker said.

A dozen missile alerts sounded, and the fast-movers burned hard toward the spacecraft carrier. It took them a minute to reach the *Decatur*, and the command center groaned when the missiles intercepted. The *Decatur*'s APS knocked out half the missiles, but many smashed into the carrier and exploded, flinging debris everywhere.

"We are seeing people die," Nicole whispered.

The EU destroyers flew over its targets and committed a twenty-eight-second burn, putting them back on intercept with the *Decatur* on their next orbit around Luna.

Alerts flashed above the *Wyoming* and the *Oregon*, detecting their burns and trajectory lines intercepting with the destroyers.

"Oh...ho ho!" Gonzalez clapped his hands. "The Luna Fleet sprung a trap on the destroyers!"

"It's not funny, Gonzalez," Vanderheiden replied. "Spacemen are dying."

Gonzalez frowned and rubbed his nose.

"Intercept in sixty seconds," Bakker said. "Damn...this general is good."

"How many times is that, now?" Vanderheiden asked.

"The *Wyoming* and the *Oregon* hit them three times this morning."

"It's Fosvik, right?" Gonzalez raised his head.

"No, he got removed from his post. General Sinclair is commanding the fleet." Bakker looked over his shoulder at Vanderheiden. "You met her, right?"

"Yes." Vanderheiden kept his eyes locked on the US gunship dots curling around the moon. "And she won't go down easily. This will be a long fight."

"Platform 1 has visual on the destroyers." Nicole flashed the telescope feed on the main screen.

"Here come the gunships…" Gonzalez stood up.

The gunships zoomed past their enemies, and the two destroyers splattered into many pieces, tumbling in different directions. A collective groan echoed across the command center.

"Damn!" Gonzalez shouted. "Look at all that debris!"

The slugs from the rail guns were impossible to see, but Vanderheiden imagined hundreds of slugs smashing into the destroyers and ripping them apart.

"They're done, right?" Bakker looked around.

"No way they are still in the fight." Gonzalez shook his head.

"How are the gunships not damaged?" Bakker asked. "Aren't destroyers supposed to be the best combat spacecraft?"

"Nothing can stop the rail-gun slugs," Vanderheiden said.

"But what about the missiles?"

"APS. Active protection system," Vanderheiden answered. "A bunch of turrets loaded with pellets placed on the gunship, able to shoot down missiles."

"And that lets the gunship get close to the destroyers," Gonzalez added.

Bakker blew out air between his lips. "I wouldn't want to be on those ships."

The hologram beeped, zooming in on the *Piedmont* carrier and its two gunships shifting course. Heads turned again.

"Where are they going?" Gonzalez wondered.

Their engine burns ceased two minutes later.

"No vessel on intercept…" Gonzalez raised an eyebrow.

"Check the ground." Vanderheiden walked around the corner of a workstation.

"Oh no…" Gonzalez raised his arms.

"What's on the ground?" Vanderheiden asked hastily.

"Marius Hills."

"They are going to bomb it." Vanderheiden ground his teeth.

25

THE GENERAL

The exciting and violent opening hours of the battle, ending with a bombing run of Marius Hills, were followed by many hours of stillness on the operations deck. While the ground war got stuck in a battle of attrition, bullet holes littering the domes and bodies dropping on dusty surfaces, both fleets had avoided each other so far. After refueling the *Wyoming*, the propellant tanker was connected to the *Oregon*, refilling its tank.

Drifting in the dark-red-lit command deck, Sinclair's undergarment was soaked in salty perspiration, and her space suit's filter system could no longer flush out the sweaty odor. A persistent itch formed between her glutes. The space suit prevented her from scratching it, irritating her. She dreamed of repressurizing the hull, taking off her suit, and applying lotion to it, in a matter of minutes. But she couldn't. The Luna Fleet remained on combat condition, requiring the cabins to be depressurized and spacemen suited up. Except for the *Decatur*, due to insufficient space suits.

Captain Audubon remained strapped into his seat in deep sleep. Asleep, too, Captain Piazza's mouth was agape, saliva drooling down her chin. Her arms and legs twitched every minute or so. All the adrenaline built up from combat had worn off, knocking them out.

Lamar, on the other hand, refused to sleep and kept sipping energy shots through the bite valve inside his helmet. He was constantly scrolling through charts of each spacecraft.

Sinclair hadn't eaten or drank anything, but she was fully awake somehow. During the many hours of respite, she kept her eyes glued on the orbital hologram, watching for any signs of movement from the *Piedmont* and its two gunships orbiting above the moon's equator.

Rubbing her bottom, Sinclair tried to find the right angle to relieve the itch but didn't find it. Second Engineer Lamar pushed away from his console and coasted next to Sinclair, looking at the orbital hologram map. "Four destroyers and both tankers taken out on three attack runs and a missile barrage... Not bad, General."

Sinclair looked at the *Piedmont*'s red dot on the map, wondering what was going through Medvedev's head. Was this a minor setback for him? Or did he think his fate was sealed but continued fighting out of duty?

Eyeing the *Nevada* dot circling back toward the moon, Sinclair was determined to drag out this lull as long as possible until Barrows returned to low orbit. Medvedev likely knew the clock was ticking. What was he waiting for? She stopped scratching.

Lamar slurped on the bite valve, and Sinclair saw green fluid flow through the clear tube. The mess hall offered two smoothie flavors, veggie and fruity, to keep spacemen fed during extended periods inside space suits.

"You know what sounds good right now?" Sinclair asked.

Lamar stopped drinking. "What's that?"

"Sausage and rice." Sinclair's mouth started salivating at the thought of the juicy meat and moist rice.

"I never thought I would love eating cockroaches." The engineer shook his head.

Both of them chuckled, Sinclair baring her teeth and Lamar heaving.

"Oh boy..." Sinclair laughed again. "I remember so many spacemen in an uproar once they realized they had been eating cockroaches for weeks."

"Sergeant Espinoza was a sneaky bastard."

Sinclair slowly shifted her eyes toward Lamar. "Because I told him to."

"You did not!" Lamar's jaw dropped, and then he laughed, slapping his thigh. "You—"

Alerts from the orbital hologram blared. Sinclair's head jerked up to the screens. Audubon uncrossed his arms and shot forward, eyes refocusing on his monitors.

"Eh—uh...enemy gunships on hard burn!"

This was an unexpected move. If Sinclair was in Medevdev's position, she would've kept her units consolidated and hoped the ground assault succeeded, held out in low orbit until reinforcements from Earth or Mars arrived or an armistice was set. Did Medvedev know something she didn't? Did he have a trick up his sleeve?

For a few moments, the gunships' trajectory shifted across the orbital map as their engine burns continued. "Who is your target?" Sinclair whispered.

Audubon kicked Piazza's leg. She didn't reply, prompting him to follow up with a harder kick. Piazza shook awake and looked around, startled. Once she regained her senses, she pulled herself closer to her console. She noticed the drool on her chin and tried to wipe it off with her hand but smacked her visor instead.

"What are your orders, ma'am?" Audubon asked.

"Stand by." Sinclair watched the trajectory lines of the gunships move.

She glanced at their tanker's data screen and saw the *Oregon* refuel at seventy-four percent completion. The assault craft carrying the Raiders were still awaiting their refuel. She chewed her lip, anxious to get her battle group moving again.

For less than a minute, the orbital course shifted into an intercept path for Sinclair's battle group.

"We are ready..." Lamar muttered.

"Stand by!" Sinclair barked.

And then the gunships shifted out of intercept course as their engine burns continued. Sinclair's heart sank.

"They are going after the *Decatur*. Damn it...they can handle destroyers"—she sucked air through her teeth—"but not gunships."

A mixture of alarmed and panicked voices hammered Sinclair's ear, causing her head to ache.

"*Wyoming*, we need to intercept the gunships now. It's our—"

"They are on an intercept course to the *Decatur*!"

"*Wyoming*, this is *Decatur*. What are—"

"The *Piedmont* is exposed. Send us in!"

"Lock it up!" Sinclair yelled. She looked at her three officers and made a cutting motion across her neck. "Get the *Oregon* fueled up ASAP!"

After pulling up the data charts on every spacecraft in battle, she typed notes on her console, scrutinizing all possible scenarios. She reviewed the flight plans of her three gunships and plotted different paths, calculating the delta-v requirements of each. Trapping the EU gunships in a pincer attack, hitting them from multiple sides at once, was needed to bring the battle in orbit to a swift ending before the *Decatur* was knocked out.

Sinclair struggled with what to do about the *Piedmont*. The carrier, with General Medvedev likely on board, was exposed and defenseless. An opportunity Sinclair hated to waste. But handling the gunships was more urgent.

"Mm." Sinclair pondered all the battle scenarios spinning in her head.

"General, we need—"

Sinclair shot up a finger near Audubon's helmet, silencing him.

With all the possible flight plans for her gunships calculated, Sinclair cracked a knuckle. She looked at the video of the *Rhode Island*, the black hexagon-shaped destroyer escorting the *Decatur*. Frustrated at herself for leaving the carrier and destroyer exposed like that, Sinclair pressed her lips together.

Sinclair looked between the *Decatur* and the *Rhode Island*. She thought of the dozens of spacemen without space suits stuck inside the carrier and the danger they were about to face. She let out a sigh and looked at her drawn battle plan, an orbital map with many lines.

She tapped her screen and messaged the battle plan to all spacecraft in her fleet.

Sinclair issued orders immediately, not giving the officers a chance to digest the plan. "Tanker, cease refueling of the *Oregon* immediately. Refuel the assault craft to fifty-three percent. I repeat, five-three percentage. Over."

"Roger that, *Wyoming*. Shifting refueling operations to the assault craft."

"*Nevada*, execute a new flight plan. We will perform a pincer attack on the enemy gunships before their third flyby of the *Decatur*."

"Acknowledged, *Wyoming*. Initiating burns now. We'll be cutting it close here."

Audubon looked up from his console, eyebrows furrowed. "This is the plan you got?"

"It's the best we got, Captain." Sinclair tilted her head and switched channels. "*Oregon*, veer off now and follow your assigned flight plan. Make sure you and the *Nevada* are in sync."

"Roger that."

"This is going to be tight." Audubon turned to the other two. "No room for error here."

"Damn...you see what the *Rhode Island* is doing?" Piazza pointed at his screen, teeth bared slightly.

Ignoring the chatter, Sinclair contacted Fabian. "*Decatur*, put your ship in lockdown. Spread our spacemen to all compartments. Switch your weapon systems to fully autonomous. You've got a nasty salvo of slugs heading your way."

"Roger that, *Wyoming*." Fabian sighed. "Godspeed."

Once Lamar and Audubon saw what Piazza was pointing out, their eyes widened. Their heads turned to Sinclair as she connected with the destroyer.

"*Rhode Island*, you got two gunships heading your way. Make a hard burn following this flight plan and launch all your missiles against the gunships in the first flyby."

There was silence on the other end of the channel. The officers on deck stared at her, knowing the order Sinclair issued would put the

Rhode Island on a suicide run, heading directly toward the gunships. A destroyer might survive against one gunship and its deadly rail gun but not two.

"Do you understand your orders, *Rhode Island*?" Sinclair asked firmly.

Major Martinez, the *Rhode Island* commander, replied, "We acknowledge your orders and will carry them out, *Wyoming*."

Sinclair's throat tightened. "*Wyoming* out."

Sinclair switched to the assault craft. "Dragon Platoon! Warm up and prepare to board the *Piedmont*. The *Wyoming* will cover your approach."

Captain Vasquez came on the line. "Roger that, *Wyoming*. We are ready to spill blood."

Sinclair turned off her comm and let out a deep breath. She watched the *Oregon* veer off and ignite its main engine. Barrows's crew began their assigned engine burn, and the telemetry numbers changed for the *Nevada*. The tanker extended its propellant line to the first assault craft as Raiders inside the red-lit cabin prepped their weapons and gear.

Sinclair frowned when she saw no movement from the *Rhode Island*.

Audubon noticed Sinclair's glower. "General...give them a moment."

"We don't have a moment!" she snapped. "The enemy gunships are on hard burn to the *Decatur*. We need to disrupt them. The *Decatur* won't survive more than two attack runs."

"General, how would you feel if General Garrett ordered you on a suicide run?"

Sinclair was annoyed. She imagined herself hesitating, refusing to immediately accept the order until she understood its justification. She'd scroll through the orbital charts, play with the velocity and altitude, and scrutinize the overall battle plan until she found an alternative acceptable to Garrett and—

And she understood Audubon.

Looking at the *Rhode Island* through the *Decatur*'s telescope,

Sinclair held her tongue and hovered her finger over the comm button. She glanced at the gunship icons, less than two hours from intercepting the *Decatur*. She chose to spare them a moment.

When her mental clock ran out, Sinclair pressed the comm button. On the queue, the *Rhode Island* blew its maneuvering thrusters, turning away from the *Decatur*, and ignited its engine.

"Happy hunting, *Rhode Island*," Audubon said.

"Thank you, *Wyoming*," Major Martinez said. "We'll give them a surprise they won't forget."

When the tanker disconnected its propellant line from the second assault craft, the *Wyoming* and the assault craft burned their engines for less than a minute, slightly altering their course to intercept the *Piedmont*. Sinclair ignored the engine burn, watching the *Rhode Island* on the orbital hologram and its missile-targeting camera.

"Missiles armed and ready to launch," Major Martinez spoke. The vessel approached the end of its slingshot approach, about to find itself in front of the enemy gunships.

The gunships emerged over Luna's rough horizon, and its port sides were visible on the *Rhode Island*'s targeting camera.

"Targets locked and...missiles away."

Each missile slid out of its cell on the destroyer's front side in a successive manner and ignited its engine, temporarily blinding the cameras.

"One minute to impact."

The two enemy gunships turned on their short axis, pointing their rail guns at the *Rhode Island* and its incoming missile barrage. Multiple flashes of light from the rail-gun muzzles broke out like fireworks. Sinclair cringed, thinking of the slugs hurdling toward the *Rhode Island*.

A few slugs hit the missiles, causing them to spin or jerk away from the barrage. Seconds later, the slugs ripped through the *Rhode Island* in multiple places, knocking out cameras and cutting off the destroyer's connection with the *Wyoming*.

Through the *Decatur*'s telescope, Sinclair watched the unrecognizable destroyer tumble downward in a violent, uncontrolled spin. The engine nozzles alternated between flickering and firing abnormal plumes. The back side of the tumbling destroyer ballooned twice its size and broke apart, sending pivots, engine nozzles, nuclear rods, armor panels, and bloodied space suits in all directions.

The missile barrage approached the enemy gunships, and their active protection systems fired hundreds of pellets, breaking the missiles to pieces. The mass cluster of debris flew past the gunships.

Sinclair could see hints of damage on the gunships, but she grimaced as the gunship spun their rail guns back toward the *Decatur*. Their gray outlines got bigger and clearer as they got closer to the carrier.

Behind each helmet visor, every face on the operations deck grew somber, staring at the *Rhode Island*'s blacked-out signal. The status card of the *Rhode Island* switched from red to black. Sinclair didn't feel any sorrow choking her throat. She could only focus on the enemy gunships.

The EU gunships' fireworks started again and lasted much longer. The exterior cameras of the *Decatur* shuddered, slugs hitting the central chassis section between the two rings. The gunships flew underneath the carrier in the blink of an eye, and the slugs ripped up the engineering module from the other side.

The broadside ceased, and the two gunships shrunk back into gray dots in the distance. Sinclair looked closely at both sections, which appeared grated but remained structurally intact. It could take another attack run or two for the carrier to be broken apart.

Sinclair felt her lungs burning and let out a gasp, not realizing she'd been holding her breath for the entire attack run.

"Status report, *Decatur*?" Sinclair asked.

"Multiple depressurizations near the rings. Hatches are holding. Reactor is stable so far. Engineers are suited up and currently assessing the damage. Over."

"Roger that, *Decatur*. Brace for second attack run. We will intercept the gunships before their third attack run. Good luck."

Sinclair turned her attention back to the *Piedmont*, seeing it grow bigger. "Raiders! Prepare for boarding."

The *Piedmont* fired its engines to full blast. Several kilometers out and approaching fast, the two assault craft veered away from the *Wyoming*, spun around, and fired a retro-burn, decelerating.

The *Wyoming* didn't decelerate, though. Sinclair could only afford one flyby of the *Piedmont* before she had to chase down the enemy gunships. Lieutenant Colonel Fabian and the *Decatur* didn't have much time.

Sinclair watched the *Piedmont* appear in the rail-gun camera. The EU carrier had a similar design to the *Decatur*, but the octagon-shaped modules were slightly bigger and painted a darker shade of gray.

"Weapons, knock out the engines."

Piazza tapped her console, and the rail gun rattled with a long burst. The slugs ripped off all five engine nozzles, splintering them into pieces, and the carrier stopped accelerating. The engines coughed out ugly plumes before shutting down.

"Dragon Platoon, the *Piedmont* is yours. Hit them fast. Hit them heavy." Sinclair clenched her fist to emphasize her point. "When they surrender, you *will* accept their surrender. Do not shed more blood than needed. Over."

"Roger that, *Wyoming*." Captain Vasquez hand-signaled for his platoon to get ready for breaching.

A hundred meters out, the assault craft shut off their engines. The turrets of the *Piedmont* opened fire, shooting pellets at the smaller vessels, leave minor marks on the hexagonal-shaped armored hulls and scrapping its black paint off.

Sinclair knew she could've destroyed the *Piedmont* in a few attack runs, but that would've put the *Nevada* and the *Oregon* at greater risk against the two enemy gunships.

The Raiders unstrapped from their seats, unracked their assault rifles, and huddled around the exit hatches on both sides of the spacecraft. Maneuvering thrusters fired, and the assault craft approached their target at a quickened pace, being sandblasted with pellets.

"Knock out the turrets!" Vasquez ordered.

A assault craft spun a quarter of a full rotation, aimed their mounted rail guns at the carrier, and fired slugs, knocking out the turrets.

The craft approached the front and rear of the carrier separately. Just when the vessels seemed about to crash into the hull, their front thrusters fired, bringing them to a standstill relative to the carrier. The surface of Luna still spun beneath them. On the queue, the assault craft' breaching mechanisms extended out and latched onto the hull of the *Piedmont* with a magnetic lock.

"Prepare for breach!" Vasquez shouted.

The breaching mechanism fired explosives into the hull, creating a circular hole big enough for one Raider at a time to float through. An immense amount of pressure roared out of the blown holes, deflected outward by the breaching mechanism.

Once the jettisoning slowed down to a whistle, Vasquez said, "Breaching! Breaching! Breaching!" The Raiders funneled through the holes rapidly and sealed them to regain control of the pressure inside the carrier.

The Raiders moved through the narrow corridors quickly, firing stun grenades into small rooms, cracking EU spacemen with gunshot wounds. A fire team traversed the exterior of the carrier, firing armor-piercing bullets into the hull. Sinclair switched her screens back to the *Decatur* and her two gunships.

"Incoming attack on the *Decatur*," Audubon reported. "ETA six minutes."

Even if her gunships burned all their propellant to change their orbital angle, it still wouldn't be enough for them to intercept the enemy gunships before their second attack. One orbit around Luna, and they would miss the gunships by a few hundred kilometers. Another orbit, a thousand kilometers. Orbital mechanics were stubborn and unforgiving. Current orbital paths finally had Sinclair's planned pincer attack falling on the two gunships just before its third flyby of Decatur.

"Bracing for impact. They are—" Fabian's voice was cut off.

The gunships appeared on the *Decatur*'s scopes for the second time, and connection was lost. Sinclair feared the gunships landed their shots too well.

"Does anyone have eyes on the *Decatur*?" Sinclair scrolled through the data.

"*Wyoming*, this is *Nevada*. We have a visual. It's still intact, but massive damage is visible. Multiple hulls compromised, and pressurized air venting in numerous places."

Sinclair cursed to herself. She wondered how many spacemen inside the carrier could've been saved from the depressurization if SPACECOM had supplied enough space suits.

Sinclair spoke through her teeth. "Captain Audubon, how is our timing with the pincer attack?"

"The *Wyoming* and the *Oregon* look good. But"—Audubon shook his head, letting out a deep breath—"we need another burn from the *Nevada* if all three of us are to hit at the same time."

"This is the *Nevada*," Barrows said. "We are nearly bingo on propellant. We can't do another burn."

Sinclair tightened her lips, tapping her armrest. Burning all of its propellant risked leaving the *Nevada* adrift in orbit around the moon, unable to avoid attacks from the Fifth Fleet.

"*Nevada*, either we make the pincer attack work or the gunships are going to destroy the *Decatur*. Execute the burn now."

"Godda—" Barrows paused. "Roger that, *Wyoming*. Performing burn now."

After the *Nevada* burned the last of its propellant, Audubon nodded with nervousness. "Looking good, *Nevada*." He turned to Sinclair. "We are good to go."

"Acknowledged, Navigations. All gunships, maintain current course. Do not deviate without my authorization."

"Roger that," Cavalieri and Barrows replied.

Entering the dark side, the moon blocking the sun, Sinclair saw to her left the *Nevada* flying toward her gunship at an angle.

"Prepare for course correction burn." Audubon tapped his console.

The nuclear-thermal engines fired, and Sinclair felt the g-force push her to the left side of her seat as the gunship steered to the right, allowing it to merge with the *Nevada* and fly in formation, ready to hit the EU gunships at their port side.

"Happy for you to join the party, *Nevada*." Sinclair smiled as the dark outlines of the *Nevada* became visible.

"Let's finish this, *Wyoming*," Barrows said.

"All systems nominal." Lamar scrolled through multiple data charts with his finger.

Sinclair popped a knuckle and winced at the unexpected sharp pain. "Status report, *Oregon*?"

"EU gunships in sight. Commencing fire in three minutes, nineteen seconds."

"EU gunships intercept the *Decatur*. ETA four minutes, thirty-five seconds," Audubon indicated.

"Four minutes from our targets." Piazza tightened her straps, licking her chapped lips.

The *Oregon* approached the EU gunships from behind, at a similar arc, so its firing window on the gunships was significantly longer than the *Nevada*'s and the *Wyoming*'s. Sinclair couldn't see the gunships from her scope when Cavalieri announced on the channel: "Opening fire."

The *Oregon*'s camera blurred from the rail gun's juddering.

After the half-a-minute-long barrage, Cavalieri reported, "Targets are spinning around, aiming at us." The *Oregon* sustained its salvo.

Sinclair was glad to have given the *Decatur* a reprieve. But now the *Oregon* was in danger. "Countdown?"

"Forty-five seconds!" Piazza replied.

EU gunships were visible on the scopes and firing slugs at the *Oregon*. "Commence fire now!"

"But—ma'am, I don't have the targeting set—"

Alerts swarmed the *Oregon*'s status card. "We've sustained damage. Continuing fire!"

Sinclair swirled her head. "Damn it, Lieutenant! Adjust it now and fire!"

Piazza tapped her console with jittery fingers, lips wet and chapped. "Targeting adjusted. Opening fire!"

Many rounds of pulsation gripped the cabin. Sinclair's jaw muscles were sore from clenching so her teeth wouldn't chatter. "*Nevada*, open fire!"

Barrows didn't reply, but the *Nevada* acknowledged by firing.

Their slugs started chipping away pieces of the gunship. The EU gunships stopped firing and turned again.

"Oh! Uh...General!" Audubon's eyes widened. "They are turning away from the *Oregon* and toward us!"

Sinclair saw it as Audubon spoke. The cone-shaped outlines of the EU gunships morphed into circles. They were aiming at the *Wyoming* and the *Nevada* now. Sparks lit up the center of the gunships.

"Incoming!"

"Keep firing!" Sinclair pointed at Piazza.

Everything happened too fast for Sinclair to process. It started with a few slugs slamming into the *Nevada*, but the shooting didn't stop. Watching debris fly away from all the gunships, it was as if a gigantic boulder slammed into her side, blowing air out of her lungs and knocking her head against the headrest. Her vision went blurry. But she heard her heavy panting and smelled her sour breath.

She tried to raise her arm but winced at a sharp pain in her left shoulder. She caressed her space suit with her other arm, checking for damage.

"Status report?" She coughed, scanning the blurry figures on the operations deck. Lamar's arms were moving swiftly across his console, and his voice came through.

"Half of our heat radiators are knocked out." Lamar's tone was urgent. "Shutting nonessential systems!"

Sinclair gripped her armrest and rubbed her dislocated shoulder. She noticed it was too quiet. And too soft. The rail gun had stopped firing. She turned her head to the fuzzy body on her left side.

"Piazza! Resume fire!"

The weapons officer didn't reply.

"*Piazza?*"

Sinclair blinked and shook her head, her eyesight less blurry each time. Piazza's helmet was cracked, with a mass of red flesh underneath the visor. Her right arm was missing, droplets of blood floating out of the ripped arm sleeve.

"Transferring Weapons to— Ah *fuck*!" Sinclair yelped, piercing pain gripping her shoulder as she shot both of her arms up to her console to restart the rail gun.

"Our heat regulators are disabled, General!" Lamar said. "We can't sustain many of rounds of—"

"Override them!"

Sinclair eyeballed the EU gunships. The *Wyoming* had just flown over them, and the opposing gunships were spinning around to fire at the *Wyoming* and the *Nevada*. Sinclair's battle group was still inside their fire window. Her blurry eyesight prevented her from reading the data text, but she tapped the screens and pressed the execute button, hoping she'd selected the correct numbers.

The maneuvering thrusters coughed and groaned as the gunship spun around to aim the rail gun at the receding target. Sinclair selected the closest gunship on her screen and jabbed the fire button. In response, the rail gun throbbed and Sinclair's teeth clattered.

The heat regulators announced it was shutting down the rail gun to prevent overheating.

"Override!" Sinclair shouted.

The operations deck continued vibrating. The spacecraft tried to shut down the rail gun again.

"Override!" Saliva splatted against the visor inside her helmet.

Sinclair looked closely at her target. Each time she blinked, the damage on the EU gunship seemed to get worse. First blink, a nasty hole was punctured in the center. Second, debris jettisoned out of the gunship's side. Third, an explosion crippled the gunship's engine section, breaking the spacecraft into two parts.

Cavalieri whopped. "One gunship down!" The *Oregon*'s black blur zoomed underneath the two EU gunships, firing slugs into the second gunship, chipping it at the corners.

"General, we can't go on much longer!" Lamar pleaded.

Sinclair watched the second gunship shrinking rapidly on the targeting camera as they orbited away from it. Half her eyesight turned dark red, and it stung her eye. She blinked, noticing a few droplets of blood floating inside her helmet.

"Ceasing fire," Sinclair whispered, shutting down the rail gun. Sinclair looked at Piazza's bloodied body and sighed.

* * *

The last EU gunship, broken but active, seemed content to keep its distance from the Luna Fleet, performing small burns periodically to avoid crossing paths with the US gunships. Cavalieri had raised the *Oregon*'s altitude to slow down her velocity so she could circle behind the enemy gunship and trail it. Sinclair ordered her to maintain a safe distance and monitor it.

Sinclair got on the channel with the ground forces. "Ground Base, come in."

A few seconds later, Dressler's distinct hoarse voice came through. "Dressler here."

"Low orbit secured." Sinclair licked a blob of blood that landed on her lip. "What's the situation on the ground?"

"Enemies have breached—Corporal! Grab that box of ammo and give it to Delta Squad!" There was a pause. "*Wyoming*, they've breached the west side and are funneling in their reserves. We are holding but are going to run out of ammunition before we run out of targets."

"Do you need support?" Sinclair glanced at Lamar, who shook his head.

"I've put together a squad, ready for a flanking attack, but hostiles have secured positions along the ridgeline. We can't move without being exposed. Requesting orbital bombardment on the ridgeline."

"Roger that, Aestuum. Stand by." Sinclair muted herself and turned to Audubon. "Put us in a stable orbit at the lowest altitude possible. We need multiple flyovers above the ground base."

"Roger that." Audubon was slow with his reply, pulling his eyesight away from Piazza's bloodied body. He typed on the console and spoke with the *Nevada* in a flat tone. The *Wyoming* extended its propellant line to the *Nevada* for a quick refill.

Sinclair gave the second engineer a side glance. "What's the problem, Lamar?"

"As long as our heat regulators are down, rail gun is limited."

"What is it going to take to fix it?"

Lamar paused. "Not short enough for us to regain full combat capabilities."

"How long?" Sinclair asked sharply. She switched the rail gun's caliber from armor-piercing to explosive slugs.

"The heat radiators need to be replaced, and the replacement stockpile is down at Aestuum. Once I get a shuttle and crew working on it...two days."

"That's too long. Make something work, Second Engineer." Sinclair lifted her head. "ETA for our flyover of Aestuum?"

"Ninety-three minutes, ma'am." Audubon was a little quicker with his reply.

Sinclair turned to Lamar. "You got ninety minutes to fix the heat regulators."

Lamar sighed heavily. "General, that's asking for—"

"Second Engineer, I will be conducting an orbital bombardment with the rail gun. Either you jury-rig the problem and we have no issues, or we have a catastrophic meltdown, damaging the rail gun. We need to close out this fight." She emphasized the last words. "Your call."

"Yes, ma'am." Lamar spun around and glided out of the operations deck.

Ten minutes before flying over Aestuum, Sinclair watched the rocky hills of Luna's dark side rotate underneath her, slowly morphing into the smooth plains of Mare Tranquillitatis—just west of the mare was the Aestuum Space Force Base.

The weapons station was empty, except for smeared blood on the headrest, after Sinclair helped Audubon remove Piazza's body.

Audubon lost his concentration frequently, and Sinclair shook his shoulder softly to make him regain focus. It was obvious he'd developed feelings for the deceased officer.

The *Wyoming* and the *Nevada* spun and pointed their rail-gun muzzles down to the surface. Lamar glided onto the operations deck and strapped himself in.

"We good to go?" Sinclair asked.

Lamar shook his head. "Let's just hope the rail gun can operate beyond its engineering specifications."

"Copy."

Less than eight minutes until they flew over the ground base, and the gunship's automated systems were in full control for the upcoming orbital bombardment, Sinclair watched the *Oregon* icon on the orbital map, on the tail of the last EU gunship.

The web pattern of the Aestuum Space Force Base came up on the thermal scope. Miniature orange figures swarmed a corner of the crater, moving underneath a hail of gunfire and surrounded by jagged craters created by explosives. There were many orange figures motionless near the domes. A kilometer south of them, Sinclair saw orange spots lined up along a ridgeline. The orange figures were lined up in parallel with the gunships' orbital pattern, making this an easy bombing run.

Excitement tickled Sinclair's stomach. She knew the battle was at the beginning of its end.

"Ground Base, this is *Wyoming*. Incoming orbital bombardment. Danger close."

The rail guns opened fire once the crosshairs hovered over the ridgeline. The explosive slugs peppered the ridgeline, causing rocks to fall off the cliff and dust to rise above the ground, and many EU marines were blasted out of place, ripped to shreds by shrapnel.

"Ridgeline is clear, Aestuum. Carry out your flanking attack now."

"Roger that, *Wyoming*." An overlap of excited chatter nearly drained Dressler's voice. "Launching our counterattack now."

Each time the gunships flew over Aestuum, Dressler's units gained more ground and more hostiles fell back to their shuttles, abandoning heavy weapons and vehicles. The *Wyoming* and the *Nevada* destroyed the shuttles before the EU marines had a chance to board them.

"You got scores of marines stranded on the surface." Sinclair smiled. "See if you can give them warm beds and food in our brig."

"Roger that, *Wyoming*. We'll take care of them."

An unencrypted communication request came from the *Piedmont*, and Sinclair raised her eyebrow. Sinclair accepted the call, and Captain Vasquez's sweaty and stern face inside his combat helmet came on the screen.

"General Sinclair, *Piedmont* is secured. The Fifth Fleet's senior officers are in custody."

"Excellent work, Captain. Who is the fleet commander?"

Vasquez smirked. "See for yourself, General." He turned his head and pulled someone by the shoulder. An overweight man with pale skin and black hair came to the center of the screen. His goatee was thick and his hair was unruly.

"General Medvedev," Sinclair said.

"General Sinclair." He spoke with a hint of resignation.

"General Medvedev, order your fleet to stand down immediately and maintain their current positions. All spacemen will be spared, fed, and sheltered on Luna. Do you accept these terms?"

Medvedev hesitated, giving a side glance, and Sinclair saw Vasquez squeeze the general's shoulder.

Medvedev turned to the other side and nodded at someone off-screen. "We accept your terms of surrender. Our lives are in your hands. I hope you are an officer of your word."

Vasquez loosened his grip.

Sinclair nodded. "Then don't give me a reason—"

"This is *Oregon*!" Cavalieri came on the channel with an urgent tone. "The enemy gunship has opened fire. Projectiles heading toward a photonic platform."

Medvedev glanced to the side again, listening to something. His eyes widened, and he glanced nervously at Sinclair.

Sinclair turned to the *Piedmont*. "General Medvedev! Order your gunship to stand down! *Now!*"

Medvedev's goatee twitched nervously as he tried to find his next words. "General Sinclair, I've lost contact with the *Klaipeda*. They are declining our connection requests." He leaned close to the monitor. "They have gone rogue."

"Bullshit! Tell them to stand down!"

"General! I'm telling the truth!" The excess skin under his goatee shook. "It is a rogue gunship."

Sinclair clenched her fist. Audubon took control of a telescope and pointed it at the photonic platform. By the time an image was generated, the platform was torn apart, slug holes covering the entire length of it. A nuclear reactor broke apart and drifted away from the platform. Sinclair bared her teeth with a wince. That was two photonic platforms hit by enemy fire.

"Enemy gunship now changing its altitude. It's—it's descending rapidly."

"System failures?" Sinclair asked.

"Negative," Cavalieri replied. "All engines firing full blast."

"The velocity and angle of this descent is too strong and steep," Barrows said. "It's a suicide plunge!"

"What's the target?" Sinclair shouted.

"The Luna Space Elevator's surface anchor."

An engine burn to exit a descent required a significant amount of propellant, and the *Oregon* was short of it. It wouldn't be able to drop quickly, hit the EU gunship, and return to stable orbit without emptying its tank.

"General Medvedev..." Vasquez pulled out his handgun and pressed the barrel against Medvedev's head. "If the gunship doesn't—"

"Stand down, Captain!" Sinclair shouted.

"But, ma'am, that gunship is—"

"Stand down!"

Vasquez whispered something and pulled his handgun away from Medvedev's head.

"This is *Oregon*. Performing engine burn to intercept the *Klaipeda*. Be advised: we are entering a decaying orbital pattern."

Sinclair ignored Cavalieri, trying to get in contact with Vanderheiden and warn him of the incoming orbital bombardment on his space elevator.

"General..." Lamar whispered.

A connection error popped up, and Sinclair slammed her fist down. "Audubon! Get me connected to VC!"

"General!" Lamar shouted.

Sinclair looked at him and saw him staring at the orbital hologram, jaw slack and blood receding from his face. She looked at the orbital hologram and immediately saw it.

"No...no..." She scrambled back on channel with the *Oregon*. "Cavalieri! Pull up. You don't have the propellant to return to stable orbit. Pull up!"

"That's a negative, *Wyoming*. We've already burned our propellant. We'll take out the *Klaipeda*."

"Chief Cavalieri. Pull up!" Sinclair gripped her console hard.

"General Sinclair...we will defend Luna. We won't let them touch the space elevator. You saw Vanderheiden's speech. It's the future of Luna."

The *Oregon*'s rail gun locked on the *Klaipeda* and fired several rounds. The EU gunship went adrift and slammed into the surface, sending debris everywhere.

"*Klaipeda* down."

Watching the gunship's altitude drop more rapidly, Sinclair felt her insides hollow out. She desperately wanted to reach out and pull the *Oregon* back up.

Cavalieri spoke again. "General Sinclair. It was an honor serving under you. We will never forget it. Abborn and Maxwell...give them hell. All the people that died today...don't let any of those lives go to waste. Keep Luna safe."

The lunar surface came up fast on the *Oregon*'s camera, craters and hills visible. Sinclair's chin tremored, her eyesight losing focus on the monitor. Tears began to form in her eyes, and Sinclair couldn't wipe them off with her helmet on.

"I promise..." Sinclair spoke softly.

The gray surface came up against the rail-gun camera fast and blacked out. The channel and camera feeds cut out. The *Oregon* crashed into the surface, flinging debris everywhere and leaving scratch marks across the regolith dirt, within sight of the kilometer-tall surface anchor.

"She's gone..." Barrows whispered.

26

THE MAGNATE

NYSE: VC 202.46 (-17.37%)

Vanderheiden froze with his mouth agape, never having seen so many red cards on the main screen in the PhotonicWay Command Center. *The Luna sector is falling apart.* He stood behind Gonzalez, who spoke incessantly into his headset and pointed at an operator across the command center frequently. Once the EU gunship destroyed Luna Platform 2, the situation inside the command center went from serious to a calamity.

Vanderheiden was still trying to wrap his mind around the fact that the employees on board were likely dead. *It was doing just fine, and suddenly...gone.* The sound of operators gasping when the platform was destroyed still rung in his ears.

A tall woman ran around Bakker's workstation too quickly and slammed into Vanderheiden's shoulder. He halted his fall by bracing his arm on the workstation behind him.

"Oh, I'm so—" She extended her arms, panting.

"Slow down!" Vanderheiden snapped at her.

The woman took a step back.

He took a breath. "Just go..." He stepped aside for her.

She walked by slowly without looking at him, mouth open.

Gonzalez spun around and slipped his headset off. "Sir, the *Blue Wake* is approaching too fast. We can't divert it to Earth. We have to decelerate it at Luna. With our current capacity, we are not going to catch all inbound spacecraft to Luna."

Vanderheiden noticed a hint of white powder under Gonzalez's nose and gestured for him to rub it off. *You said you were sober.* Gonzalez pressed a finger to his nostril, looked at the tip of his finger, and his eyes widened. He quickly rubbed the rest of the white powder off with his hand and put his headset back on.

Vanderheiden glanced up at the Luna hologram, with four photonic platforms orbiting it. Luna Platform 2 was destroyed by that EU gunship, and Luna Platform 4 was offline due to minor damage from the opening hour of the battle. PhotonicWay was a highly complex and delicate operation, requiring platforms to be in the correct orbital positions and inbound spacecraft approaching on schedule and at the correct velocity and trajectory. The system was not suited for war.

Two platforms failing at Luna unleashed a large ripple effect across the entire PhotonicWay. Now, many Luna-bound spacecraft were at risk of not receiving power to decelerate, in jeopardy of flinging off into space with no hope of return. Other spacecraft were being diverted to Earth, straining the capacity of the eight-platform photonic system hovering in medium earth orbit.

"All manned spacecraft must be caught. All unmanned vessels get low priority." Vanderheiden pointed at the spacecraft cards. "If it requires sacrificing an unmanned vessel and letting it drift into deep space, do it. We will send the bill to the government. This is their mess."

Vanderheiden ignored an incoming call on his hand terminal.

"We've already done that." Gonzalez shrugged. "We still don't have a free slot in the Luna sector to decelerate it."

"Then find more spacecraft to divert!" His hand terminal beeped persistently.

Gonzalez nodded and turned back to his workstation, relaying orders to his operators. Vanderheiden pressed his fingers into his eyeballs to relieve a headache pressing against his skull, trying to ignore the incoming call. He answered it after a sharp sigh.

"What do you need, Cooper?"

"Vanderheiden, have you seen the latest stock numbers? Our stock is dropping...seventeen percent and falling!"

"Look, Cooper, we have a serious situation at the command center we're working on. The battle over Luna disru—"

"We need to implement the cost-cutting measures Arellano scoped out and pause the space elevator project. We need to stabilize this stock price now."

Vanderheiden curled his upper lip. "Cooper! The stock will have to wait. We have more pressing matters to deal with here."

"Vanderheiden! You need to fix this! If we—"

Jabbing his finger at the hand terminal, he ended the call. "Damn him!" He looked at the cards flashing yellow and red.

Operators continued walking and jogging around the four rows of workstations, conversing in urgent voices. Gonzalez was running different scenarios with Bakker and Nicole, trying to find a way to decelerate the *Blue Wake*.

As the minutes rolled by, the number of red cards went down from twelve to six. The *Blue Wake* still flashed red. But the majority of the cards were yellow. *Better than a board full of reds.* Vanderheiden eyed Gonzalez and his team. *Keep working it.*

"Look, we have an abundance of slots in the Earth sector." Nicole hovered over Gonzalez's shoulder. "Easiest option is diverting as much traffic to Earth as we—"

"No!" Gonzalez interrupted. "That's just leaving us with more problems later in the week. We must maximize the capacity of—"

A screeching whine from everyone's hand terminal stole attention away from the conversation. People pulled out their devices and read the alert.

"Oh my God."

"Goddamn..."

"Oh shit!"

Vanderheiden read the notification, and his heart skipped a few beats.

> MISSILE THREAT INBOUND TO HOUSTON. SEEK IMMEDIATE SHELTER. THIS IS NOT A DRILL.

Vanderheiden looked out the large glass windows. *How many missiles? Where are the targets?* His mind ran through several locations of importance. Government facilities, military bases, spaceports, and nuclear power plants. When he thought of the VC headquarters, his spinal cord shivered. *We are a vital part of the space economy.*

"We need to go!" A man bolted from his chair and ran. Another jogged to the door, followed by a third. It cascaded into a dozen people scrambling to leave, tripping over each other. Many other employees stood frozen, watching as it nearly turned into a stampede. Vanderheiden bared his teeth, furious at the chaos.

"Stop!" he yelled. "Calm down!"

With the obnoxious tone still blaring from hand terminals, the panic came to a standstill and all heads turned to him. He drew in a deep inhale through his nose, then looked around the command center at each employee and up at the cards flashing red.

"I'm staying here," he announced to the command center. "If you choose to leave, I will not hold it against you. If you want to leave, line up in an orderly fashion and walk out...*slowly*. This is like a fire drill."

People glanced at each other and took a few steps toward the exit.

"I'm not leaving." Gonzalez didn't look up from his workstation.

A few employees continued walking out, but many others headed back to their workstations, silencing their hand terminals.

"I'll take my chances," Nicole whispered.

Bakker pointed at the main screen. "They need our help."

Vanderheiden sat next to Gonzalez. "What's going on?"

"Okay, we got a spacecraft we can divert. *Spacecraft 56*."

"A government vessel. What are you waiting for? Do it!"

Nicole popped over Gonzalez's workstation, holding her headset away from her ear. "Vanderheiden. I got Mr. Blackburn on the line." She winced as if someone were yelling into her ear. "He is... demanding to know why his spacecraft is being rerouted. He wants to speak with you."

"Which spacecraft is his?"

"It is...the *Wrath of Carbon*."

"Is it manned?"

"No, sir."

Vanderheiden waved her off. "No, I won't take his call."

Eyes wide, she inhaled and put her headset back on. "Mr. Blackburn? Yes, Mr. Vanderheiden is unavailable right now. Unfortunately..." Her voice trailed off as she walked away.

Gonzalez leaned in and whispered, "What about *Freighter 4*? It's on a supply run to—"

"I know what it is for," Vanderheiden hissed. "Bring it to Luna if you can. The moon has much rebuilding to do after this battle. They are going to need the space elevator."

"So, I'll have to reroute another passenger vessel." Gonzalez pointed at a small icon on his screen.

"Do it."

Bakker came over to Gonzalez and Vanderheiden. "We got a problem..."

Vanderheiden scoffed. "Just spit it out."

"*Spacecraft 56* is refusing our commands, saying they can't be diverted per federal laws."

"Well...what about the *Blue Wake*?"

"Both vessels are approaching the same platform. One has to veer off."

Vanderheiden stood up from the chair. "Then make *Spacecraft 56* veer off. Put them in a holding pattern around Earth, and we'll loop them back to the moon in a few days."

"I'll try again."

Vanderheiden's hand terminal beeped with a call, and he pulled up the caller ID.

"Gabriella," Vanderheiden answered, "if this is about Cooper..."

"Vanderheiden...I've been monitoring the command center. I know you have your hands full, so give me a minute. You need to hear what I have to say."

Anytime Gabriella put her foot down and demanded a word, Vanderheiden knew it was important. "Okay."

"Our stock is dropping. Shugart's stock is rising because the war is going to boost its defense business. They are going to attempt another hostile takeover. Cooper is already whispering with other shareholders and is going to use this opportunity to impose more control over the company. I'm making my rounds with several of them to push back against Cooper. I need you to get things straightened inside our company before Cooper gains more support on the board. Good luck at the command center."

Gabriella ended the call. Vanderheiden put the hand terminal down and ground his teeth, trying to fight off the sharp pain inside his skull that seemed to be getting worse by the minute. *How much worse can things get?*

"Veer off!" Gonzalez yelled into his headset. "*Veer off!*"

Gonzalez's unnerving voice shook Vanderheiden from his thoughts. He looked up at the orbital map, showing *Spacecraft 56* still on approach to Luna Platform 1.

"They aren't acknowledging our commands, Gonzalez," Bakker said.

"Shut off that platform!" Gonzalez threw down his headset and ran around the workstation, thrusting his finger at the main screen. "Don't give *Spacecraft 56* any power! They are disobeying our commands!"

"We can't do that," Nicole replied. "We would have to override the platform's software."

Snarling, Gonzalez rested his hands on his hips and dropped his head. The platform fired its laser beam, sending power to the government vessel and starting its deceleration.

Vanderheiden saw the *Blue Wake* still continuing its approach, its dotted line going straight into the lunar surface. "Tell the *Blue Wake* to veer off!"

"It's too late," Gonzalez whispered, looking at the ground. "We already put them on orbital-insertion trajectory..."

Vanderheiden felt a cold flush. "So...how are we going to decelerate it?"

Gonzalez turned to him, face white and lips quivering. He tried to speak, but no words came out.

"Is there another platform that can beam it power?" Vanderheiden looked at the hologram.

Gonzalez spoke in fragments. "Not...w-with Platform 2 gone."

Vanderheiden's jaw dropped as he watched the *Blue Wake* speed toward the moon's surface. The command center went silent. Nicole whispered a prayer, and Bakker rubbed his face, dark bags under his eyes.

The *Blue Wake* icon disappeared when it touched the moon's circle. No one spoke for a minute. Vanderheiden's back neck muscles trembled more, and his fists clenched harder as the silence dragged on.

Gonzalez turned around and walked back to his station. "Continue your tasks, people. We have more spacecraft to take care of."

Vanderheiden looked up, seeing the *Spacecraft 56* hovering leisurely above Luna. He screamed, muscles and veins straining against the skin of his neck.

"I want to know *who* was in that government vessel!" He turned to Gonzalez, small bits of saliva flying out of his mouth. "Drag their asses over here! I don't care if it is a senator or an accountant."

His heartbeat pounded against the back of his eyes. He pressed his finger to Gonzalez's chest, who flinched at each word Vanderheiden roared. "*You* drag their asses down here and demand an explanation for disregarding our commands! PhotonicWay is ours, *not theirs*!"

With a deep frown and puffing, Vanderheiden swept his eyes across the command center, seeing faces frozen in shock. Vanderheiden's neck muscles loosened, and he relaxed his clenched fists. *Goddamn...*

He turned back to Gonzalez. "I'm sorry." Vanderheiden gripped his shoulder. "I shouldn't have yelled at you. You didn't deserve that." He turned to the rest of the large room and spoke louder, eyeing as many employees as he could. "None of you deserved that."

"I..." Vanderheiden pursed his lips and walked out of the command center. "I will take care of this." *I will make them pay.*

27

THE GENERAL

"Damn...how many survived that?" Second Engineer Lamar looked at the screen.

The *Decatur* looked like a meteoroid shower had hit it. Holes of all sizes covered the entire spacecraft carrier. A few modules appeared unscathed, but others seemed to have been pulled through a metal shredder. Liquid spewed out of the propellant tanks, and pieces of debris clouded the carrier, threatening the spacemen and droids conducting repairs.

"Fewer, if they don't get those rings spinning again and pressurized." Sinclair pointed at the rings.

Without gravity, wounds couldn't drain. Without air pressure, space suits prevented medics from treating the wounded. Sinclair hoped the casualty situation was manageable. But once she looked at the entire spacecraft carrier again, she doubted it.

"Months..." Lamar muttered. "Months of repair."

"Is the carrier totaled?" Sinclair asked.

Lamar tightened his lips.

Guilt clenched her stomach. Should she have done something different? Maybe pair the *Decatur* up with a gunship instead of a destroyer? That would've left the Luna Fleet with weaker offensive capabilities, prolonging the battle. Seeing the damage the *Decatur* had suffered zapped away all the glory Sinclair thought she would've felt after winning the battle. It was a strange and conflicting feeling.

Sinclair let out a breath, turned around in midair, and ordered Audubon: "Navigations, start docking procedure."

Audubon raised his arm to the controls. "Starting docking procedure."

Sinclair looked across the operations deck at Piazza's body, strapped to the hull. Sinclair looked away when she glimpsed Piazza's dead eyes behind her cracked and bloodied visor.

The *Wyoming* docked with the spacecraft carrier. Sinclair thought it was a miracle some of the docking ports were still operational.

"Captain Audubon, you have command of the *Wyoming*. Transfer casualties to the *Decatur*, restock on ammunition, refill our tank, and get the hull repaired. Understood?"

"Yes, ma'am." His face was gray and sullen.

Sinclair reached out, gripped his space suit, and squeezed hard enough to touch his shoulder. "We aren't out of this mess. Let's secure Luna first, and then we can mourn the fallen."

"Yes, ma'am." His voice was unchanged.

She gestured for Lamar to follow.

"General, shouldn't I stay here and oversee the repairs?"

"Negative. I have a different task in mind." Sinclair pushed herself off the wall toward the exit. "Follow me."

The two glided through the gray tunnel toward the exit hatch. Aside from a couple of holes punctured by slugs, the *Wyoming* was in decent shape. Engine and rail gun were still operational. Spacemen worked to seal holes and repair damaged instruments.

A spaceman welding a panel saw Sinclair and nodded. "General."

Another saluted her. "Ma'am."

Sinclair and Lamar exited the gunship, glided down the passageway, and came do the air lock on the *Decatur*. Neither side had pressure, so Lamar opened the hatch with ease.

Light fixtures flickered, exposing white walls smeared with blood. The red alarm flashed, making the crystalized droplets of blood floating around the compartment look like black beetles. Many wall panels flashed alerts.

Sinclair heard her breathing get heavier inside her helmet. She looked to her left and saw a spaceman, his body bending at unnatural angles and spinning. The young man's eyes were wide open, blood covering his face, hands light blue. Despite wearing his black uniform, a large, moist hole was visible in his lower torso.

Lamar drifted toward the body. He secured the young man to the hull, closed the private's eyes, and bent his head down for a moment.

The engineer turned around and nodded. Sinclair pulled a handle, propelling herself toward the front section of the spacecraft carrier, toward the command deck.

They reached the secondary medical bay. They approached the hatch, and Sinclair frowned at the wall panel, which showed no air pressure on the other side.

The hatch opened, unveiling a maelstrom of medics and wounded spacemen. Despite hearing nothing, the body language of the wounded produced phantom screams in Sinclair's mind.

Engineers worked furiously, welding thick panels over the holes in the hull. The doctor hovered over one engineer, pointing at the hole. The engineer turned around, shaking his hands. They must've been speaking on a separate comm channel.

"Doctor, status report?" Sinclair drifted toward him, trying not to bump into the medics.

Dr. Naish changed his comm channel and raised a finger. "One moment, ma'am."

Sinclair looked to her side and watched a medic shake a patient's shoulder. After no movement from the patient, he grabbed a resuscitation device and placed it around the torso of the patient. He pressed a few buttons, and the device pressed up and down on the wounded's chest, performing chest compressions. Watching each compression go down the patient's torso made Sinclair's chest feel tighter.

"General, the casualty situation is critical," Dr. Naish's voice blurted out in her ears. "More wounded are coming in than we can treat. No air pressure, so we can't treat many of the wounded. Access to the artificial rings is compromised, so we can't reach the primary medical bay. I *need* gravity and air pressure." He shook his head. "I don't know how many more casualties we'll come across once we gain access to the rings and the front section of the spacecraft carrier."

Sinclair struggled to reply, and her eyes drifted toward what was supposed to be an empty corner. Instead, body bags were stacked one on top of the another, strapped to the wall. She counted fourteen. All these spacemen had followed her command during the battle. They had followed Sinclair's decision to disobey Abborn's stand-down orders. Dozens of young lives, maybe over a hundred, lost under her command. The responsibility fell on her shoulders, and the weight got heavier every minute.

"Manage the situation as best as you can, Doctor." Sinclair grabbed a wall handle and sprung toward the next hatch.

Sinclair and Lamar reached the command deck. Legs floating upward, Lieutenant Colonel Fabian hovered over another spaceman's shoulders, looking at the consoles.

Sinclair tapped his foot. Fabian's pale and sweaty face looked back. He reoriented himself to face her. Sinclair saw that half of his right arm was missing. A sealed tourniquet covered the stump.

Sinclair stared at his arm for a few seconds. Fabian shrugged. "I haven't gone into shock yet. The painkillers are holding everything at bay."

"How did it happen?" Lamar drifted next to Sinclair.

"Last attack run, shrapnel slicked it off clean," Fabian said.

Sinclair blinked. "Give me a sitrep."

Fabian floated over to the command console and, for a split second, tried to catch the console to stop his glide with his missing arm before he quickly used his other arm. He powered up a hologram of the *Decatur*.

"The casualty rate is coming in at around forty percent." He glanced at his arm. "Including myself. We managed the first two attack runs well, but the third one set up a chain reaction of failures. Losing pressure in multiple compartments was when things got bad.

Engineering module is damaged, and nuclear reactor is barely below the red line."

Sinclair tightened her lips, frustrated many spacemen either lost or were going to lose their lives because of a space-suit shortage.

The lieutenant colonel pointed at the chassis near the two rings. "The central corridor here has been nearly destroyed, cutting off the connection with the rings. No power is getting through. Hence, the lack of rotation."

"Goddamn..." Lamar leaned closer to the center console. "How bad is it?"

"Come with me." Fabian rounded the center console and exited the command deck. Sinclair and Lamar on his tail, he moved down the corridor toward a closed hatch. Breathing heavily, Fabian hunched forward and gripped the hatch bar. He squinted his eyes and blinked like he was struggling to see.

"Fabian?" Sinclair asked.

Fabian's body jerked like he was surprised. He shook his helmet, glanced both ways, and tapped the wall panel. Sinclair and Lamar glanced at each other.

"That's how bad it is." Fabian pushed himself to the side when the hatch opened. "Those gunships were gunning for our rings."

The exterior hull was nearly gone, making the two large rings visible. Crushed metal, ripped cables, and pieces of foam floated around where a hull used to exist. No one was getting through without their space suits getting ripped by jagged edges. All that kept the front half of the ship connected to the back half were a few metal struts. Sinclair imagined taking a power tool, sawing off all the struts, and disconnecting the two sections in a matter of minutes, crippling her spacecraft carrier, leaving her fleet choking for supplies.

Sinclair nodded. "How long will it take to repair?"

"Weeks." Lamar shook his head. "Months."

Fabian signaled his agreement with a nod.

"Well, that leaves us with one other option." Sinclair pressed her tactical armband. "*Nevada*, this is *Wyoming*. Come in."

Lamar turned back to inspect the damaged hull.

Barrows's voice came online. "This is *Nevada*. I am reading you."

"Give me a sitrep."

"Refueling is complete. Orbital patrol has resumed. The enemy destroyers and gunship have shown zero flight changes."

"How are the wounded?"

"We've lost one." Barrows sighed. "The other three are hanging on, but they need medical attention soon."

Sinclair wished she had a shuttle to spare or a fully operational medical bay on board the *Decatur* to use. It felt cruel deciding who lived and who died with only brief hesitation or thought.

"Continue your patrol, *Nevada*. Situation on the *Decatur* remains critical."

"Acknowledged," Barrows said. "Any word on Cavalieri and the *Oregon*?"

It was like a wrecking ball slammed into Sinclair. Since the shooting stopped, she'd focused on assessing the casualty situation, repositioning the fleet to secure Luna, and kicking off recovery efforts. She hadn't taken the time to digest the fact that Cavalieri was dead, sacrificing herself to protect the Luna Space Elevator.

"No word on the *Oregon*," Sinclair said.

"Roger that, *Decatur*. Over and out." Barrows cut the connection.

"What's the only other option, General?" Lamar asked.

Sinclair locked eyes with the engineer. "The *Piedmont*."

* * *

"Ma'am, I advise you not to board the *Piedmont*." Dressler had a large bruise covering half his face, and his swollen jaw made his words sound hoarser. "You are taking a risk boarding the EU flagship. It could be rigged for sabotage."

Sitting inside the cramped interior of the transport shuttle, Sinclair's heart raced harder, watching the *Piedmont* get bigger on the telescope. The gray spacecraft carrier looked intact and functional, except for the two assault craft attached at awkward angles to both ends of the large spacecraft like giant leeches. Pieces of debris hovered around where the assault craft connected to the vessel. The flagship had a longer length than the *Decatur* but only one artificial gravity ring.

"Noted, Colonel. The *Decatur* is in critical condition, close to totaled. The *Piedmont* is our only opportunity to recover. If we get killed, we have capable officers to take over. Barrows, Cavalieri, and Fabian will carry—" She froze.

Dressler frowned after a moment. "Understood, ma'am."

Sinclair blinked, pushing Cavalieri out of her mind. "I want to speak with General Medvedev face-to-face and understand why that gunship didn't surrender. We need to assess the condition of their vessels. I'm not expecting reinforcements from Earth or Mars soon, and we are down to only two gunships. We need to replenish our fleet numbers."

Sinclair and Lamar sat in one row. Colonel Dressler and three Raiders sat in the row opposite of them, fitting into the small seats with their armored space suits and assault rifles. Two of them had bullet and shrapnel marks on their chest armor and helmets.

Sinclair found it strange that Dressler had joined the boarding party. He could've sent one of his captains and overseen recovery efforts from the ground base.

The soft bump signaled the shuttle docking with the *Piedmont*. Sinclair and Lamar unbuckled from their seats. Raiders lined up near the hatch, warming up their weapons.

After cycling the air, the Raiders raised their assault rifles at the hatch. The hatch opened, and two Raiders, armored space suits peppered with bullet holes and medical dressings, smiled back.

"Welcome aboard!" Captain Vasquez said.

Dressler floated through the hatch first, using his jetpack, and shook hands with the Raiders. "Outstanding job, men." He slapped both of their shoulders. "You fucked them up good."

Vasquez pointed at the other Raiders gliding through the docking hatch, eyeing their battle marks. "Looks like you guys got tickled pretty good."

"I was going to say it looked like you guys survived a catfight," a Raider said. "Who was the bitch?"

Vasquez pulled his head back, roaring with laughter.

After Vasquez's chuckling subsided, Dressler's face turned hard. "Who did we lose?"

Vasquez tightened his jaw muscles. "Russo, Kyle, Utterback, and Rojas."

"Damn..." a Raider said.

Sinclair floated through the hatch.

Vasquez went erect. "General."

"Excellent job securing the *Piedmont*." Sinclair looked up and down, inspecting the flagship's interior. There was less debris and no large holes from rail-gun slugs in the hulls. There were small bullet holes and fire marks from grenades and flash-bangs. Sinclair couldn't smell from inside her space suit, but she imagined the reek of gunfire. "Take us to the command deck."

"Yes, ma'am." Vasquez turned to the Raider next to him. "Take point, Sergeant."

Following the sergeant, everyone navigated through the modules. Raiders used their jetpacks to navigate easily, while Sinclair and the engineers grabbed handles to glide forward.

Bullet holes and blood smears decorated the walls. Sinclair could reconstruct how the gunfights had played out. She saw a few rooms covered in shrapnel marks and bloodied body parts, like the Raiders had tossed grenades to clear the room. Some passageways were spotless, and others were covered in bullet holes, showing where firefights occurred.

"How many enemy casualties?" Sinclair asked.

"We took down twenty tangos during the assault," Vasquez said.

"Where are the prisoners?"

"We confined all sixty-three prisoners to the mess hall and secured weapons in our assault craft."

Sinclair grabbed a bar and pulled herself forward to keep up with the sergeant. "Are the wounded receiving medical attention?"

Vasquez took a second to reply. "Negative, General."

"Have your team secure the medical bay and allow them to treat their wounded."

Dressler jumped in: "General, we need to keep the prisoners confined to the mess hall. We can't give them a chance to regroup and fight back."

Sinclair reached out for a wall with her hand and feet to stop her glide. She turned around to face Dressler. "They are prisoners of war. We will give them the medical treatment they are entitled to. Get it done."

Dressler stared at her with his cold eyes. The longer Dressler took to reply, the tighter Sinclair's jaw felt.

He blinked and turned to his Raiders. "Secure the medical bay."

Sinclair released her jaw, spun around, and pushed forward.

Approaching the command deck, the number of blood marks and bullet holes dwindled. Sinclair imagined the terrified spacemen had started surrendering in doves as the Raiders slashed through their defenses. At that point, Medvedev probably wished he'd kept a squad of marines on board, instead of committing all units to the Aestuum assault.

They went through an air lock and entered the pressurized command deck. A fire team occupied the chamber, which had a similar layout to the *Decatur*'s command deck. A Raider, without his helmet, bared his teeth in pain as another immobilized his arm with a white tourniquet.

Sinclair took her helmet off and inhaled air that smelled of sweat. She turned to Lamar. "Look through the data and find something. I need to know what state this fleet is in."

"Yes, ma'am." Lamar floated to the consoles.

"Captain Vasquez, bring General Medvedev to the command deck."

"Yes, ma'am." Vasquez and another Raider exited the chamber.

Sinclair saw the command seat, a swivel chair, placed at the center of the deck. She didn't like that, imagining herself swinging her head in all directions to speak with her subordinates in the middle of a chaotic battle. She would've passed out from dizziness.

She nudged her foot over the wall and glided to the seat. A photo was attached to the armrest. Medvedev, a lean man with thick black hair and a slightly amused look, stood behind a laughing woman and three boys. She took the photo and slid it into her chest pocket.

Captain Vasquez reemerged inside the command deck entrance, gesturing with his head for someone to enter. She heard a wet cough. The same man from the photo, but with a thick goatee and packing several extra kilograms of weight, floated onto the deck. With an expression that hinted at uncertainty, General Medvedev scanned the chamber. His brown eyes locked on Sinclair when he saw the two white stars on her chest. His gaze shifted between Sinclair and Dressler, who stood behind her. For a split second, he let slip a perplexed look. Sinclair imagined she looked like a small girl compared to the two giants, Dressler and Lamar.

He coughed and brought his hands behind his back with a raised chin. "General Sinclair." His Russian accent was thicker in person compared to on a comm channel.

A second EU officer, short and bloated, drifted onto the deck. His chapped lips twitched, his eyes locking on each Raider on the deck. He didn't stop moving his hands, like he was looking for a fight. Raiders noticed it and kept their eyes on him.

"General Medvedev"—Sinclair twisted her gloves off—"I have occupied your flagship and neutralized many of your vessels in lunar orbit. Do I have your surrender?"

"What happens if we surrender?" Medvedev asked.

"We will classify you and the rest of your spacemen as prisoners of war placed under my protection and offer basic care."

Medvedev's lips parted. "Why do I hear a *but* coming?"

"It depends on how you answer my next question, General."

The other officer looked around. Medvedev didn't move a muscle.

"Ask—" He hacked loud, rattling coughs. While rubbing his chest, a few more coughs broke out. He cleared his throat after the coughing subsided. "Ask away."

"Why should I not treat you as a war criminal and prosecute you?"

The Russian didn't reply, but his face hardened.

"I can have you and your officers locked up for attacking the PhotonicWay and bombing civilian targets on the surface. Hundreds of civilians are dead." Sinclair raised a finger. "A few minutes *after* you announced your surrender, one of your gunships attempted to bomb the space elevator. I could have you—"

"Spare me the high moral standing!" Medvedev followed with a curse in Russian. "We are no different. Let's not forget who bombed the Three Gorges Dam and drowned thousands of people during the war. That was a civilian target, but that didn't stop General Shugart!"

He swung his finger across the command deck. "During the war, while your country sat behind your two large oceans, Europe brushed closely to nuclear winter and saw widespread devastation. And then—"

His breath cut short, and he heaved into a succession of coughs.

"General Med—" Sinclair tried to interject.

He raised a finger, shaking his head.

"And then"—he wiped his mouth with the back of his hand—"your country had the *audacity* to hold our economy, our livelihoods, hostage until we agreed to cede full control of Luna over to you. So... spare me the lecture! If you're going to charge me, *do it*!"

"You done?"

The obese officer with chapped lips crept forward. "Watch your words, lady..."

"Look at where you stand." Dressler flicked a switch on his holstered pistol. "I know who will be at the bottom of the queue if we experience a food shortage."

Medvedev raised his arm in front of his subordinate. "Not now, Gromék..."

"Save your words, General." Sinclair took her eyes off Gromék. "Your attempt to conquer Luna failed. Do I have your formal surrender?"

"Yes, you do."

"Excellent." Sinclair crossed her arms. "What are your government's next moves?"

"I can't disclose that."

"Can't or won't?"

Medvedev looked at an empty corner of the command deck. He suppressed a cough.

"I see." Sinclair eyed Captain Vasquez. "Take them back to the mess hall."

After they left, Sinclair leaned toward Dressler. "Start transporting the prisoners down to the ground base. We need them off before we transfer the *Decatur* crew over. And have Dr. Naish examine Medvedev. His coughs didn't sound good."

"Roger that, ma'am," Dressler said.

She floated toward Lamar, who had his sweaty head inside a wall panel. "What have you found?"

He strained to pull his bald head out. "They are in pretty good shape. The *Piedmont*'s cargo bay is fully stocked with goods. We just need to reseal the breaches, clean up the interior, and it'll be in fighting condition."

"What about the destroyers and gunships?"

"Two destroyers and one gunship are still active. They are stranded either with no propellant or substantial damage."

Sinclair chewed her lip. "Are their vessels compatible with our systems?"

Lamar gave her a quizzical look. "Their engineering and weapons systems are similar. However, we would need to purge the software, so...yes, they are."

"Excellent." She twisted her gloves back on. "Get these vessels converted over to our systems and begin repairs. Salvage everything else for spare parts."

The second engineer ran his hand across his bald head. "Without the Craven spacedock, that would take months to complete. Six... eight."

"Then there is no time to waste, Lamar." Sinclair grabbed her helmet and floated to the exit.

* * *

Sinclair struggled to think, sleep deprivation grinding her cloudy mind to a halt. Without the normal twenty-four-hour cycle, she'd lost track of time and wasn't sure when she had last slept. Despite touring the extensive damage the ground base had received from the battle, she remembered little of it. She was unsure if she'd walked through the medical bay to check on the wounded. She lay in bed in her private quarters, watching the newsfeed.

"*—was the first full-scale military engagement to take place beyond low earth orbit. The situation is still developing, but all signs point to substantial damage sustained between the opposing fleets. Casualty numbers continue to climb. Officials on both sides have called for a de-escalation of the situation, but both militaries remain on full alert and missile threats continue to be issued to—*"

Sinclair muted the newsfeed and opened her inbox, blinking to make the text clear. There were hundreds of unread messages. She ignored messages from close friends, former classmates, fellow officers she barely knew, and a few congressmen. She opened a message from Garrett.

> OUTSTANDING JOB, SINCLAIR. IT WON'T GET EASIER.

She shook her head, struggling to understand his cryptic message. The fogginess in her head didn't help, so she closed the message.

A picture of her emerged on the muted newsfeed. It was taken after receiving her two stars. She hated the picture because she seemed displeased, recovering from a stomach flu the previous day. She unmuted the newsfeed.

"*—interim commander of the US Luna Fleet when the battle broke out. At age fifty-three, she is one of the youngest generals and is well known for her strong advocacy for gunships and photonic propulsion.*"

Comments flooded a corner of the newsfeed, praising Sinclair for the victory. One comment called her the Protector of Luna. Another said that she was a leader this country needed.

She muted the newsfeed again and tried to connect with the *Oregon*. Nothing came back through the radio. Ground units were driving to the crash site. Her chest grew heavy. She told herself to accept that Cavalieri was dead.

She'd worked hard her entire career, honing her skills to prepare for battles. But she didn't feel any satisfaction from her victory. Only sadness filled her chest as she thought about the hundreds of lives lost. Was it the right call to open fire on the Fifth Fleet? It didn't feel glorious seeing many spacemen dying or in agony over geopolitics. No one walks away from war eager for more.

Tears pooled in her eyes. She ground her teeth and clenched her fists. It was too much for her to hold at bay. She lost her composure and started heaving, letting out a few wails. Tears continued building in her eyes, with little gravity to pull them down her cheeks.

Hiccups now popping out of her lungs, she curled up in her bed and took long breaths. She inhaled again and exhaled. She repeated this several times until her muscles loosened.

Her hand terminal pinged with an urgent notification. She wanted to forget about the space force. But her gut told her to open it. She sat up and opened the message.

> GENERAL SINCLAIR,
>
> AFTER YOU EXECUTED AN UNAUTHORIZED COMBAT OPERATION IN THE LUNA SECTOR, AGAINST DIRECT ORDERS FROM SPACECOM, YOU ARE HEREBY RELIEVED OF LUNA FLEET COMMAND, EFFECTIVE IMMEDIATELY.
>
> GENERAL ABBORN

28

THE MAGNATE

NYSE: VC 169.01 (-16.52%)

"The stock is still dropping!" Cooper slammed his hand down on the table. "This is a crisis of confidence!"

His shout rattled Vanderheiden's headache, fueling his irritation for the bickering director. He leaned back into his leather chair and looked up at the photonic platform statue hanging from the ceiling of the Executive Chamber. *My company only got to Mars, and the Luna Space Elevator is near completion, but the board has descended into the abyss of bickering.* He sighed. *What's next? They overthrow me?*

"A lot of what's happened has been outside our control," Gabriella said. "Our stock will recover. Could be weeks. Could be months."

"Not good enough!" Cooper flicked his hand. "Have you checked Shugart's stock? With war breaking out, defense contracts are flooding out of the Pentagon and filling up their balance sheet." Cooper swung his head back to Vanderheiden. "And know you what that means?"

"They'll attempt another hostile takeover." He brought his eyes back down.

"Exactly."

"Look..." Vanderheiden massaged the tight muscles above his

ears. "We are stabilizing Luna operations. Luna Platform 4 is about to restart. It will be months before we can replace Platform 2, given we committed the bulk of our resources to the space elevator. But we can manage Luna's traffic with three platforms."

Cooper lowered his chin. "No, what is going to restore shareholders' faith in this company is turning around and delivering strong profits next quarter."

Vanderheiden frowned and looked around the table. Scharre Sr. stared at Cooper with an amused look, almost sinister, with his gigantic eyes. Arellano watched the stock tracker on her hand terminal. On the hologram, calling in from Sinus Medii, Brunelli held a deep scowl, arms crossed.

"And what do you suggest?" Vanderheiden asked.

"Halt the space elevator construction," Cooper said. "Taking that cost item off the balance sheet. Now."

"Don't touch my space elevator, Cooper!" Brunelli uncrossed his arms. "Do you hear me?"

"Settle down," Vanderheiden snapped. "Cooper...the surface anchor has been built. We are about to deploy the cable, linking it between the surface and the orbital anchor. After that, we have to reinforce the cable and raise the commercial station to the hundred-kilometer altitude." He raised three fingers. "We are three months away from mankind's *first* fully operational space elevator."

Arellano stopped looking at the terminal. "Our stock price reflects the shareholders' faith in our Luna Space Elevator, not the Photonic-Way. Cutting the project will only make things worse."

"You should not have promised the space elevator." Cooper shrugged.

"Oh, damn you, Cooper!" Vanderheiden pointed his finger across the table. "We announced it because you were unsatisfied, threatening to force leadership changes!"

Gabriella scoffed, shaking her head at the activist investor. "Not sure where you were when Shugart was at our gates, threatening a hostile takeover."

Scharre Sr. tapped his fingers on the table. "We have to think about Luna. Completing the space elevator will expedite recovery efforts on the moon. The bombing runs destroyed a quarter of the Luna industrial base. It'll be months before it is back up to full capacity."

"The space elevator is the future of this company." Vanderheiden emphasized the words. "I mean...damn it! I'm trying to help the Lunarians, and I don't need people like you breathing down my neck!"

"What I think we have is a leadership problem. On top of all these problems, you are now engulfed in bribery allegations." Cooper waved at Vanderheiden. "Another unnecessary problem."

Vanderheiden clenched his fist. *Damn you, Cooper.* Gabriella rolled her eyes, and Arellano eyed her boss with an uncertain look.

"There you go," Scharre Sr. said with his Southern drawl. "I was wondering when you would bring that up."

"This is serious!" Cooper said. "He bribed the National Medical Service!"

Vanderheiden could only laugh in disbelief when news broke of him allegedly bribing NMS to get Emily treatment for Creutzfeldt-Jakob disease. *Not a news report I expected to read this morning.* Unclenching his fist, he lowered his voice. "Again...allegations are false."

"Doesn't matter." Cooper waved his arms around the Executive Chamber. "Investors are seeing chaos at Luna. Costs continue to climb. And the company's CEO is being subjected to a criminal investigation." He pressed his finger against the table. "What we need...is a leadership change."

Vanderheiden straightened his back.

"Let it all out, Cooper." Scharre Sr. smirked. "Tell us what you really want."

Cooper ignored him. "Stop the space elevator, or I will resign from the board and demand a merger with Shugart."

Scharre chuckled. "I want to see you do that..."

"Stop it, sir," Gabriella hissed at her father-in-law.

"Damn you, Cooper!" Brunelli shook his fist. "You will have to take me down if you take him down!"

Vanderheiden's breathing quickened. *This is my company.* He narrowed his eyes across the table at Cooper. His anger locked up his jaw.

Cooper sneered at him. Before Vanderheiden could shoot out of his chair and roar at him, Arellano cut him off.

"Everyone!" Arellano turned on the wall monitor to a newsfeed channel. "We need to watch this."

On the screen, standing at the podium at the White House's Rose Garden was President Barbour. Behind her were congressional representatives and business leaders, Tsung being one of them. Vanderheiden could see Contador, the bald senator with spectacles, at the edge of the video. He hunched forward, scanning the crowd like he was trying to measure something with his eyes. Everyone else on stage seemed pleased with themselves. The bright sunlight illuminated one side of their faces and darkened the other side. The newsfeed replayed clips of the press conference, the bottom screen captain reading in bold red letters: "Industry Champions Act Passed."

A news reporter said: *"In the aftermath of the Marius Hills Massacre and the outbreak of violence between US and EU fleets over Luna, Congress has passed, with bipartisan support, the Industry Champions Act. This bill will give the executive branch unprecedented power to seize assets 'vital to the national security of the nation.' President Barbour signed the bill into law this morning."*

The video switched to President Barbour. *"We face the genuine possibility of war with the European Union,"* she said in her charismatic tone. *"Our nation has experienced a crippling recession, driven by excessive competition, opportunistic businessmen, and predatory bankers. The needs of the people are more important than the needs of shareholders. Now...is the time for the federal government to step in, consolidate critical economic sectors, defeat our foreign adversaries, and bring stability to this glorious nation."*

"Consolidate critical economic sectors?" Vanderheiden spread his arms on the table.

Barbour raised a finger. "*The first phase of this act is to appoint industry champions, companies appointed by the federal government, to oversee the consolidation of their respective industries. We will transform them into national companies owned by the federal government. We will structure them with the needs of the people as the utmost priority, not the shareholders.*" She gestured to the three business leaders behind him. "*I am pleased to announce the first set of industry champions. Stephen Toll of Tenet Bank will lead the consolidation of the financial sector. Shankha Kayal of Guardian Energy will lead the consolidation of the energy industry.*"

Vanderheiden didn't need to hear what sector Tsung would take over.

"*From Shugart Technologies, Cheryl Tsung will merge the space industry.*"

It felt like a heavy ball had been dropped on Vanderheiden's back. *And just like that? Shugart takes control of my company with the government's backing?*

Each CEO stepped up to the podium and said a few words. Vanderheiden didn't hear the first two, Barbour's announcement still ringing in his ears.

Minutes later, Tsung stepped up with a satisfying smile. "*I am honored...to be at the helm of the Space Development Authority. I will adhere to my patriotic duty, serve my country, and listen to the needs of our citizens.*" She dragged out her last words. "*Thank you.*"

Vanderheiden ground his teeth, sharp pain stabbing a back tooth.

The news reporter resumed her narration. "*This bill represents a strong rebuttal against the list of demands issued by the Space Magnates demanding lower taxes and deregulation. The story development continues. Next, we will cover—*"

Vanderheiden turned the newsfeed off. Everyone seemed to have lost their voice, staring at the blank screen. Even Cooper said nothing.

After a long minute of audible breathing around the table, Vanderheiden turned to Cooper. "I will *not* stop the space elevator."

Blinking, the director gulped and locked eyes with him.

"So be it." Cooper pocketed his hand terminal and stood up. "Let it be known that because of the current CEO's ineffective leadership and inability to adhere to the wishes of the shareholders, I resign from the board, effective immediately."

He pushed his chair in, took long strides toward the door, and left the Executive Chamber. Every person in the room watched him leave.

"Damn it..." Gabriella mumbled. "There goes a third of our board's support."

* * *

"I cannot believe this!" Dr. Raymond's voice blurted out of the speakers on the table in the Executive Chamber. "With a bill like this, you'd think it would've been leaked to the public. Those dirty politicians were waiting for the right moment to pass it."

"I'll tell my family's legal team to drop everything and fight this." Gabriella typed a message on her hand terminal.

Dr. Raymond continued her rant. "It is not right for the government to swiftly pass a bill within a week and seize my company the next day!"

"Do you think this bill would hold up in the Supreme Court?" Vanderheiden asked.

"I doubt it." Gabriella shook her head. "Laws like this have been passed, especially during wars and economic crises. But never one of this scale."

"But are they going to compensate us?" He opened his palms. "What does this mean for our companies?"

"No details on that," Dr. Raymond said. "Shugart lawyers are coming to my office tomorrow. My legal team is digging through the act."

"Good afternoon, people," Blackburn spoke on the call.

"Blackburn!" Gabriella tried to sound happy. "Glad for you to join."

"To say these are troubling times would be an understatement," Blackburn said.

Scharre Sr. broke his silence, rubbing his chin. "Are we responsible for this? Did our list of demands trigger this?"

More people from the Luna Business Association joined the conference call.

"I don't think we are to blame," Gabriella said. "This is just poor timing. We may have been the last straw. The politicians must have thought the time was ripe to pass this bill."

"We must issue a strong rebuttal," Blackburn said. "We must stand our ground!"

"I agree," Vanderheiden said. "Which representatives voted for this bill? I never thought Congress had the numbers to pass this kind of bill."

"It was bi-partisan," Gabriella said.

Vanderheiden felt stumped. "So, you are telling me all the money we spent providing to campaigns and lobbying politicians was for naught?"

No one replied to his question. *I could've spent those millions replacing Luna Platform 2.* Vanderheiden sighed. *What a waste.*

Gabriella pressed her hands together at the fingertips. "A few weeks after we published our list of demands, tax collectors and financial regulators came knocking at the Scharre conglomerate, asking to look into our accounting books for bogus reasons. Our legal team kicked them out. Has anyone else dealt with that recently?"

Vanderheiden remembered Arellano coming to his office and telling him antitrust regulators had requested a meeting. She told him legal had it handled.

"Yes, but it was the antitrust folks," Vanderheiden replied.

Others shared similar experiences, and Vanderheiden felt his jaw drop. The worst story he heard was Dr. Raymond sharing how government lawyers had threatened to suspend Valkyrie Labs' intellectual property protection.

"Shit..." Scharre Sr. shook his head. "They are trying to crack down on us. Scare us into withdrawing our demands. President Barbour is good."

Senator Contador is good, Vanderheiden thought.

"A democratically elected government is capable of this?" Scharre Sr. said.

"Of course, they are!" Blackburn retorted. "Democracy doesn't always work out."

Imagining Contador and Tsung taking control of Vanderheiden Corporation and grinning at the lucrative assets made Vanderheiden seethe.

"We have to publicize these investigations," Dr. Raymond said.

"Not only that"—Blackburn spoke with a bitter tone that made Vanderheiden cringe—"we must escalate our war against the government."

Gabriella frowned. "Don't call it a war..."

"There is no one in the government who will support us." Blackburn raised a thick finger. "No one! We are on our own. If we are to stop the government from confiscating our companies, we must make it hurt." He raised his fist. "Hard measures are required."

"And how do you suggest we do that?" Gabriella asked.

"Lock down our facilities. Prevent federal agents from entering our premises. Transfer our assets to Luna."

"They would arrest us for that," Vanderheiden said. "People could even die if they sent in a SWAT team."

"We are not rebels," Dr. Raymond said.

"Like I said...hard measures. All my assets are at Phantom Torch. I want to see SWAT try to take it."

"Don't forget about the Raiders."

"I wouldn't count on that." Blackburn smiled. "My inside sources say there are talks of mutiny inside the Luna Fleet."

"No, we are not doing that." Gabriella waved her arm. "We must continue dialoguing with the government and overload the courts."

"Do as you wish, Gabriella." Blackburn crossed his arms. "I'm locking down my facilities. I have private mercenaries to lend if anyone needs them."

It felt like smoke came out of Vanderheiden's ears. *Why are businessmen always the bad guys? Maybe this bill will be a good thing. Show the people what it is like to have businesses run by clueless politicians.* He thought of bureaucrats trying to decipher a balance sheet or orchestrate the PhotonicWay Command Center. *Blackburn's hard measures seem just. But is that too much?*

"Any idea when these confiscations will start?" Dr. Raymond asked.

No one spoke. Nobody ended the call. Only the network static spoke.

29

THE GENERAL

Sinclair bent down toward the hand terminal on her desk. "I restored our Luna operations! I defeated the Fifth Fleet! The United States holds Luna." She pointed at her chest. "And they want to take away *my command*?"

Garrett blinked a few times on the video, showing his annoyance. "You finished?"

"No, I'm not. So—"

"Stop. Just stop."

Sinclair held her tongue, holding back the urge to rant. She paced her private quarters, which were about the size of an office cubicle, while Garrett appeared to be sitting in his office at a log cabin. He was looking off to the side, rubbing his cheek deeply. There was a three-second delay in their connection.

"This is a good thing, Sinclair. It means Abborn fears you."

"And Maxwell." She paced faster, taking three steps before turning and walking to the other side. "Look! We need to take this public. Expose their incompetence!"

He shook his head. "No, we need to keep this internal. Let me reach out to my connections at the Pentagon and make them fully appraised of the situation. Rally support around you."

"Of course." Sinclair rolled her eyes. "You want to keep it quiet."

"Sinclair! Going public is risky. You lose control of the narrative once it is out in the open."

Sinclair studied Garrett closely for a moment. Retirement had changed him. His neck and acne-scarred cheeks appeared thicker. His hair was gray, and he had bags under his eyes. Sinclair wondered if he was having difficulty with retirement or had just gotten out of bed.

"How are things back home?" she asked.

"Great." Garrett chuckled a little too long. "Oh...things are just great!" He shook his head.

Sinclair stopped pacing. "What's going on, Garrett?"

"Ginger left me, so I'm just sulking in retirement while we are at war."

"I'm sorry about Ginger."

"The Continental Missile Shield is failing to intercept many of the hypersonic missiles. A lot of the bases on the eastern seaboard are getting hit hard." He rubbed his eye socket with the palm of his hand. "A hundred dead at Port of Houston."

"That's war." Sinclair paced the room again. "We deal with it."

"Did you see the memo warning about soldiers deserting from their posts en masse?"

"I never thought highly of the army." Sinclair shook her head. "Just a collection of criminals and civilians with no other career opportunities. Like many of the enlisted up here."

"It makes me wonder what kind of morale is persistent across the military. We are in the early stages of war, and I would've expected civilians to flock to the recruitment offices to sign up." He raised his arms. "Instead, they are in the streets protesting against anything and everything! Do people want to defend their country?"

"Well, I would—"

"And this Industry Champions Act..." He sighed. "It is not good. Not good. We got people flooding the streets protesting it. And then we got counter-protesters coming out. This country is turning into a dumpster fire with its polarizing politics. It's madness..."

"Industry Champions Act?"

"It grants the government unrestricted power to seize companies they deem vital to the national economy."

"And that's legal?"

Garrett held his shrug for a few seconds.

"Hey, Sinclair..." He straightened his back. "I need to go take a walk. It was great talking to you. Again...phenomenal job taking down the Fifth Fleet."

Sinclair's heart swelled with pride. "Thank you, Garrett."

"Even if you lose your command, you'll be remembered as the general who defended Luna. You'll hold sway over many people. Hell" —he chuckled—"you could run for senator and give Maxwell a hard time."

Sinclair laughed hard at the thought of sitting on the Senate Committee on Armed Services, looking down at and scolding Maxwell. She held the back of her hand to her mouth, trying to control her laughter that echoed around the room.

"Thank you, Garrett." She smiled. "I needed that."

"Anytime, Sinclair." He cut the connection.

The pleasing thought of lecturing Maxwell slowly morphed into the dreadful image of him arriving at Luna to take over Sinclair's command. Her stomach tightened at the thought.

She pulled up the archive of video logs for the *Decatur* command deck and scrolled through the recordings until she came across her conversation with Abborn after intel reports of the Fifth Fleet's TLI. A paused video showed a split screen, Abborn standing in his office on one side and Sinclair floating on the command deck on the other side. The audio sounded gibberish, and both generals moved unnaturally as Sinclair shifted the time marker in the video. She kept moving the marker until she found the specific words Abborn spoke.

"—order you to stand down and allow the EU fleet to enter Luna if they kick off a TLI. Negotiations will play in our favor. EU is sending half of their fleet to—"

She adjusted the time markers to capture the entire conversation and made a copy. She drafted an anonymous message and attached the video.

"We are doing this my way, Garrett." With a single beep, she sent the encrypted message to Greenwood, the journalist from *The Overseer*. She smiled deeply, eager to hear what justifications Abborn would come up with this time.

* * *

The hangar bay was the size of a sports field, the best place to be if any spaceman was claustrophobic. Half a dozen armored rovers lined up on one side of the hangar bay. At one corner, piles of metal planks, plastic boards, and torn wires reeked of burnt plastic and charred metal. A few spacemen and many droids funneled into the hangar bay and dropped the scraps onto the growing piles.

Scores of body bags covered the other side of the hangar bay. Two spacemen in space suits unloaded one black bag at a time from the rover and laid them gently on the ground. Many bags outlined the shape of a human body. Some had abnormal shapes, like limbs were missing.

Medics in white uniforms navigated between the bodies, opening each bag, scanning the deceased's microchip in their neck, punching in details on their hand terminals, and resealing the bag. Sinclair counted four rows, with about close to twelve bags in each row.

She approached a medic. "Lieutenant, what will happen to the deceased?"

The medic typed on her hand terminal. "Once all the bodies are consolidated, we will transport back to Vandenberg."

The war had brought cargo traffic between Earth and Luna to a near standstill, so Sinclair knew the bodies wouldn't be moving soon. "No, bury them here."

The medic raised an eyebrow. "But, ma'am, the policy is—"

"I set the policy. These spacemen died protecting Luna. We will bury them here." Sinclair pulled up a map on her hand terminal and pointed with her finger. "Put them on the ridgeline. That way, they can watch over the Aestuum Space Force Base."

"Yes, ma'am." The medic nodded.

"Where are Chief Engineer Cavalieri's personal items?"

The medic pointed at a row of black containers lined up against the wall. "They will be in one of those."

Sinclair inspected each container until she found Cavalieri's name on a metallic name tag. She opened it and chuckled when she saw a paperback book lying on top of clothes titled *Chronicles of Admiral Cordova: The US Naval Admiral Who Defied Washington.* She couldn't believe Cavalieri violated regulations by bringing a paperback to space.

She caressed the book, stroking each page like she hadn't felt paper before. She opened it and found pages covered in handwritten notes. *History repeats itself... Pivotal moment in weaponry technology... Still a viable tactic today... Reminds me of my general... I can't imagine fighting on the ground. I prefer the comforts of the spacecraft...*

Sinclair stopped reading and went back to the previous comment. *Reminds me of my general.* Sinclair assumed Cavalieri was referring to her. She read the section near the written note.

> AS THE WAR DRAGGED ON AND MANY FLEETS AND ARMIES PERISHED IN INEFFECTIVE OFFENSIVE OPERATIONS, CORDOVA AND HIS PACIFIC FLEET WERE CONTENT ON A STRATEGY OF CONTAINMENT AGAINST THE CHINESE NAVY. THIS WAS A BLATANT CONTRADICTION OF ORDERS FROM WASHINGTON DEMANDING THE RECONQUEST OF LOST TERRITORIES.

"Well...that is not the case anymore," Sinclair whispered. "My career is over."

"What did you say?" Barrows asked. Sinclair hadn't heard him approach from behind. She closed the book with a thump and put it back in the container.

"Just talking to myself." She turned to Barrows.

Barrows looked at the black container, and the frown on his baby face deepened. "Are those her items?"

Sinclair nodded.

"I can't believe she is gone." He exhaled.

"Miss her bugging you to get tattoos?"

Barrows chuckled and grabbed the book by its spine. "She will be missed."

Sinclair rested her hands on the container. "She died protecting Luna."

Barrows gently placed the book on top of the clothes. He muttered something incoherent.

"Something on your mind, Colonel?"

"It's my fault."

Sinclair furrowed her eyebrows. "What is?"

"Cavalieri is dead because of me. If I had taken down both of the tankers, she would still be here." He clenched his fist hard enough for white knuckles to emerge. "It's all my fault. I *should've* taken down those tankers."

Sinclair licked the back of her teeth. Barrows's performance wasn't flawless, but he had success. She thought over her words, needing her best gunship officer not to fall into the abyss of anger and regret. She nearly fell into it after the *Imperator* but Garrett pulled her out.

"Colonel...we all made tough choices that day. I gave the order to redirect the missile barrage against the first group, which allowed the *Piedmont* to drop their marines to the surface unchallenged. We prioritized taking down the destroyers first over the gunships. I left the *Decatur* paired with a destroyer, not a gunship. Dozens of spacemen died on that carrier because the destroyer couldn't beat the two gunships. Barrows. Look at me. Were those mistakes? We'll never know."

Barrows curled his lips, eyes widening with anger. "We all know things would've turned out differently if I did my attack run correctly."

"No, you don't."

The colonel struggled to find words.

"We are at war." Sinclair gripped his shoulder. "There will be many bad days. It's not about being perfect and avoiding mistakes. It's about living with our decisions, right or wrong, and focusing on the current day. Our fleet came out on top despite being outgunned, outnumbered, and...basically abandoned by our country, so we must've done some things the correct way, right?"

Barrows looked both ways and bared his teeth. "We defended Luna, and Abborn *strips* you of your command. Why?"

"We technically disobeyed his orders."

"They attacked us! This war—"

Barrows cut off his words when he saw Lieutenant Colonel Fabian walk into the hangar bay.

"Mess hall! Ten minutes!" Fabian ordered the medics working the body bags. He nodded at Sinclair and Barrows and walked out, seemingly indifferent to his right arm being missing.

Rubbing his nose, Barrows stumbled over his words. "I—I thought it would've united the country, you know?" He waved in the general direction of Earth. "But people are tearing up the streets, protesting whatever they are protesting about, being shot by the police."

He rested his hand on his hip and his other arm on Cavalieri's container. "Even my children are asking why I'm fighting this war, and my wife is asking when I'll come home."

Sinclair wanted her to tell him to keep his lack of faith to himself. She didn't need someone dampening the pride her fleet had finally discovered after winning the battle over Luna. But she couldn't help but agree with him. It didn't seem worth it to venture out into the wilderness, putting your life on the line for your country, only to turn around and find it burning.

"Colonel, every soldier will question his duty at some point in their life. This is your time. Think about the Luna Fleet. We are responsible for the spacemen under our command. We are responsible for the Lunarians. Think about them."

"What happens when Maxwell arrives?"

"I shall transfer my command over, and Maxwell will run the fleet the way he sees fit."

"But what about me? What about everyone else?"

"I don't know what his plans are. But you and I are the most experienced gunship officers now. The space force will put you to use somewhere." She imagined Maxwell assigning Barrows to tanker or logistics duty.

"We shall see in a few weeks." Barrows tapped the container, saluted Sinclair, and walked off.

Sinclair watched Barrows march out of the hangar bay, wondering how many others shared similar frustrations. She saw the positive vibe everywhere she went, especially after their victory. But was it their country they were passionate about? Or was it Luna?

* * *

Sinclair sat at the desk in her private quarters, fingers hovering over the keyboard of her hand terminal. She didn't want to write this letter. Every ounce of her body wanted to write a scathing letter to Maxwell. He earned none of her respect. She doubted he would even read the letter. But tradition demanded the incumbent commander of a fleet write a personal letter to the succeeding commander.

GENERAL MAXWELL,

WHILE WE DON'T AGREE ON MANY THINGS, WE MUST KEEP THE LUNA FLEET STRONG. I HOPE THE RECENT BATTLE SHOWED THE FEASIBILITY OF GUNSHIPS, AND DESPITE YOUR ADVOCACY OF DESTROYERS, I HOPE YOU WILL AT LEAST KEEP THE GUNSHIPS MANNED AND IN FIGHTING CONDITION.

COLONEL BARROWS IS YOUR BEST GUNSHIP OFFICER. LT. COLONEL FABIAN WILL KEEP YOUR SPACEMEN IN LINE. SECOND ENGINEER LAMAR WILL KEEP THE SPACECRAFT RUNNING. COLONEL DRESSLER IS DIFFICULT TO WORK WITH, BUT HE KEEPS THE RAIDERS SHARP.

GOOD LUCK WITH YOUR NEW COMMAND,

GENERAL SINCLAIR

Sinclair printed the document, folded the sheet of paper, and slid it into an envelope. The door alerted her to someone seeking entrance.

"Enter."

Fabian entered and saluted with his missing arm. Sinclair hadn't gotten used to seeing half of his arm gone.

"General, I request your presence at the mess hall."

"How urgent is it?" Her eyes felt heavy, eager for a nap.

"It'll only take ten minutes, ma'am."

Sinclair stood up, zipped up her black combat uniform, and checked her hair. She exited her quarters, following Fabian.

Fabian walked with a slightly awkward posture, without his full arm to balance himself. The corridors, recently repaired with fresh wall panels and light fixtures, were eerily quiet. No spaceman marching to their assigned posts or fixing damaged wall panels. No facial expressions of subtle contentment after a major victory. Only droids continued working.

"Where is everyone, Lieutenant Colonel?"

"The mess hall, ma'am."

She guessed it was a change-of-command party, but it was too early to have that party, given General Maxwell was weeks out. She scrambled to outline a change-of-command speech in her head.

They entered the mess hall. Hundreds of spacemen overcrowded the large room, causing the environmental system to churn loudly. All eyes were locked on Sinclair. Many had injuries, ranging from broken arms to bandaged necks to missing legs. She was shorter than many of them, so most looked down at her, making her feel vulnerable.

The tone in the room was strange. There was no clapping or hollering. Only stern looks on everyone's face. Sinclair didn't like this and fought the urge to step back.

"General Sinclair," Fabian announced. "I have something that needs to be said in front of the spacemen of this fleet."

He put himself in front of Sinclair, with the sea of spacemen behind him. Her senses went on high alert. She clenched her muscles and scanned the room, ready for something to fly at her.

"Before you joined the Luna Fleet, crimes and drug use were rampant, food supply was poor, things were toxic between officers and enlisted, and our fleet was combat ineffective. Many of us lost hope...until you boarded the *Decatur*."

Sinclair loosened her muscles slightly.

"Against all odds...you turned things around. You removed the officers and NCOs who mistreated us, cracked down on crime, and provided us with a better food supply." He smirked and glanced back at the spacemen, raising his voice. "Though I will say, I wasn't a fan of you sneaking cockroaches into our burgers." Laughs echoed across the mess hall. Sergeant Espinoza raised his shoulders, ready for something to hit him. Sinclair smiled.

Fabian's smile faded away. "You led us to victory."

Her eyes filled with tears, turning all the faces into fuzzy circles. All the spacemen stared at her. Their faces didn't carry sorrow or anger. They stood at attention.

"You are the best general we could ask for." Fabian raised his voice. "This decision is unanimous among all of us. We will *not* accept General Maxwell's command."

A lightning bolt struck through Sinclair's chest. This was mutiny.

Fabian dropped his arms to his sides, snapped his feet together, and raised his arm to a salute. "General Sinclair, you are our commander. We pledge our loyalty to you. We will serve you to the end."

Fabian snapped to a hard salute. Behind Fabian, hundreds of spacemen saluted, feet snapping against the lunarcrete floor.

30

THE MAGNATE

NYSE: VC 132.11 (-21.83%)

Everything Vanderheiden had worked for the past twelve years came down to this moment. He'd bet the entire company on this endeavor. His employees believed in the mission. *This is what I was born for. To free mankind from the chains of gravity.* Once the Luna Space Elevator went online, he would be immortalized as the man who'd built mankind's first of many bridges to space, opening the solar system to all. *This is to be my legacy.*

"Orbital Anchor?" Brunelli's voice came through the speakers of the Executive Chamber.

"Go," an engineer from the orbital anchor replied.

Vanderheiden turned away from the windows overlooking the humid woodlands of Houston and joined the directors and company chiefs seated at the table facing the large monitor crammed with numbers and videos of the cable deployment operation.

"Surface Anchor?" Brunelli continued down the checklist. The chief technology officer and two engineers were on a webcam positioned in the lower right corner of the large monitor, overseeing the cable deployment from the Luna Space Elevator Operations Center in Sinus Medii.

"Go."

"Descent drone?"

"We are ready!" Vanderheiden smiled at the employee's enthusiastic voice.

"Traffic control?"

"All clear."

"Emergency units?"

"Go."

"We have a go from all units," Brunelli declared. "Initiating the descent."

Vanderheiden's eyes shifted to the external camera of the descent drone. The miniature spacecraft was attached to the bottom end of the cable. The titanium cable reached up over a vast distance to the orbital anchor suspended 56,000 kilometers above the moon. The drone was designed to pull the cable down to the surface and control its descent, allowing it to land inside the surface anchor.

The engines fired, vibrating the camera. The altimeter, displaying the drone's altitude, showed it hovering eighty kilometers above the surface, at the edge of Luna's gravity well. Once the descent drone went below the well, the moon's mass would start pulling it down. Vanderheiden knew the descent would start off slowly, but as the drone went deeper down the gravity well, the acceleration would pick up.

He looked at the video of the surface anchor and admired the sight, wishing he could be at Luna to watch this operation in person. Constructed out of titanium, the surface anchor looked like the internal structure of a skyscraper, wide at the bottom and narrow at the top. Rails went up the four sides of the tower to allow cargo and personnel to transfer between the surface and cable. One side was exposed to the sunlight, making it difficult to see the struts and rails on the dark side. Located at the center of Luna's closest point to Earth, the tower appeared to be pointing at the planet, telling everyone to go home. The only object missing from the tower was the cable reaching into orbit.

Seventy kilometers.

Arellano repeatedly tapped her hand terminal, refreshing the stock tracker, almost frantically. Vanderheiden sighed, reached out, and flipped her hand terminal face down gently. Arellano blinked, startled by the act.

"Please enjoy the show," Vanderheiden patted her shoulder. "If we are successful, the stock won't matter."

Arellano looked at him for a moment before letting out a deep breath and nodding.

Sixty kilometers.

Vanderheiden surveyed the rest of the table. Gonzalez was unable to remain still, rubbing his jaw or adjusting his sitting posture repeatedly. Some directors' eyes were glued to the screen, somewhat awestruck by the operation.

"I'm just glad Cooper isn't here," Vanderheiden whispered to Gabriella. "I wouldn't be able to stand him if he were in this room."

"He wanted to observe the operation from here." Gabriella smirked. "I told him not to bother."

"Thank you."

Scharre Sr. leaned over to the two. "I'm sure that bastard regrets his resignation."

Forty kilometers.

Vanderheiden pulled out the red rubber ball from his leather jacket pocket and squeezed it hard, wishing the altimeter would turn faster.

With each kilometer taken off the altimeter, the Executive Chamber grew quieter and quieter.

Twenty kilometers.

The cable unwrapped beneath the orbital anchor with blinding speed as the descent drone gained velocity. It looked like a fantastical beast's black heart pumping fast. Vanderheiden clutched his rubber ball harder, feeling aches in his palm.

Fifteen kilometers.

What if we fail? What if the government takes it all away from me? He shook his head, trying to wipe away the thought of federal agents or soldiers barging into his bedroom and slamming him to the ground as Susann screamed. *I can't let them do it. They'll have to do it over my dead—*

Gabriella gripped his upper arm tightly. He stopped caressing the ball and let it drop on his lap.

Ten kilometers.

"It's almost here!" Brunelli announced.

Five kilometers.

Vanderheiden's heart started pounding hard. *Here we go.*

At the two-kilometer mark, the landing thrusters ignited, and the flash was hard to miss on the surface anchor camera. The cable was too thin to see, but the drone was dropping fast.

Another engine fired at the final kilometer, and the drone decelerated rapidly, seemingly hovering over the lunar surface without dropping. It guided itself toward the tall white tower.

Vanderheiden's chest grew tighter. *Land...please land in the tower.*

Once the tower secured the cable, there would be an enormous amount of tension placed on the cable. As long as the tensile force meter on the top of the main screen stayed either green or yellow, the cable was safe. If it turned red, the cable would snap.

I can't watch. I can't watch, he repeated to himself, his breathing heavy and forced.

Like a swing set, the drone swerved toward the tower and fell inside the structure, the engine light disappearing into it. Vanderheiden closed his eyes, refusing to look at the tensile-force meter color. *Please...*

The silence felt stifling. No one spoke. Many breaths were held.

"One moment, please..." Brunelli announced.

Gabriella's grip tightened. "It's yellow."

Vanderheiden imagined the cable groaning and the tower creaking, desperate not to let go of the cable. It seemed like many minutes to him, but he refused to open his eyes. Gabriella's death grip turned his arm numb.

"Another moment, please!" Brunelli asked.

"Oh God...come on!" Gabriella whispered.

Vanderheiden's chest gripped him so hard, he thought he was having a panic attack. *We failed... We failed...*

"Is it green?" Vanderheiden asked.

Gabriella didn't reply.

"I have confirmation," Brunelli said in a steady tone. "Cable is secured."

The room exploded with cheers, applause, and whistles. Vanderheiden collapsed into his seat, resting his head and arms on the table.

* * *

"They are in the front lobby, sir..."

Vanderheiden barely made out the administrator's words amid the loud celebrations in the Executive Chamber.

"Who?" Vanderheiden asked loudly.

"Mrs. Tsung and multiple executives from Shugart Technologies."

Phantom alarms rattled his ears. *Shugart?* He heard a muffled voice in the background, like someone was talking to the administrator.

"Uh..." she corrected herself. "Their company is now called the Space Development Authority. They are not to be referred to as Shugart Technologies."

"Wh—" Vanderheiden shook his head, walking away from the triumphant crowd. "But it is Tsung, correct?"

"Yes, it is."

"Keep them in the lobby." He marched back to the table. "Do not let them out of your sight!"

Vanderheiden ended the call. "Silence!"

The directors and company chiefs turned to him. Once they saw his sour expression, the smiles fell off their faces.

"Shugart is downstairs in the lobby." Vanderheiden rested his fisted knuckles on the table. "Clear the room. Now."

An hour later, Vanderheiden sat down on one side of the long table in the Executive Chamber, flanked by his directors. They said nothing to each other. Everyone knew why Shugart was here. Vanderheiden braced his palms on the table. *They'd come to confiscate their platinum prize.*

An executive assistant opened the door, and many executives enter the room. Vanderheiden only recognized the last two. The lanky lawyer walked in, scrolling on his hand terminal without a glance at the directors. Tsung entered, looking like the queen of the land. Every finger held a piece of jewelry, and a terrible amount of makeup covered her face, failing to hide her age. Walking toward the empty chair across from Vanderheiden, she kept her chin high and held her sneering gaze at him.

The Shugart executives sat down. The bright-orange sun hovered behind the Shugart executives, creating dark silhouettes. Vanderheiden still could see the white edges of Tsung's eyes, like she'd finally found her long-sought treasure.

Vanderheiden looked around the room. The Shugart executives wore amused expressions, looking across the other side of the table. Gabriella studied each executive. Scharre Sr., eyes bulging as always, stared at Tsung.

"What can we do for Shugart today?" Vanderheiden was done with the silence.

"Don't play ignorance with me, Vanderheiden," Tsung replied. "You know why we are here. We are now called the Space Development Authority. I made it clear to the lady down in the lobby." She pressed her lips. She leaned back in her chair and waved at the lanky lawyer.

Vanderheiden remembered the lawyer and his thick-rimmed glasses from the previous time Shugart was at the headquarters proposing a merger. *If they confiscate us, that merger might've been a good deal after all.*

The lawyer spoke in a mechanized tone. "Under the authority allowed by the Industry Champions Act, th—"

"I'm sorry...what is your name?" Vanderheiden interrupted.

"Graves." His eyes flicked up. "The Space Development Authority is issuing its formal notice that Vanderheiden Corporation is now under the ownership of our corporation, effective immediately."

He pulled out a sheet of paper from a black folder with "SDA" printed on it and slid it across the table. "Each shareholder will receive a compensation of seventy-five credits per share at the end of the business week."

Scharre Sr. grunted. Without taking his eyes off Tsung, Vanderheiden could hear a mixture of shock and anger from his flanks. He took the paper, glanced at it, and slid it back across the table. *You think you can take my company at such a bargain price?* "We do not accept this offer."

"It is not an offer, Vanderheiden," Tsung said. "It is compensation for my corporation taking ownership of Vanderheiden Corporation. This"—she waved her arms around the room—"now belongs to us."

"Don't get ahead of yourself, Tsung. My lawyers are busy at court stopping this illegal law."

"Charming but futile." Tsung flung her fingers at him like he was an annoying fruit fly. "The Industry Champions Act shields us from judicial challenges. Take the compensation and enjoy your retirement."

The way she spoke made Vanderheiden want to yell at her. He rose out of his chair, his broad chest pressed forward.

"You don't issue orders around here. Until you give the respect we've earned, you are not welcome here." He extended his arm to the door. "Get out."

"You don't give the orders anymore." Tsung didn't move. "I own this company, Vanderheiden. Pack your items and leave." Her eyes swept the table. "You aren't part of the new corporation."

"Are you serious?" Vanderheiden screwed up his face. "We built this company. You don't just get to take it away." He jabbed a finger at her. "*You*...had a chance to be a part of it. But you turned down the offer. And you don't get to go to the government to fix your mistake."

"Save your words, Vanderheiden." Annoyance flashed across Tsung's face.

"Get out...or I will call security."

"Now, that would be illeg—"

"Get out!" Vanderheiden jabbed the screen on his hand terminal.

Uniformed security with "VC" on their chests burst into the Executive Chamber, scanning the room for a disturbance.

"Please escort them off the campus." Vanderheiden swept his finger across the table.

"What is this?" Tsung stood up, talking over him.

"What's going on here?" a security guard asked.

Gabriella stood up, whispering into his ear, "Vanderheiden, don't escalate this."

"Do not..." Tsung curled her lips at Vanderheiden.

"Get out!" he screamed.

Vanderheiden and Tsung yelled and talked over each other. Arguments broke out across the table between the others. Some stood up and threw curses. The security officers took a few uncertain steps forward.

"Quiet!" Gabriella brought the room to silence. She brought her hands behind her back. "Everyone from Shugart shall leave at once."

"I don't believe you understand the situation here, Ms. Gabriella Soto." Tsung twisted a ring on her finger.

"It's Mrs. Scharre." A corner of Gabriella's mouth curled up. She turned to the security officers. "Who is your employer?"

The head of security raised an eyebrow. "You guys."

"Excellent." Gabriella nodded and pointed with her chin at Tsung. "Please take these folks and escort them off the campus."

Many of the executives stood up and walked to the door. Tsung remained standing in her place, staring at Gabriella with an unblinking gaze.

"Ma'am..." A security guard rested his hand on her shoulder.

"Don't fucking touch me!"

"Get out, Tsung," Vanderheiden said.

She jerked her head back to him. "I don't think you under—"

"Get out!" Vanderheiden slammed his fist down on the table.

Tsung sucked her lips in, blinking. She kept her distance from the security guard when she got up and left the Executive Chamber.

* * *

"I said..." A director turned away from the windows overlooking the sprawling corporate campus surrounding the administrative buildings. "Are you two pleased with yourselves for signing the list of demands?"

"I heard you the first time." Vanderheiden flicked his gaze toward the director, who was starting to remind him of Cooper.

"You should've informed me of that decision beforehand." He raised a fist to his forehead. "I didn't put a substantial amount of money into this company for you to risk it for your own political desires."

"Political desires?" Vanderheiden chuckled. "I have no interest in becoming a politician. I enjoy running a business and getting stuff done."

"Please...don't tell—"

"We *had* to do something." Gabriela stood up from the table and wiped dust off her black jacket. "Year after year, the government was throwing more taxes and regulations at us, grinding our business and the economy to a halt.

"Look, it was just irresponsible to—"

"Zip it, everyone!" Vanderheiden shouted. "We are on the same side here. Let's talk about how we are going to stop Shugart from confiscating our company."

Scharre Sr. grabbed the sheet of paper the lanky lawyer slid over. "Seventy-five credits? That is less than sixty percent of our current market value right now! In the middle of a recession! What makes them think they can"—he spat the word—"*compensate* us for that amount?"

"Corporate Transparency Act," Arellano replied.

The chief financial officer stood at the door. Gonzalez was behind her, eyes flickering around the room.

Arellano walked to the table. "That number made no sense at first, but when I reviewed our historical financials connected to the PhotonicWay to develop a counteroffer, that's when it clicked." She turned on the hologram, displaying financial charts. "It is the total cost of building and operating the PhotonicWay."

"What?" Scharre Sr. was perplexed. "Since when did the cost determine a company's value? Did I miss a memo?"

"That value will not fly in court," Gabriella said. "We all know it."

"I agree." Vanderheiden pointed at Arellano. "We need to throw everything we got at the court. Pull every legal maneuver possible to delay this confiscation. We must buy ourselves as much time as we can."

"You heard them..." Gabriella pointed at the empty chairs. "The Industry Champions Act shields them from judicial challenges."

"I want to see them try." Vanderheiden scoffed. "File the legal injunction." He turned to Gonzalez, who pulled out a chair to sit down. "Gonzalez, grab the master key and transfer control of the PhotonicWay to Sinus Medii. Get on the first shuttle out of our spaceport to Luna."

Gonzalez nodded. Vanderheiden pointed at the speaker. "Brunelli, have a team at Luna ready to secure the master key once he arrives."

"I'll be there," Brunelli said in a harsh tone. "No one is taking that key for us."

"That's right." Vanderheiden nodded. "Shugart can claim they own VC, but that means nothing if they don't control the PhotonicWay."

"What about our bank accounts?" Arellano asked.

"Transfer them to your local branches at Luna. We need to pull our financial assets before Tenet Bank locks them down."

He scanned around the room, and saw that looks of defeat still covered many faces. "There have to be more things we can do." He slapped his palm with the back of his other hand. "I want options!"

Gabriella sighed, tightening her lips. “What if we offer multiple seats on the board to the government, turn VC into a state-owned company, allowing us to be independent of Shugart? We can use the Luna Space Elevator as leverage.”

Vanderheiden scratched his beard. *The government being the one and only shareholder. An annoyance, but we would still run VC.* He shook his head. “That’s a bitter pill we may have to swallow.”

Scharre Sr. got up and walked up to Vanderheiden, his eyes unmoving. “I want to make this clear: Once the government gets a seat on our board, their influence will only grow. And they would eventually push us off the board.”

Gabriella shrugged. “It is better keeping some sort of control instead of handing everything over to Shugart and losing our family’s investment.”

Vanderheiden saw it as an acceptable arrangement, as long as he could continue expanding the PhotonicWay and build more space elevators. *But she is right. How much time before I’m no longer CEO? Would Senator Contador even accept that arrangement?*

“Do we know where Cooper stands on this?” Scharre Sr. asked. “Is he supporting the confiscation?”

“I doubt it, if Shugart is buying at seventy-five credits,” Gabriella replied.

“Not if Cooper and his partners got some cash underneath the table from Tsung.”

Gabriella shook her head. “Cooper may be ambitious, but illegal isn’t his style.”

Vanderheiden asked, “Are the lawyers still on the line?”

Affirmatives were spoken.

“Get a corporate governance restructuring proposal drafted that we can take to the government. Let’s see if they’ll accept us as a state-owned company independent of Shugart. You have twenty-four hours.”

His hand terminal pinged with an urgent message from Susann.

> GET TO THE HOSPITAL NOW! EMILY FELL INTO A COMA.

He felt blood pulling back from his face, and his lips shuddered. *No, she was given two years.* Looking up, he saw Gabriella and others looking at him with concern.

"What is it?" Arellano asked.

"I—I...need to go." Vanderheiden slowly rose from his seat and walked unsteadily out of the Executive Chamber.

31

THE GENERAL

The swarm of droids and fresh armor panels covered sections of the *Piedmont* damaged during the battle. The first ring was spinning at normal speed, generating artificial gravity for the wounded spacemen unable to be transported down to Aestuum. The bottom of the spacecraft carrier was softly lit by the gray moon 120 kilometers below it.

Sinclair readjusted the gun holster strapped to her thigh and looked down at Luna one last time, assuming it was the last time she would set foot on the celestial body. She had a feeling her next stop would be Fort Leavenworth.

The *Montana*, the tapered, cone-shaped black gunship, hovered at a distance, waiting for docking clearance. Sinclair found it ironic that Maxwell, a staunch advocate for destroyers, traveled to Luna in a gunship.

Strapped to her seat in the transport shuttle approaching a different docking port, Sinclair got on the comm. "*Piedmont*, what's the holdup with the *Montana*?"

"Unexpected delays due to the repairs," Lieutenant Colonel Fabian replied.

Sinclair heard a smile in his voice. “Lieutenant Colonel Fabian… you will grant docking permission now. The next fleet commander is on board that gunship. This is not the time to protest.”

“Acknowledged,” Fabian replied a few seconds later. “Granting permission now.”

Sinclair imagined Maxwell fuming inside the *Montana*, complaining to one of his cronies about the delay. She had to make sure this transfer of command went smoothly. A more agitated Maxwell was a more irrational and vengeful Maxwell. The Luna Fleet didn’t deserve that kind of fleet commander.

“General?” Dressler sat next to her, his recoilless assault rifle strapped across his chest.

“Yes, Colonel?”

“Is my unit being rotated out of the fleet as well?”

“Not that I’m aware of.” Sinclair shook her head. “Why are you asking?”

“Blue Platoon from Squadron 2 is on the *Montana*. I just picked up their transponders.”

Sinclair pursed her lips. Given the space force only had just over three hundred Raiders, transferring Raiders to Luna seemed illogical. SPACECOM would keep the Raiders close to low earth orbit, where the next stage of the war was expected to flare up.

The transport shuttle docked with the *Piedmont* before the *Montana* did. Sinclair entered the command deck. Fabian and his subordinates in the room stood by their stations, heads held high. Dressler and his Raiders drifted to the back wall. Sinclair floated near the command console, waiting for Maxwell to arrive.

Maxwell rushed onto the deck, trailed by a Raider fire team and three senior officers. Sinclair knew he was already over the edge.

“Who is the traffic controller here?” Maxwell swung his flustered face around the deck.

A corporal pushed away from his station. “Corporal Burchard here, sir.”

Maxwell pointed at him. “Have him arrested for disobedience.”

A Blue Platoon Raider crossed the chamber and twisted the corporal's arm. Sinclair heard one of Dressler's Raiders rustling behind her.

"General, take it easy," Sinclair said. "These spacemen have been through—"

"You will remain silent, Sinclair." Maxwell flicked his deep-brown eyes at her. "I will deal with you in a minute."

He scanned the room, hesitating when he saw Fabian's missing right arm.

"Effective immediately, the Luna Fleet is under my command." He looked past Sinclair. "Colonel Dressler, you report to me now."

Sinclair sighed. "General Maxwell...there is no nee—"

"Silence, Sinclair!" Maxwell's booming voice bounced around the command deck. "You are no longer a general. You are a criminal! You will be *silent*!"

"A criminal?" Fabian jabbed his chin forward.

Maxwell twisted his head. "Was I speaking to you, Lieutenant Colonel?"

Fabian sucked his lips between his teeth.

Maxwell moved closer to Sinclair, close enough for her to smell his coconut cologne. Her stomach cringed at the scent. She clenched her fists behind her back hard.

"What are my crimes, Maxwell?" she asked.

"That is an unnecessary question, Sinclair." He smirked. "You oversaw the shooting of civilians at Marius Hills. You violated direct orders from General Abborn to not engage the Fifth Fleet."

"That is one way to look at it, ain't it?" Sinclair whispered.

"You're at the end of the line." Maxwell raised his voice. "You and I might have never seen eye to eye. You may not agree with my methods of running the space force. But remember this..." He pointed at his chest. "Who was the one who fought for diplomacy and restraint?" His finger turned toward Sinclair. "And who was the one calling for violence?"

Sinclair clenched her teeth hard and imagined Maxwell's white teeth shattering under the pounding of her knuckles. Her neck shook as her anger built up.

"You are the warmonger, Sinclair. I am the peacekeeper." Maxwell spun around in midair. "Have General Sinclair arrested!"

Two Blue Raiders came forward, extending their arms out with handcuffs. Sinclair heard clicks behind her.

Fabian approached Maxwell. "This is not right."

"Back to your station!" Maxwell shouted.

"We need General Sinclair!" Fabian pointed at her.

"Stand down! Or I will have you arrested!"

"Step aside, Fabian," Sinclair pleaded.

Fabian hesitated and looked at Sinclair, blinking a few times. He looked back at Maxwell.

"That's right." Maxwell nodded. "Step aside, cripple."

Fabian roared and lunged forward. He tackled Maxwell, sending both of them tumbling across the deck.

"You mother—" Maxwell flew a couple of fists into Fabian's rib cage. Fabian only screamed, hurling fists at Maxwell.

Rolling backward in a wrestling match with Fabian, Maxwell pulled a black object from his leg. He brought his arm forward, and sharp gunshots rang out. Blood flew out of Fabian's back, and he went slack, floating softly to the ceiling. Maxwell untangled himself.

Something clicked inside Sinclair's chest, and what unfolded next felt like an out-of-body experience. She drew her handgun, vision narrowed on Maxwell. She wasn't sure what words boomed out of her throat.

Maxwell turned to her, his dark face going slack once he registered Sinclair aiming her gun at him. Three rounds blew holes in Maxwell's torso, flinging him back to the wall and splattering blood on the white panels.

Sinclair swung her handgun toward the Blue Raiders.

"Put your weapons down!" She gripped his handgun with two hands, vocal cords trembling. "Don't do it! *Put your weapons down!*"

The Blue Raiders half raised their assault rifles, swinging their heads between Sinclair and Dressler's fire team behind her. After a few seconds, the Raiders jerked their rifles up.

The room exploded with sharp cracks and blinding muzzle flashes.

Sinclair tucked and pulled herself behind the command console. She felt something hot rip through her leg. Her ear canal rattled with waves of gunfire engulfing the room.

"Shift left!" someone yelled.

More gunfire shrieked behind Sinclair. She curled up deeper underneath the console. Bullets hit plastic panels and metal struts. Screens shattered, and control panels blew sparks. Raiders groaned and yelled as the gunfire escalated. The room became engulfed in smoke and bullet holes. The depressurization alarm boomed and flashed.

The gunfire ceased abruptly.

"Sergeant! You still up?" Someone spoke but Sinclair couldn't recognize the voice with her ears ringing from the earsplitting depressurization alarm.

"I'm up, sir!" The voice was muffled.

"Corporal! You alright?"

"Fucking bitch... They got an artery." The voice came from another corner of the room.

"Sergeant, attend to him!"

Sinclair gripped her handgun, close to her chest. She panted hard, swearing to fire all bullets before they took her. She heard groaning as the ringing in her ears died down. A jetpack gave multiple bursts of air.

"Put the gun down, son." A deep voice spoke. "Put it down."

"All this"—someone coughed and struggled to breathe—"for her?"

"Don't do it, son."

"Fuck you!"

Three gunshots barked. Sinclair emerged from her cover and trained her gun at a Raider in black-and-gray-camouflage armor, but lowered it once she registered the soldier to be Dressler.

Dressler pointed his RG-79, smoke leaking out of the muzzle, down at a Raider whose face appeared to have been smashed in with a sledgehammer. He swung his weapon around the room. His dark face was hard and focused. The command deck was covered in blood, bullet holes, and shattered displays. Some Raiders in black armor floated lifelessly.

"You alright, General?" Dressler glided over and checked her leg. "You are bleeding, ma'am. Put pressure on it. Here...give me your handgun."

Sinclair shook her head and holstered it. Dressler guided her hand to the wound and pressed on it. "Sergeant! Put the *Piedmont* on lockdown and undock the *Montana*."

"Yes, sir!" The Raider flew across the room and punched his fingers hard on the docking controls.

Sinclair screamed when a blinding pain gripped her leg after Dressler pressed harder on her wound.

"Keep it tight, ma'am." He patted her shoulder. "It's alright. You're still alive." He raised his finger to his earpiece. "Dragon-1...spin up all units and deploy them to the *Piedmont*. Full combat package. Copy?"

Sinclair looked up and saw Fabian floating against the ceiling, blood oozing from his back into a black orb, no gravity to pull it down. Dressler followed her eyes. He let go of Sinclair's hand and grabbed Fabian's leg, pulling him down.

Dressler pressed a finger to Fabian's neck for a few seconds. "He's dead."

A groan, followed by a cough, was made. Sinclair jerked her head toward the sound and saw Maxwell wincing, his bloody teeth bared.

Sinclair pressed off the wall with her good leg and pulled her handgun. Each breath grew heavier as she got closer to him. She knew Maxwell would somehow escape justice for this. Abborn would force his patrons to turn a blind eye or fabricate a cover story. Sinclair shook her head, clicked the safety button off, and raised the handgun to Maxwell's head.

The wounded general closed his eyes and looked away, panting harder.

"Don't do it, General." Dressler came to her side.

Sinclair's hand shook, struggling to keep the metal sights lined up on Maxwell.

"He is unarmed." Dressler rested his hand on her arm. "Don't lose your honor."

Sinclair squeezed the trigger a few millimeters back until she felt the trigger's resistance grow stiffer. If she pulled the trigger a millimeter closer, Maxwell would no longer be a threat to her spacemen.

"You are our commander," Dressler said. "Don't take that away from us."

She closed her eyes, hand trembling and teeth clenching.

And, with a deep exhale, she released her finger.

"Get him to medical." Sinclair snapped the handgun back in her holster. "He won't get the easy way out."

* * *

After the Dragon Platoon arrived in their assault craft, they swept through the entire carrier, module by module, gathering up Maxwell's spacemen and placing them in the mess hall under guard. Sinclair wasn't taking any chance and assumed all spacemen from the *Montana* were in the fold of Maxwell's violent plot.

Down to only two functional gunships and unwilling to let go of the *Montana*, Sinclair negotiated with the gunship's crew. Short of patience, her blood vessels pulsing hard for vengeance, Sinclair threatened the crew with violence unless they turned over the *Montana*. The crew quickly capitulated.

It surprised Sinclair how easily Maxwell's Raiders had been disarmed. Sinclair speculated much of it had to do with Dressler's reputation and word spreading on how he gunned down Blue Raiders inside the command deck.

Resting in what had been Medvedev's private quarters, Sinclair floated inside her sleeping bag strapped to the wall. Her gunshot wound was aching, and the medical bay was short of painkillers. She could hear and feel the vibration of the construction shuddering through the walls of the *Piedmont*. She focused her mind on finding a rhythm to the pounding and drilling, trying to distract herself from the pain.

Sleep refused to drown her, and her mind spun in a vicious cycle, running through vivid memories of the *Imperator* blowing up, the spaceport atrium littered with dead bodies, destroyers torn apart by rail-gun slugs, the *Oregon* crashing into the lunar surface, and gunshots blowing Fabian's back open. Sinclair pressed her eyes with the palms of her hands, trying to press the violent images away.

Sinclair huffed and unzipped the sleeping bag. She kicked the wall and curled up into a slow spin inside the small compartment, her blonde hair trailing behind her head like a flag fluttering against strong winds. The injustices couldn't go unpunished. The government must pay for ordering Fosvik into the Marius Hills Massacre. Abborn must bear the consequences of advocating for destroyers and refusing to support the Luna Fleet when the EU Fifth Fleet burned for Luna. Maxwell must answer for his violence.

The somersault flushed the tension from her body. The more she thought about it, the more she wondered why she even cared about the United States. Despite over twenty years of service, she had only gotten stabs in the back as inept generals, crony oligarchs, and corrupt politicians benefited themselves at the expense of everyone else. Supporting a government willing to shoot its own citizens, stripping away their freedom through illegal laws, and abandoning soldiers to fend for themselves was not worthy of her service.

It was the hardworking people and businesses of Luna she felt proud of defending. Despite challenge after challenge being thrown at them, they stood back up and rebuilt their cities. They fed and supported her fleet. She felt an obligation to protect them, and the United States Space Force was only a hindrance to that obligation.

If Sinclair was going to do what she was going to do, she needed a new set of allies. She pulled her hair back in a tight ponytail, zipped up her black uniform, and pulled out her hand terminal. There was only one organization that could support her.

She started the video recording. "Mr. Vanderheiden, this is General Sinclair. I put more thought into the employment opportunity we discussed years ago. I have a counteroffer to make..."

32

THE MAGNATE

NYSE: *Error Detected*

An encrypted message popped onto the screen, and Vanderheiden swiped it away. His eyes were locked on Susann's message. *Emily fell into a coma?* His knee shook with impatience. *A coma?*

The cabin lowered the intensity of the sound when the VTOL engines thundered against the air. Giovanni sat in the cabin with Vanderheiden, looking out the window. The sun was setting, making the many brake lights and headlights of cars on the roads easy to see. The parking lots of churches and charity centers were lit by overhead lights, showing long lines encircling the buildings and enormous crowds hugging the entrance.

The landing pad on top of the hospital flashed as his VTOL approached. Protesters with signs and flares surrounded the medical center, facing police officers in riot gear. Multiple police cars lit up the building with red and blue lights. Vanderheiden couldn't tell what the protest was about. *These days, it could be anything or everything.*

After landing on the rooftop and taking the elevator down, Vanderheiden walked through the hallways, followed by Giovanni.

The hospital was still a mess. Patients sat on chairs or lay on the floors in the hallways. Garbage cans overflowed with trash. Supply closets were bare. Doctors and nurses didn't wear latex gloves. Many of their eyes looked like they were trying to disconnect themselves from reality.

Susann marched from the opposite end of the hallway. She had her dark hair pulled back and had no makeup on.

"What's going on?" He grasped her arm. "I got your message."

"Emily is in a coma," Susann said, her eyes turning watery. "It was just...sudden, and the doctor can't explain why."

Vanderheiden sighed. He couldn't remember his last conversation with Emily, given she had been asleep during his past few visits.

"Things don't look good around here." He glanced both ways down the hallway. "Can we move her to a different hospital?"

She shook her head. "It's worse at other hospitals. I drove to them."

His throat tightened. "Susann, please don't drive in this area. Use the VTOL instead."

"If you are worried about the protesters, I can handle them."

"But you are my wife, and I have a target on my back." He waved in the air. "Politicians are asking people to confront businessmen in the streets, demanding them to go along with the confiscations. You know how some people can get nasty about that."

She glanced over his shoulder. "Thanks for looking after him, Giovanni."

The bodyguard nodded and went back to scanning the hallway, eyes twitching with alertness.

Vanderheiden reached for a kiss to her cheek, but she spun around and walked away. He blinked and followed her to Emily's room. Giovanni stood outside the door.

A convoluted collection of medical equipment surrounded Emily. At least three instruments were hooked up to her. A plastic tube went into her mouth. She was pale, almost blending in with the white bedsheets. He felt his heart cramp. It was one thing hearing that his daughter was in a coma, but it was different seeing it.

Susann sat in a chair next to Emily. Her head rested on her hand, clutching a tissue. Vanderheiden took a few steps forward.

Susann looked up. "Do you have the treatment?" Her eyes were red and she looked exhausted.

"I do not." He stopped walking. "Emily is still low on the queue."

"Then why are you here?"

"Our daughter is in a coma," he whispered.

"There were so many days I could've used your help, but you were *too busy* with your hobby."

"My hobby? It's my job..."

Susann sprung out of the chair and smacked him in the shoulder. "Your job is to be a father!" She smacked him again. "You are wealthy!" Another smack. "What's the point"—a third smack—"of it all if you can't get Emily the treatment?"

Vanderheiden raised his arms to block her swings. "Damn it, Susann! I'm your husband! Don't *smack* me like that!"

She stopped swinging and stared at him, her face reddening.

"Ask the government." He readjusted his leather jacket.

She let out a sharp gasp. "Why weren't you here?" Her lips twisted, and tears swelled in her eyes. "There were so many days I could've used you by my side. We promised to be there for each other."

He stepped forward to embrace her.

"Get out!" Susann flung her arms to the sides. *"Get out!"*

He flinched back, mouth open. They stared at each other. Susann's face was flushed and tight. Vanderheiden sighed and walked out of the room. He gestured for Giovanni to stay put and walked into an unoccupied patient room.

The way Susann crumbled before him still stung. *She is struggling, and I should have known. Why is everything falling apart?* He paced the room, his heart beating in panic. *I'm not a good father. I'm not a good husband.*

Vanderheiden ground his teeth. The company he'd founded and had dedicated years of his life to was being taken away. He was so close to completing the first space elevator in human history. *So close.* Susann chastised him. His daughter lay in a hospital bed, dying. The government failed to treat his daughter, and yet they had the audacity to take away his lifelong project.

His fists shook, forearm muscles training. His lungs exploded, and he let out a maddening roar. He punched a hole in the wall. And another hole, followed by a third. Blood oozed out of his knuckles. He kicked the closet door, feeling pain on his toenails. Screaming, he swept glass containers off the cabinet with both arms, shattering them across the tile. He ran over to the bed, knocked the medical equipment down, and slapped the mattress. He roared again, feeling his lungs cramping.

"Mine! Mine! *Mine!*" He slapped his hands on the bed.

He panted hard and slouched his shoulders. His heartbeat echoed from the tip of his skull to the bottom of his feet. The medical devices on the floor beeped. He stomped one of them to stop the bothersome noise. A mixture of liquid dripped off the counter. Needles and cotton pads were scattered across the floor.

He leaned against the wall and collapsed to the ground, heaving. He gasped and tried to let out a cry, but nothing came. His vision narrowed into a dark tunnel as he stared at the broken glass containers he'd thrown. *I did all this to save Emily.* He squinted his eyes shut. *But I have failed.*

His hand terminal beeped with an urgent message, pulling Vanderheiden out of the darkness in his mind. He pulled it out and saw it was a second notification from the encrypted message. He opened the message, seeing a video recording of a US Space Force officer with thin lips and blonde hair pulled back.

Her cheeks were more swallow compared to when he'd met her at the soccer game. General Sinclair must be on a military spacecraft from the looks of the metal panels he saw in the background. He pressed play.

"Mr. Vanderheiden, this is General Sinclair. I put more thought into the employment opportunity we discussed years ago. I have a counteroffer to make. The US government's confiscation of your company, under the Industry Champions Act, is illegal."

She paused and turned away from the camera, looking around for her next words.

"I can offer your protection against the act. As of this moment, I am in control of Luna. Move your company to Luna, and I will give you the freedom you seek. I will adhere to the list of demands the Space Magnates asked for. This offer is to all magnates. I invite everyone to Luna to discuss this opportunity. I ask for a quick response. Time is not on our side. Discretion is of the utmost importance."

The screen blacked out.

Vanderheiden didn't move. The tensions and aches that burned his body bled out of his arms and legs. The headache no longer stabbed his skull. *Move to Luna? Maybe. Just maybe.*

Sharp sounds and loud words came from the hallway. Vanderheiden put his hand terminal away and stepped out of the room. Giovanni wasn't by Emily's room. He looked down the hallway and saw his bodyguard lined up with hospital security officers. Protesters stood in front of them, yelling.

Vanderheiden ran to the window, looked down at the parking lot, and saw police officers standing clear of the protesters funneling into the hospital entrance.

"Oh no..." he whispered.

Sprinting out of the room, he remembered the mess he'd made. He pulled his terminal out to send a large tip to the National Medical Service, but hesitated. *Screw it...they can use my tax credits.* He stepped out into the hallway and walked toward the crowd.

"Vanderheiden!" a protester shouted. "We saw your VTOL! We know you are here! Come out and explain why you won't give your company to the people, you greedy capitalist!"

You mean give it to Shugart? Vanderheiden stopped walking.

The crowd became more agitated when they saw him. Giovanni and hospital security officers continued holding the protesters back.

Vanderheiden stepped backward and bumped into Susann.

"Why aren't you in the room?" he hissed and then shook his head. "Forget it... Get Emily to the VTOL!"

"Why? She is in a coma!"

He gestured violently at the protesters.

"Let's keep it civil here, people!" Giovanni yelled. "We are at a hospital!"

Vanderheiden grabbed Susann's arm. "Now!"

She ran back to the room.

The crowd shouted and cursed at Vanderheiden. *How do they expect me to cooperate if this is how they treat me?*

A man shoved a security officer, who pushed him back.

"Please leave!" a nurse yelled over the counter. "Our patients are ill!"

A protester pointed at Giovanni. "You are part of the problem!"

Vanderheiden had never been in a fight in his life. Growing up, he'd experienced his fair share of playful wrestling but never a fist-fight. He clenched his fist, hoping he was ready for his first one. He took a few steps back.

A black stick swung out of the crowd and hit a security officer. He dropped to a knee, blood dripping down his brown hair. The attacker swung again.

Giovanni opened his jacket, drew his handgun, and fired two rounds into the attacker's chest. The shot echoed down the hallway. Blood splattered on the faces of the protesters. The attacker collapsed to the ground, arms and legs twitching.

"Get back! *Get back!*" Giovanni stepped back, gun pointing at the legs of the crowd. The security officers drew their guns, glancing at each other.

The crowd pulled away, like an invisible force was pushing the two groups apart. Everyone froze, staring at one another. Vanderheiden took a few more steps back, his gut screaming at him to run.

One protester took a cautious step forward. Another took a step. A few followed them. Giovanni and hospital security didn't react.

"Get them!" someone in the crowd yelled.

The crowd burst forward like a tsunami.

"Run!" Giovanni swung around.

Vanderheiden sprinted down the hallway. Panting, he was relieved to see his family entering the elevator. Emily was in a mobile bed, assisted by two nurses.

"Get to the rooftop!" Vanderheiden shouted. "We'll meet you up there!"

"Michael!" Susann stretched out her hand to grasp him.

The elevator doors closed and beeped.

"Giovanni! Up the stairs!"

"Go! Go!" Giovanni sprinted down the hallway, staying ahead of the protesters.

Vanderheiden swung the door open, and the metal door smacked against the concrete wall. He ran up the stairs, skipping every other step.

A gunshot echoed from below him. The shell clinked on the ground.

Vanderheiden didn't look behind him, concentrating on each step. He kept his breathing steady and purposeful.

Another gunshot, followed by the clink.

Running up the stairs felt like a sprint workout, and thinking of it that way helped his nerves stay under control.

Beneath him, two gunshots barked, and multiple clinks sounded against the concrete floor.

He ran out of steps and pushed through the exit door, coming out onto the rooftop. The strong wind and the VTOL engines hitting the air knocked him to the ground. The engines drowned all other sounds, ringing in his ears. It was nighttime, so only the VTOL and light fixtures lit up the rooftop.

Susann and the nurses pushed Emily toward the VTOL. Emily's brown hair flew everywhere.

The elevator door was still open. He charged for it and pressed the hold-door button repeatedly.

Giovanni came out of the exit door, slammed it shut, and pushed his shoulder against it.

Vanderheiden cupped his hands around his mouth and yelled, "We have to go!"

"No! Get the VTOL ready!" Blood vessels popped in Giovanni's neck as he held the door. "Wave your arm once it is ready for takeoff!"

"You promise?"

"Yes! Go! Go!"

Vanderheiden ran across the rooftop. His family was in the VTOL. Once they secured Emily, the nurses stepped back from the aircraft. Vanderheiden pushed them into the cabin, knowing they were in danger as well. One of them yelped.

He jumped inside and pressed the emergency takeoff button on the VTOL controls. A circle spun on the console screen, and the engines roared.

Susann stroked Emily's hair, whispering into her ear. Vanderheiden looked back at Giovanni. He still held the exit door closed.

The console beeped, ready for immediate takeoff. Vanderheiden stepped off the aircraft and waved at Giovanni.

He nodded and holstered his handgun. He took a few deep breaths and then sprinted for the VTOL. A massive crowd flooded out the exit door behind him, like fire ants leaving a compromised anthill.

Vanderheiden stepped back in and offered his hand. Giovanni grabbed it with a sweaty hand and pulled himself in.

The VTOL ascended. Vanderheiden wished it would climb faster. When it cleared the edge of the building, he relaxed.

"A Molotov!" Giovanni's eyes widened, and he drew his handgun.

Vanderheiden snapped his head back to the roof and saw a person holding a Molotov cocktail, a cloth covered in flames hanging from the top of a glass bottle. He was charging for the VTOL. Vanderheiden felt déjà vu, thinking he recognized the way the person ran.

Giovanni extended his arms out and fired three shots, muzzle flashes lighting up the cabin. The individual completed the throw before collapsing to the ground with two red holes in his torso.

The dark bottle with a fire tail flew toward them and hit the side of the aircraft. The engines drowned out the sound of the glass shattering.

The fire burned the exterior, visible through the window, casting everyone inside the cabin in shades of orange. Susann wrapped her arm around Emily, horror on her face. The nurses screamed.

The jet engines blew the fire out. The aircraft was several meters clear of the rooftop, where the crowd gathered, shouting curses and flashing hand signals. Vanderheiden closed the door and collapsed in his seat. He saw Giovanni shaking, both hands grasping his handgun.

"I shot four of them." His teeth were clicking.

"Giovanni..." Vanderheiden reached across the cabin. "Put your gun away."

Giovanni seemed surprised to find a gun in his hands. He holstered it.

Vanderheiden grasped Giovanni's arm. "Thank you."

The trembling bodyguard only nodded.

Vanderheiden looked out the window, half of it charred from the fire. Down on the streets, police in riot gear fired tear gas at larger crowds. Rioters threw some of the tear-gas canisters back. Flares burned inside the crowds. In other blocks, flames engulfed stores and cars. Streets were littered with debris and motionless bodies. A massive fire consumed one government building. Many districts were completely black from the lack of power, and small sparks popped inside those dark blocks.

Vanderheiden pulled out his hand terminal and replayed Sinclair's message. He fast-forwarded the recording.

"—is illegal. I can offer your protection against the act. As of this moment, I am in control of Luna. Move your company to Luna, and I will give you the freedom you seek. I will adhere to the list of demands the Space Magnates seek. This offer is to all magnates. I invite everyone to Luna to discuss this opportunity. I ask for a—"

He paused the recording and looked out the window. Emerging from the VC spaceport on the coastline, far enough away that it was behind the planet's curvature, was a rocket firing its engine. It illuminated the clouds in the nighttime sky, carrying Gonzalez and the master key to orbit.

No one is taking my company. No one is telling Valkyrie Labs how to distribute their CJD-VL. Fingers shaking, he pressed the reply button and started recording. He looked at his daughter lying in a comatose state. *I will save you, Emily.*

"General Sinclair...I accept your offer."

33

THE GENERAL

"*General Sinclair...I accept your offer.*" Vanderheiden nodded. "*Name the date and location. The Space Magnates will be there.*"

The video was shaky, and the background noise sounded like Vanderheiden was inside an aircraft. The businessman looked shocked but focused, like a soldier who'd just gotten his first taste of combat.

The screen blacked out. Sinclair turned off the hologram and looked across the table at the four top senior officers of the Luna Fleet. Behind the general was a long, narrow window revealing the permanently black sky overlooking the plains of lunar dust encompassing the Aestuum Space Force Base and its many domes.

Having rushed back to the ground base amid retrofitting the *Piedmont* spacecraft carrier, Lamar was still in his space suit, irritated. Colonel Barrows's eyes were wide and he couldn't sit still. Colonel Dressler stood in the back of the room, arms crossed, stoic as a statue. He scrutinized everyone, like he was trying to uncover a mole. Lieutenant Colonel Audubon sat with a slight slouch, his curly black hair hanging over his forehead, seemingly indifferent about being in the room.

"Offer protection against the Industry Champions Act?" Barrows asked. "Wh-what does that mean?"

"We're going rogue, Barrows." Lamar untwisted his gloves off.

"No..." Barrows flinched and spun his head to Sinclair. "You don't mean that, do you?"

"Yes, Colonel, that's exactly what I mean," Sinclair replied. "Our country is fracturing. It's everyone for themselves now. We must pick a side now, and the Space Magnates represent hope for our fleet, not the US government."

"Look, General..." Lamar wiped sweat from his bald head. "The spacemen declared loyalty to you. They didn't agree to become deserters."

"And I swore to look after each one of you." Sinclair pointed at the officers. "This is necessary to protect our future. Abborn and SPACECOM don't care about us. They don't deserve our loyalty. They left us at the mercy of the Fifth Fleet."

Barrows stood up and circled around the table, toward the window. "Even if we declare independence, go rogue"—he waved his arms—"whatever we are calling this, what happens to our supply lines? What's stopping Abborn from sending in the Orbital Fleet? What about General Fassbinder and the Mars Fleet?"

"That's why we need the Space Magnates. They'll keep us supplied and fed. We've defended Luna and we will defend it again. We also have the EU vessels for extra firepower."

Barrows took a few shaky breaths and stared at the dusty surface outside, his eyes desperately searching for words.

"What if we asked the Mars Fleet to join us?" Lamar rested his hands on his space suit's neck seal.

"That crossed my mind." Sinclair turned to the second engineer. "If they left their theater to join us, that would raise alarms at the Pentagon and leave Europe unchallenged on Mars. If we approached General Fassbinder and he refused, we've exposed ourselves prematurely, and two fully equipped fleets will charge us from both directions."

"I know a few spacemen in the Mars Fleet," Lamar replied. "They are disgruntled like our spacemen were when you came here last year. They may be open to your plan, General."

Sinclair shook her head. "It's an unnecessary risk."

"Stop this!" Barrows smacked his hands on the base of the window. "Why are we talking about this? We are talking about *treason*! I have family back home. We can't betray our country!"

"They betrayed us first!" Sinclair shouted.

Barrows flinched away from her.

"Maxwell came here and killed Fabian!" Sinclair continued raising her voice, her throat tender. "The government abandoned us! We defended Luna, and they tried to take away our command!" She pounded her chest. "We *earned* this command!"

Barrows raised his hands. "You have every right to be—"

"Do you know who has supported us the entire time we've been here? *Huh?*" Sinclair jabbed a finger toward the window. "The Lunarians! Even after we stormed their spaceport and shot several of them! They've helped rebuild our fleet and kept us fed. They have earned our protection, and I will give it to them!"

Sinclair took a step toward the table. "Are you with me?"

Lamar and Barrows glanced at each other. Dressler kept his eyes on Sinclair. Audubon continued staring at the wall.

"Fuck it." Lamar shrugged and grabbed his helmet. "Luna is my home. I'm in."

"Audubon?" Barrows asked.

"I'm with General Sinclair." The lieutenant colonel lifted his head, and his soft, watery eyes turned hard. "They must pay for Piazza's death."

"Jesus Christ..." Barrows shook his head. "Dressler?"

The Raider didn't speak, still standing against the wall next to the door. He looked deeply into Sinclair's eyes. She felt uncomfortable, like he was formulating plans to kill everyone in the room for the crimes they were conspiring to commit. He could save his own skin, order Raiders to barge in at any point, arrest Sinclair, and turn her over to Abborn. She glanced down at the handgun holstered to his thigh.

"This isn't about nations, ideologies, or profit." Dressler pushed himself off the wall with his foot. "It's about victory. Victory or defeat."

Dressler walked around the table, the other four watching his movement. "Like the general said, this nation is falling apart, and we must pick a side. I intend to pick the side that will emerge victorious. We belong to the battlefield. I will serve the commander who will lead us to victory." Dressler raised his finger toward Sinclair. "General Sinclair is that commander."

Sinclair throttled a sigh building in her throat. "Thank you, Colonel."

Dressler gave a small nod and then snapped his eyes to Barrows.

Sinclair followed his eyes. "Barrows, are you in?"

The senior gunship officer rested both hands on the base of the window, shaking his head. "You've been planning this for years, haven't you?"

He turned around. "You shifted our food supply to Scharre Farms to reduce our reliance on Earth. Was that to make it easier to break away from the United States?"

Sinclair opened her mouth, but Barrows cut her off, taking steps toward her.

"You ordered Vasquez to assault the *Piedmont* with minimal collateral damage, putting them at risk. Was keeping the Fifth Fleet intact part of your conspiracy to expand the Luna Fleet?"

He took another step forward. He was within arm's reach of Sinclair now and looked down at her. Sinclair wished they were in zero-g so she could hover above him. She stood her ground and didn't blink.

"This decision to commit mutiny was not driven by events that forced your hand." He pointed at her and spoke in a bitter voice. "You...have been conspiring for years. You are ambitious with no lines to cross."

He expanded his arms out. "We are just tools for your own political ambitions. You...are no different from the other generals. I thought you were different."

Sinclair wasn't sure. She believed the plot had formed somewhere in her subconscious. She was always independent-minded and disliked people telling her what to do.

Barrows slowly pursed his lips, and his eyes hardened on Sinclair. "No...I will not end my family's generations of military service for the United States. I will not betray my country. I will not— Oof!"

A black-and-gray blur slammed Barrows onto the table. Dressler twisted Barrows's arm behind his back and pulled him down by his neck to the hard surface. Lamar stepped back with disbelief, and Audubon remained seated, eyes widening.

"General?" Dressler jerked his head up, keeping Barrows restrained. "We can't let him loose."

Sinclair looked down at Barrows, his baby-shaped face seething red. She cringed, wishing it didn't have to be this way for him. "Send him to the brig, Dressler. Keep him isolated."

"Yes, ma'am." Dressler pulled out his electric baton and electrocuted him. Barrows shuddered into unconsciousness, and his eyes rolled back.

"Goddamn it, Dressler!" Lamar stepped forward. "Go easy on him!"

"We are not taking any chances here!" Dressler barked at him.

Sinclair tightened her fists. "Dressler, take a platoon over to the Billionaires' Crater and secure it for our meeting with the Space Magnates."

"Yes, ma'am." Dressler heaved Barrows over his shoulder with a grunt and departed the room.

Sinclair felt pity for Barrows weigh heavily on her chest. She was devising a conspiracy to go rogue, and she'd just lost her best gunship officer.

Lamar pulled up his hand terminal. "General...if we do this, I will need to rework the fleet's network. SPACECOM could easily take control of our spacecraft if they knew our plans."

"How hard will it be to alter the codes?" Sinclair asked.

"Depends on how many engineers I have working on this."

"Pick two you trust and get it done."

"Yes, ma'am." Lamar marched out of the room.

“Lieutenant Colonel Audubon!” Sinclair yelled

The lieutenant colonel snapped out of his seat at attention. “Ma’am.”

“You are now my deputy. Take command of the fleet. Monitor the scopes closely and report any changes in the Orbital Fleet’s behavior.”

“Yes, ma’am.” Audubon saluted and left the room.

Alone now, Sinclair turned back to the narrow window. It didn’t seem real, but after decades of hard work and unyielding determination to gain four stars on her shoulders, she was a rogue soldier. The United States would brand her and all officers of the Luna Fleet as traitors. She felt tension in her back, coming from the obligation to protect her spacemen from the crimes she was about to commit.

Convincing the senior officers to support her plot wouldn’t be the hard part. The hard part would be convincing the dozens of Space Magnates to put their companies at risk. Either she received the support of the Space Magnates and gained access to their economic resources or the Luna Fleet would quickly descend into starvation, disorder, and mutiny before the Orbital Fleet swept in and arrested all spacemen.

34

THE MAGNATE

NYSE: *Error Detected*

We're going to Luna?" Susann stood in the foyer, which was cluttered with small containers.

Vanderheiden walked down the steps, trying to ignore the commotion engulfing their villa as Giovanni and his security team packed up the family's personal items. His head no longer ached, and he felt elevated by a new sense of purpose. A new opportunity to regain control of his future and save Emily. He had forgotten how clear one's mind was supposed to be.

"It's not safe here anymore," Vanderheiden said. "Our address got leaked."

"Don't fool yourself, boss." Giovanni walked by with a container in each arm and set them down. "The government posted it on the network."

"But what about Emily?" Susann pointed up the stairs.

"You saw what happened at the hospital." Vanderheiden reached the bottom of the steps and dropped the containers he carried. "We can't stay here. We have a medical clinic in Sinus Medii near the surface anchor. She will be cared for."

Susann didn't reply. She narrowed her eyes at him, her frazzled brown hair making her look like she was about to snap. Vanderheiden tucked his chin in slightly.

"You aren't doing this for Emily." Susann crossed her arms. "You're escaping the government, aren't you?"

"I have to." Vanderheiden sighed. "Our livelihood is under threat. I can't let them take my company."

"What about our daughter? She needs you here."

"She is coming with us."

"She *needs* her father."

Susann grabbed his arm with a tight grip and pulled him into his office, away from the security team. She closed the door, turned around, and looked at Vanderheiden with moist red eyes. "Your company doesn't matter. Emily does. Bribe someone in the NMS. Buy the treatment off the black market."

She will do anything for Emily. Vanderheiden blinked. *Anything.*

He pulled out his hand terminal, opened a message from his inbox, and handed it to her.

Susann looked at him with an inquisitive look. She took the hand terminal and read the message. Confusion contorted her face, and her lips quivered as she read through the message.

"They promise to move Emily to the top of the queue if you cease your legal efforts against the Industry Champions Act," she whispered. "When did you get this message?"

"Yesterday after federal agents raided the headquarters."

She held her mouth open for a moment, lips trembling. "Are you going to do it?"

Vanderheiden crossed his arms and clenched his jaw. "I will not."

Susann's expression turned dark. "You *choose* your company over *your own daughter*?"

Vanderheiden grabbed the terminal and pointed at it. "This is extortion." He spoke in a calm, calculated voice. "I will not bend to Shugart or anyone. Thousands of employees depend on me. Hundreds of customers need the PhotonicWay and the Luna Space

Elevator. Many investors put their money at risk to build this company."

He took a deep breath. "I am not simply going to roll over and let them take my company. It would be an utter...betrayal of all of them if we accepted this offer."

"But this is our daughter!" Susann squealed.

"And how *dare* they hold our daughter's life hostage!" Vanderheiden roared.

Susann's voice shrank to a whisper. "So, we are going to let her die?"

"I will not let her die. I am still a father." Vanderheiden gulped. "Dr. Raymond is the key."

"The Valkyrie Labs CEO..."

"Yes. She is a Space Magnate. General Sinclair has promised to support our list of demands. If the general delivers, Valkyrie Labs regains full control of CJD-VL distribution. And then we will get Emily's treatment."

Susann relaxed her shoulders and straightened her back. "Promise me you will save Emily."

"I promise."

Susann sighed. "Then we will go to Luna."

"Gabriella." Vanderheiden heard Giovanni's voice muffled by the office door.

"Where is he?" she asked sharply.

Vanderheiden left the office. As soon as he closed the office door behind him, Gabriella came up to his face. "We need to move."

"We're working on it." Vanderheiden swept his hand across the foyer.

"The board is asking for your whereabouts."

"Hold them at bay. We need to know what Sinclair will offer."

"Her message was clear." Gabriella interlocked her fingers in front of her. "Declare independence. Separate Luna from the United States."

"Do you think the board will go along with it?"

"There will be a divide." She shook her head. "Cooper will try to file an injunction against you, but as long as we stick together, hold the master key, and shift our financial assets off Earth, there is nothing they can do."

"What about the other Space Magnates? Do you think they will support Sinclair?"

"Blackburn and the radicals will go for it. But I'm worried about others, such as Dr. Raymond." Gabriella pursed her red lips. "However, when the government is about to take away your businesses with no recourse, the most extreme option looks attractive. But how many are willing to go through with it?" She shrugged. "We will find out soon."

"What about your family?"

"Mr. Scharre and my wife are already at Luna in the Costa Crater, waiting for everyone. The Scharre family built its wealth through Luna. If Sinclair can deliver on her promise, they will back her." She glanced to the side. "Though I'm worried about a few of his children, such as Junior."

Giovanni stepped in between the two. "We need to leave in minutes. My team can only hold off the federal agents at the spaceport gates for so long." He picked up a container. "If we are to leave before they seize your spaceport, we leave *now*."

* * *

"Welcome to Marius Hills, Mr. Vanderheiden. Enjoy your stay." The bored customs official pressed a button, and the console chimed.

"Thank you." Vanderheiden grabbed his hand terminal, walked past the booth, and entered the Marius Hills Spaceport atrium, joining his family, company chiefs, employees, and the security team. He glanced back at the customs official, who raised his hand for the next person in line. *Which side will he choose when Luna secedes from the United States?*

The large entourage gathered their items and walked toward the tunnel connected to Marius Hills City. Susann, bedridden Emily, and VC employees were headed to the surface anchor while Vanderheiden, Giovanni, and Gabriella were needed at the Billionaires' Crater.

Floors and walls of the domed atrium had been stripped down to barebones. Carts roamed in all directions, carrying tools and materials. Construction workers poured fresh lunarcrete. Sparks flew as droids welded walls and structs. The environmental system ran at full capacity, but it still smelled like burnt metal and sweaty odor. It was loud enough to rattle Vanderheiden's head, and he couldn't hear himself think.

Many of the walls were fully restored, except for a five-meter section near the tunnel entrance connected to Marius Hills City. The lunarcrete wall was riddled with what appeared to be bullet holes. *A memorial for the people killed during the massacre.*

The workers and droids bore the logos of Blackburn Materials, Lawrence Resources, Castlereagh Manufacturing, and many other companies. *Ironic for politicians and newsfeeds to praise the government for leading the recovery effort.* It was the companies and their employees that did the funding, coordination, and heavy lifting of the Marius Hills reconstruction.

"Vanderheiden?" someone shouted from the construction site.

Vanderheiden froze, watching a bald man with a long beard emerge from the crowd and march toward him. He recognized Logan from his previous trip to Luna and the interview on *Samantha's Corner* after his public announcement of the Luna Space Elevator.

Giovanni stepped in front of Vanderheiden and raised his hand. "That's close enough!"

Logan stopped at a distance, his chest up and chin held high. "Are you Vanderheiden?"

"Yes, I am," he replied cautiously.

"What are you going to do about this Industry Champions Act? The other Space Magnates that came through here haven't said anything."

Vanderheiden was uncomfortable with his tone. He looked around the atrium and noticed dozens of Lunarians watching their conversation. He chose his words carefully.

"The Industry Champions Act is in direct violation of our list of demands," Vanderheiden said. "We are seeking political and legal solutions to counteract the new law."

He took a step toward the tunnel, uncomfortable with how the Lunarians stared at him.

Logan raised an eyebrow and cocked his head. "We need something better than that!"

"Don't let them take our companies!" someone behind Logan shouted. "Luna doesn't belong to the United States!"

Vanderheiden stopped walking again, feeling the countless eyes falling on him, sensing their judgment. *They are testing me.* He took a vigilant survey of the large crowd surrounding them. *Wondering if I'm a selfish billionaire or a business magnate who will take the high road.*

He saw farmers who kept his employees fed, welders who built the space elevator cable, electricians who kept the domes wired, doctors and nurses who provided much needed health care, nuclear engineers who powered many cities, and countless other Lunarians who made the Vanderheiden Corporation possible. *Who make my legacy a reality.*

The Luna Space Elevator wouldn't have been possible without them. Yesterday, when they traveled to Luna on the PhotonicWay, Brunelli called Vanderheiden to report that the primary spacedock, called 100K Station, had been successfully raised and locked into space elevator cable a hundred kilometers above the surface. The climber ascent and descent tests to and from 100K Station remained the final steps before the space elevator was declared fully operational.

Turning to his entourage, Vanderheiden watched Susann grip Emily's hospital bed tightly, stroking their daughter's hair. *This isn't just about saving Emily or protecting my company.* He looked back at the larger crowd. *It's also about them.*

It was about the many Lunarians whose well-being was threatened by the government. *They helped secure my legacy.* Vanderheiden took a deep sigh, feeling a new duty grip his conscience. *Now I must return the favor. Take the high road.*

"You are right!" Vanderheiden announced. "Luna doesn't belong to the United States. Marius Hills City, PhotonicWay, Copernicus Quarter, the Luna Space Elevator..." He swung a finger around the crowd. "All of you built it. We will not let the government take what is yours by right. As long as I am standing, I will fight for your future. A safe and secure future!"

Vanderheiden raised a fist. "Luna...is *yours*!"

Cheers roared, its echo bouncing around the dome. The commotion turned into a chant.

"Vanderheiden! Vanderheiden! Vanderheiden!"

Logan extended his hand with a broad smile. Giovanni looked at it and then glanced at Vanderheiden over his shoulder. Vanderheiden nodded, lowered his fist, and shook Logan's hand.

"Lunarians are here for you," Logan whispered into Vanderheiden's ear. "Contact us if you need our support."

"Vanderheiden! Vanderheiden! Vanderheiden!"

* * *

To an average person, the Billionaires' Crater was an extravagant project funded by wealthy people with too much money on their hands. To Vanderheiden, Costa Crater was an audacious effort to build a large park with a pressurized atmosphere inside the crater with a reinforced glass dome built over it. Costa Crater was envisioned to hold trees, creeks, ponds, lawn, beaches, and livestock, offering Lunarians an escape from the dark and barren lunar surface. The dome had been partially built when the recession hit, and the tax increases had caused funding to dry up. Now it stood silent, no construction drones at work.

Many apartments encircled the dome, rented out by millionaires and billionaires. As the rover got closer, Vanderheiden could see half a dozen other armored rovers surrounding one apartment and assumed it was Scharre Sr.'s, as the elder banker had agreed to lend his home to Sinclair for the secret meeting.

A garage door beneath the apartment opened, and the rover

rolled down the ramp toward a parking lot filled with other rovers. After the garage closed and the air repressurized, Vanderheiden, Gabriella, and Giovanni stepped out. A door opened, and several soldiers with assault rifles spread out across the garage.

"Inside, please," a Raider ordered.

Vanderheiden's chest tightened, thinking it was a sting operation. But he calmed down when he saw the Raiders standing with relaxed demeanors, not pointing their weapons at them. Their helmets hung from their hips so their concentrated faces were visible.

The three stepped inside, finding themselves in a small lobby. Blackburn, Dr. Raymond, the Castlereagh sisters, Xin, and many other Space Magnates waited by a second door.

"Welcome to Luna." Blackburn nodded.

Dr. Raymond said, "I hope this general is legit, Vanderheiden."

"I hope so, too, Doctor," Vanderheiden replied.

The second door opened, and a tall, dark-skinned Raider stepped into the lobby, and looked each magnate in the eye. Past the second door was a set of stairs. The Raider officer raised a finger to his ear and nodded.

"The general is ready for you." His voice was hoarse. "Step inside, please."

The magnates exchanged looks, hesitating to move. One by one, many eyes turned to Vanderheiden. He froze, finding himself unable to take a step forward. *What is Sinclair's plan? Did she already have power brokers in Washington ready to grant them autonomy?* At the soccer game, she hadn't come across as someone with deep political connections. *Or is it a military option she has in mind?*

He felt relief when Gabriella broke the lack of motion and entered the door first, going up the stairs, head leaning forward. The other Space Magnates followed her.

Vanderheiden sucked in a breath. *I am about to enter a meeting to discuss what is essentially a rebellion.* If this plot failed, he hoped history would at least be empathic to their cause and allow future generations to understand their motivations. He didn't want history to simply misrepresent them as unethical businessmen or irrational anarchists. *It is the intention that matters, not the result.*

The high-ranking Raider cleared his throat, shaking Vanderheiden out of his thoughts. It was only him and the Raiders in the lobby now. Everyone else waited for him. General Sinclair waited for him.

He straightened his back and walked up the set of lunarcrete stairs, each step feeling heavier and the walls seemingly getting narrower and ready to swallow him. He entered a large room with a circular table and an observation window overlooking Costa Crater, showing the crater's dark bottom and the outer edge illuminated by the sun. The unfinished rooftop looked like giant metallic fingers reaching out from the lunar surface toward Earth.

All the Space Magnates were seated, looking at him.

A petite blonde officer with a crude scar covering part of her neck walked up to him. *Those burning eyes.* Clear memories of the soccer game flooded his mind.

"Vanderheiden." General Sinclair offered her hand.

35

THE GENERAL

"General Sinclair." Vanderheiden clenched the general's sweaty hand.

There were more gray lines in Vanderheiden's brown hair and beard. The skin around his eyes was darker. However, he seemed alert and composed, like a hardened veteran. She imagined if they had met at the soccer game now, it would've been quiet inside the executive suite. Vanderheiden nodded and took a seat next to Gabriella.

Sinclair clasped her hands behind her back and walked around the table in front of the large observation window that looked down on the unfinished park inside the crater. She wished the flutters in her stomach would go away. It was strange to be more nervous now than during the hours leading up to the Battle of Luna. She wanted Garrett in the room with her. Her mentor never stopped pointing out her spotty diplomatic skills. He would've known how to handle this.

But she was on her own. She had to do this herself.

Sinclair looked around the room, noting the names of each Space Magnate. Gabriella was easy to remember because of her salt-and-pepper hair and thick-rimmed glasses. Scharre Sr. looked terrified of being here, or maybe that was just how his bulging eyes made him seem. Blackburn, bald and burly, gave eager stares around the room.

She saw the Valkyrie Labs CEO but couldn't recall the name of the doctor with a gap in her front teeth. The Castlereagh sisters sat next to each other, but one sister stared at Sinclair with revulsion. Sinclair assumed she was Amanda, who had nearly died in the Marius Hills Massacre.

Sinclair took her eyes off Amanda. Who held sway among the Space Magnates? How much influence did Vanderheiden hold? Who did she need to focus on? Which ones could she ignore?

Dressler entered the room and punched the panel, sealing the door and locking it. With an assault rifle hanging off his shoulder, he stood next to the door, alert, and nodded at Sinclair.

"Thank you." Sinclair spread her arms, swinging her gaze across the circular table. "You came here because I offered protection against the Industry Champions Act. The act is illegal and violates your rights as citizens. In the next few months, they will confiscate every one of your companies."

She raised a hand, saying the words in her head before speaking. "I can offer you protection from the abusive government of the United States. At this moment, I command one of the strongest military forces in the solar system."

A few magnates leaned forward, and Sinclair felt confidence raising her voice. "What I'm proposing is the formation of the Luna Free State. We break away from the governing system of the United States and form an independent nation, with your businesses as the foundation. My military will offer—"

"I didn't come to Luna to take part in a rebellion!" The doctor stood up with revulsion. "I thought you were offering us a political solution!"

Sinclair's neck tightened. "This is not a rebellion. This is the moon's return to a celestial body open to all, safeguarded by the Luna Fleet."

"Don't lie to—"

"Dr. Raymond, stop," Blackburn replied. "You were naïve to think a space force general would offer a political solution."

Many around the table exchanged troubled glances. The flutters in Sinclair's stomach buzzed stronger.

"Let the general finish." Blackburn nodded at Sinclair.

"Political reform is what we should continue pushing for!" Dr. Raymond planted both hands on the table. "We are already criminals for being here, talking about...rebellion."

Blackburn uncrossed his arms. "There is no hope for political reform. Each day, the Industry Champions Act weakens us. Either we declare independence and protect our companies now...or never."

"We are talking about war." Dr. Raymond curled her fingers. "War!"

"Raymond!" Blackburn barked at her. "Let the general finish her proposal. The Protector of Luna has earned that privilege."

Dr. Raymond looked down at him for several seconds. She sat down with reluctance.

Thrown off her word trail, Sinclair measured each word before she spoke. "This strategy can succeed. Revolutions are successful in power vacuums. The United States and the European Union are at war with each other. This gives Luna an opening."

She walked around the room, squeezing her petite figure between the chairs and lunarcrete wall. She raised four fingers. "There are four key elements to a successful revolution: loyalty of the military, legitimacy of the rebellion, control of the newsfeeds, and control of the economy."

She looked at Dressler. "I have the loyalty of the Luna Fleet. Violent protests are waging across our country. The legitimacy is there. For control of the newsfeeds, we need to manage an effective public relations campaign to garner support for our uprising. I will need your support in this area."

She stopped behind Blackburn. "That brings us to the last element: control of the economy." She pointed with both fingers across the room. "That's where each one of you come into play. Before we declare, we must—"

"We don't control the economy," Gabriella interrupted. "The zero-g manufacturing complexes in low earth orbit are the key linkage between Earth and Luna. Whoever controls that controls the cislunar space."

Sinclair nodded. "And that is why I suggest we launch a preemptive strike against the Orbital Fleet in low earth orbit."

"A preemptive strike?" Dr. Raymond was on her feet again.

"Let her finish!" Blackburn slammed his fist on the table.

Sinclair felt the floor slipping out from under her. She was losing control of the meeting. She powered up the hologram in the center of the room, illuminating everyone's face. The hologram displayed Luna and her fleet orbiting it.

"We launch an EU gunship, manned by my spacemen, into a trans-Earth injection maneuver, under the cover of EU prisoners having escaped and trying to join up with remnants of the EU fleet. Closely behind, we launch our own vessels, informing the Orbital Fleet we are in pursuit." The hologram shifted to Earth, showing spacecraft entering orbit around the planet.

"The Orbital Fleet will deploy spacecraft to intercept the EU gunship. My vessels will bring up their rear." The hologram showed the Orbital Fleet spacecraft between the EU gunship and Sinclair's spacecraft.

"Once in position, all three of our vessels will fire on the Orbital Fleet and neutralize them. Our combined forces will then overwhelm the remaining elements of the Orbital Fleet and occupy low earth orbit, giving us control of the cislunar economy."

The room murmured. Blackburn nodded with a satisfied grin, his eyes ravenous.

"This is a rebellion," Dr. Raymond said.

"We cannot be the aggressors," Gabriella replied.

Sinclair swallowed. "It is necessary to ensure our independence."

"I will not support a preemptive strike." Gabriella shook her head. "If we carry out this kind of operation, we'll be labeled as the aggressors and lose legitimacy."

Blackburn replied, "The governments will cave in if we control the manufacturing complexes."

Gabriella ignored him, continuing to look at Sinclair. "I will support the proclamation of a free state...but no preemptive strike." She tapped the table with her finger. "We are businesses, not a military."

Sinclair didn't want politics to derail a sound military strategy. "Blackburn is right. If we gain control of the manufacturing complexes, we control the economy. Fortifying Luna and trying to outlast the governments won't work. We don't have the resources to win a war of attrition. We must make a preemptive strike and cripple their forces."

Up on her feet now, Gabriella's jaw tightened. "If we become the aggressors, we will squander any political support we have and lose this war." She pointed at Sinclair. "You said a key element of a successful revolution is legitimacy. We lose that if we are the aggressors."

Sinclair fumbled to come up with a response, wishing for Garrett's guidance. Doubt flooded her mind, and she struggled to put a sentence together.

"Political support doesn't matter." Blackburn shrugged with annoyance. "Power is determined by who holds the guns."

Gabriella blinked at him.

Sinclair concluded Blackburn and Gabriella held the most sway among the Space Magnates. Vanderheiden sat silently, listening to the debates. She determined him to be a wild card now.

Gabriella raised her arms, looking side to side. "Will anyone else speak out against this aggression?"

"I agree with Gabriella," Scharre Sr. said, his bulging eyes tracing the table. "If we decide to be the aggressors, I will not be a part of this. Either we hold our ground here or I return to Earth and continue pushing for political reform."

Blackburn rose from his seat. "Political reform is no longer an option. No matter how much money we throw at our lobbying friends, the government will never change. They will always be leeches on us. If we are to do this, we must ensure the government cannot retaliate against us."

Dr. Raymond was red. "Blackburn! You want to be responsible for starting a war and having blood on your hands?"

"They started this!" Blackburn got in her face. "I will not let them take what I built!"

"But we can't do it with violence!"

Multiple arguments erupted, voices overlapping each other. Sinclair tried to follow the conversations, but the voices echoed in the observation room, making it hard to follow what everyone was saying. Dressler stepped forward, like a displeased father ready to shout, bringing silence to the room. Sinclair shook her head.

Acid grew in the back of her throat over the need for the Space Magnates' agreement on her military operation. She wondered if this was what it felt like dealing with congressional committees in Washington, DC. No wonder General Garrett had little praise for Congress.

Sinclair still needed the many Space Magnates to support her plot. She had to tread carefully. The industrial base was key to fueling her war machine and boosting her chances of winning the war. Some of these magnates could cripple the rebellion if they withdrew their support. Gabriella controlled a sizeable chunk of the agriculture sector. Vanderheiden dominated space transportation, and the Luna Space Elevator was close to completion. Blackburn made up the vast majority of manufacturing. And topping all of them, Scharre Sr. controlled Luna's financial system through the Scharre Bank.

"Compromises are necessary to develop a political network," Garrett had said a couple times. Sinclair needed to find that compromise. She was threatened with the loss of the financial and agricultural sectors if she pushed for a preemptive strike, leaning on Blackburn's support. If she aligned with Gabriella and Dr. Raymond, she could lose Blackburn and other manufacturing companies, leaving her with no ammunition to arm her gunships or panels to replenish the armored hulls. Was a compromise possible? Or would she have to pick a side and force the other into submission?

People talked over each other as the voices grew louder. What would happen next if this summit fell apart? She had already committed treason by holding this meeting, with dozens of witnesses able to share the story with federal investigators. The room grew hot, and Sinclair wiped sweat off her forehead.

"I will say this one last time," Gabriella stressed. "If we go forward with a preemptive strike, I will leave."

Blackburn's face turned purple, and he bared his teeth. "You all don't have what it takes to seize the freedom we seek. A preemptive strike is necessary to protect our future!"

He strolled toward her. "Gabriella, if you are going to play the ultimatum card, I shall play it as well. We do a preemptive strike...or I'm out."

Gabriella tilted her head toward Blackburn. "Never bluff with me."

She grabbed her bag and walked toward the hatch. Dr. Raymond and several other magnates got up, following Gabriella. Scharre Sr. rested his face in his hands. Sinclair felt the bottom giving out underneath her.

She locked eyes with Dressler, the words to order him to force them back to the table materializing in her throat. He seemed to have read her mind, and drifted his hand to the electric baton strapped to his hip.

"Enough!" Vanderheiden yelled, rising from his seat. "No one is leaving this room until we have an agreement."

36

THE MAGNATE

NYSE: *Error Detected*

This is a disaster. Vanderheiden ground his teeth, watching Dr. Raymond follow Gabriella toward the closed door. *An absolute disaster.*

If Dr. Raymond didn't support the Luna Free State proclamation and break Valkyrie Labs away from the National Medical Service's draconian regulations, how would he save Emily? The thought of his daughter succumbing to Creutzfeldt-Jakob disease while the Space Magnates bickered over their future launched him out of his seat.

"Enough!" He pushed himself up, kicking the chair back, and pointed at Gabriella to sit back down. "No one is leaving this room until we have an agreement."

Gabriella's neck tightened, but she didn't speak. The others following her froze. Vanderheiden turned to General Sinclair. *I'll take it from here.*

Gabriella and the others returned to their seats. Watching them take their seats, Blackburn's face remained purple, his hands clenched in heavy fists. *How the hell am I going to unite the Space Magnates?* Vanderheiden thought.

"I will not return to Earth without a plan to save our companies. The government will not take my company." Vanderheiden pointed at the large window showing the partially completed dome roof reaching over the crater. "People are in the streets, throwing their anger at anybody. Launching a preemptive strike will unite them against us, giving them a common adversary. The government will get a blank check to crack down on us." He waved his hand. "We will not do a preemptive strike."

Blackburn opened his mouth, but he was cut off by Vanderheiden raising his finger. He turned to the other side of the room, where Gabriella, Dr. Raymond, and others sat. Sinclair stood in the center, unmoving. "There is no more hope for political reform. Democracy has failed us. We are in the twilight years of a once great nation. Let's not get caught in its collapse. This is our chance to break away and decide our future." *My daughter's future.*

"Enough monologuing, Vanderheiden," Blackburn growled with annoyance. "What are you proposing?"

"The Luna Space Elevator."

"What about it?"

"You advocated for preemptive strike to maintain access to the zero-g manufacturing complexes. What if we built our own complexes?"

Blackburn chuckled. "It took years, decades, to build those."

"That was before the space elevator existed," Vanderheiden replied. "We could build those complexes in months with it."

Blackburn's side of the room went silent.

I got you. Vanderheiden smiled. "Once we build our own complexes, we redirect our raw material supply to them, leaving the ones in low earth orbit dry. The government would be in a difficult position, unable to impose an embargo on us without dire economic consequences."

"What about the rest of us?" Dr. Raymond asked. "How is that going to protect our companies?"

"We fortify Luna and issue a formal declaration that we are no longer bound to the laws of the United States. Then we sit back and wait for their next move." He pointed at Sinclair. "The Luna Fleet will protect us."

"A fortress strategy..." Dr. Raymond said.

"Yes," Vanderheiden replied.

Blackburn turned to Sinclair. "Without the preemptive strike, what are our chances of winning the war?"

Sinclair raised her chin. "Tactically speaking, a preemptive strike will raise our chances of having a short and decisive war." She paused for a few seconds. "However, the political cost could be high."

Blackburn sucked in his thick lips.

"I have a sufficient number of vessels to protect Luna," Sinclair said. "The space elevator will enable us to build more. We hold the home-field advantage. We defended Luna once, and we'll do it again."

Blackburn and the other manufacturers whispered to each other. After a minute, Blackburn pulled from the group. "Everything depends on the space elevator. We need more assurances for our security. That is why we still advocate for a preemptive strike."

Damn you, Blackburn. Vanderheiden glanced at Gabriella, and both of them held their stares. *Time to give a concession?*

Before the summit, Vanderheiden, Gabriella, and Scharre Sr. had agreed to a list of concessions they were willing to put forward to unite the Space Magnates. *I will not return to Earth only to be dragged to a guillotine.*

"What if we offered, evenly split between all members in this room, a ten percent revenue share of the Luna Space Elevator? In return, you agree to the fortress strategy."

Blackburn crossed his arms and leaned back with a hint of amusement. "I need something more enticing." He twiddled his fingers. "An offer we can't turn down."

"What else do you need?" Gabriella asked.

"Twenty percent. And"—Blackburn smiled, his eyes gluttonous, glancing at the other manufacturers—"fifty percent of the Luna Space Elevator's capacity reserved for military use."

"Now, you are just getting greedy, Blackburn," Vanderheiden

scolded. "War production only brings more business to your companies."

"We must fully support Sinclair's forces!"

"Ten percent revenue share," Vanderheiden countered. "Twenty-five percentage military use, and any increase must have a two-thirds vote from the Space Magnates."

A few turned to Blackburn.

"Fifteen percent revenue share," the bald and burly man said.

Vanderheiden walked around the room. "Twelve percent revenue and twenty-five percent of space elevator reserved for military use." He extended his hand. "Deal?"

Blackburn stood up and grasped Vanderheiden's hand tightly with a smile. "Deal."

Vanderheiden turned around and raised his voice. "All in favor of the fortress strategy?"

He waited a minute for everyone's response. *I can't have any of them feeling forced into this plot.* He feared some magnates would seek immunity from the government to save themselves once things got difficult. *Who will cave first?* One by one, many nodded slowly.

But Vanderheiden only noticed Dr. Raymond trembling. "Dr. Raymond? We need your pharmaceuticals. We can't do this without you." *My daughter needs your CJD-VL.*

"Come on..." Blackburn leaned closer to her.

"We are going to be prosecuted as criminals." She shuddered.

"The government is run by criminals!" Blackburn asserted. "They are the ones who started this!"

Vanderheiden stepped in front of Blackburn and opened his palms to the doctor. "All we are doing is declaring independence. It is up to the government to decide if they will accept it or respond with force." He waved at Sinclair. "She will protect us."

Dr. Raymond brought her hands to her cheeks and rubbed them for a moment.

After a minute of watching her nervousness, Vanderheiden looked around the room. "Will anyone step forward to help out? I've already made a concession. Someone...needs to step it up if we are to make this work."

"I'll buy out Valkyrie Labs," Scharre Sr. said.

Vanderheiden snapped his eyes to him. *Don't aggravate her. My daughter needs her.*

"No!" Dr. Raymond dropped her hands. "You won't take a piece of my company!"

"Then join us..." Scharre Sr. rose slowly, offering his hand.

"Fine!" She exhaled. "Count me in."

She is already unsteady about this. Vanderheiden turned to the general. *I must monitor Dr. Raymond closely.* "General Sinclair, on behalf of all Space Magnates, we accept—"

"Not Sinclair!" a woman behind him yelled. "Not the Butcher of Marius Hills!"

Sinclair widened her eyes and twisted her lips. She raised her hand to the door, shaking her head. Vanderheiden looked behind, noticing the Raider took a few steps toward Amanda.

"Damn it, Amanda!" Blackburn roared, marching around the table toward the Castlereaghs. "Don't spoil an alliance we are about to make!"

Vanderheiden spun, seeing Amanda pull her arm out of her sister's grasp and fast-walk toward Blackburn.

"We cannot partner up with a general who killed dozens of Lunarians!" Amanda said.

"Do not put your need for revenge above everything else!" Blackburn stabbed a finger in her face.

Amanda didn't flinch. "You were not there when the Raiders gunned them down!"

"Don't forget it was Lunarians who shot Lawrence." Alexis came to her side. "He died in your arms."

Vanderheiden got lightheaded at the thought of his friend dying, blood spilling out of his neck. The hardness in Amanda's face dissipated, and she fell silent, her eyes drifting to her hands.

Blackburn smirked, looking down at her.

"I'm sorry," Sinclair said.

All the magnates turned to the general with a mixture of surprised reactions.

"We can discuss the appropriate judicial measures after Luna Free State is secured," Sinclair said. "But, for now, my fleet is your only chance to gain that independence."

Alexis guided her sister back to her seat. Vanderheiden walked to the general.

"We accept your offer...on one condition."

Sinclair raised her chin. "Name it."

"All strategic decisions must have approval from the majority of us."

Sinclair tightened her lips and looked around the room. "That's acceptable if my fleet gets something in return."

"Okay..." Vanderheiden spoke slowly. "What do you have in mind?"

"All my spacemen must have a stake in the future of Luna. Your companies are a key pillar of the moon. If you agree to allocate ten percent ownership of all companies represented in this room to the fleet, you have a deal."

"Yes, we can give you ten percent of our shares," Vanderheiden said. "But we have to agree on how the shares are allocated to your spacemen. We can't have senior officers hoarding them at the expense of the junior and enlisted."

Sinclair slowly took her eyes off Blackburn. "That's a fair deal."

"Excellent. What's our next move?"

Sinclair returned to her seat. "Our supply lines will be critical to surviving, at best case, a limited economic embargo. Worst case, total war. I need a full understanding of what resources will be vulnerable when our supply line with Earth is cut off."

She touched her chin. "Let's see...Blackburn Materials and Castlereagh Manufacturing for our raw and high-tech materials. We are covered there. How does our energy grid look?"

Gabriella said, "Our energy production is split between solar farms and nuclear reactors. Blackburn and Castlereagh can replenish solar farms, while Vanderheiden Corporation can construct new nuclear reactors for any of the cities here."

"Excellent," Sinclair replied. "Propellant. Our engines can use either methane or hydrogen. Hydrogen can be extracted from the water ice deposits inside the lunar crust. Methane grants our spacecraft more delta-v, so we need to secure an alternative supply. Where can we procure methane?"

"Mars," Vanderheiden replied. "It's within reach of the PhotonicWay."

"Yes, but the US and the EU control that planet."

"What about Titan?" Vanderheiden said. "Saturn's moon is awash with methane. My company has the capability to get a photonic platform deployed to Titan. That can be our next project."

"Hold off on that." Sinclair held up her hand. "We should still approach the European Union and negotiate access to methane. We have a common enemy now."

Vanderheiden heard the boldness in her voice. This was now a military discussion, not a political dialogue.

"It's risky." Gabriella shook her head. "Europe could pull us into their war against the United States. The PhotonicWay can be used when we run out of propellant."

"We still need propellant to transport between the surface and orbit," Sinclair replied. "And I doubt there are enough photonic engines to convert all of our spacecraft."

"Then the Luna Space Elevator is key," Vanderheiden said.

"We have a bigger problem than energy and fuel to worry about." Gabriella straightened her back. "Food."

Sinclair tightened her lips. "Yes."

"Damn..." Blackburn replied.

Vanderheiden looked at Gabriella. "What's the problem? You have farms across Luna and in orbit."

"Phosphorus is our problem. It is the key fertilizer for our farms, and Earth is our only source in the solar system for it."

Blackburn wiped dust off his table. "So, the governments can defeat us through starvation. We need to carry out that preemptive strike to bring this imminent war to a swift conclusion."

"Absolutely not!" Dr. Raymond shouted.

"Victory is given to the strongest, not those morally justified," Blackburn said. "I'm not about to starve to death!"

Vanderheiden signaled the two to be silent. "Gabriella, how can we secure a supply of phosphorus?"

"We could secure enough supply to last us twelve to eighteen months before the supply goes bad. Some of it will have to come from the black market, given the government oversight of the suppliers. We need to purchase phosphorus from a supplier not owned by the government to avoid raising suspicions."

"What happens when we run out?" Blackburn asked.

"Then we pursue the military option to secure a stockpile," Sinclair replied. "Gabriella, how long will it take to procure that supply?"

"Give me six months," Gabriella answered.

"Let's get it done in three." Sinclair pointed at her. "All of us will lend ships if needed. Fake an emergency to expedite the process."

"I can claim my supply was tainted and required a full replenishment."

Sinclair touched her chin again. "So, food and propellant are our problems here. The parameters are fluid right now. The progress of the US-EU war will be the key factor. For now, all of us here need to start altering our supply lines to reduce dependence on the United States."

"We are doing this." Blackburn bobbed like he was thirsty for the upcoming struggle. "We *are* doing this!"

Vanderheiden looked around; everyone seemed to be in shock over the fact that they were about to commit a rebellion. *I will do it to save Emily. And mankind's future in the solar system.*

Gabriella stood up. "Well, it is time to get to work. First, draft a public statement. The last thing we need is the government turning to us as a common enemy and uniting the people." She looked around the room. "We need a spokesperson."

People exchanged looks. With a wide grin, Blackburn looked at the general. "I nominate General Sinclair."

Sinclair snapped her head to him, her frown deepening. She stood like a droid perplexed by a simple task it wasn't programmed for. "Why me?" she croaked.

"You hold the most credibility among everyone in this room." Gabriella gestured to Blackburn. "You are the Protector of Luna. People were in the streets chanting your name after you won the Battle of Luna."

Sinclair straightened her back, but the frown persisted. "Fine."

37

THE GENERAL

When Sinclair stepped into the holding cell and saw Barrows in handcuffs, chained to the table, her heart twisted inside her rib cage. It was like seeing a close friend bearing the punishment for something she did. Barrows had a patchy beard covering up his baby face, and he sat with his back erect, watching Sinclair with a cold look.

His eyes lowered to her left shoulder, and he noticed the patch of the United States flag was missing, replaced by a yellow-and-black flag.

"I see you haven't changed your mind." He sighed, making no effort to hide his disappointment.

"Looks like you haven't changed your mind, either." Sinclair sat down at the table and crossed her legs.

"Do you know how far back my military heritage goes?" Barrows shot his chest over the table, baring his teeth. "Generations of military service unbroken since World War II. Nearly two hundred years, General!"

"I could name a list of leaders from military families who betrayed their countries for a more honorable cause. At least, that's what Cavalieri would—"

"Don't bring her into this!" Barrows pounded the table with his handcuffed fists. "You will not tarnish her name with your treason!"

"Stand down, Colonel!"

His breathing quickened, and the knuckles on his trembling fist turned white. "I will not betray my country."

Sinclair tilted her head to the side. "Even after what our country did? Even when our corrupt and incompetent government betrays the Constitution and removes the guardrails of democracy? When superior officers come and shoot their own spacemen?"

"Every nation has its dark times." Barrows frowned. "I will not be the soldier who abandons his country when things get tough."

Sinclair didn't reply, using the silence to push down the urge to plead for his loyalty. For years, she'd mentored him and transformed him into arguably the best gunship officer in the United States Space Force. She needed him if she was to see through the rebellion. It would be such a waste of his potential to be rotting in a cell when a war raged on. His wife and children didn't deserve that.

"I need you, Barrows." Sinclair crossed her arms. "You are my best combat officer. I need someone to watch my back."

"What happened to you?" Barrows shot out of his chair, his hands still chained to the table. "I stood by you. I *looked up* to you. You were the best general we had. You...you were supposed to lead the United States Space Force!"

Sinclair uncrossed her arms and rested them on the table. She gestured at the chair and waited for Barrows to sit back down.

Once his bottom was back on the chair and his breathing had returned to normal, Sinclair replied, "I don't care about being the space chief anymore. Once Maxwell shot Fabian, all that went out the air lock. It's not about gaining power for the sake of power. Ambitious people tend to lose sight of why they are seeking power, and that corrupts them. I lost sight of that for a while. If you are going to seek the top, do it for something good."

Sinclair waved her hand in the air. "All of this I'm doing...is for our spacemen. To protect our spacemen and give them a noble cause to fight for: the safety and security of Luna. The moon is key to stretching mankind's footprint across the solar system. It is my duty to protect Luna and make sure it doesn't fall into the wrong hands. And I intend to carry out that duty until my end on the battlefield."

Barrows kept his cold eyes locked on Sinclair. She got up and scooted her chair in. "You are welcome to join my side again, Colonel Barrows. I will have a gunship waiting for you to take command of." She raised her finger and extended it hard. "But I will only accept you if you are fully committed."

Barrows didn't reply, his eyes only growing more bitter.

"We'll talk again, Colonel."

She left the holding cell and heard the door slide behind her and close with a hiss.

* * *

The top officers of the Luna Defense Forces assembled at the Aestuum Command Center, surrounding the command console that beamed a holographic projection of Luna.

Colonel Dressler, in full combat gear, stood next to Sinclair, ready for the next battle that could be days, weeks, or months away. As long as she remained a competent fleet commander, Sinclair concluded Dressler would stand by her side for the duration of the rebellion.

Sinclair felt less certain about Chief Engineer Lamar and Colonel Audubon, who were standing on the other side of the command console. She'd trained Cavalieri and Barrows and served with them for years. They should be here with her. But Cavalieri had given her life for the security of Luna, and Barrows sat in the brig, ideologically split with Sinclair. So, she had to settle for the charismatic Lamar and the quiet Audubon. Not her preference, but that's the deck of cards she held.

Sinclair checked her tactical armband. "Officers, in a few hours, the Proclamation of Luna Free State will be broadcast. This will trigger a political crisis down in the States, and we have to be prepared for a military response. Our objective is to ensure Luna's independence and protect it against any aggressors."

The hologram spun to show three groups of combat vessels. "Operation Fortress Luna. Our fleet will be broken into three groups to maintain a defensive perimeter around Luna. Two will be positioned in low lunar orbit and change their orbital patterns on an irregular basis to confuse any adversaries. The third group will be our reserve and remain in position in high orbit at Lagrange Point 2, on the far side of Luna."

"So, this is a defensive operation." Audubon scratched his cheek. "No offensive moves?"

"There will be no preemptive strike, if that is what you are asking."

"Well..." He spoke softly. "It is the quickest and cleanest way to cripple Orbit Fleet's capability to launch an attack on us."

"General," Dressler said, "I can sneak two fire teams inside the Orbital Fleet, sabotage their operations, and make it look like the actions of rogue elements inside their fleet."

"Too risky." Sinclair shook her head. "You were in the room with the Space Magnates. They were against any preemptive strike. If we did so, many would withdraw their support, cutting off our supply lines and leaving us crippled in a matter of months. The Orbital Fleet could then sweep in for the final blow."

"The Space Magnates dictate military strategy now?" Dressler raised his voice. "We are military officers. We make these decisions, not boardroom seat warmers."

"The government has to be the aggressor." Sinclair's nostrils flared out. "The first attack we launch will be in response to their aggression. If we attack first, we'll be labeled as terrorists and wipe out any political support we have back home."

Audubon rested his hands on the console. "If we launched a surprise attack and defeated the Orbital Fleet, the war would be swift and we limit the bloodshed. If we don't do this, we could prolong the war and see more body bags in our hangar bay." He pointed at his chest. "And *that* will be on us. It is morally justified to launch a preemptive attack."

Images of body bags filling up in the hangar bay flooded Sinclair's mind, and pressure built up in her throat. Was Audubon correct, or was his quest for revenge for Piazza's death clouding his judgment? She needed to keep a close eye on him.

"What is the makeup of our fleet?" Dressler asked.

"The *Montana*, the *Nevada*, and the *Wyoming* gunships are fully operational," Lamar replied. "The *Decatur* remains heavily damaged, and we are likely to scrap it. For the EU spacecraft, the *Piedmont* and the two destroyers have been restored and are functional. Their sole gunship will take several weeks to repair."

"Prioritize that gunship," Sinclair said. "There is a reason I made you Chief."

"Yes, ma'am."

"So, we only have five to six combat spacecraft to defend Luna... against the Orbital Fleet's dozen." Audubon sighed. "We get lucky once, not twice, General."

"And don't forget the Mars Fleet," Lamar added.

"That's why we need to pursue an alliance with Europe," Sinclair replied.

"Europe?" Audubon pulled his hands from the console like it had suddenly turned hot. "We are going to just...forget about the hundreds of lives lost in battle and become allies with the European Union?" he spat. "Just *forget* about it?"

"The enemy of my enemy is my friend." Lamar crossed his bulky arms.

"That can go the other way around," Sinclair said. "The US and the EU could sign an armistice and turn their guns against us. We need to secure that alliance with Europe before cooler heads prevail between the two nations."

Audubon's breathing grew heavy.

Dressler stepped away from the console, came to the colonel's side, and rested a hand on his shoulder. "Who do you want revenge against: Europe for blood drawn on the battlefield, or the United States, which abandoned us? You can't have both."

Audubon snapped his head up at Dressler's last statement. He moved his stare from the Raider to Sinclair.

Sinclair watched Audubon contemplate the two choices. She did not want Dressler to throw another gunship officer into the brig. Her spacemen needed to be inside the operations decks of gunships and destroyers, not resting their bottoms on the lunarcrete benches inside the brig.

"So be it." Audubon's breathing returned to normal. "We must seek that alliance."

"Good call." Dressler patted his shoulder. "We are in this together. We must cover each other's sixes."

The tall Raider frowned at Sinclair. "But the Space Magnates won't go for it. They don't want Luna dragged into a war."

"Give it time," Sinclair said. "They may oppose it now, but when the sanctions and embargoes inflicted by the United States start to hurt us, the magnates will welcome an alliance."

The three officers nodded their heads in unison.

"Any questions?" Sinclair asked.

"What is the lucrative incentive you spoke of the other day?" Lamar asked. "It might be the only thing that'll keep certain spacemen invested in this plot."

"The Space Magnates have agreed to allocate ten percent of their company equities to our spacemen," Sinclair replied.

"All the companies? Vanderheiden, Blackburn, the Scharre conglomerate...all of them?"

"Yes."

"Billions..." Lamar whistled. "That's billions of credits."

Audubon's mouth dropped open, and Dressler blinked with a twitch of his neck muscles.

"And how will that be distributed?" Lamar asked.

"It will be allocated and adjusted based on each spaceman's rank," Sinclair answered.

"General...I strongly advise against that."

"Why?"

"Fundamentally speaking," Lamar said, "it is a struggle between the haves and have-nots that's tearing the United States apart. Let's not give our spaceman something to brawl over."

"Do you have an alternative?"

"The shares need to be distributed equally, regardless of rank. And for any spacemen killed in battle, their shares will be passed on to their next of kin, not back to fleet command."

"I'm with the chief here." Audubon nodded, his black curly hair jiggling. "Rank doesn't matter here. All of us are putting our lives on the line."

Sinclair thought for a moment. "We can do that, but the fleet commander retains the voting power of all shares. I must maximize my influence over the Space Magnates."

"For how long?" Lamar asked.

"When the United States recognizes our independence, I will release the voting power of all shares not allocated to me."

Dressler turned to face Sinclair. "And is that when the Space Magnates will pursue judicial measures against my Raiders for Marius Hills? Like you promised to them at the meeting?"

Sinclair turned off the hologram. "I said what they wanted to hear. We need their support." She turned to the Raider and leaned her head forward. "As long as I'm the commander of the Luna Defense Forces, no one will pursue criminal charges against my spacemen, including Captain Brawner."

* * *

The shuttle engines fired and kicked Sinclair into her seat. The vessel vibrated as it raised its altitude. Luna grew small behind them. The engines cut off and weightlessness returned. The shuttle maneuvered itself into a line formation with other shuttles, hundreds of meters apart. Several kilometers in the distance was the *Piedmont*, barely visible to the human eye.

Craters passed beneath. The surface anchor was easy to spot if you knew which craters and unpaved roads to find. If she looked through a thermal-imaging telescope, she would spot the orbital anchor around Lagrange Point 1 and a thin cable stretching down to the surface anchor in Sinus Medii. A hundred kilometers above the surface was 100K Station, the spaceport attached to the space elevator cable and anchored by three titanium cables to the surface.

Sinclair unclipped her harness and let herself float. Chief Engineer Lamar and a few of his engineers were in the shuttle with her. If what Vanderheiden said was true about a trip up the space elevator being a fraction of a launch service cost, the possibilities of what her fleet could build were endless.

She opened a schematic drawing of a gunship on her hand terminal. "Chief, come here."

Lamar pushed against the hull to float toward Sinclair. "Yes, General?"

"Check out these schematics I drew." She sent the file to his hand terminal. "Once the space elevator is finished, we need to build a new class of gunship. Play with the length of the rail gun. Double its length...or triple it, if you can."

Lamar's face lit up as he scrolled through the drawings. "Oh yessss...the—the space elevator would raise the limit of how big our gunships can be." He pointed at the schematics. "This kind of size is possible. We can go bigger than what you are asking for, but I need to see how the space elevator performs first."

"See how the performance projections of the gunship look if you swap about the nuclear thermal engines with a photonic engine," Sinclair said. "Play with it and come back to me." Lamar nodded eagerly and floated back to his seat.

Her hand terminal pinged, notifying her the broadcast was about to go live. How would Garrett react to it? Like Barrows, Garrett had patriotism in his blood, so he likely would consider her a traitor. Deep down, she hoped his affection for her would override his patriotism. She chuckled at the thought of Garrett walking up to Abborn, laughing in his face, saying he'd underestimated Sinclair.

The *Piedmont* was visible on the screens. The spacecraft carrier was fully restored with fresh armored plates. The new white-colored plates not matching the spacecraft carrier's original gray color made it look disfigured. The artificial gravity ring spun at normal speed. Many gunships and destroyers were docked to the spacecraft carrier, waiting to be boarded by its new crews. Those vessels were covered with fresh armored plates as well.

Despite the obvious repercussions of this decision, it felt liberating to Sinclair. She no longer felt restricted by superiors and rival officers jealous of her. Thinking about becoming the top military commander of the first nation outside Earth sent shivers down her spine.

But the decision felt justified.

All monitors and hand terminals flashed a yellow-and-black image, followed by a video displaying Sinclair from head to shoulder. Watching the video play, Sinclair looked closely at the dark shades she applied under her eyes and the touch-up on her cheeks and decided it was a mistake to put makeup on. She wished she ignored Gabriella's advice on cosmetics.

A yellow-and-black flag waved behind her. The Space Magnates had chosen a rarely used color combination for flags to distinguish themselves from other nations and ideologies. They believed a red-white-blue combo, which represented democracy and freedom, lost its true meaning.

Sinclair, in the video, started talking. "*My name is General Vivian Sinclair, and I am commander of the Luna Defense Forces. I speak to you today as a voice of Lunarians and a representative for the Space Magnates. Today, I am issuing the formal declaration that Luna ceases to be a territory governed by the United States. We are now the Luna Free State, an independent state.*

"*This proclamation is in response to years of violence and persecution against Lunarians by the corrupt and oppressive government of the United States. The government imposed unjustified and draconian taxes against us. The government confiscated people's property indiscriminately and without due process. The government allowed crime, hatred, prejudice, and corruption to spread throughout the country, enriching those with strong political connections at the expense of the common man, woman, and child. The government refused to come to Luna's aid when it was attacked. The government plundered, tortured, and killed Lunarians for expressing their dissent.*

"The Luna Free State will be self-governed by the people who inhabit it. Do not disrupt commerce traffic. Do not impose taxes and regulations against Luna-based entities. Do not discriminate against Earth-based businesses that conduct trade with Luna. Do not interfere with the Luna Space Elevator. Do not interfere with the PhotonicWay. If these conditions are honored, we will adhere to existing agreements with Earth-based entities.

"If any of these conditions are infringed upon, it will be considered a violation of our sovereignty, and we will respond accordingly. We will defend the moon. We will defend our right to freedom and self-governance. Do not test our resolve."

The monitors blacked out. Seconds later, the shuttle jerked when it docked with the *Piedmont*. Sinclair felt her lungs burning and exhaled when she remembered to breathe.

Across the solar system, she imagined all the missile cells of destroyers and rail-gun barrels of gunships swinging toward Luna.

38

THE MAGNATE

NYSE: *Error Detected*

This section of the lunar plains was empty and dusty when Vanderheiden, Brunelli, and VC engineers visited it for the geological surveys nearly two years ago. Now, the one-kilometer-tall surface anchor stood on the ground, the titanium cable reaching from the top into the pitch-black sky, surrounded by construction droids, many domes, and half a dozen roads twisting in and reaching out in multiple directions.

Unbelievable. Vanderheiden stared at the immense structure through the window from the common room at the Sinus Medii Medical Clinic. *Two years ago, this was only a dream.*

He turned away from the reinforced window and held a metal cup underneath the water dispenser. Clear liquid came out in a soft trickle. After the cup filled up, he took large gulps, feeling his dry mouth turn soft, quenching a deep thirst. He placed the empty cup underneath the dispenser again and looked over his shoulder, seeing Gabriella watching Sinclair's public broadcast repeat on the monitor built into the lunarcrete wall.

"Mark my words," he said, "Sinclair is going to become a warlord."

"I don't like it either, but Sinclair is right." Gabriella didn't take her eyes off the newsfeed. "A lucrative incentive is key to maintaining the support of the Luna Defense Forces."

"But Sinclair controls ten percent of all our companies now." He watched the waterline rise to the top of the cup. "That's enough voting power to alter the balance of power in the boardrooms." *And she is just a military officer, not a businesswoman.*

"I agree," she replied. "We must exercise control over Sinclair."

Vanderheiden took a sip, still feeling the craving for more water that tasted like gunpowder. He watched the monitor, noting Sinclair's harsh look and neck scar as she announced the Proclamation of Luna Free State.

"Key to influencing her is controlling the economy," Gabriella said.

"Blackburn will be the biggest supplier of the war materials. That'll give him the most sway over Sinclair. He'll try to sideline the Castlereaghs and other manufacturers." He inhaled. "I just know it."

"But we have the Luna Space Elevator. Blackburn and the Castlereaghs may build the war materials, but they'll need the space elevator to transport it. Sinclair will need it to construct her new combat vessels at the 100K Station." Gabriella took her eyes off the monitor and pointed out the window. "That's our leverage."

"And your family's bank," Vanderheiden added.

"The future of Luna comes down to the space elevator. You hold the most power of any of the Space Magnates. I promise you...others, especially Blackburn, are plotting ways to counter your influence."

People gunning for my wealth and power? Nothing has changed. "We can't let that happen." He waved his arm. "You saw how eager he was for the preemptive strike."

"Let me talk to the other magnates." Gabriella stepped away and paced the common room. "If I can rally enough of us, we can counter Blackburn's voice and dictate the future of Luna."

Vanderheiden finished his drink and tossed the cup into the recycler. "How is the board taking all this?"

"Furious...as expected," she replied. "Our stock price was falling when the government shut down the stock exchange. No one is happy right now."

"I don't care how they feel. I don't care where the stock price is. Will they continue to support us?" Vanderheiden pointed at Earth, which hovered directly above the space elevator. "Or will they push me off before I can build the Earth Space Elevator?"

"Push *us* off," Gabriella corrected him. "If the directors are thinking far enough ahead, they know it would be unwise to abandon the company that built the first space elevator." She stopped pacing the room. "Get the space elevator operational, and you'll make my job easier."

"No shit!" Vanderheiden hissed.

"Easy..." Gabriella raised her hands. "We are on the same side."

"Where is Cooper?"

"He didn't make it to Luna."

"Damn it..." Vanderheiden cursed to himself. "You were supposed to make sure all directors were in Luna before the proclamation went out. I don't care if he resigned. He still holds a major voice on the board."

"I got eight of the twelve directors here."

"The missing directors are probably receiving visits from federal agents and being interrogated. I need to know what Cooper is doing." Vanderheiden rubbed his forehead, feeling the anxiety pulse in his head. "That bastard is probably negotiating immunity with the government right now and spilling secrets to Shugart to save his own skin."

"Give Cooper a chance," she said. "He dislikes the government just as much as you do."

Vanderheiden turned around and walked to the window. Far out in the distance, the base of the surface anchor hid behind the curvature of Luna. He saw a hint of the red container with strobe lights move on the rails, climbing up to the top of the surface anchor.

"The ascent test is about to start." Vanderheiden smiled. *And then the future of Luna truly begins.*

"Are you coming to the operations center?" Gabriella asked. "The company could use your presence."

"No, Brunelli achieved the descent test. He can handle the ascent without me." Vanderheiden glanced at the closed door across the hallway. "I need to be with Emily."

"Are you sure?" Gabriella slanted her head. "You've worked hard and taken a huge risk building the space elevator. You don't want to be there for the celebration?"

"Don't worry about me. Emily's room has a window, so we can watch the ascent test from here. Susann insisted we get that room."

"Susann knows you well. You are a fortunate man." Gabriella patted his shoulder and left the common room.

* * *

Dr. Schalberg stood by the end of Emily's bed with a soft smile. "She will make a full recovery from her comatose state."

"I thought Creutzfeldt-Jakob was to blame for this." Susann sat on the bed next to their daughter. "Do you know what happened to her?"

Emily remained asleep, but there was no longer a tube going down her throat. Some color had returned to her skin, and she wasn't perspiring much.

"I, uh..." The doctor swiped through something on her hand terminal, shaking her head. "There were unidentified chemicals found in her bloodstream." She raised her finger. "But her body has flushed most of it out, which is positive news."

"Did they give her the wrong medicine, tainted fluids, or..." Vanderheiden trailed off, sitting in a chair by the wall close to Emily.

"I am at a loss, sir." Dr. Schalberg sighed. "I wish I could fully diagnose what happened to her. But I can say with high confidence that whatever happened to her wasn't natural."

"They nearly killed our daughter." Susann curled her lips.

"Emily is under the best care Luna offers. Lunarians take care of each other." The doctor winked at Vanderheiden. "Once Dr. Raymond arrives with the CJD-VL treatment, we can start the procedure."

"It's happening." Susann exhaled with relief. "It's finally happening."

Dr. Schalberg nodded and left the room, the door sealing shut.

Vanderheiden felt relieved about Emily being at Sinus Medii Medical Clinic after what he'd seen at the Texas Medical Center. The private professionals here seemed human, unlike the government zombies. Her doctors were sharp and on a mission, and the nurses were accommodating and supportive. They were short on specific drugs and clothes, but the war was to blame for that. *I'm just glad NMS doesn't get to fiddle with health care on Luna.*

"We should've brought Emily here in the first place!" Susann rested her forehead on her hands.

"This is why I supported the proclamation," Vanderheiden said.

"Look, please don't lie to me." Susann raised her head. "You threw your support behind it because you didn't want your company to be taken away."

"That contributed to my decision," Vanderheiden conceded.

"Did you at least consider what this meant for us?" Susann pointed at the bed. "For Emily?"

His neck stiffened. "It wasn't a simple decision."

"Let me make it clear what it means for everyone else." Susann stood up, clenching the aluminum wrap of a snack she'd eaten. "I'm now stuck on Luna, and you know me...I don't like leaving Earth. Emily is going to be blocked by every academic institution."

She tossed the wrapper toward the recycler, but it bounced off the wall instead. "This damn gravity!" She growled, curling her fingers.

"You are right," Vanderheiden whispered. *I don't want to have this argument. Not right now.*

Susann looked at him, trying to figure out if he meant it.

Vanderheiden's hand terminal beeped with a message from Gabriella.

THE ASCENT HAS STARTED.

Vanderheiden stood up and walked to the window. The window frame was much smaller than the common room, but he could still see the surface anchor. He placed his hand terminal on the frame of the reinforced glass and opened the altimeter to track the ascent test progress. The cable picked up reflections off the sun, like a blade slicing through the black sky. The red container sped up, propelled by the electromagnetic rails attached to the cable.

"Why did you do it?" Susann came to his side. "Why throw yourself into a political issue that could lead to a civil war?"

"How would you feel if you dedicated twelve years of your life to building something, sacrificing time with our family, straining our marriage...only for someone else to sweep in and take it from you, saying it doesn't belong to you?" Vanderheiden turned to her. "How would you feel?"

"Pissed off?"

"*Fucking* pissed off!" he shouted. "I built the PhotonicWay. I'm about to complete a space elevator. I have built a legacy that'll last generations, only to be called evil...greedy...corrupt."

The red container became smaller and smaller as it fast-tracked up from the surface. Vanderheiden almost couldn't see the red object anymore. The altimeter displayed five kilometers.

Vanderheiden continued. "Recessions, crises, wars, massacres... everything is falling apart. The interests of the few have hijacked the system at the expense of the many. I tried to be a good citizen, but the government and the oligarchs *stabbed* me in the back. I will no longer bow to them. The only people I care about are my family, my customers, my employees, and my shareholders. They are the reason for my legacy, *not* the government, and *despite* the government."

"Can we trust this General Sinclair?" Susann asked. "The security of Luna will come down to her fleet."

"I don't know..." He thought about his conversation with Gabriella and envisioned ways to hold influence over her. "What I know is Sinclair fighting for our side is better than the other side."

The door opened, and Dr. Schalberg and two nurses entered to the room, followed by Dr. Raymond, carrying a small container taped with medical warnings.

"Hello, everyone." Dr. Raymond smiled.

"Do you have it?" Susann approached her.

"I do have it." Dr. Raymond patted the container and then turned to Dr. Schalberg. "Are we ready?"

Dr. Schalberg nodded and gestured for the nurses to prepare Emily. One nurse went over to the medical machines behind Emily's bed and inputted commands. The other nurse pulled Emily's sleeve up, applied sensory pads, and checked her intravenous line.

Setting the container down on the table hanging off the foot of Emily's bed, Dr. Raymond unclipped the latches, opening the container to reveal a syringe and a small glass bottle with a thick amber-colored liquid.

The parents took seats by the wall near Emily. Susann interlocked her fingers tightly. Vanderheiden glanced at the altimeter on his hand terminal leaning across the window, reading fifteen kilometers. *Eighty-five kilometers to go.*

"Before we begin, let's go over how the CJD-VL treatment works." Dr. Raymond picked up the glass vial. "We will administer the treatment via IV to Emily every other day for thirty days. After that, it will be every month for the rest of her life."

She set the vial down and pointed at the nurses. "Since we are rebuilding Emily's nervous system, the treatment will cause pain, so she will have to be sedated each time we administer it."

Dr. Raymond closed her eyes for a moment. "I have to disclose there's a minor risk that Emily's body will reject the treatment. We will have to monitor her for fifteen minutes after they administer the treatment." She nodded at the medical staff. "I have briefed Dr. Schalberg and her nurses on the corrective actions if necessary."

"What do we do in that case?" Susann sat on the edge of her seat. "How will we cure her disease?"

"If Emily rejects it, then we will discuss the next steps." Raymond rested her hands on the bed's side rails. "For now, let's focus on administering the treatment."

Susann gave a sharp sigh, but Vanderheiden thought he was the only one who heard it. He grabbed her hand and squeezed it. Susann clenched it harder, her pulse bouncing against his skin. Vanderheiden closed his eyes and took in a deep breath. *I have fought so much for this moment.*

He opened his eyes and saw the altimeter. Thirty-four kilometers.

"Let's begin." Dr. Raymond pulled rubber gloves on, inserted the needle into the vial, and extracted the amber liquid, filling up the syringe to the top line. Dr. Raymond came to Emily's side. The Valkyrie Labs CEO handed the syringe over to Dr. Schalberg, and she inserted the needle into Emily's intravenous line. The amber liquid disappeared as Schalberg pressed the black plunger with her thumb.

"Set for fifteen minutes," Dr. Schalberg commanded, and a medical screen chirped, flashing *15:00*. "Start the timer."

Dr. Raymond closed the container, snapping the latches back in place, and walked to the door. Vanderheiden quickly rose from his seat and followed her out of the room, catching her in the hallway. "Dr. Raymond."

She turned around, eyebrows raised, waiting for a question.

"I don't know what I can say to show how much gratitude Susann and I have." Vanderheiden placed his hands on his hips. "You know we can pay the full cost of the treatment."

"I don't need your money." She shook her head slowly. "I owe you."

"But you saved my—"

Dr. Raymond shot up her palm and set the container down on the floor. "When I started Valkyrie Labs, I wanted to develop drugs to cure patients neglected by the legacy pharmaceutical labs."

She pressed her finger against her eye, wiping something away. "But I lost my way. I bent to the will of the shareholders and their demands for greater profit. I put up no fight against NMS, letting those...cruel bureaucrats decide who received the drugs, not Valkyrie Labs or the doctors."

She looked away from him, covering her mouth. She took a few deep breaths. After she looked up, her moist eyes locked on the Luna Space Elevator through the window.

"You inspired me." She walked into the common room, staring at the space elevator. "Your company was banking forty percent profit quarterly from the PhotonicWay. Your future was secured. You could've rested on your laurels." She pointed a firm finger at Vanderheiden. "But you put your company, all of it, at risk to build the Luna Space Elevator. You did it because it was the right thing to do. It was what society needed. Not because it was the most profitable decision."

"Well..." Vanderheiden walked toward her. "The space elevator boosted my stock and will generate significant profit."

"But you risked bankruptcy! You almost lost your company to Shugart! The board was a few votes short of kicking you out!" Dr. Raymond snapped at him. "Very few business executives will do that. You reminded me that running a business isn't just about profit."

She let out another long breath and pressed her fingers against her lips, leaning against the glass. "We aren't just responsible for our companies anymore. We are responsible for Luna. With this proclamation, we've put all Lunarians at risk. It is our duty to serve them. There are some of us who will forget that. I won't let them forget."

Dr. Raymond turned away from him, picked up the container she'd set on the floor, and walked out of the medical clinic.

We are responsible for Luna. Vanderheiden felt Dr. Raymond's words grip him. He was driven to rebel against the government to save his company and Emily. But he hadn't fully processed the fact that the livelihoods of a quarter of a million people were in his hands. In the hands of the Luna Defense Forces and the Space Magnates. *There are some of us who will forget that.* If they failed, many Lunarians risked starvation, persecution, and violence. Others would go to prison branded as traitors.

Vanderheiden shook the thoughts away and returned to the room. He found Susann sitting next to Emily, stroking her arm, staring at the timer count down the seconds. Dr. Schalberg and the nurses examined the medical data, eyes squinting. Vanderheiden watched Emily's chest for a moment, waiting for it to rise. He finally saw her chest inflate when he briefly became alarmed.

Walking over to the window, Vanderheiden saw eighty kilometers on the hand terminal. The red container was not visible, too far up in the black sky for the naked eye to see. His eyes traced down the cable to the towering surface anchor.

For nearly two years, every minute of every day, his sole purpose had been acquiring CJD-VL and building the Luna Space Elevator. He did it in the face of boardroom skirmishes, government crackdowns and confiscation, Shugart's hostile takeover attempts, and Lawrence's heartbreaking death. Feeling proud of himself for overcoming that, he looked at Emily and Susann. *But I have put everyone in danger now.*

Dr. Schalberg walked over and whispered, "Five minutes."

Vanderheiden nodded. Ninety kilometers.

He'd saved his company and his freedom but had now put Luna at risk by declaring it a free state. Recalling Sinclair's public broadcast and how she promised a military response to violations of Luna's sovereignty didn't settle his restless nerves. *Is Luna a death trap?*

Agreeing to Shugart's compensation offer, accepting CJD-VL from NMS and the conditions they imposed, and relaxing at their villa outside of Houston seemed like a rational decision. *Avoid the challenges of the world and live a peaceful life...*

Vanderheiden thought he'd made a dreadful mistake. *What have I done?* He placed a palm against his eyebrow, grinding his teeth.

"The future of Luna comes down to the space elevator," he remembered Gabriella saying. "You hold the most power."

His trembling stopped, and Vanderheiden pulled his face from his hand, looking at the Luna Space Elevator. *No, the future of the solar system comes down to the Earth Space Elevator.*

Ninety-five kilometers.

My legacy is not complete. The only glimmer of hope for peace between the United States, the European Union, and Luna came down to the Earth Space Elevator. A behemoth bridge between Earth and the rest of the solar system, bringing its wealth and opportunities to all of mankind. Vanderheiden sucked in a deep breath through his nose. *That is my mission.*

Multiple beeps blared, and Susann let out a shriek.

Vanderheiden spun around, his heart ramming up against his

throat. Susann clutched Emily's arm with both hands, gasping erratically.

No... Vanderheiden stumbled toward his unmoving daughter. *Not after everything.*

His lips quivering, he turned to the doctor, demanding to know what happened, and froze.

Dr. Raymond smiled and shook hands with her medical staff, their faces beaming with joy. A nurse turned off the beeping timer.

"It's okay," the doctor said after she registered the anxiety on Vanderheiden's face. "The treatment is working."

Vanderheiden grunted and let out a sigh. "T-thank you so...much."

The medical staff powered down a few medical devices and departed from the room, leaving the Vanderheidens alone.

He pulled a chair up to the bed, placing one hand on Emily and the other against his mouth to hold all the emotions in.

"We did it," Susann whispered, rubbing Emily's arm.

He clenched his teeth, trying to keep the bubbling emotions sealed.

The altimeter honked and flashed *100 kilometers* in green text.

We have saved Emily. Vanderheiden gasped. *We have built the Luna Space Elevator.*

Out came a cough first and then a few wheezes. Susann wrapped her arms around him, and that's when it felt like a dam burst open. Vanderheiden cried. Tears fell and rolled down his cheeks, soaking his beard and Susann's shirt.

"It's okay." Susann tightened her arms around him when the sobbing intensified. Her sturdy embrace prevented him from sinking to the floor.

His chest hurt so bad, he thought he was going to pass out. Susann's hold kept him grounded and upright.

"Thank you," Susann whispered. "I'm proud of you, Michael."

Vanderheiden continued sobbing. And he wept for a long time.

39

THE SENATOR

Senator Contador exited the West Wing, and the soggy humidity only made him take quicker steps toward his vehicle, its door held open by Torrez. He took a white handkerchief from his jacket pocket and patted away the sweat droplets from his bald head. Glancing to his side, he saw President Barbour surrounded by an entourage of agents and advisors, walking across the hot asphalt toward the press group and waving at bystanders behind the security fence. *Wave harder. It might save your presidency.*

He stepped up into his black vehicle and pulled the door shut, not giving Torrez a chance to close it. "I will meet with the general." Contador frowned at Dean, his chief aide, sitting in the other passenger seat. "Now."

"Yes, Senator." Dean pulled out her hand terminal.

Contador watched Barbour speak to the press, moving her arms in a reassuring manner. The senator took his glasses off and wiped them with a separate handkerchief from his other jacket pocket. He didn't want the handkerchief damp with sweat smearing his glasses.

He noticed the vehicle was idle. "Get us out of here, Torrez."

"Sorry, sir. Security protocol. We aren't leaving until the Secret Service lets us."

Contador hissed as he watched General Abborn and the other military chiefs emerge from the West Wing. "I don't need my intelligence lowered by these incompetent drones."

Dean and Torrez both stifled a chuckle. *I'm glad I can be humorous.*

"How was the meeting, sir?" Dean adjusted her auburn braid.

"Take a good guess. Barbour sure knows how to put on a good show for the cameras but she is useless in the Situation Room." Contador pointed at the crowd. "Abborn and the others seem to think it is just a protest by the Space Magnates, with a rogue general giving vocal support."

Contador turned his head away from the window, back to Dean. "They don't understand the Space Magnates just declared independence for Luna, just like the Thirteen Colonies did on the Fourth of July. Only, this time"—he pointed at his chest—"we are the British monarchy and they are the Continental Congress. This is a rebellion, and we must crush it with our full military might! Do *you* have the general on the line?"

"I do, Senator."

"Good. Tell him to meet me at the Second North Atlantic–Eurasian War Memorial in thirty minutes." He looked through the windshield to see if the security bars were down. "I will not be waiting."

After the Secret Service finally let them exit the White House premises, Torrez floored the acceleration pedal, speeding the vehicle down Constitution Avenue toward the Potomac River. Many intersections and openings were occupied by armored vehicles and antiair missile systems, all cordoned off by soldiers and green wooden barriers. The soldiers had bored looks on their faces, kicking small rocks, whistling songs, and sweating under the scorching sun.

Pedestrians walked by the military zones without a second look. Construction droids broke up a concrete sidewalk, sending white dust everywhere. A man and woman with three kids smiled for a camera shot of the World War II Memorial behind them. Contador frowned. *We are at war, and you decide to take a vacation?*

"I have Tsung on the line, Senator," Dean said.

Contador pressed the monitor hard enough for the front seat to bounce forward. Tsung's face occupied the screen, and she smiled like she was pleased to receive a call from Contador. *But are you?* She was inside an office at a mountain retreat, probably in the Appalachians.

"Senator, what can I do for you?"

His fingerprint smear on the screen covered her left eyebrow, like she had a mole forming, and he pulled out his handkerchief to wipe off the distraction. Tsung raised an eyebrow, wondering why Contador hadn't spoken yet.

"Tsung, is Vanderheiden Corporation firmly under the control of the Space Development Authority?" He tucked away the handkerchief in his jacket.

"The headquarters and all ground-based assets are under our control."

"Those are irrelevant, Tsung. Do *you* control the PhotonicWay?"

She held her smile, but Contador noticed her gulp. "Unfortunately, Senator, those remain out of—"

"Three months ago, you were given the green light to acquire Vanderheiden Corporation. Why was it not done? Why didn't you just walk into their headquarters, hand the check to the board, and take over?"

"Senator, you have to understand the business world runs on transactions through consent by both parties and without coercion. I had to be delicate and acquire VC without alienating the employees. Loyalty to Vanderheiden runs high in that company."

"This is not time to be...*delicate*." He spat the word like it shouldn't exist in the dictionary. "I told you the negotiations were all a ploy. I knew something was up when the Space Magnates scrambled to Luna and met with Sinclair."

Tsung dropped her smile and didn't try to hide her irritation. *You probably think I'm one of those clueless senators who lacks a dose of reality outside the Beltway. Think again...*

"Did you call me just to vent your disapproval of my conduct, Senator?"

"Yes, and another thing..." Contador stretched his arm over to Dean, and she placed her hand terminal on it. He read through the military contract, originally signed by Shugart Technology but now transferred over to the Space Development Authority. "I understand you have four new gunships you are under contract to build and six destroyers. Is that right?"

"Yes, Senator." Tsung crossed her arms.

"And you are"—he glanced at the timeline chart—"three years behind schedule on the gunships? But no issues with the destroyers?" There was a hint of sarcasm in his voice.

"That's correct. The gunships are more challen—"

"Here is what's going to happen." Contador pointed at the camera above the monitor. "You are going to halt all work on the destroyers. Their uselessness was clearly demonstrated during the Battle of Luna. You are going to get those gunships back on schedule."

"You don't get to make that call, Senator." Tsung narrowed her eyes.

"I am close to the defense secretary and many of your board members, so do not expect their support when your position is challenged. Another thing you should be aware of: There will be no more price increases to accommodate any schedule delays you have. It is no longer a cost-plus contract. The price is now frozen."

At this point, Contador knew he was crawling inside Tsung's skin. Her nostrils were flared, and her blushing was visible underneath her layers of makeup.

"Am I clear, Tsung?"

"Yes, Senator."

"Will you carry out my requests?" He leaned closer to the monitor. "Or do I need to find someone else who will get it done?"

The muscles around her nose twitched. "Yes, it'll get done, Senator."

She cut the connection before giving Contador a chance to reply. He growled.

Driving down Independence Avenue, Contador pondered Tsung's

fate. *Has her time come or does she get a reprieve?* The number of ill-guided and oblivious people in the situation room made his stomach rumble. *Was it a mistake assassinating General Shugart to elevate her?*

Circling the Tidal Basin, he rubbed his deep dimple softly, turning each item in his head up and down. *We will not win this if the key leaders aren't removed. Who do I replace them with? How do I do it? Mm?*

"It is time to pull the plug on Aguirre." He said without taking his eyes off the man-made reservoir. "Release his sex tape. It's time to remove him from the administration."

"You want to take down the vice president?" Dean frowned. "Won't that create internal turmoil? We need unity."

"I don't care. We don't need unity. We don't need stability. We *need* power." He raised his clenched fist. "We need to dominate. The VP is a weak link. We need to make sure Congress will back Governor Watkins. He will be an asset to us." He stroked his dimple again. "I just need to figure out what to do with Barbour."

"Should we at least try to negotiate with the Space Magnates first?" She leaned on her armrest. "We can't fight Luna and Europe at the same time. The military has done well against the Europeans so far."

"*General Sinclair* has done well against the Europeans," he corrected her. "No. We will crush the Space Magnates. Set an example to all who dare to challenge the power and authority of the United States. Luna will not escape my grip. It is key to controlling the solar system...and I will not have it taken by capitalist pigs or tyrannical generals!"

"I think you are overextending yourself." Dean interlocked her fingers in a pleading way. "You are picking every battle. Your hand will be exposed sooner rather than later."

"I've said I always need a devil's advocate inside my office, but I'm starting to question your loyalty." He rested his lanky fingers gently on Dean's hands. "Do we have a problem here?"

She tucked her chin into her neck and pulled her hands back. "We don't."

Are you a weak link? Contador looked out the window and saw the Second North Atlantic–Eurasian War Memorial approaching.

Enclosed by a sea of grass, the three-meter-tall pyramid of black granite had the names of the fallen and missing engraved on all four sides. It was sparsely crowded, and people stopped by each of the statues and standing stones marking the boundary of the memorial.

The general was nowhere to be seen, and Contador felt his patience dry off. The senator eyed the black pyramid and the sunlight reflecting off a corner edge, creating a yellow line. *How many names will be engraved on the next memorial? Thousands? Tens of thousands? Hundreds?* He took a deep breath and squinted his eyes at the sun. *If this government has strong and competent leaders, this war will be short but victorious.*

A large man emerged from behind a standing stone and walked toward Contador. The way he sauntered showed how heavy his beer belly was. The senator sighed. *For once, can I have a general who is patriotic, competent, and healthy? At least Garrett checks two of the boxes.*

As Garrett came closer, his thick eyebrows nearly covering his eyes, Contador found Sinclair in his mind. *The great things we could've done if she'd chosen our side...*

"Senator Contador." Garrett wore khaki pants that weren't ironed and a button-up shirt. Contador measured him, observing how he was holding himself. He seemed a little gray, like a piece of his soul was dying one day at a time.

"How is your wife doing? Ginger, correct?"

"I don't know. You'll have to ask her." He looked away. "Separated."

"I see." He needed to know if Garrett was the general that would save this nation. *The army generals and navy admirals are getting on my nerves, begging to be given the reins to lead the war effort.*

"General Garrett, I am in need of an honest opinion." Contador held his hands in front of his abdomen. *I need to know if you have the guts to wage unrestricted warfare. Crush Europe. Crush the Space Magnates. Are you the general this nation needs?* "What is your assessment of the war today?"

"Don't you have General Abborn to ask? Or Maxwell?" Garrett titled his head, his thick neck bending with it. "Oh wait..." He smirked.

"Maxwell can *rot* in his cell, for all I care!" Contador snapped. "His actions gave the Luna Fleet a reason to go rogue!" He closed his eyes and sighed. "Abborn is a liability. Despite our victory at Luna, we are at a stalemate everywhere else."

"That's correct."

"I am in need of your advice." Contador waved his hand toward the murky sky. "Can we win this? Can we defeat the European Union and subdue the Space Magnates? You know Sinclair better than anyone else."

"I still find it ironic you want my advice." Garrett pointed at his civilian clothes. "I was forced into retirement...by you. Why should I help you?"

Clenching his teeth hard, Contador was sick of this dance. *If hurting my pride is what it takes...*

"Clearly, you have more merit than I give you credit. It was a mistake to push you out. I will admit that." He pressed his palm to his chest and bowed a centimeter forward. "Please accept my apology. All I ask is that you don't hold a grudge against me. Let's work together and set the ship straight."

"Work together?" Garrett's eyebrows shot up, fully revealing his eyes.

"Let's answer my question first."

"Okay, Senator. Okay." The general nodded and paced around the concrete they stood on. "The Europeans lost the bulk of their space fleet when the Fifth Fleet attacked Luna. We have control of low earth orbit. Their remaining fleets will be on a defensive posture. It is now a war of attrition down here on the ground."

The general continued pacing, the sunlight creating black shadows over his eyes. "That's a simple task, but it won't be easy. Sinclair and the Space Magnates will be trickier. I see three scenarios here. First, Sinclair allies with the EU and invades low earth orbit. We will crush them with the Orbital Fleet's numerical and defensive advantage. Sinclair isn't fool enough to do that. Second scenario: Sinclair attacks Mars. We will respond by deploying the Orbital and Mars Fleets to defeat her in a pincer attack."

He stopped pacing, standing in front of Contador. "The third and most probable scenario: They fortify Luna and hunker down. We impose a *complete* economic embargo and threaten starvation. We'll see how long the Space Magnates last with their businesses in shambles and their food supply cut off."

Contador was pleased Garrett had suggested starvation. *Seems I did underestimate you after all. How foolish of me.* "General Abborn is not willing to do that. He believes the Luna problem is a political problem, not military."

"That man is an idiot." Garrett shook his head. "Sinclair walks her talk."

A couple walked toward the two, seemingly obvious to the sensitive conversation. Torrez shooed them away.

"What if I reinstated you and made you Chairman of the Joint Chiefs? I will pull Congress's support behind you, and you wage unrestricted warfare against the Space Magnates. Five stars waiting for you, General Garrett." Contador gestured at him. "All you have to do is say yes, and I will make it happen."

Garrett straightened his back, and the color gradually returned to his face, like a new purpose in life had formed inside him. He twisted his lips side to side. *Trying to figure out if this is another political trap or an opportunity worth taking? There are no hidden knives here, this time.*

"What about Barbour?" Garrett asked. "She is advocating for a softer approach, and I'll be reporting to her."

"I'll deal with her."

"Why don't you be president instead?" Garrett chuckled.

"That's not how I work." *True power belongs to those who wield it from the shadows.*

Still not hearing an answer from Garrett, Contador chose to sweeten the offer. "I can offer you wealth. A board seat on the Space Development Authority."

"I'm a patriot." Garrett recoiled. "I'll do this for my country, not self-enrichment. I'll do it, but under two conditions."

"Name them."

"I decide what happens to Sinclair."

"Hm...trying to protect your protégé?"

"Former protégé." Garrett's eyes widened. "Anyone who calls me a traitor, guilty by association, can choke on their words."

"Fair condition." Contador leaned his head forward. "And the second?"

"Productions of destroyers are to be canceled and all resources pooled into building more gunships."

Contador smiled. *And that is why I rule this nation. I'm steps ahead of everyone.* "Done."

He raised an eyebrow. "Just like that?"

"Just like that."

Garrett smiled. "Then we have a deal."

"Excellent." Contador offered his hand, and Garrett's bulky hands gripped it.

Watching Garrett walk away with purpose, disappearing behind the pyramid, Contador wanted to smash his glasses and punch himself in the face. *I was such a fool to support Abborn and Maxwell. How did I not see who Garrett and Sinclair were?* He felt fortunate to now have a general in his corner who had a good grasp of Washington politics and was willing to pull the gloves off to crush the rebellion. *But will I be able to control him? As long as I am alive, corporations and militaries will not rule this country. I must not let democracy fall.*

He pulled out his hand terminal. He saw multiple messages with large documents attached. He opened one file, and it displayed a 3D model of a cable stretching from Earth all the way up to a space station in geostationary orbit. The file was labeled "Earth Space Elevator" and the "VC" logo was stamped on the top corner of the screen.

"Now I understand why you want control of Luna, Mr. Vanderheiden." He closed the file and gave a satisfying sigh. *I know everything that's happening in your company. Not every director is loyal to you, Mr.*

Vanderheiden. It's easy to get people to spill secrets once families, dark secrets, or financial assets are threatened.

He put his hand terminal back in his pocket. *You think you've made the bold move, Mr. Vanderheiden?* He walked back to his vehicle, followed by Torrez, as the sun fell behind the pyramid, creating a black triangle silhouette. *Well, you are wrong. I make the bold moves.*

ABOUT THE AUTHOR

Saul Rayburn is a sci-fi author. SPACE MAGNATES is his debut novel, first book of the Space Magnates trilogy.

In addition to writing, Saul enjoys swimming, pickleball, coffee, traveling, and video games. He lives in Texas with his wife and two dogs.

You can subscribe to his email list at subscribepage.io/saulrayburn

You can also visit him at the social media links below:

facebook.com/saul.rayburn
instagram.com/saul.rayburn
patreon.com/saulrayburn

ACKNOWLEDGMENTS

I must take a moment to thank a special group of people who helped me through the various stages of writing this book. I give my most sincere thanks to:

The beta readers who read a rough draft of this novel and offered critiques to help elevate my story: MASON BELL, SARAH LEWIS, MARIE LEWIS, RANDALL EKSTROM, and SARAH BETZOLD.

The design artist who took the time to draw an excellent and beautiful book cover, allowing me to dedicate my time to the writing: CHERIE CHAPMAN.

The copy-editor for correcting all my grammar errors, sentence structure issues, and misspellings: MICHELLE HOPE.

And last, my wonderful wife and two loyal dogs for tolerating my early morning wake-ups to write, hearing my frequent complaints about the difficulty of drafting a novel, and offering only encouragements.

All of you helped make this novel a reality. Thank you.

Made in the USA
Middletown, DE
06 July 2024

56971538R00234